Three warm and entertaining novels by Joyce Dingwell, a favorite author from Harlequin's Romance Library

A Thousand Candles... Rena had never liked her, so Pippa chose to ignore her cousin's real motives for inviting them to Australia. Anyway, for the sake of her young brother, Davey, she felt they ought to go. Once there, however, surprises came thick and fast! (#1615)

The Mutual Look... Exchanging the pastures of England for the paddocks of Australia after her retired employer had asked her to accompany the horses he was sending to his nephew there—proved far easier than Jane Sidney had believed possible. The only trouble was her attractive but arrogant new employer, William Bower. (#1738)

There Were Three Princes... Verity had gone to Australia because of her younger brother. As long as he needed her she would stay. But her life became suddenly complicated by the three Princes—Matt, Peter and Bart—only one of whom, she was told, was available! (#1808)

**Another collection
of Romance favorites...
by a best-selling Harlequin author!**

In the pages of this specially selected
anthology are three delightfully
absorbing Romances—all by an
author whose vast readership all over
the world has shown her to be an
outstanding favorite.

For those of you who are missing
these love stories from your
Harlequin library shelf, or who wish
to collect great romance fiction by
favorite authors, these Harlequin
Romance anthologies are for you.

We're sure you'll enjoy each of the
engrossing and heartwarming stories
contained within. They're treasures
from our library... and we know
they'll become treasured additions
to yours!

The fourth anthology of
3 Harlequin Romances by

Joyce
Dingwell

Harlequin Books

TORONTO • NEW YORK • LONDON
AMSTERDAM • PARIS • SYDNEY • HAMBURG
STOCKHOLM • ATHENS • TOKYO • MILAN

These books by Joyce Dingwell were originally published
as follows:

A THOUSAND CANDLES
Copyright © 1971 by Joyce Dingwell
First published in 1971 by Mills & Boon Limited
Harlequin edition (#1615) published August 1972

THE MUTUAL LOOK
Copyright © 1973 by Joyce Dingwell
First published in 1973 by Mills & Boon Limited
Harlequin edition (#1738) published December 1973

THERE WERE THREE PRINCES
Copyright © 1972 by Joyce Dingwell
First published in 1972 by Mills & Boon Limited
Harlequin edition (#1808) published August 1974

Cover photograph © Larry Dale Gordon/The Image Bank
of Canada

ISBN 0-373-20074-9

First edition published as Harlequin Omnibus in November 1977

Second printing March 1978
Third printing April 1979
Fourth printing July 1983

Contents

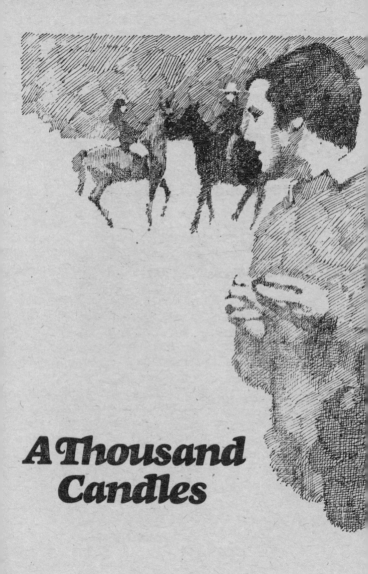

A Thousand Candles

Pippa wanted no more complications. She'd traveled to Australia, seeking one more spring for her little brother, Davey, who according to the doctors was in the last year of his young life.

That's why she tried to discourage the stranger on the train from describing his home. Clement Crag, however, was not a man to be put off easily. "Sure, there's spring up there, scrubber, the most spring in all the world," he promised Davey. "You'll see."

Davey was filled with new confidence. But Pippa was afraid to hope.

CHAPTER ONE

Davy's small nose pressed against the train window had changed into a squashed marshmallow. His eyes never left the passing scene, but his mouth whistled tunelessly da-da-da-da-da-da. Six da's, and Pippa knew what they meant. Almost visibly he had fondled the words when she had explained them to him, smiling back at her when she had finished: 'I like that, Pip.' Dear little boy, dear little brother, he was his father's own son when it came to expression, though ... achingly ... little use that gift would be.

She, the daughter, had taken after Mother, nothing in particular, Aunt Helen had fondly admitted to her sister, adding, 'But if you're half as sweet ...'

Pippa's own memory of her mother was vague, only to be expected when Mother had died ten years ago and she had only been ten herself. Davy had been born and Mother had died. Then, soon afterwards, Father had died, and Aunt Helen had taken the two of them, Pippa who took after her mother and was 'nothing in particular' and Davy who would have been a poet like Father if he had grown up.

Only, and Pippa looked at the small marshmallow nose, he wasn't going to have the time.

That was why she was here now. In this Australian train. Why otherwise would she have come to Australia? She had no Australian links, save Uncle Preston who was not really an uncle but her mother's and Aunt Helen's cousin, and Uncle Preston's daughter Rena.

Admittedly she knew Rena slightly. They had attended the same English school. Uncle Preston had done well in

Australia, so well that flying his daughter back and forth for her education had meant nothing at all. The identical choice of schools had been coincidence. Uncle Preston had selected it because of its prestige, but Pippa had achieved it because of an entry exam. She was not particularly smart, but she had a deep sense of responsibility, responsibility to Aunt Helen who was devoted and kind, and responsibility to Davy who was dependent and small. The selection board had said to Aunt Helen and Aunt Helen had passed it on to Pippa: 'She showed such anxiety in her papers we really felt she must have her reward.'

The reward, of course, had been only the bare subjects, no extras; they would have to be paid. There was no money to pay them, so Pippa had done without the music and dancing that most of the others ... and certainly Rena ... had enjoyed.

She remembered her first meeting with Rena.

'Has your second cousin Rena Franklin looked you up, Pippa?' Aunt Helen had asked one day.

'No, she's a boarder, and boarders and day girls don't mix much.'

'Then you must look her up. After all, you two girls are related. Then that poor child, all the way from Australia!'

Only Rena hadn't been a poor child. She had made that obvious without saying a word. When Pippa had proffered shyly: 'I'm Pippa Bromley, a kind of cousin,' proffered it humbly as well as shyly, for Rena was exceptionally pretty, exceptionally vivacious, and, even in a similar gym tunic, exceptionally exclusive, Rena had simply looked Pippa up and down and said: 'Oh.'

Looking back now Pippa smiled slightly and could not blame her. I was, she remembered, a frog of a child. Aunt Helen always had had to buy uniforms that had been discarded by girls who had left and they certainly shouted it. Then those corrective glasses she had worn, so big and round! Then those rabbit's teeth behind that brace! Yes, no wonder Rena . . .

The way it is in big schools, the two had seen little of each other after that meeting. Pippa had sometimes said uncertainly, 'Hullo, Rena,' and Rena had condescended a nod in return.

Rena had been whisked away quite soon and finished in Switzerland, and that had been the end of Pippa's brief association with Mother's and Aunt Helen's cousin's child.

Yet here she was travelling to Rena's home in this Australian train!

She had been told that she and Davy would be met at the airport and driven by Rena to Tombonda, but at Mascot there had been a further message telling them to find their own way. Fortunately, Pippa learned, it was not a long distance from Sydney. Tombonda in the Southern Highlands was only a matter of some three hours, and with a fare to match. Otherwise, Pippa had thought later at Sydney's Central Railway, she might have been in a spot. It sounded ridiculous after a flight from England, but that had been Rena's gift.

Over the telephone, *London* telephone, Rena had said, 'I've seen my air agent, Pippa, and you have only to state your name.' Then she had added enthusiastically, '*And Davy's.*'

It was the undoubted keenness for Davy that had won Pippa. She might have demurred for herself, but to hear someone ask for Davy . . .

It had all started when Rena had called in at the cottage one day when Pippa was at work.

'She's in London shopping for a week or so.' – Still flitting back and forth, Pippa had envied. – 'She happened to be passing through our village, and decided to say hullo. I will say, Pippa,' Aunt Helen had reported, 'she was taken with Davy.'

'*Rena* was?' Pippa had been surprised.

'He's a winning little boy,' Aunt Helen had reminded her, but a little surprised herself.

Pippa had been more surprised when Rena had rung soon after and said what she had.

'Oh, Pippa,' the clear cool voice had greeted, 'would you remember me, Rena?'

'But of course, Rena. And lately, I'm told, you visited Aunt Helen.'

'Missing you, dear, but' . . . a pause . . . '*not Davy.*'

So Aunt Helen had been right. She had been interested in Davy.

'A darling little boy,' Rena had said. 'But so pale.'

'Yes.' Because she knew the end to that now, Pippa had found no words to say.

Then she had heard *Rena*'s words, Rena telling Pippa that she and Davy must come to Australia. *Soon.*

At another time she might not have listened, or at least only half listened, she might have answered politely, 'Yes, some day perhaps,' thinking 'Never at all.'

But, because of Doctor Harries, of what he had told her, had told her only this afternoon, she *had* listened. Then said: 'Yes.'

'Yes, Pippa?' Aunt Helen had looked incredulously at her niece after the phone had gone down.

'Yes, Aunt Helen. – Where is Davy?'

'Feeding the birds. He can't hear, he's at the other end of the garden.' Aunt Helen had drawn aside the curtain to show Pippa.

But Pippa had had to accept her aunt's assurance that he was out there, for she couldn't see for tears.

'What did the doctor say?' Aunt Helen had asked

quietly, but her voice had told Pippa she already knew, for they both had sensed for a long time that Davy was only on loan to them, that he was that shorter thread in the pattern of life.

'He put it gently,' Pippa had said brokenly, 'but it still meant the same. He – he said that this was the last spring.'

It was April. Pippa thought she had never known a more tender English April. Walking to the station each morning she had felt the magic . . . but with it a pain beyond belief. From the leafy ledges had come the twitterings of birds, from the grass-hidden roots of bramble and hawthorn the stirrings of little creatures, dew gemmed the delicate lace the field spiders threaded on the briar. Yet Davy was not to see it again. It was the last spring.

Then Rena had rung and said what she had and standing and listening and waiting to insert a polite 'No'. . . . 'Thank you very much for the thought' . . . Pippa had remembered that down there, down under, it was different from up here, that winter came in June, that summer came at Christmas, that autumn, never fall there for nothing fell, came when the buds were bursting here. That September, not April, was the first of spring.

September. Only five months away, and Doctor Harries had estimated around nine . . . ten perhaps . . .

There could be another April for Davy. April in September. September, the first of spring.

'You'll be alone when it happens,' Aunt Helen had said afterwards.

'Yes. But you do see, don't you?'

'Yes. And Rena was certainly very nice when she called, and undoubtedly she took to Davy. It should be all right. After all, she is a relation.' If there had been a note of uncertainty in Aunt Helen's voice it had only been

13

faint. Not like the blunt warning that Janet had blurted out. Janet had been at the school, too, a kind of in-between Rena and Pippa, less extras than Rena, but certainly more than Pippa, and Janet had looked incredulously at her old friend when she had been told Pippa's plans.

'Australia! Rena Franklin! Wake up, Pip.'

'It will be all right.'

'Leopards don't change their spots.'

'I never knew Rena that much.'

'I did, and I can tell you—'

'And I can tell you,' Pippa had prevented, 'that you could be wrong. I changed. Remember the little owl I was? Or was I a rabbit? Not that I'm much different now but I don't have corrective glasses and braces any more. At least I'm different there.'

'Yes, a great deal different, and it's worrying me.' Janet had looked consideringly at the slender girl with the soft quiet face, the soft brown hair and the hillside green eyes.

'Worrying you? What on earth for?'

'Who ... or is it whom? ... not what,' had corrected Janet dourly. Then she had answered barely: 'Rena.'

'You're worrying because of Rena?'

'Yes. And I'm very sorry you're going. Why must you, Pip?'

'In Australia September is the first of spring, and Davy ... well, Davy ...'

'I see,' Janet had nodded. 'Well, good luck, Pippa.' But Janet's voice had sounded as though she strongly doubted that luck.

Pippa had gone to the air office as Rena had instructed her and the tickets had been handed over. Good-byes had been said ... if Aunt Helen had held on to Davy longer than she had to Pippa the little boy had not noticed it ...

14

then, with a minimum of trouble, for which Pippa mentally thanked Rena, they had set off.

Rome ... Karachi ... New Delhi ... Bangkok ... Darwin. It had gone like a dream. Only after Darwin had Pippa felt any cobweb of doubt. The brown grass far beneath them was so unending, so – so unchangeable. Did summer ever leave such terrain, she doubted, and if it didn't, and if there was no winter, how could there be spring?

Then Mascot was coming up and Pippa's cobweb was being brushed aside in the busyness of collecting bags and getting ready to be met.

Not being met had been another doubt, but at least Rena had not forgotten about them, she had left a message.

Then soon after the Southern Highlands train had left Central, had spun through suburbs whose colourlessness could have been suburban colourlessness anywhere, the cobweb had gone completely, gone in ferny hillocks, in turfed fields, in belts of green treetops, ponds of cloud-reflecting water ... most of all in the apples, pears, damsons and greengages, the medlars and walnuts that *had* to have a awakening otherwise they would not be there. That was when Pippa had happily told Davy that here 'September is the first of spring' and he had started his da-da song.

'It's like home.' Davy had unsquashed his nose for a moment to say this of the Southern Highlands and to accept a railway lunch-box sandwich. He had always been an outgoing little boy and he asked companionably of the only other traveller in their compartment: 'Is it like your home, too, sir?'

'Not on your life, cobber.' The passenger who had been reading ever since he had stepped into the compartment just as the train had moved out from Sydney folded the paper and put it down.

'Then what is your home like?' asked Davy with interest.

The man ... large, rather too large for a narrow train compartment, Pippa thought ... so darkly bronzed you felt yourself to be almost of a different race, began packing a pipe with such loving care that Davy forgot his sandwich to watch in fascination. The man waited until he had completed the packing to his satisfaction, then lit up and said to Davy: 'Big.'

'Big country?'

'That's it.'

'What else?' asked Davy.

'Real hills, not these pretty ups and downs they call hills down here.'

'Yes?'

'But only hills in the distance, mind you; around us is dead flat. Red, gold and purple hills. Rocks sticking out of them like bare bones.'

'Yes?'

'Flowers you've never seen before, cobber, Salvation Jane ... though that's only a weed ... mulga when it comes into its yellow, wild iris.'

'Yes?'

'Empty miles, burning heat, scrubbers and brumbies.'

'*Please.*' Her lips thinned, Pippa leaned across and put a slab of railway cake firmly into Davy's hand. At the same time she drew his attention to a riding school they were passing, and once more Davy's nose became a squashed marshmallow. He was thinking, she sincerely hoped, of nice dapple greys and cute chestnuts, not scrubbers and brumbies.

'Sorry if I widened the horizon,' drawled the brown man, weaving out smoke now but carefully directing it

16

away from her.

'I'm sorry, too,' said Pippa shortly. 'When something can't be, why begin it?' She compressed her lips again.

'You have the wrong slant there,' the man answered. 'Nothing never "can't be", miss.'

'I don't wish to discuss it with you.' She took up a magazine.

'You really mean you're beaten,' he grinned. 'Oh, yes, you are. You've laid down your guns.'

'I'm reading.'

'But you've never seen a word. Look, I don't meet many people, not where I come from, so when I do meet them I like to talk. That's why I've trained it today instead of taking my car. To talk.'

'Then I'm very sorry. There are other compartments.'

'This one will do.'

She ignored him and proceeded to read, though ... maddeningly ... not seeing a word.

'Big country, you said?' The riding school was past and Davy was back again.

'That's right, little scrubber.'

'Those scrubbers, are they—?'

'They're wild cattle, wild from years in the bush. To run a steer down you have to do it in full gallop, flick it by its tail and then pin it to the ground.'

'Look, Davy,' called Pippa desperately, 'I'm sure I saw a bear in one of those trees.'

The nose became a marshmallow again and the brown man mouthed silently but unmistakably, so unmistakably Pippa could not ignore it: 'Liar.'

'I beg your pardon,' she said icily.

'So you should beg it. Liar. Rail backwards, we used to say as kids. You knew there's none down here.'

'How would I? I'm—'

'A pomegranate. Yes. But surely you'd still know koalas don't run wild any more. A few on the coast north of Sydney, some in Queensland, but not in this bit of England.'

'Bit of England?'

'It *is*, isn't it? The young scrubber just said so. Home, he said. And that's why you like it to the exclusion of any other place, isn't it? You just don't want to spread your wings. Also' ... accusingly ... 'that's why I can't widen his horizon.' A nod to Davy. 'The moment I open my mouth it's "Please.... please ..."'

'Please,' said Pippa again, but frigidly, definitely, closing the subject for all time this time ... or so she thought.

For quite calmly he leaned across and took the magazine away from her, placed it face down.

'Where I come from we pass the time of day,' he told her, ignoring her indignation at his action.

'Where I come from we do, too.'

'You surprise me. I wouldn't have thought it.' He gave an impudent grin.

'What you think or don't think doesn't concern or interest me.'

'It mightn't concern you, but I bet it would interest you. Why don't you give it a go?'

'I am not interested,' she said furiously.

'The boy was.'

'*He can't be.*' The words, the aching words were out before Pippa realized it. She gave a little involuntary cry and put her hand to her mouth. Now, surely, he would leave her alone.

But not the brown man.

He said slowly, so slowly she saw at once he understood and she wondered at the intuition in such a big, tough person: 'The way I look at things you must live life as

18

though it's lived for ever.'

'And when it isn't?' she asked in little more than a whisper.

'Then you live it all the more. – The young 'un, isn't it?'

'Yes.' She wondered why she admitted it to him, a stranger.

'Care to tell me?'

'No. I mean . . . I can't. I mean . . .'

There was a pause. 'Look.' He broke the pause. 'Look, you get back to your magazine.' He handed it to her. 'I'll give him some living for half an hour. No, don't be scared. I won't disturb him.'

'I . . .' She did not know what to say; she felt very close to tears.

'Read,' he advised, sensing the tears, and she got behind the pages, not seeing a word, only hearing his voice, then Davy's entranced little voice, then his again, Davy's, and then somewhere in the conversation, in answer to Davy who seemed since he had started that da-da song to take a lot of interest in spring: 'Sure there's spring up there, scrubber, the most spring in all the world. Well' . . . a grin . . . 'sometimes. One week the ground is stony and bare, but the next it's knee-high in grass. Then there's mulga. Wild Iris.'

'Salvation Jane,' came in Davy, knowledgeable now, 'only that's a weed. Did you know, Crag, that—'

'Crag?' Pippa put down her magazine, and the brown man explained, 'On my invitation, miss, you have to call each other something.'

'But Craig . . . he means Craig, of course.'

'Crag, not Craig. That's the name I go by.'

'Unusual.'

'Not really. It's a "met" name out west. The Crags were pioneers.'

19

'But Davy ... but my brother used it as a Christian name.'

The brown man smiled. 'I was baptised Clement. Me Clement! Clement Crag! Oh, no. I soon put a stop to that.'

'Did you, Mr. Crag?'

'Crag,' he invited, 'like the scrubber just said.'

'Because you *are*?' For some reason she had to bait him.

'Only in the wrong hands, in the right ones I'm pretty level going.' He looked at her and she saw that his eyes were almost the brown of his skin, more bronze than dark.

'Did you know, Crag,' Davy was trying to continue, not interested in their interchange, 'that in England, where we come from, everything is different from here? It's summer in winter and winter in summer and—'

'And it's autumn when the leaves fall,' the man said.

'Yes,' nodded Davy, 'and spring is in April.'

'And did you know,' came in the man, 'that this year you get two bites of the cherry?'

'What do you mean?'

'September is the first of spring here,' said Crag, 'so with your spring already in England you'll be having double spring.'

'At your place,' said Davy wistfully, 'it would be double double spring, because you said it's the most spring in all the world.'

'That's right, scrubber. If you and your sister feel like a bigger helping still on your plates, you come up to Falling Star.'

'Is that its name?'

'Sure is.'

'Would there be room?'

'For a scrubber your size!'

'For Pippa, too.'

'Pippa?'

'Her.' Davy indicated. 'My sister.'

'Pippa.' The man appeared to taste it. 'Our mornings at Falling Star begin at piccaninny daylight, not seven, but yes, scrubber, room for Pippa, too.'

'So you know that poem,' said Davy, pleased with his new friend. He explained of Pippa: 'She was called that because she was born at seven and had eyes like hillsides.'

'Still has, I reckon.' The brown man was looking at Pippa, and, embarrassed, she looked away.

'Also,' continued Davy importantly, 'our father was a poet.'

'Then that settles it. A poet's son would have to come to Yantumara.'

'Is that Falling Star?'

'Sure is.'

'We're going to Tombonda,' grieved Davy.

'That means a hill. I'm going, too.'

Pippa's mouth, open to say as quietly but as finally as she could, not to put such wild ideas as going up north to a cattle station ... it sounded like cattle ... into the boy, closed again. Going to Tombonda, too!

'But that's not your country,' Davy was protesting jealously, jealous for the country he had just heard about, 'you're scrubbers and brumbies and—'

'So was my father's country until he got too old to run a steer down at full gallop, and then—'

'Flick it by its tail and pin it to the ground.'

'Yes,' nodded the brown man. 'So he came here for a rest.'

'And you've come down to see him, Crag?'

'Not any more, scrubber. He sees it all at the one time now from a good viewing cloud up there. No, I've come to

21

check the place, and to' . . . He stopped. Presently he said, 'Look, Davy, there's a wombat for you.' As the nose became a marshmallow again, the man turned to Pippa and finished: 'And I've come to ask that girl next door what gives. Because' . . . paying no attention to Pippa's implied uninterest . . . 'when I come to Tombonda when I'm old I want someone carrying on, like I did for my father, up at Falling Star.' He stopped. 'Do you follow?'

'It doesn't concern me,' Pippa said coldly.

'But do you see?'

'It doesn't concern me,' she said again.

Another pause . . . then again he broke it.

'Then would it concern you if I asked *you* to come instead?' He was attending his pipe again, not looking at her.

'What?' Pippa sat straight up.

'Because,' he went on, '*she* isn't coming or she would have been there by this time, and time runs out.' He said it quite unabashed.

'Are you the same person who just quoted that we live for ever?' Pippa demanded, still taken aback by his impudent proposal. 'Are you saying instead now that time runs out?'

'No,' he answered, 'but I am saying that the time for living life as it should be lived runs out, Pippa.' – Pippa, indeed! – 'That that right design, God's design, of man and woman, then later' . . . a significant nod in Davy's direction . . . 'has to have its start.'

He was unbelievable. The subject was unbelievable.

'With Davy,' she inserted incredulously at last, 'assuming that children are your theme—'

'They are.'

'You'd overcome time.' Really, she froze, this person . . .

22

'That was what I was thinking,' he nodded frankly, 'a family readymade.'

'But not for long.' She bit on her lip as the words escaped her.

He held up a big hand cancelling what she had said, cancelling it so definitely she almost could have believed him. Only, of course, she mustn't . . .

'Besides,' he resumed, 'I've quite taken to the little scrubber. So after I see Rena—'

'Rena?' she gasped.

'That's where you're going, isn't it? Franklins. Has to be, it's the only other property at Tombonda. The rest of the district consists of railway cottages and a few shops.' He looked musingly at her for a few moments. 'You know, Pippa,' he shrugged, 'you being here makes sense, or at least the young scrubber does.' He gave a short laugh.

'I don't understand,' Pippa said.

'Well, I hope you keep that up. It's not a good understanding, I reckon. – Tombonda's the next stop. Only short intervals down here. Not like our part of the world.'

'The big country?' Davy was back with them again.

'That's right, scrubber. There we don't deal in miles but thousands of square ones. Gear ready? We get off now.' The brown man was swinging the bags down, swinging Davy down, swinging . . . and Pippa rankled but had to comply . . . Davy's sister.

There were two cars waiting beyond the small neat station, one empty, the other attended and ready to go. The first was a distinctly muddy landrover that looked as though it had seen a lot of action. The other was a well-polished sedan that looked like Rena. Pippa was not surprised when a driver came forward from the sedan and claimed them.

Crag ... a ridiculous name ... went to the jeep and stepped into it without opening a door. He did not move off until after they had moved. In the rear vision mirror Pippa watched him behind them. He followed until their car swept at length into Uncle Preston's park-like property on the station side of a wooded hill.

The driver, seeing the direction of Pippa's gaze, said: 'Crag's is on the other side, and that's Crag now, he comes down now and then.'

'From the big country,' said Davy.

'That's right. Miss Rena meant to meet you today, miss, but at the last minute her father wasn't the best.'

'It didn't matter, we enjoyed the train.'

'Yes, and we met Crag,' Davy put in.

The driver looked as though he was going to say something, but evidently he changed his mind. He was emerging from an avenue of camphor laurels now and coming to a halt. The halt was by a large, dark-red brick, two-storeyed house named Uplands. It was the sort of house that Pippa rather had imagined as Rena's background – rich-looking, prosperous. The perfect scene for the girl now coming out of the front door and down the steps to meet them. Second cousin Rena. Very little different really from the attractive, somehow exclusive even in gym tunic Rena who had condescended now and then at school to smile and nod.

But she was smiling winningly now, running to welcome them ... except that the smile stiffened when she turned at last from Davy to Pippa, and slowly, estimatingly, consideringly looked Pippa up and down.

'You've changed,' Rena said.

Helping the driver with the bags, Pippa heard herself babbling about the corrective glasses having corrected, the brace having braced, and she wondered why she was being

24

apologetic. Anyone would think I'd become a swan from a duckling, she thought wryly, whereas I'm simply a little less the owl and the rabbit than I used to be. It occurred to her ludicrously that she was using up a lot of creatures, and she gave a little laugh, but Rena did not laugh back. She was still looking her over, but when Pippa turned directly on her, feeling rather embarrassed by the close regard, to make some diverting . . . she hoped . . . remark, her second cousin went up the stairs and stood for a few moments talking to an elderly gentleman who had come out on the patio to watch them.

That they were speaking of her was obvious by the quick flick of Rena's eyes in her direction again, then a shrug and a nod from the man.

He was thick-set and stolid, but something about the features acclaimed Rena to be his daughter.

'Uncle Preston.' Pippa prompted herself to go up the steps to the man and hold out her hand.

'None of that, m'dear.' He smiled expansively at her. 'We're kin, remember.' His eyes roved over her.

'Far off,' she said faintly, not liking his rather un-uncle look.

'Not too far for this.' He kissed her appreciatively, his daughter looking on with cool amusement.

'When you're ready, Pippa,' she said, 'Daddy will show you where you're to sleep.' Her glance went briefly to him.

Pippa turned back for Davy, but Uncle Preston had his hand under her elbow and was guiding her forward, squeezing her arm jocularly every now and then. Something seemed to be amusing him and he chuckled to himself.

'That took some of the wind out of her sails,' he ho-ho'd. 'But' . . . proudly . . . 'being my Rena she soon showed who's Miss Fixit.'

For some distasteful reason she could not have put a finger on, Pippa did not ask the obvious questions. She permitted herself to be propelled up a wide staircase, then along a passage to a back room, for most obviously and most indisputably it *was* a back room.

She did not mind that. After all, she had had back rooms all her life. Indeed, all Aunt Helen's rooms could have been classed as back rooms, their old cottage being small and cheap as it was.

But this room fairly cried out back room. It was as bare as a ward and held only a bed, a chest of drawers and a chair. The window was narrow and it missed the rural loveliness of the Southern Highlands, that treesy, hillocky charm that could have been home. Instead it looked down on an incinerator, several waste-bins, a mulch heap and a woodpile. Also quite unmistakably the room ... now Pippa had turned back from the window ... had not been prepared.

Uncle Preston was chuckling again; again he was looking Pippa up and down.

'What's she like? That's what I asked her.' He ho-ho'd once more. He came nearer to Pippa. 'Do you know what she said?'

'What, Uncle Preston?'

'Do you know what that know-all girl of mine said? She said "Oh, just a little brown thing." '

'Well, I have brown hair,' Pippa said sensitively, not liking being the pivot of his attention.

'Yes, and you're small. But good things come in little packets, m'dear, and those eyes! And that sweet little face! Did I say welcome?' He leaned over, but Pippa prevented quickly, 'Yes, Uncle, you did.'

He was easy to divert, thank goodness. He started chuckling over Rena again, whom obviously he both doted on and quarrelled with. 'Didn't expect a winner like you. That'll upset her applecart.'

'I'm not.' In an inspiration Pippa added, 'I mean not like your daughter.'

They were the right words. Uncle Preston expanded visibly and agreed, 'No. My Rena's got it, hasn't she? So she should, she's had a fortune spent on her.'

He was extremely proud of Rena, Pippa decided, but he would often disagree with her for the simple reason that they would be one of a sort, the sort, Pippa thought a little sinkingly, that years ago, and she recalled it now, Aunt Helen, usually the most discreet of people, had said: 'Not the side of the family you want for yourself.'

The arguments the pair must frequently have staged were proved in Uncle's next words.

'A fortune,' he growled resentfully, 'but fortunes run out, and if she keeps on with this silly whim she's got now. . . . That's why you're put here, girl. Tucked safely away where you can't be seen.' He waved his arm round the room. 'She didn't expect you to be like you are. Oh, yes, I know my daughter.'

'It's quite sufficient,' said Pippa of the room, 'but where is Davy's? I always sleep near Davy.'

'Not necessary any more, Pippa.' Rena had joined them and at once her glorious golden colouring lit up the drab interior. Pippa saw Uncle Preston looking adoringly at his only child.

'*I* am taking over from you, pet,' Rena said smilingly but definitely. 'Poor little Pippa, tied down all these years.'

'It hasn't been a tie, Rena, and I would prefer—'

'But she's not going to, is she, Daddy?' A quick sharp look at her father. 'She's going to relax. *I* am having darling Davy near me. No, no more words. Our little Martha has done her share of work. Unpack your things, pet, and then come down to tea.'

27

Pippa stood for quite a while after Rena and her father had left. Her impulse was to go after them and have an understanding at once, tell them that Davy was *her* responsibility, that—

But it seemed rude. They had paid the fares out, expensive fares, they had taken them under their roof. Not that Pippa's corner was an attractive one, indeed it was quite unattractive, but it was still not costing a penny, and Rena was certainly taken up with Davy.

She was glad after she had placed her things and gone down that she had not insisted on that understanding. Rena stood at the bottom of the stairs and she took Pippa's arm and led her to a suite.

Davy was sitting on a padded window bench playing with an expensive mechanical toy, and while he was so absorbed, Pippa let her glance rove round. She would have been unfair had she not allowed a cry of pleasure. The room was perfect for a boy. The furnishings were many-coloured, but brightly and youthfully so. The pictures were pictures boys liked. Not only these, but Rena had shown nursing sense in including a divan as well as a bed, almost as if she had known that a delicate child must rest other hours than the expected night hours.

There were plenty of cupboards for books and toys and the wide-flung windows were cheerfully curtained.

'Rena, it's perfect! Quite perfect.'

'It should be,' grumbled Uncle Preston, who had come behind them, 'not only cost me a packet to renovate but I had to pay a nurse as well for advice.'

'Daddy, be quiet!' Rena sounded annoyed; she probably wanted the praise for the arrangement for herself, but Pippa felt a warmth for her second cousin for going to the trouble of seeking skilled advice.

'This was where you were to be,' Uncle Preston was saying, nodding to an adjoining room, which, though no larger, was much more attractive than the room upstairs. 'That's what you get for not being that little brown thing, m'dear.'

'We'll have tea,' Rena said abruptly. She gave her father a hard stare and he said no more.

A maid brought tea and cakes to the patio. Uncle Preston criticized the cakes as he munched them, saying they must have cost a few pennies to make 'with that butter and all'.

'My father is mean,' said Rena quite coolly. 'He counts the cents.'

'If I hadn't, young woman, you wouldn't be where you are. Then where's that, anyway? Hanging up your hat to a—'

'*Daddy!*'

Uncle Preston was silenced. But not for long. He explained to Pippa how thrift had got him on in the world.

'I started in business as a boy, and then—'

'Then you're not a farmer, Uncle Preston?' Pippa looked beyond the patio to the rural setting.

'Lord, no, I only bought Uplands because her ladyship—'

'That's enough, Daddy!' Rena gave another of her hard stares.

Pippa said a little awkwardly that for a man of commerce Uncle Preston had shown excellent farming sense since the Southern Highlands appeared so lush and rich, but he laughed and brushed that aside.

'No real farms here, girl, it's more a showplace. Oh, yes, you'll see fine orchards, prize cows and horses, but mostly it's a retreat for retired country folk who have had their day out west but can't face the confines of the city now they're on in years. It's quite a rich area, in its residents as well as its soil. Social, too.'

Uncle Preston's description tied up with their train companion's account of the district, thought Pippa, though certainly that brown man with his pipe could never be described as social.

Davy was rubbing his cake into crumbs and Pippa could see that Uncle Preston was watching him. Rena would be right, she thought, he would be mean in the little things; that was how he had got on. Her brother was tired, she decided. He needed rest.

She got up, saying she would see to him, and Rena nodded casually . . . then suddenly, at the same time as a car pulled up on the drive, she jumped to her feet, fairly hustled Pippa out, and said, 'No, *I* will. You go upstairs.'

'But, Rena, I—'

'Daddy, take her.'

'But it's the doctor, Rena,' Uncle Preston objected, looking through the window, 'and it's me he's come to see.' He sounded peeved.

Pippa, looking at him, could well believe he was the reason for the doctor's visit. The chauffeur had said he was not the best, and she had noticed when they had arrived he had a bad colour. Now, away from the sun, that pallor was even more pronounced.

'Glen will see to you *afterwards*, Daddy. Do as I say. Do it now.'

In another minute both Uncle Preston and Pippa were in the hall.

Pippa could hear steps, she could hear a clear, pleasant male voice, then Rena's high smooth voice in gentle response.

'Ho-ho,' said Uncle Preston scornfully . . . he seemed to ho-ho a lot . . . 'now she's put that plum in her mouth, and for all people, *him*. I can't afford him, Pippa. You may think I was joking when I said that before about my

30

present circumstances, about fortunes running out, but I wasn't. She, of course, will never believe it, never having been deprived in all her life. But it's true. Look, Pippa, I'll put you in the picture, this picture my spoiled girl means to paint.'

But Uncle Preston didn't. Not then. His daughter came to the door, and something had happened in the few minutes that had elapsed between their hurried retreat and the doctor's arrival. Rena wore a charming butter-cup-hued overall, a nursing-type overall. With her shining golden colouring she looked quite beautiful.

And not just beautiful but dedicated as well. Rena's eyes were soft and docilely downcast. Her smile was sweet.

'Doctor Burt will see you now, Daddy. Take my arm, dear.'

She took it for him and led him back through the door, closing the door definitely before Pippa could glimpse this Doctor Burt.

The mysterious Doctor Burt. Pippa could not help but think that as she climbed the stairs. He must be a very exceptional man to ring that change so soon. One minute a pretty, petulant, headstrong girl, the next minute a tender nurse.

Pippa crossed to the window and looked curiously out, hoping to catch a glimpse of Doctor Burt, but—

She saw the incinerator, the waste-bins and the mulch heap instead.

CHAPTER TWO

Pippa did not see Doctor Burt in the days that followed, even though he called regularly because Uncle Preston had had another turn.

'What's wrong with your father?' she asked Rena on one of the few occasions she met up with her cousin.

Rena shrugged, if perhaps not actually callously then certainly carelessly. 'Something or other,' she said, and her answer was at a complete variance to her attire, for, as well as the nursing uniform, Rena now had taken to wearing a professional veil whenever the doctor called. She said it was to keep her hair, that gleaming gold hair, away from her face, but it was still a very becoming veil. 'When one grows older things happen,' Rena said vaguely about her parent.

She was not so unkind as simply untouched, Pippa decided. Like Pippa, Rena had no mother, her maternal parent, too, having died early in her life, but unlike Pippa she had no Aunt Helen. Pippa could find a great pity in her for that. Rena might have a father, but Uncle Preston was entirely a business person, never, Pippa remembered distantly yet with love, like her own father. Preston Franklin had a fatherly regard, but it was mainly a massive paternal pride, pride that Rena was a Franklin after himself.

Pippa thought of Uncle Preston as someone who once he got something into his mind would not let go of it. For instance, his comfortable status (even though he complained about reversals) must have come through long hard application as well as a natural acumen. She felt he had passed that iron determination on to his daughter, and whatever it was ... though that should be *who*ever it was, thought Pippa, for unmistakably it was this Doctor Burt ... she wanted, she would leave nothing undone not to get her own way.

For some reason part of that programme was to have *Pippa* away. Had she not been the owl, the rabbit so long, Pippa might have been complimented over this, but she had no illusions about herself. She was that 'little brown thing' that Rena had described to her father.

So far, apart from not wanting her present, Rena had been quite friendly to Pippa. Having her father to complete her little act whenever Doctor Burt attended, she had had no need yet to deprive Pippa of Davy, for Pippa felt she knew now why the pair of them, Rena's distant English cousins, were here in Tombonda. It was that determination of Rena's, that iron resolve to get what she wanted. Evidently she had tried other methods with the elusive doctor, then recognized the possibility of this one. Shrewdly she had built up a scene for herself ... Uncle Preston had said painted a picture ... and she had had the money to do it, to bring the two of them, though only one really was needed, *Davy*, over from England. She never really had taken to Davy, Pippa knew now. She didn't dislike him, she simply had no feeling about it at all, but he had happened at a right moment, and she had grabbed what offered. Just now she could play the humanitarian role without the little boy, her father could complete a tableau set out for this Doctor Burt, but when Uncle Preston was around again Pippa had no doubt that Davy would take his place, and much more picturesquely, for there was something infinitely winning in the tender caring of a child.

What was he like, this doctor, for Rena to be so keen? So keen even that she did what could have been termed 'homework' on him. She sought out Pippa and asked her advice on nursing.

'I was a typist, Rena.'

'But you've looked after Davy.'

'Never professionally.'

'Only a few things, Pippa, sensible, convincing things will do.'

'Convincing to whom, Rena?'

'It's really nothing to do with you, Pippa. You've been brought over here free and you are enjoying free board, so I hardly think—'

'I didn't mean it like that. I mean what manner of person is to be convinced. If it's someone who understands a nurse's duties—'

'It's Glen Burt,' said Rena quite calmly. A pause. 'I'm marrying him.'

No 'I hope to'. No 'If I do'. Had Uncle Preston been like that when he decided to be a business success?

'Glen is not the usual type,' Rena continued. 'I mean not – well, not like Dom Hardy.' Domrey Hardy shared his overseer duties between the Franklin property on this side of the hill and the Crag property on the other, the Southern Highlands estates not being large enough to warrant an individual man. Pippa had met him and been favourably impressed. He seemed the born all-round farmer, she thought, the right man for a mixed district like this where piggeries, dairy farming, poultry runs and orchards found the weather equally favourable. She felt sure he would have had his own farm had he had the means.

'Dom is transparent, you can see what he's thinking, and that is of me,' Rena said with the lack of pleasure that beautiful *accustomed* girls often show.

'But Glen,' she continued, 'is unaware of me. He is so dedicated, so lit up. It's different to meet a man like that.'

34

'You've been spoiled, Rena,' Pippa smiled tolerantly. She suddenly found herself thinking of Crag, and wondering how apparent *he* had been. Was that over-apparency the reason he had come back from his 'Big Country' to Tombonda to see what had happened between himself and the girl next door? Had he been too easy for Rena? Would Rena tell him so when he asked her as he had told Pippa on the train that he would; 'What gives?'

She had not seen Crag yet, though Davy had spoken of him persistently and longingly. She had had the idea of walking the little boy over the hill to renew the acquaintance, for Davy had certainly made an idol of him, only she had been forbidden. It was ridiculous, really, and she didn't understand it, but on the first morning that she had visited Uncle Preston in his sickroom, an approved visit since Doctor Burt was not expected until noon, she had said in answer to how she was filling in time a casual, 'Looking around, Uncle Preston. This afternoon I thought I'd take Davy over to the next estate.'

'Crag's?'

'Yes.'

'*No*, my girl.'

'No, Uncle Preston?'

'*No*.'

'But, Uncle Preston—'

'*No*. Do you hear?'

'Yes, I do.' She couldn't see any reason, though, but Uncle Preston was not supposed to talk much, so she had left it at that. Evidently Rena was unconcerned where she went so long as she was not around when Glen Burt was here, but Uncle Preston had been quite emphatic.

'I suppose I have been spoiled,' shrugged Rena, continuing on with her musings. 'I know I'm attractive. And that's what challenges me. He ... Glen ... doesn't notice.'

35

'Do you love him or are you enjoying the challenge?' Pippa dared.

'They're both the same when you've been bored like I have.'

'Oh, Rena—' began Pippa, but Rena broke in irritably:

'Give me some nursing hints.'

'I only took an aide course,' demurred Pippa, but as Rena stuck out a stubborn lip she complied.

'A nurse needs to be adaptable, tactful and discreet. Her patient is her first concern.'

'Something more concrete. I could pretend all that.'

Pippa told her about room temperature, the storing of medicines, the necessity for a stock of good temper and patience, the need to concede yet stand firm.

'Something definite,' Rena demanded.

'I've only dealt with children, with Davy.'

'That's what I want, because Father will be up again very soon, and I'll have to use your brother. Oh, don't look like that. I wish him the best as you do, but if I can avail myself at the same time, I will. *Tell* me something, Pippa.'

'It's as well to be able to amuse a sick child,' Pippa said leadenly. Why had she ever come here? she wondered.

Rena must have seen she had gone a little too far. 'Tell me about Davy,' she asked quite gently. 'What exactly is it?'

'An incurable circulatory disease. That is, incurable now.'

'You mean something might be found?'

'I tell myself so, and no one really can say definitely these days, but—' Pippa looked away.

'All this will interest Glen.' Rena became brisk again. 'He wants to do research. That costs money, and you'd think he'd be aware that I could help him.' She looked around at her affluent home with satisfaction. 'Tombonda,' she went on, 'is only till Glen goes to Europe, or America, or – or somewhere *right away*.' She said the last almost with passionate fervour, and Pippa looked at her in puzzlement. 'Right away,' her cousin repeated.

Pippa thought of how she had declared that love and challenge were the same when you were bored and she wondered had the doctor been any other man who had not thrown his heart at Rena's feet would any other men be as attractive to her cousin? Undoubtedly, her thoughts ran on, Crag Crag's failure with Rena had been his over-susceptibility. Perhaps if she saw the brown man before he returned to his Big Country, to his Yantumara, Falling Star, she could put him wise. A pity for such a family-anxious person to waste 'time for living life as it should be lived' by making wrong moves.

That afternoon Pippa saw Glen Burt. She was gathering flowers to brighten her room when his car pulled up. She got behind a shrub, knowing that Rena would be angry if she was around, but she had a good look at him.

She liked him instantly, and she would have loved to have talked to him about Davy. There was a gentleness yet a strength to him, she thought. No wonder that Rena...

Rena sought her out later and said quite frankly: 'Father's to be up and around again quite soon, indeed, he'll be allowed on the patio tomorrow, so I'll be using your brother. I'm not asking "Any objection?" because even if you had one, like Dom always has objections, I wouldn't listen.'

She always brought Domrey Hardy into it, Pippa mused. She answered her cousin: 'That's all right, Rena, so long as Davy has attention.'

'He's going to have heaps of it,' Rena assured her.

Uncle Preston was out on the patio the next day as promised, and during the morning he had a word with Pippa.

'You've stopped away from next door as I said?'

'Why, yes, Uncle Preston.'

'You're entitled to a reason.'

'I think I am. You see, I met Mr. Crag on the train coming down to Tombonda, and Davy has been asking about him.'

'Then Rena can take him over.'

'I think,' Pippa said clearly, 'that that might be suitable, for Mr. Crag said on the journey that he wanted an understanding with Rena.' Actually he had said he wanted to know 'What gives?' but he had meant an understanding.

She waited for Uncle Preston to explain, and, always the business man, he did.

'They had a semi-agreement,' he grunted. 'It was just after Rena had that fall off Bunting, I remember.' – Bunting was one of the ponies – 'I thought everything was set between the pair of them, and I was pleased, even though ...' Uncle Preston was silent for a moment. 'Yes, I was pleased,' he took up again, 'because Crag could keep my girl in the way she was accustomed.

'Then that fellow, that doctor fellow joined the act,' he went on. He glowered.

'And Rena fell in love with him?'

'I don't know about this love,' grumbled Uncle Preston testily.

'You must do. You married Aunt Millicent.'

'She was suitable,' he replied. – That was typical of Uncle Preston, and Pippa half-smiled.

'You don't find Doctor Burt suitable?' she asked.

'He's a dreamer. You only have to look at him.'

'I haven't,' admitted Pippa. Well, actually she hadn't, only between the boughs of a shrub.

'Then you will,' he promised.

'Rena doesn't want that, though I don't know why.'

'Don't fish for compliments. You're pretty, Pippa. Not a beauty like my girl, but lots of men like a quiet type like you. She doesn't want you because she's afraid Glen might be one of those men. Which would suit me. Oh, yes, you'll meet Burt, my girl.'

Uneasily Pippa had left Uncle Preston. At no time had she expected to be rapturously happy in Australia, so long as Davy was contented had been all she had asked, but this in-between position in which she found herself, in between Rena and her father, was certainly something she had *not* anticipated.

That she had not dreamed up the situation was established at once by Rena meeting her in the hall just beyond the patio.

'I know what he said,' Rena pounced at once.

'It was unimportant, Rena.'

'Not unimportant to me. I told you I was going to marry Glen.'

'Yes, I heard you, but I can't see where I come in.'

Rena looked hard at her but did not explain. 'I meant it, Pippa. *I* am marrying Glen. So I don't want you in this.'

'I don't want to be in it, either, I just want a quiet life with Davy.'

'Then you've come to the wrong place if you interfere. Father doesn't want Glen for me, so he's encouraging you to step in. But I won't have it, Pippa. Do you understand?'

Pippa said, confused, 'He's forbidden me to take Davy over to Crag's.'

Rena shrugged carelessly at that and the shrug

39

prompted Pippa to complain: 'You tell me to keep away from the doctor, yet your *father* tells me to keep away from your neighbour. What am I to do?'

'What I say, of course.'

'And that is to—'

'To see Crag. To do what you like with Crag. I don't want him.' A toss of the golden head.

About to add, 'Neither do I', Pippa said impulsively instead, 'But you did once.'

'I don't know if I did,' Rena shrugged again. 'I think it was just – just—' But she did not finish it. She set her lips instead.

Pippa broke the little silence that followed by repeating, 'You must appreciate my position, Rena. Your father forbids me to see Mr. Crag. You forbid me to see Doctor Burt. I have no particular desire to see either, so what gives?'

What gives? Crag Crag's drawled words. She thought of Davy's Big Country man and wondered why she had copied the foolish phrase.

'Oh, just make do with Dom,' advised Rena crossly, for the overseer was coming up the drive now. Quite rudely the girl turned and left Pippa to greet the young farmer alone. Dom took it philosophically. 'Always,' he sighed, 'Rena is running away from me. It was just a buying authority I needed. Something dull to do with pigs.'

'Only *you* don't find it dull?' deduced Pippa sympathetically.

'No,' he admitted, 'I love what I'm doing.'

'Except that you'd sooner be doing it for yourself?'

'And with—' he began impulsively. Then he stopped.

It came to Pippa that if anyone could help her in her odd position, the in-between uncertainty in which she found herself, in between stubborn Uncle Preston and determined Rena, it could be this kind young man.

'Mr. Hardy—' she ventured.

'Can't it be Dom?' he smiled. 'Admittedly we're not the wide untrammelled west—'

'The big country.'

'Yes, but even in these Southern Highlands formality is out of place.'

'I'm Pippa,' she agreed warmly, for she couldn't help liking him. As he nodded back, she began again, 'Dom—'

But she wasn't to ask his advice or help or information, because Rena's imperative voice called to her through a window.

'Where's Davy?' Rena asked sharply.

With a little gesture to Domrey Hardy, Pippa went inside. Rena met her as she came through the door.

'Glen is coming at once to give Father a final look-over before he's allowed right out of the house and around the grounds again. Daddy's obviously thriving, so no doubt Glen will make this a last visit unless he's called out especially. But he's one of those righteous doctors you can't call. I mean he wants to know if it's absolutely necessary.' A little rueful laugh. 'What a man! So I thought I'd present Davy today, start a new programme of events. But the wretched boy is missing.'

'Davy isn't here!' Pippa said urgently.

'Oh, don't take on, Pippa, he can't have gone far. The trouble is where? Glen will be out in half an hour.'

Pippa turned on her furiously. 'I don't care when he comes out, Rena, all I care is that Davy is missing. Have you looked in his room?'

'And your room and every other room. The garden. The orchard. I even went down to the chicken run. That deplorable boy—'

'He could have gone into the planting.' Like most of the estates in the Highlands area, the Franklin property included a small afforestation section where softwood was being raised. Though it was called the planting, the trees had been in for some years, and were fairly well advanced, mostly pine, already spreading their branches to meet and form a concealing green tent. Pippa had walked through once and nearly lost herself among the identical trees. If Davy had ventured in—

Brushing past Rena, Pippa ran out of the room, then out of the house, down past the cultivation, the stables, the piggery, orchard, the resting paddocks.

'Davy,' she called, 'Davy!'

She was aware that in parkland like this there was little fear of the boy being lost, that Rena was probably right when she had contemptuously dismissed, 'Oh, don't take on, he can't have gone far.' But even in a little distance the strain could be too much for her brother in his delicate state. Also, if he had ventured into the planting ... the forest, he called it ... he could have panicked when he found himself, as Pippa had, walking round in circles, and, being a child, not had the sense to know that in such a small afforestation it was not far to the open fields again.

Reaching the deep green and plunging into it, Pippa called once more, 'Davy! Davy! It's Pippa, Davy. Stand quite still then shout out my name, darling.' She waited, but there was no answer.

She combed the woods thoroughly. At any other time she would have rejoiced in the cool pine tang of the needles brushing her face, the soft carpet of the fallen ones beneath her feet, but not now.

Stumbling over roots she kept up her searching and calling, then found she was climbing a small rise. At the bottom of the rise a little stream purled by, and now she found a new fear. She ran forward and was relieved to see that the brook was quite shallow, but often deep

pools formed at intervals, she knew, and she looked
nervously up and down stream, wondering which way to
search.

Then to her surprise she saw a patch through the trees.
She must be out of the planting, but on the other side to
Franklin's. Crag Crag's side. Sobbing a little in relief, she
ran forward, past more tilled ground, some of it under
cultivation, then at last she saw the house, not elegantly
two-storeyed like Uncle Preston's but leisurely and spreading. The sort of a house you expected from a big country-
man. Strictly Western-style.

Snatching a breath, she began to run again, but already
she had run too fast for too long, and a sharp pain halted
her. She refused to accept the pain and pushed herself
forward once more, her heart pumping so acutely in its
effort to cope that at last she was forced to stop definitely,
not only stop but sink to the ground.

When Crag joined her a moment afterward, he just
left her like that, wisely waiting for her to recover, checking Davy, who was by his side, that he did the same.

Davy's scolding, 'You naughty girl to run like that, you
always tell me not to' were the sweetest words Pippa felt
she had ever heard. She knew she was going to cry, and
that was something she never did in front of Davy, but
how to stop the relieved tears?

Then she found she could cry in safety, for the brown
man was telling Davy to come and see something, and
they were both gone. By the time they returned, her
breath had returned, and her eyes were dry. Davy forgot
about his admonishment in the excitement of whatever it
was the man had shown him, but Crag Crag found time
to say as they followed Davy, who was leading the way
triumphantly to the Crag house: 'He's right, you know,
you were a naughty girl. Why?'

'I thought you understood the position,' she said stiffly,

and she nodded briefly to her brother. 'I told you in the train—'

'Oh, that.' He gave a hunch of his great shoulders. 'But you were worrying for yourself, not for the scrubber. What good could that do?'

'It was Davy concerning me, of course,' she defended. 'He could have got lost in the planting and worked himself up to a pitch which could be dangerous. Then there's a stream and—'

She stopped. Stopped her progress as well as her answer to him, for he had paused to pack his eternal pipe, and halted her with him. She felt infuriated with him for his calmness, for his deliberation. Except that Davy now was too far ahead she would have grabbed her brother's hand and returned him at once and without any more explanation to Uplands.

'Look,' said Crag Crag, still doing his packing and tapping thing with the tobacco, 'you shouldn't have run like that, it did nobody any good. It did Davy no good . . . you worrying over him never does any good. Children live in the present, not the past nor the future. They're such little scrubbers they have nothing in the past to regret and nothing in the future to fear, so they're content.

'Then' . . . giving her no chance to edge in . . . 'it did you no good. You're still out of breath.

'Then' . . . lighting the pipe he had been busy on . . . 'it did me no good.' His match made a little scratching sound.

'I fail to see where you come into it.'

'Shall I tell you, then?' He had started walking once more, had taken her along with him, but now he stopped again. Stopped abruptly.

'No,' she said hurriedly, not knowing why her heart was keeping up its thumping so long. 'No, it doesn't matter. I'm sorry I was so foolish, and I do see your point.

44

It would have put you out had I collapsed in your grounds.'

He did not comment on that at once. He looked her burningly up and down, then he said deliberately: 'When I was at school we used to call kids like you stinkers. You know damn well I wasn't thinking of that.'

Now was her turn to ask, 'What, then?' but Pippa blurted instead, 'Davy has reached your house.'

She saw that the house was named briefly (and rather clownishly, she considered) simply: 'Ku'.

'Meaning shelter,' the brown man said, guessing her scorn. 'That's what it is for me. *Home* is up north, at Falling Star.'

'Rather elaborate for a mere shelter,' she remarked. 'Oh, naughty Davy, he's gone in.'

'He was there before, so why not now? It was the scrubber who saw you running out of the planting.' They had reached the wide verandah by this, and he stood aside and nodded for Pippa to climb shallow steps into a long cool hall.

'It's not like Uncle Preston's,' Pippa murmured, for she could think of nothing else just then to say.

'It's the same as the big country house. Big country men only know one style – long halls, rooms each side, verandahs all round like the brim of a hat. Makes for coolness, only coolness isn't needed much here, not in the Southern Highlands.' He laughed. 'But it didn't matter to my father, for being a big country man he naturally put in chimneys everywhere. They all go out and up. It's not what you'd call perfect planning building a cool house and having to make it warm, but I'm glad he built big country style, I like the look of a fire.'

'So do I,' chirruped Davy from the fireside of the room into which Crag had led Pippa, 'especially when you make toast.'

45

'Davy,' reprimanded Pippa, 'you shouldn't have run away like this. Why did you?'

'I didn't want to see another doctor. I'm always seeing doctors. So I thought I'd ask Crag. But Crag's been telling me about Manager and how he had this bad leg.'

'Your Falling Star manager?' asked Pippa politely, and Davy went into peals of laughter.

'No, he's a bay, and so is Major, but Captain is grey, and Taffy is—'

'Get back to Manager,' said Crag.

'Well, Manager had to see the vet. Then he had to see him again. And again.' A big breath. 'Then again. But in the end—'

'In the end?' Pippa's throat was dry.

'He won a hurdle. They have these races up in the big country, you know. Real jockeys and pretend jockeys ... I mean not jockeys who are jockeys all the time. The real jockeys wear silks, but the others wear overalls or jeans or crash helmets even. So Manager won by not missing out on the vet. And I'll do the same, Pippa, because Crag says—'

Crag says. Crag says. The little voice went on and on, not giving Pippa a chance to insert, 'Yes, dear, but now we have to go home.'

At length she did, though. She said accusingly to Davy: '*Your* vet is at Uplands right this minute and you're not there to be checked, so you'll never win a hurdle.'

'Reckon he will from now on, though, eh, scrubber?' drawled Crag. 'Reckon he'll remember Manager.' He looked narrowly at Pippa, asking: 'Is this vet one Glen Burt?'

'Yes.'

'Then I reckon I needn't drive you back. I reckon Rena will be scorching up the drive any minute now.' A short knowing laugh.

Davy's attention was on a racing manual Crag had handed him, so there was no need to talk carefully. Pippa knew that when Davy read he read with all of him, everything else was excluded.

'I expect she will,' she agreed. 'She plans to use Davy.'

'You don't object?'

'Not so long as my brother has attention.'

'What about you?'

'What do you mean?'

'You don't want attention yourself? This doctor's attention? You see, I've met Burt.'

'I haven't.' Her colour was high.

'Then when you do you mightn't like the way Rena has things worked out.'

'Oh, really—'

'Yes, really. He's an exceptional fellow. Handsome, too. You mightn't like sitting back while Rena does a maternal act in flowing veil and what-have-you to spring a trap that could have been yours.'

'Actually you mean *you* don't like it,' she said angrily. 'Not from Rena.'

'Me?' He was patently surprised.

'Oh, don't give me that,' flung Pippa. 'You said yourself in the train that you had to see Rena to find out what gives.'

'Remember what I say, don't you,' he said, absurdly pleased, or anyway, Pippa found it absurd.

'Also,' she continued coldly, 'Uncle Preston told me of your semi-agreement with Rena.'

'Not semi on his part,' grinned Crag. 'Old Preston was all for it. That is' . . . thoughtfully . . . 'failing—'

He did not finish, and Pippa said as she had before: 'Really.'

'Don't repeat that any more,' appealed Crag. He waited, then: 'Look, Pippa' ... *Pippa*, Pippa revolted ... 'I'll put you straight. There *was* a semi-agreement. I'm sick of being a bachelor, and I don't mind admitting it.'

'Time running out and all that?' caustically.

'Exactly. But I still wasn't so keen that I would have rushed into it. As it happened I didn't need to. *I* was the rushed one.'

'That's very ungallant. It's also untrue.'

'It's not ungallant. Rena Franklin ran after me like you just ran after the scrubber. Oh, I was flattered all right. Just down from the bush and a girl storms me. A beautiful one. Only—' A quiet smile.

'It's not true,' interrupted Pippa. 'You rushed Rena, and she got sick of it. Everyone rushes her, except Glen Burt, and that's why—'

'You believe that?' He looked at her incredulously.

'Why not?'

'You wouldn't think of believing that she's running away instead?'

'You just said she ran after you.'

'Yes, but she didn't mean to catch up. Oh, no, not our Rena.'

'I simply can't follow you,' Pippa said after a little pause. 'It's all so contradictory. You said she rushed you, then you say she was running away. It makes no sense. But I do advise you' ... briskly now ... 'to — to court Rena differently. Don't be so — so susceptible. *Then* you might win.'

'And you think that's what I want?'

'You have said so, haven't you? You spoke about that design of man and woman' ... her cheeks flushed ... 'and how it has to have its start.'

'Reckon I did say that,' he nodded, 'only I was forgetting something else, something the old man once told me.'

'Uncle Preston?'

'My old man. My dad. His life and my mother's life together was the only kind I wanted.' He took up his pipe. 'I asked Dad once how – well, how you *knew*.' He turned the pipe over in his big hand. For Crag Crag, Pippa thought, he actually looked shy.

'Yes?' she asked gently, wondering at her gentleness.

'He said . . . my father said it was a thousand candles.'

'All lit up?' Davy was looking up from the horse book now.

'All lit together, scrubber. Reckon I forgot it for a while, but do you know what' . . . he was lighting the pipe now . . . 'I've remembered it again.'

'Absence doesn't always make the heart grow fonder,' nodded Pippa crisply, 'now that you're near to Rena again you've remembered it.'

'Rena?' If she hadn't been worried how Rena was going to react to Davy's absence and not reacting properly herself, Pippa would have said there was a negation in his voice.

'Here she is now,' advised Davy, peering out of the window. He added wickedly, 'Purple with rage.'

Rena certainly looked angry, thought Pippa, joining Davy, she was flushed and actually tousled. She put her arm protectively around her brother.

'She spits, but so far she doesn't bite,' advised Crag calmly from his side of the room. 'I had a wild cat like that once at Falling Star.'

'Did you, Crag?' came in Davy eagerly. 'Tell me about it.'

'Later, scrubber. You take your sister out to the kitchen and help her make a pot of tea. I'm going to spread oil.'

Out in the large galley ... big country style again in its capaciousness, in its large centre table ... Davy said, 'I didn't see any oil. I wonder if he's spreading it now.'

'Yes,' contributed Pippa, 'I wonder.'

But by the quietness in the room they had just left, in spite of Crag Crag's refusal of Rena, Pippa had more an impression of candles. A thousand candles as two people looked across a space at each other.

All lit together.

CHAPTER THREE

ON their way back to Uplands, Pippa was relieved to find
her cousin almost mellow. After Rena's angry expression
as she left her car on the drive to storm into Crag's Ku ...
purple with rage, Davy had said ... she had trembled for
her brother. Davy had literally never known an admonishing word, not a seriously admonishing one, all his small
life, and the words Rena had seemed about to throw at
him had raised all sorts of fears for that sensitive little
boy. But either the tea she had brought in or the oil Crag
had spread ... Davy was still puzzling over that oil ...
had done something. Rena now was quite relaxed.

'It's always the way with Crag,' Rena said quite amiably, negotiating a bend, 'he calms me down. Actually
we two would make good chemistry.'

It seemed an unromantic way to put it, Pippa thought,
she preferred candlelight, but she supposed it came to the
same thing. Rena's happy mood also meant no scolding
for Davy, and for that she should be pleased, and she was,
of course, except ... well, except ... Her lips moved unconsciously. She was not aware she spoke.

'Pippa,' came in Davy from the back seat, 'why did you
just say candlelight twice? It's daytime, and anyway,
there's 'lectric here at Tombonda.'

'Yes, darling.'

'And 'lectric, too, up at Falling Star. They have plant,
Crag told me. It's not like a plant in the ground, it's a
machine plant, Crag told me.'

'Yes, darling,' Pippa said mechanically. She was
pleased there was no reckoning from Rena, but somehow
she still felt oddly heavy.

'Our Davy,' Rena was saying cheerfully, 'wasn't needed after all. Glen spent a long time on Father.'

'How is he?'

'Oh, quite all right, I should say,' vaguely. 'After Glen finished the examination I got our doctor on to the topic of Davy, and succeeded in interesting him enough to come out if . . . when . . . he's asked. I'm sure of it.'

'Doesn't a doctor always do things like that?'

'I told you before, Pippa, Glen is the frightfully dedicated type. He wouldn't come just for a fee, there'd have to be a proper reason. I told him what you told me about Davy – that circulatory thing. He was certainly keen. I should say he'll come whenever I ring.'

'Thank you.' Pippa's voice was dry.

'The trouble is,' Rena continued, self-absorbed as usual, 'he'll have to meet you, and you know how I feel about that.'

'I don't know why.'

'Oh, come off it,' said Rena slangily, 'you must look in the mirror sometimes. You're pretty, Pippa, something I never expected, otherwise I wouldn't have had you here. Surely someone somewhere at some time must have told you that.'

'No one did.'

'It takes some believing.'

'Then you'll just have to believe.'

'You mean you've reached the age of twenty . . . you'd be that, Pippa, you were some years junior to me . . . and no man has told you!'

'None.'

'It takes some believing,' Rena said again.

'It's true. I haven't met anyone. My life has been taken up with—' Pippa gave a brief indicative nod of her head.

'A child can't take up that much.'

52

'*Love* can.'

'Then preserve me from it!'

'But you already have it, haven't you? Or is it – challenge? Oh, I'm sorry, Rena, I'm speaking out of turn.'

'You are,' said Rena, 'but after all I started this. Frankly, Pippa, I don't know much about – well, about what you just said, I – I mean—'

'You mean love?'

'Yes. You see ... well ...' Suddenly and unnecessarily Rena put her foot down on the accelerator and the car fairly leapt ahead, Davy, taken unawares, tumbling forward. Pippa caught him before any damage was done. Rena tossed, 'Sorry.' As Pippa righted Davy again she saw that Rena wore an oddly pinched look.

To bridge an awkward silence Pippa asked, 'What am I to say to Uncle Preston if he questions me? He was very adamant that I didn't go over to Crag's.'

'I doubt if he'll ask you now he's allowed outdoors again. My father is primarily a business man and he'll be so anxious to check up whether Dom Hardy is still ministering his estate as it should be, that he hasn't been giving more time to Ku than to Uplands, that he'll probably forget all about it. That's typical of Daddy. Pennies first. Which reminds me, *you* can be of use to our overseer, Pippa. Father will like that. So will I. At least it will keep you from Glen.'

'Rena, I told you I have no wish to know this Doctor Burt.'

'What about his knowing you?'

'I can't help that, and I'm sorry. If I could help it I'd—'

'Yes, I suppose so. But he'll certainly want you for data on Davy. Apart from giving it to him, Pippa, just don't linger, will you? Just – just watch it.'

It seemed incredible to Pippa that Rena's lovely red

mouth could form these slangy threats. Only that somewhere somehow they rang false, she could have felt angry with her cousin.

'How can I help Dom Hardy?' she asked instead.

'The Southern Highlands comprise the perfect stud for pigs, cows, horses,' shrugged Rena, 'and blessed events always call for help. If you consult Dom Hardy's official calendar you'll see quite a birth list ticked up.' She paused. 'Also, can you ride?'

'How well would I be required to?'

'He'll tell you.' Again the shrug. – What an odd girl she was, hard, yet somehow defiantly, determinedly so. It puzzled Pippa.

When they reached the house Uncle Preston was out walking round the different sections, as his daughter had said he would, and when Pippa joined him he did not question her about Ku. Instead he kept up a grumble about his monetary affairs, the same grumble Pippa had heard before, mostly concerning his daughter and her blithe refusal to realize their present position.

She took the old man's hand to help him over some uneven ground, noticing how thin it had become during his illness. 'Down to your last million, Uncle,' she teased.

'You can laugh,' he retorted, 'but I'm genuinely concerned. For some time now the market in which I'm vitally involved has been ... But what's the use of telling you?'

'Often telling helps.' But Pippa said it without much feeling. Always she had been poor, really poor, and looking around this beautiful estate she had to smile wryly at Uncle Preston's idea of straitened circumstances.

The old man continued his grumbling. 'How could Rena face up to it?' he said.

'But this place alone—'

'Wouldn't keep her in shoes. Rena has been used to everything, *everything*. That was why I was resigned about Crag for her after ... well, once I knew, once I could see that—' As he had previously, Pippa recalled, Uncle Preston did not finish his thought. Returning to Crag again, he sighed regretfully: 'There's money there.'

'Rena-money,' smiled Pippa, and her uncle nodded.

'I thought that least she would be right that way, then what does that minx do but play up again.'

'The doctor?'

'Yes.'

'No doubt you've spoiled her, Uncle.'

'No doubt,' he admitted ruefully. 'I wasn't a young parent and she was an exceptionally beautiful girl. Yes, I spoiled her, Pippa. Still, it's only recently she's been like this. Always capricious, of course, but not like this. She used to lead me a merry dance, that was my Rena, but sometimes I think it was only after her fall off Bunting ...'

He had said something about this before, Pippa remembered. She asked: 'Was she hurt?'

'Never Rena, she's a perfect horsewoman, even handles falls.' He chuckled.

There was a silence, and Pippa broke it with the information that Rena had suggested that she help the overseer with the Uplands estate. As Rena had said, her father was pleased.

'Yes,' he nodded practically, 'there's enough idle hands at Uplands. Though I've no doubt that that wasn't her reason, not Rena's, she just wanted you out of the way when the doctor fellow calls.'

'I have to see Doctor Burt some time, he'll want information about Davy.'

'Then you'd better look your worst,' ho-ho'd Uncle Preston.

Feeling uncomfortable at the turn of the conversation, Pippa said there was no time like the present to offer her services to the overseer. She helped Uncle Preston to the patio, touched by his exhaustion after such a small expedition, then went to the back of the house and across the lawn to the stables.

Domrey Hardy was sitting in his office absorbed in estate affairs when she entered, but he looked up and smiled and cleared a chair for her.

She told him that it had been suggested that she help him.

'Mr. Franklin back on the job again,' he nodded.

'No, actually it was Rena who told me, but Uncle Preston was quite pleased.'

'Yes. Rena.' Dom looked down at his papers again.

A silence grew. Pippa broke it at length by saying briskly: 'I believe you have a string of happy events, Dom.'

'That's right.' Dom came out of his absorption and was the alert overseer again. 'Candytuft foals in a month. The piggery will be a nursery in several weeks. As for Velvet—'

'With a name like that Velvet must be the cow.'

'Yes, and she's predictably unpredictable in her timing. She could be right this minute, next week, next month. No official forty weeks for our girl, she shortens or lengthens the period to her own liking.'

'Doesn't a bull calf generally take longer?'

'Yes. But I sometimes think rules were made to be broken by our Velvet. Also, going on previous confinements, she's touchy. We have, of course, a good vet, but Velvet usually chooses a moment when a vet isn't available.'

'I might be able to help.'

'The idea is attractive, but have you helped before?'

'I lived in a country village and at least I was aware,' Pippa replied.

She next brought up the subject of riding. 'Rena said I might be of use there, and that you'd let me know.'

Dom had put the pen he had been doodling with back on the stand and he folded his arms on the desk. He was looking across at Pippa yet not looking at her somehow. 'Determined, isn't she?' he said quietly.

'What, Dom?'

'You're not to upstage her. That's it, isn't it. – Oh, I'm sorry, Pippa, I'm talking rot.' He tried to brush it aside, but Pippa persisted.

'What is it, Dom?' she asked again.

When he did not reply, she said: 'It's Rena, isn't it?'

'Yes.'

'What did you mean by upstage?' – Crag had said almost the same thing, she recalled, only he had expressed it: 'Springing a trap that could have been yours.'

Wretchedly Dom said: 'She's determined not to have you around when Burt's around, which means she's determined on him, and when Rena's determined . . .' He said it almost unemotionally, but Pippa saw that his knuckles in the big capable farmer hands were white from the tightness of his clenched fists.

At once he said again, 'Sorry, Pippa. Sheer rot. Of course I can do with you. How well do you ride?'

'How well is required?' She had asked that of Rena and Rena had said that Dom Hardy would explain.

'The Southern Highlands is the home of the pony clubs,' he told her. 'With a moderately bracing climate like we enjoy, how could it not be the perfect place? So we train for shows, for all the equestrian gatherings. We try to impart the usual accomplishments . . . canters, trots, even dressage.'

'Uplands' horses?'

'No, we accept outside pupils and train them for their owners. This, incidentally, is strictly my own business, Pippa, I pay Mr. Franklin for the exercise space and the stabling.'

'But he seemed pleased I could help you.'

'Well, some of the income goes back to him, so although it's my part of the concern it's to his advantage for it to prosper.'

She nodded, then remarked, 'Uncle Preston says he's in a bad financial position.'

Dom gave a short laugh at that and said nothing. He took Pippa out to a pretty cream pony which he said he was training for a client for the next Royal Show.

'Rickaby needs exercise around your weight, Pippa. Care to try him?'

'I haven't any gear, not even a pair of slacks.' She had brought none. They had not seemed necessary.

'That's all right, there's plenty in the change room.' He nodded back to the stables.

As he saddled the pony, Pippa returned to the stables, found the change room and changed. The clothes that were hung there were all very good. Rena's? And had Rena ridden since her fall from Bunting?

She asked Dom this when she came back again. He was bent over the pony, but he straightened at once. 'Did Rena tell you about that?'

'No. Her father mentioned that she had had a fall.' Pippa did not add that Uncle Preston had complained that his daughter had not been the same since. Instead she said, 'These must be her clothes. They're good.'

'Then if they're good they would be hers,' he said abruptly. He came round to leg Pippa up. His face was unrevealing – intentionally so, Pippa thought.

It was a puzzling situation, but once she was on the pony's back she forgot the puzzle. She always had loved riding, and in the village where they had lived it had not been such an expensive pleasure. Though ... smiling ... she had never ridden in a kit as well tailored as this.

She trotted round for a while, then, encouraged by the fact that months out of a saddle had not lessened her ability, she ventured down a track leading from the circle that Dom had flattened out from other exercising. What happened next was entirely her own fault. She should have realized that a 'boarder' here simply to learn the tricks, not present just for the fun of it and certainly not for exploration, would not comprehend the un-even ground as the track petered suddenly out, the bushes began to encroach, the trees crowd in, a dividing fence imprison. The gully creek was her final undoing. Ordi-narily it would have been a charming spot, Pippa thought briefly, a place where tranquillity would be the keynote, no sound except the chirping of crickets, the song of a bird, the tinkle of the brook, but it was new and strange to the cream pony, and like all highly bred animals he was over-sensitive to unaccustomed things. Perhaps he saw a shape in the shadows that Pippa could not see, something that frightened him, for, rearing up, he turned and streaked, quite out of control now, away from the shad-owy gully. Unfortunately the path the pony took was right beside the boundary fence. Several times Pippa brushed it quite roughly. She thought ruefully that Rena's expensive gear would suffer. But at least, she thought, too, it was better that than the pony.

Now the animal was fairly flying, and though she had always enjoyed a brisk gallop, Pippa had never been good enough to cope with anything like this. She gave up trying to check Rickaby, show him who called the tune, her only thought now was to hold on. Hold on. Hold on, she said desperately as the pony fairly flew over the ground.

She could hear hooves digging in; she would not have thought the little light fellow could have made such a din. Then she saw something streak past her, a second horse, a much larger mount than her own, which would account for that noise. But she had no time to look properly, she was too concerned with her own inability to deal with the racing cream, too aware of the fellow's knowledge, as horses always have such knowledge, that she had lost her touch.

'Pull in!' the voice called authoritatively. Even in her despair she recognized the voice as Crag Crag's, and she called back pleadingly, 'I can't!'

'Then hold on. I'm coming. And when I say Clear, clear your feet from the stirrups. But hang on, Pippa, he'll rear.'

She obeyed mechanically, held on mechanically, freed herself when he called out as he turned his own mount and doubled back to reach over and grab her rein. As he shouted 'Clear!' the cream fellow rose on his hind legs and Pippa felt herself slipping, but her feet at least were free and she was able to be lifted out of the saddle and deposited in front of Crag, then, a few moments later, dropped to the ground.

'Reckon,' said a slow voice, 'you'll have to do better than that when you ride after a scrubber up at Falling Star.' Crag Crag took out his pipe and began his packing act.

His unshakeable calmness usually irritated her, but now it gave her the time she needed to catch her breath. She did not pick him up over his assumption that she would be going to Falling Star, she was too grateful she had not fallen herself. She found a log and sat on it while he secured Rickaby.

'Damn silly thing to do,' he said, when he came back again, 'these are strictly ring ponies, not ring-bark.'

'Ring-bark?'

'Well, you've nearly done that to yourself.' He was looking at the jodhpurs that had received the impact of the boundary fence. They were torn, frayed and rubbed.

'Rena's,' she said forlornly.

'But the skin underneath is yours. Best you give it some attention, girl.'

'I'm all right.'

'If you are it's more than you deserve to be. You should know these fellows are only spit and polish boys, not like—'

'I know, not like the ones who carry you full gallop to flick a scrubber down and pin it by its tail.'

'You remember!' he said with delight.

'Oh, you – you fool!' Pippa replied. She got up and brushed herself. 'I must get back. Dom will wonder where I am.' It occurred to her that she must seem very churlish seeing that but for this man she might not be returning at all, so she added humbly, 'I thank you very much.'

'That's all right.' He grinned. 'I was only thinking of the Franklins. It puts people out to have someone collapse on their grounds.'

'*You* remember.' It was Pippa's turn. They both began to laugh.

'Well,' said Crag, 'that's better than crying, anyway. You better get up as you said. But soak in the bath to-night. Nothing like heat for a graze. Have you anything to apply?'

'The clothes got the impact.'

'You'll find you got impact, too, beneath those clothes. Have the doctor look you over. No.' A brief grin. 'It's Burt, isn't it, so that would be out because of Rena. But

61

see to yourself all the same.'

'I will, and thank you again. By the way, how was it you were here to rescue me?'

'You were rescued, isn't that enough?'

'Do you make a habit of going down gullies in case maidens come along on runaway horses, Mr. Crag?'

'No, Miss Bromley' . . . he knew her name! . . . 'but I do go along the fences at times. It's a bad habit I got into at Falling Star, where it's deadly important.'

'Why?'

'Dingoes.'

'But are there sheep at Falling Star?' At least she knew that dingoes must be kept from sheep.

'No, but it's important that I keep the dingoes on my side for the southerners who do have sheep.'

'That's considerate of you.'

'I've plenty of consideration. Could you do with some?' He was tapping the tobacco down now, and something about that deliberate finger made Pippa feel uncomfortable.

'I'd better go.'

'I'm not stopping you,' he grinned.

'Certainly you're not.'

'I wouldn't be too certain,' he proffered, and his laugh followed her as she grabbed Rickaby's rein and led him back up the hill. What a man! she thought, as she had thought before.

Dom was not around. She was grateful for that, and unsaddled Rickaby at once and rubbed him down. In the change room she examined the jodhpurs and found them frayed and worn but still fit for use. However, she would have to tell Rena. As for herself, the skin was rubbed, as Crag had said, and she had no doubt she would tingle when she got into the hot bath he had advised, but she had come off fairly well.

62

As soon as she got to the house she sought out Rena and apologized about the riding kit.

'It doesn't matter, it was only old stuff I left there. You said you fell?' Rena's eyes were oddly narrowed.

'Yes. My own fault. I shouldn't have taken Rickaby down the gully.'

'Then you weren't with Dom Hardy when it happened?'

'No.'

'No one to pick you up?'

'Yes. Mr. Crag happened to be examining the fence.'

'And he picked you up?'

Something in Rena's voice brought Pippa's eyes flicking up to the girl's blue eyes. They were beautiful eyes, large, heavily-lashed ... and just now bright with tears. Tears? Rena in tears?

But the next minute Pippa told herself she must have imagined it.

'You want to be careful,' Rena said flippantly, 'when you fall. Sometimes it's not just the ground that's hard.'

'What do you mean, Rena?'

'Sometimes it's ...' But Rena did not finish. She simply turned and left.

Pippa staring after her thought that as well as being lovely, Rena could be a very strange girl.

All that week Pippa helped Dom. No blessed events occurred, but there was plenty to do in the stables. Dom had six 'pupils' to learn the niceties of show business. How to canter winningly, come to a gentle halt; remain quiet and erect while a judge circled you.

It was fascinating work, and now that she had learned her lesson not to explore with these strictly arena creatures, Pippa got on quite well.

One afternoon Dom brought an intended rider along

with the 'pupil'. Marilyn was the daughter of a couple who had bought a house in the neighbouring Highlands town of Bilgong, and it was expected that Southern Highlands children ride. Marilyn had lived in a city flat and never ridden, and she looked with frank dislike on the mild little chestnut her parents had purchased for her.

Davy would have helped, only Pippa kept Davy and the horses away from each other. The boy had no fear, but Pippa had fear for Davy. He had to have a restricted life, and a pony ride was one of those many restrictions.

'At least get on Billy Boy, Marilyn,' pleaded Pippa.

'No.'

'At least pat him.'

'He'll bite me.'

'He won't. He likes apples to bite, not little girls.'

'In fact he's frightened of little girls,' said a voice, and Crag Crag joined the group. 'I have the same trouble sometimes up at Falling Star with the piccaninnies.' Crag looked at Marilyn. 'Do you know piccaninnies?'

'Yes,' Marilyn said.

'Well, my scrubbers . . . do you know scrubbers?'

'No.'

'I can tell her.' It was Davy by Crag's side, but then where else would Davy, given the chance, be?

He proceeded to do so.

'Only these are scrubbers who've learned better.' Crag took on from Davy. 'They've learned enough to go after other scrubbers. See?'

'Yes. But I still wouldn't like them.' Marilyn wrinkled her nose. 'They're dangerous.'

'They think *you* are,' corrected Crag. He went up to Billy Boy. 'Look, mate, she won't hurt you. I know how you feel, but she's quite safe.' He turned to Marilyn. 'Silly, isn't it, Billy Boy being scared of you like this.'

'Is he?' Marilyn's eyes were wide.

64

'Yes. But perhaps I can help him by letting Davy show him how safe children really are.'

Pippa gave a half-step forward.

'Can I? Can I, Crag?' Davy's voice was eager.

'Reckon I'm not your boss, scrubber, your sister's that.'

'She'll say no.'

'Reckon she mightn't.' Crag turned to Pippa and said in such a low voice that only she could hear it: 'Reckon she could feel, that living for ever means rides on ponies, too. Reckon she could if she'd only give it a try.'

Pippa faltered, 'He'll get excited.'

'But he'll enjoy it. Better to fill up a cup even if it overflows than leave it empty.'

'I – I don't know.'

'You know,' he said, waited a moment, then swung Davy into the saddle. Davy was ecstatic. His ecstasy showed so much that Marilyn became querulous.

'It's my pony,' she cried, 'it's my turn!'

Davy was put down and Marilyn was put up.

'That was beaut, Pippa,' Davy said. No harm seemed done.

A lot of good was done for Marilyn. When Dom came over later, Davy and Crag having left, he was pleased with the result.

'It was Mr. Crag really who won the day,' reported Pippa.

'Oh, he's still around, is he?'

'Did you expect him to be gone?'

'He doesn't like the city. He calls the Southern Highlands the city. He never stops longer than he can help. I wonder why he's extending now.' Dom stood silent a moment, his lips pursed.

He came out of his thoughts to ask Pippa if she would come and look at Velvet with him. On his calculations

Velvet was not ready yet, but Velvet had her own ideas.

'If you've any way with cows, Pippa, tell her to hang off, her vet's out of town.'

'You said that picking times like that was a favourite pastime with Velvet.'

'Yes,' sighed Dom. 'It would be just like her to do it again now.'

When they reached the cow her spasm was over and she was contentedly ruminating.

'That's Velvet for you,' said Dom bitterly. 'I really believed she was beginning. I suspect her of staging these alarms especially to keep us on our toes.'

Pippa was squatting beside Velvet, a pretty, rather small cow, who wore a bell locket and had big plum eyes. She examined her as she had seen neighbours in the village examine their cows.

'She mightn't be pulling our legs,' she told Dom, 'she could be on the way. I'd ring that vet if I were you.'

'I rang,' he said dolefully, 'he's out of town.'

'Any other vets?'

'Several in the Highlands, but they're all away. There's a Sydney conference, and seeing it only means a day away from their practices it's being well attended. Also, Velvet was declared only last week as a month off.'

'Could be, too,' agreed Pippa. 'Anyway, she seems all right now.'

'It was just an act she was putting on,' declared Dom determinedly. 'Wasn't getting enough attention. Look here, my girl' . . . to Velvet . . . 'if you moo me back here again, I'll—'

'Moo-oo!' cried Velvet.

'She's an actress,' repeated Dom, 'she has to project herself. Sorry to have brought you along, Pippa, we'll leave this female to chew it over on her own.'

'Moo-oo!' protested Velvet, but they laughed and

went off.

But not far. Velvet gave a very loud 'Moo-oo', and going back just for a final look and an admonishment, Dom called, 'By jove, she's right, Pippa, she's on the way, well on it.'

Pippa hurried to his side. The little cow had got on to the job in a hurry as soon as they turned away. The feet were protruding from the unborn calf.

'It shouldn't be long,' said Pippa, but Dom groaned.

'It could be an hour, more, she's only small but she has big children. The vet was trying to keep the size down, but Velvet's a cunning girl, she's always so proud of herself I wouldn't put it past her rejecting his size-determining medication when our backs were turned again, spitting it out again. This girl knows more than she should.'

He was on his knees, manipulating, massaging, soothing. He kept it up until his arms protested, then Pippa took over.

They did this in turn for well over an hour. Dom was getting worried.

'If only she'd co-operate,' he despaired.

'I think it's a bigger calf than ever before,' Pippa offered, 'I think as you said that Velvet spat out that medication.'

'Can you keep going while I see if Ferguson is back from Sydney yet? I feel this needs more than we can give.'

Pippa nodded, and Dom ran across to the office. He was gone some time, which she knew was not a hopeful sign. Evidently Ferguson was still away, and he was trying other districts.

As she manipulated, massaged, edged downwards, encouraged and persuaded, Pippa saw a car go up to the house. The doctor, she thought, calling on Uncle Preston.

She had a sudden idea.

'No go.' Dom was back again. Pippa only gave him time to say that, then she interrupted his explanation again of the city conference with the breathless . . . for it was no easy job massaging and manipulating Velvet . . . announcement that Doctor Burt was up at Uplands.

Dom caught on at once.

'Of course,' he said. 'Hang on, Pippa.' He was away in a flash.

Pippa was talking to Velvet now, soothing, 'Good girl' . . . 'Not long' . . . 'Just another try.'

The feet of the unborn calf still stopped there.

'Darling, *try*,' urged Pippa.

Velvet looked reproachfully at her, then gave a large moo-oo, and it was happening at last. There was no need for the thin, disinfected rope that Dom had ready, the little fellow, cow or bull calf Pippa had no time to discover yet, was on the straw floor of the light, airy calving pen. After all that fuss no trouble at all. Also, Pippa said severely to Velvet, not such a remarkable size. Velvet ignored her. She also ignored her plum-eyed baby, which she should have started to lick. Pippa knew from her country days that when a mother did not lick her calf she had to be encouraged to do so by sprinkling a little salt on the baby. Dom had thought of everything; he had the salt at hand.

Pippa bent over to take it up.

'Moo-oo!' called Velvet.

'Yes, pet, you've been wonderful, but just now it's baby's turn.'

Baby's turn! But which baby? For another set of little feet were protruding.

'Twins!' Pippa exclaimed, delighted.

She knew how unusual it was, and longed for someone to help . . . and join . . .

in the miracle. But immediately there was much to do. Too much for one pair of hands. With one arm Pippa held off the first baby, who had got to its feet already and was actually searching clumsily for the teats, and with the other she went through the first ritual again, that massaging, soothing, encouraging. She hoped help would not be long.

It was longer than she anticipated. Had she known Dom would not return for what seemed hours but, of course, wasn't, Pippa knew she could not have coped. She learned later that Uncle Preston had had a minor relapse and Doctor Burt had needed Dom's aid to take him upstairs. As soon as he was able, Dom had told Glen Burt what was happening, and they had hurried back, but by then. . . .

The second calf was born, daintier than the first . . . a girl? . . . and this time, without salt, Velvet was licking her child. The first one had found the teats and was sucking contentedly.

'You clever Velvet,' Pippa awarded, 'a Silk and a Satin at the one go. Yes, we'll call them that.'

One arm around the new baby . . . the old baby was looking after itself . . . and one arm proudly fondled the mother. Elation and triumph shone in Pippa's hillside green eyes, not only the wonder of birth but the miracle of two small offerings. *Two*.

She was laughing maternally, at Silk's floppy wet ears, at Satin's astonished expression, at Velvet's assured look as her tongue darted back and forth in her cleaning duties when the two men came into the calving pen.

She looked up in triumph, waiting for their applause, feeling, with Velvet, the need of a pat, a 'Good girl', a 'Well done.'

They did not speak. Had she stood there, she might have been silenced, too, in the moving picture of a soft-eyed girl and a cow and two calves. And life itself.

But instead she sat waiting, wondering uneasily was something wrong? something amiss?

At that moment Rena, who had caught up with the men, pushed past them, took a long hard look at the scene, then said thinly, 'You can come with me to the house, now, Pippa. I need you there.'

CHAPTER FOUR

As Pippa walked from the stables back to Uplands beside her cousin she darted a nervous look at the cold, set face. Nervous, because Rena's tone had insinuated a reckoning, and although Pippa had never found herself in such a position with Rena, all at once she was remembering with distaste Janet's warning, ex-schoolmate Janet who once must have crossed swords with her cousin because she had warned: 'Leopards don't change their spots.'

Rena was not beautiful now, she noted, or if she was it was hard to find beauty in that bleak look. What on earth had she done, Pippa wondered, for Rena to be furious with her like this?

She must have wondered it aloud, though she hadn't intentionally formed the words, for Rena stopped abruptly, stopping Pippa with her, and accused, 'You're the sly one, aren't you? Timed that beautifully, didn't you? Arranged yourself sweetly, made everything look your doing—'

'What are you talking about, Rena?'

'As though you don't know!'

'I don't . . . unless you mean . . .'

'I mean the happy event. Happy, anyway, for you.'

'Oh, Rena, don't exaggerate, I had no idea that Velvet was going to—'

'But Velvet did, didn't she, and you acquitted yourself admirably, didn't you, and – and—' Rena's voice cracked.

'I should think you would be pleased I was there,' endeavoured Pippa. 'After all, calves are an asset to a farm,

Rena gave a dismissive gesture. 'Oh, that,' she put aside. 'Anyone would think you were being merely farm-minded.'

'I was. What else?' – But even as she asked it, Pippa put herself in Rena's place, and she knew how Rena felt.

In Rena's opinion she had 'upstaged' Rena . . . that had been Dom's phrase . . . because Rena herself had wanted to score on the maternal angle, paint a pretty picture with the help of Davy to impress the doctor, but Pippa had beaten her to it and of all things with two calves. The absurdity of the position brought a laugh to her lips.

'Rena, you're quite ridiculous. How appealing could I possibly look squatted down beside a cow? How on earth could Doctor Burt—'

'Doctor Burt?'

Rena looked at her quite stupidly for a long moment, looked at her as though she didn't understand her. Then she said, 'It wasn't that, it was your know-allness with Dom Hardy. He would appreciate that. He would like a girl who was resourceful.'

'Of course he would. He's a land-man and—'

'And you're a land-woman.'

'No more than I was a nurse. I wish you'd make up your mind what I was, more than that what you want me to be, because I'm certainly confused, Rena. I just don't understand.'

'There's nothing to understand,' Rena said dully.

'The way I see it there is,' persisted Pippa. 'Not only must I watch my step with Glen Burt for you, it seems to me I must also keep my distance from Mr. Hardy.'

'I never said so. I – I—'

'But you've just criticized me for helping him.'

'Nothing of the sort. I – why, I loathe the man. You have a vivid imagination, Pippa, but then your father was

72

'It was Davy who took after our father,' said Pippa quietly. She asked: 'Where is Davy? Did Doctor Burt see him?'

'Not yet. He was to, but Father suddenly had this thing.'

'Badly?'

'No. Just a minor turn. He's in bed now, and will stop there a day or so. I think it's just a case of trying to make up for his last rest. Every minute must pay. That's typical of Daddy.' She paused. 'Davy should be around somewhere.'

Pippa asked could she help now with Uncle Preston, but was told no. Considering that ostensibly she had been brought up from the calving pen for this explicit cause, Pippa felt like demanding the real reason why she was here. Really, Rena would be restricting everyone soon. She turned to demand an explanation, but found to her surprise that Rena's lips were thinned no longer, but full and soft and trembling. Her lovely eyes were bright with unshed tears.

'Why, Rena—'

'Oh, go away. *Go away!*'

Pippa went.

She wandered around aimlessly, feeling an anticlimax after the earlier events of the day. She felt she wanted to talk about it all. Uncle Preston's door was closed, so obviously he was resting. She was sorry, because she knew that at least he would have liked to have heard about Velvet, even if the resultant glitter in his eyes was the vision of cents and dollars and not the miracle of birth.

Where was Davy? She looked in his favourite haunts to no avail, then decided to go down to the planting in case he had decided to visit his 'best friend' once more. Only this morning as she had dressed him Davy had spoken proudly of: 'My best friend, Crag Crag.'

She crossed the fields, then plunged into the cool green, not aware that although there was no panic now, Davy knew his way and would not lose himself, that she was running. Then, out of breath, she did realize it, and she stopped abruptly. Why, she demanded of herself, am I hurrying to Crag like this? Is it because he's the only one available to be run to, or is it— No. No, of course it's not.

She made herself turn back.

A voice halted her, and she whirled round again. Crag Crag was standing beneath a pine and watching her.

'The scrubber's not with me, if that's what you've come about,' he said. 'On the other hand, if it is Yours Truly you're after' ... he pushed the ridiculous ten-gallon hat he wore, ridiculous, anyway, for cool Tombonda, back over his head ... 'if it's me, I'm here.' He grinned foolishly.

'I – I was looking for Davy.'

'Then he's at the calving. Oh, yes' ... taking out his pipe and tobacco ... 'the news has got around. The scrubber was with me when we heard, so we strolled across. He was so enthralled I left him there. After all, birth is a first importance, isn't it? And not just one young feller but twins! Congratulations, Pippa.'

'You should give those to Velvet.'

'I did, but she – and Hardy – referred me to you. You did a fine job, girl.'

'It was an honour,' she said, rather pink with pleasure, 'to be there at the arrival of Silk and Satin.'

'Suitable names,' he agreed. 'You're an artist as well as a midwife. But you'll need to think of something less fal-utin' when my Daisy calves.'

'You're having a blessed event, too?'

'At Falling Star, not here. And being Falling Star it will

be on a much leaner scale. We run to muscle, not beauty, up top.'

'And you actually have a cow there?'

'Yes. Daisy, as I said. Original, isn't it?' he laughed. 'But having a cow up there _is_ original. Most often you don't. But Daisy's a tough old girl. Her offspring may lack your Silk and Satin beauty, but they'll wear.' He packed the pipe, tapped it to his liking, then lit up. 'Were you coming over to see me as well?' he asked.

'No.'

'I don't think that's entirely true. I think you were. I think you wanted to tell me, to shout it. And why not, Pippa? Birth is—'

'A first importance,' she quoted him.

'Yes, but something more.' He searched for words.

'A thousand candles?' she asked.

He shook his head. 'That's reserved for something else. But I tell you this: it's morning's at seven, all's right with the world, isn't it, and that, I believe, is how you're still feeling, and what you want to share. Right, girl?'

It was unbelievable. He couldn't know. He couldn't possibly understand this elation she had. – But he did.

'Yes, Crag,' she said.

They sat down on the cool piney ground. Although even the tallest trees were still comparatively small to the height they would eventually reach they made a sound like the sea.

'I love it.' Crag sat back and sighed contentedly. 'It's the one thing Falling Star never has – pine song. The only time at Yantumara when the wind can gossip like this is after the floods when the tall grasses have sprung up. But here in the planting the breeze and the trees can always talk away the hours, and when the wind changes direction it's like bells. Why are you looking at me like that?'

'You could be my father talking.' She thought of Davy who had inherited her father's gift, and her eyes began to blur.

The deep leaves seemed to draw a veil around them, the air was softly dim. He put out his big hand and placed it across hers. He left it there and she did not withdraw her own fingers. Presently, warmed, the shadow gone, she began telling him about the day's events. The satisfaction she had known. The thrill.

'If only—' she finished.

'If only?'

'If only Rena wasn't angry,' she said unhappily.

'That figures,' he said.

'But she told me it wasn't because of Doctor Burt and – and any "upstaging", and somehow I don't think it was.'

'No?' he encouraged. 'What, then?'

'Somehow I think she was annoyed because I – well, I helped *Dom*.'

'That figures, too,' he said.

'I don't understand.'

'You don't have to, Pippa. Also you don't need to do anything about it ... *until Rena starts restricting me.*'

She looked at him in surprise. 'You're never restricted by Rena.'

'Not yet.'

'Crag, what do you mean?'

'Leave it at that,' he advised. He got up and pulled her after him. 'Coming up to Ku?'

'I came for Davy and you said he'd stopped at the shed.'

'Does it have to be Davy before you come to the house?'

'Yes.' She was still confused at what he had said, that restriction he anticipated, and her answer was curt.

'Well, you're direct enough,' he shrugged. 'It's enough to set me packing my bags again for Yantumara.'

'Why are you stopping this long?' Dom had wondered that. 'You said you only ever stayed briefly.'

'That's right.' In spite of the shade he had pulled the brim of his ten-gallon over his eyes. He seemed about to say something, then he seemed to change his mind. 'Put it down to the scrubber and what goes with him,' he smiled.

'What *can* go with Davy?' Pippa cried brokenly; the comfort she had known a little while ago when he had put his big hand silently over hers was not there now. She turned blindly away, avoiding him, darting back through the planting before he could stop her. By the time she had reached the fields she was composed again. Never must Davy see tears.

Not that Davy would have seen anything except the two little calves. He was down at the calving pen as Crag had said, and he was enchanted.

He walked back to Uplands with Pippa, his little hand warm in hers. He was full of talk about Crag's Daisy up at Falling Star, and how Daisy must have two calves, too. 'At least,' he added. He skipped in his pleasure.

Dom had informed Pippa when she had collected Davy that the vet was expected from Tombonda, having returned from his conference and having been informed of the double birth. Dom then passed on Doctor Burt's congratulations to Pippa for a good job done.

It would have made for complete satisfaction, Pippa thought, had she not dreaded a second scene with Rena. However, when she and Davy entered the house Rena was sweetness itself. She even found an opportunity to explain her behaviour to Pippa. 'I was worried over Father,' she said, and had Pippa not been so anxious to accept this, she could have thought that it was the first time that Rena had ever shown such concern.

But when later she was permitted to visit Uncle Preston, she was ashamed of any doubts. He looked ill, more ill than she had anticipated by that 'minor turn' of his daughter.

She sat by his bedside and told him all about Velvet, and as she had thought he was very pleased.

'At the price of calves,' he said, 'that makes...' He stopped his calculations to ask: 'Not identical twins, I hope?'

'No, Uncle, a cow and a bull calf. Why do you hope against identicals?'

'They're taken automatically by the Scientific Breeding Group for further study. The fee for unidenticals by private sale is much more to my liking.'

'You and your money!' she teased him.

'It's all too true, Pippa.' He pleated the top of the sheet with thin fingers; he had lost a lot of weight. 'That last investment of mine was a wrong 'un, the first you could say in all my life. What a time to pick to mess things up! But then I've messed things all through. A man doesn't see that when he's doing it, only when it's done, and it all lies there behind him like a book with its pages upturned. I messed up Rena. She's spoiled. She'll never be able to take what's coming now.'

'Uncle Preston, I'm sure you exaggerate.'

'Then that makes you and my girl too. The trouble was I lost my touch, I took my finger off the button, you might say, when I let Rena persuade me to leave the city and settle down here. Things ... *my* things haven't gone well since.'

'This place is thriving.'

He shrugged irritably. 'That's Hardy's kingdom, not mine. Did you know, Pippa, that it was because of Hardy that we initially came to Uplands?'

Pippa had not known. Having only met with these relations so recently she had taken it for granted that Uplands had always been their home. Or one of their homes.

'Oh, yes,' said Uncle Preston, 'it was only after my girl met Dom Hardy in England a few years ago that it became top of her list. I had the idea for a while ... I really thought ... I hoped ...' His voice trailed off and he was silent a moment.

'But Dom Hardy isn't English, Uncle.' Pippa broke into his thoughts.

'He was taking a trip, a "gen" trip he called it. You must have noticed how English-like are these Southern Highlands of New South Wales. Hardy noticed and was taking farming tips.'

'And you met him?'

'*Rena* and I met him.' A pause. 'Straightway that girl had a new theme.'

'A farm.'

'That's it.' Uncle Preston laughed indulgently, but he cut the laugh short. 'There I go again, always spoiling her. I shouldn't laugh over my own mistakes.'

'So you chose one that Dom recommended?' asked Pippa.

Uncle Preston nodded. 'It quite suited me apart from Rena insisting on it. Not so far from Sydney so that I couldn't keep my finger on the button ... or so I thought. But a business man needs to keep the button right there beside him, not three hours away. I found that out. Either I slipped in my judgment or—'

'Does it matter, Uncle Preston?' Pippa asked gently. 'Does a little less money matter?'

'That wasn't all the judgment I lost,' he said bluntly. 'You see, I thought ... I was sure ... But I was wrong.'

Pippa herself thought that never until she had come to

79

Tombonda had she heard so many conundrums. Dom
uttered them. Crag did. Now Uncle Preston was saying
them. And they were all to do with Rena. What was it
about Rena?

To divert the old man she began telling him about her
riding episode earlier in the week, and how she had
foolishly taken the horse down to the gully.

He nodded, but she could see he was not attending . . .
that is until she finished ruefully with her tumble, and, for
conversation, how Rena had advised her afterwards that
sometimes it was not just the ground that was hard.

'She said that?' he came in quite sharply, and the
sharpness surprised Pippa.

'Yes, Uncle Preston.' She looked wonderingly at
him.

'What else did that girl of mine say?'

'That was all. She just said that it was not always the
ground that was hard.'

He was quiet for a while, then he mused: 'She fell herself once, you know.'

'Yes, you told me. You said that after that she was—'

'She was more Rena than before,' he finished for Pippa.
'More capricious. More self-willed. Less what I was
hoping, hoping for her and—' He closed his eyes for a
moment, then opened them again. 'She even got an urge
to leave here, leave Uplands. But for once I didn't indulge
her. I felt I had moved enough, that I was too old to
begin again. Pippa' . . . abruptly . . . 'what do you think of
Hardy?'

'Your overseer?'

'Yes. What do you think of him, girl?'

'He's great,' Pippa said warmly, if a little surprised at
the sudden turn in the conversation.

'Apart from that would you say he was – well, a stubborn kind of fool?'

'Never a fool, Uncle Preston.'

'But stubborn? Proud? Determined?'

'Yes, all of those,' Pippa nodded. 'Very stubborn, proud, determined.'

Another silence crept into the room. It was so long that Pippa suspected the old man had fallen asleep. She sat on for a while, wondering whether to tiptoe out or wait for him to wake up again.

He settled it for her.

'I'm awake, girl, but don't stay on.'

'No, Uncle Preston.' She got up. 'Anything you want?'

Uncle Preston said an odd thing, and Pippa was to remember it afterwards.

He said: 'You've given it to me. Close the door after you. Thanks.'

The next day Pippa met Glen Burt. Already Davy had become friends with him, telling his sister that he was a pretty good vet ... Pippa told herself she must have a word with Crag Crag about that ... and that he intended to do what the doctor told him, because Crag's Manager had done that and look what Crag's Manager had won. – Always Crag came into it, Pippa sighed.

'Yes, darling,' she nodded, 'but please not vet.'

'I told Doctor Glen and he didn't seem to mind.'

No one seemed to be minding, not even Rena when she presented her doctor to Pippa. She was all sweet concern, tender solicitude. Almost Pippa could have convinced herself that that warning that Rena had issued to her regarding the young medico was imagination.

The meeting was in Davy's room, Rena sitting at the window with the little boy, and looking lovely enough, Pippa thought, to stir anyone's heart. But Doctor Burt's attention was only on Davy, a fact that Rena should have

81

appreciated as a point against Pippa even though at the same time it would have to be considered as something against herself. When, after a quick check of the child, the doctor gave Rena a meaning look, Rena rose at once, the perfect intuitive nurse, and took Davy outside. That she stopped in the garden where she could be seen as she lovingly and very winningly tended the little boy dimmed none of her touching devotion.

Glen Burt said, 'I haven't had an opportunity to commend you on your handling of that cow, Miss Bromley. You seemed to know what you were about.'

'I was a country girl.'

'Still, not all country people. . . . You weren't working for an English veterinarian, by any chance?' He smiled, and added, 'I know from your cousin that you're not a nurse.'

Pippa supposed that that would be one of the things that Rena would take care to tell him. 'No, I wasn't,' she said, 'I was a clerk.'

'I was hoping from your coolness that you might have been one of our brigade.'

'Either animal, vegetable, mineral,' she laughed, and he laughed with her, but his good-looking face soon becoming serious again.

'I really meant,' he explained, 'that you might be able to give me some data on Davy.'

'But I can do that, of course.'

His smile was polite now. 'Of course . . . though what I wanted—'

She understood that he did not mean the usual surface details but deeper personal medical points, and who knew Davy better than Davy's sister? In a quiet, concise manner she tabulated everything she had learned from Doctor Harries about Davy. Doctor Burt listened intently, nodding his dark head now and then.

'Thank you,' he said when she had finished. 'That's what I wanted but scarcely expected.'

'Davy is all I have,' she said, 'so I had to know.'

There was a silence as Glen Burt made notes in a small book.

Pippa steeled herself to say, 'I know already that for Davy it's prognosis nil, Doctor.'

He looked up from the book and answered, 'I wish I could deny that.'

'But you can't.'

'Instead of saying No I'll say that sometimes in spite of facts, in spite of all a doctor knows, it doesn't always happen as a doctor believes.'

'Thank you.' Her smile was bleak. With an effort she said conversationally, 'Rena has told me that your ambition is research.'

He closed the book, then nodded to Pippa. 'Being a G.P., particularly a country one, will be something that will always be immensely valuable to me, but I have to admit that research is the only thing I really want.'

'Then you'll be leaving the district at some time?'

He smiled faintly. 'It takes money for that kind of dream.'

Pippa remembered Rena's: 'Glen wants to do research. That costs money, and you'd think he'd be aware that I could help him.' Instinctively her glance flicked outward to the golden girl on the lawn, now kneeling beside Davy to adjust the strap of his sandal.

The doctor saw the glance. Quietly, so quietly she could almost have imagined it, he said, 'No.'

'What, Doctor Burt?'

'Thank you for your concise information on your brother. I receive new reading every day, and I shall be on the alert especially now for anything pertaining to Davy.'

'Yes,' she said, but knowing, as he knew, that he had not answered her question.

They joined the others on the lawn.

When the doctor had gone, Rena changed her role of nurse to Davy to that of examiner of Pippa. She demanded what, where, how.

'It was all medical talk, Rena.'

'I expected it to be.' Rena's mouth thinned. She added, 'But tell me all the same.'

'He just said that Davy . . .' Pippa had to turn away.

Rena at least had the grace not to press her, but she still waited, so Pippa repeated Glen Burt's remark on wanting research but not having the money.

'You see,' triumphed Rena.

Pippa did not proceed to that odd 'No' from the doctor when his glance had followed her glance, she let Rena bask in the assurance of her money and what it could do. But most of all her cousin seemed to find delight in the fact that research would take Glen . . . and his wife as a matter of course . . . right away.

'*Right away*,' Rena repeated, almost hugging the words.

'But, Rena, you go away often. You could go now.'

'But I'd be expected back. This is my home. This is where I live with my father. When you're married, you belong to the one you're married to, so you don't come back, you're not expected. It would have been no good with Crag, for he returns regularly to Ku, and always will. I have to be away. *Away*.'

'But why?' Pippa looked at her, confused. 'You can't dislike the place, for you chose it.'

Rena had gone quite white. 'Yes, I chose it, but now I hate it. I hate it!' Almost choking on that last 'hate', Rena turned and left.

Glen Burt attended Uncle Preston several times during

the following week, and on each occasion had a look at Davy. He had an idea to try him on remedial exercises, but was very anxious to select the right ones, for he believed that wrong movements could deter the boy.

Rena offered sweetly to supervise these exercises, and who more able, Pippa thought; she had had the most expensive ballet tuition.

'No, Davy's sister, I think. The way she reported Davy to me I knew she understood even Davy's smallest muscle. This is what I'm after, Miss Bromley.' He had drawn a stick figure to demonstrate, and beckoned Pippa over. With a sinking heart, for she had glimpsed the quick look in Rena's face, Pippa tried to follow the text.

As far as she could see it ran the same gamut as the things that Crag often recommended. Crag wanted Davy to step out of himself, be more the boy and less the small ornament, or so he expressed it, only there to be touched gently, dusted and replaced. He had said, Pippa recalled, that little scrubbers had nothing in the past to regret and nothing in the future to fear, meaning, she interpreted, that Davy should live more *ordinarily*, and that was what Glen Burt, in medical terms, was saying now.

Part of the exercises involved walking while practising deep breathing. Pippa selected this one and took Davy across to Ku. – Or at least they started in that direction. As they passed through the planting she assured herself that it was because Davy was so eager for this particular exercise and so lacklustre as regarded the arm flinging and toe touching, which, after all, was only childlike, that she had chosen it, but when Davy acclaimed delightedly, 'You're skippety-hoppity, too,' of her twinkling progress, she could not deny it.

'It's the pine needles,' she told him.

'No, it's Crag,' he said. 'You're wanting to see him like I am. I love the pine needles, though, and I'll miss them up at Falling Star.'

About to argue that it was not Crag, Pippa said urgently instead: 'Darling, we're not going to Falling Star.'

Her brother answered, unconsciously adopting Crag's slow, deliberate drawl, 'I reckon we might, though, because that's what my best friend is waiting back for.'

Pippa halted, and halted Davy with her.

'I think we'll see the calves instead,' she said abruptly.

Davy was in a predicament. Silk and Satin of the wet noses and insecure legs or his best friend? His best friend would still be his best friend, he must have decided, but Silk and Satin grew every time you looked at them, and soon, according to Dom, they would be almost as big as their mother, the bull calf even bigger. Davy said judiciously, 'I think Crag will understand,' and agreed to be led instead another way, also to co-operate with deep breathing.

While he fondled the twins, the mother looking on implacably, Dom showed Pippa the gymkhana programme for the forthcoming Southern Highlands Pony Gathering.

'I'll be entering in practically every event,' he said, 'and I'm counting on you to stable for me.'

'I'm glad you didn't say ride. I didn't do so well last time, did I?'

'This wouldn't be down a valley,' he smiled, 'but in the parklands of the Pony Club, which are as smooth as a billiard table. Also, the owners of the ponies will be doing most of the riding themselves. Nevertheless there will be some events, Pippa, that perhaps—'

She smiled back and half-agreed, then joined Davy in the adoring of the small animals.

On Doctor Burt's insistence a nurse had been brought

in for Uncle Preston. Pippa had heard Rena protesting to Glen that she could manage her father herself, but he had stood firm, suggesting gently but adamantly that she was too close to Preston Franklin to be of real impersonal value, and in nursing an impersonal approach was a very essential thing.

Rena had been unsure whether to pout or take the doctor's ruling as a compliment to her as a devoted daughter, and while she had hesitated, Glen Burt had contacted a nursing bureau and succeeded in engaging Sister Bruce, a reliant person with sufficient years to assure Rena that her hesitancy had been a right move.

Rena now concentrated on Davy, and was always with him whenever the doctor called.

It was simply too much, Pippa thought. Surely Rena, an intelligent girl, must see that she was overdoing it, must sense eventually that she could never win with such obvious tactics. Undoubtedly if you loved a man you had every right in the world to fight for him, but when was possessing a fair fight? Then did Rena really love Glen? *Did* Rena?

Pippa could not have said why she held that doubt, Rena had said a hundred times how she felt to Glen, but still the feeling persisted, that feeling that Rena was forcing, or trying to force, the issue, forcing it with more urgency than emotion, and because of this when the young doctor spoke to Pippa as he did, Pippa did not feel so distressed as she might have had she felt that her cousin really cared.

Glen drew Pippa into the garden following one of his visits . . . Rena on the mats she especially had sent for and doing gradual push-ups with Davy, and looking, and no doubt aware of it, very lovely as she did so . . . and began with a tentative: 'What do you think of this exercise régime?'

'I suppose anything that builds up strength must be of some benefit,' Pippa said.

'Yes.'

There was a pause, then:

'Miss Bromley . . . Pippa . . .'

'Yes, Doctor Burt?'

'Could you say Glen?'

'Yes, Glen.'

'I . . . Well . . .' Another pause.

'Yes, Glen?'

'It's difficult to put into words.'

'Davy?' she said hollowly. How often had she said her brother's name tonelessly like that?

'Oh, no.' He hastened to reassure her. 'It's – Rena. Much as I dislike any such move I – I feel I must give up your uncle and your brother as my patients.'

'But, Doctor – but, Glen—'

He poked at a blade of grass with the toe of his shoe. He seemed wretched, but nonetheless determined to say what had to be said.

'Why does she go on like that?'

About to pretend that she didn't understand him, instead Pippa said quietly: 'Rena?' She knew he was aware that she understood his trend.

'Yes, Pippa. She . . . oh, this is very embarrassing for me.'

'Can love be embarrassing, Glen?'

'Rena doesn't love me, any more than I love her, but for some reason she – well, she—'

'Yes,' nodded Pippa. Again she spoke quietly.

'But, Glen,' she said presently, 'you're a doctor, your work comes first. Oh, I can understand how you feel, but – well—' She searched for words, found none, so made a little helpless gesture towards her brother.

'I can't work as I want to work with Miss Franklin

acting as she does,' he said bluntly. 'I'm a dedicated person, Pippa, I always have been. I have no time for all this.' He spread thin sensitive hands.

'Rena could find you time.' Pippa felt she was entitled to say that, for hadn't Rena already said it? 'She has enough to let you follow the path you want to, Glen.'

'But I wouldn't want it. Not without . . .' He turned to Pippa. 'You see, there's someone else. She was at university with me. Nothing has ever been said between us, otherwise I would have said it to your cousin, but the way I feel about Jennifer and the way I sense she could feel about me . . .'

There was a pause, then Glen Burt spoke again.

'We never actually discussed things, but we both knew what we wanted from our years of study, and I believe we both knew whom we wanted it with. It's Jennifer some day, I hope, Pippa. It *has* to be Jennifer. — So you see how I feel now.'

'You said before that Rena was only playing a part with you, then wouldn't that make it easier for you to tell her what you have just told me?'

He gave another movement of his hands. 'Is anything easy with Rena?' he asked. Then he said the same as Crag had said. 'How can you tell her when she's running away?'

'Running away, Glen?'

'I feel that. I suppose I'm crazy.'

'Someone else said it. But — but from whom?'

Almost as if answering the question Domrey Hardy joined the two of them on the lawn.

They talked a while, then, believing that Dom wished to consult Rena on farm matters, Pippa nodded to the two exercisers, but Dom did not even glance in that direction.

'It was you I wanted to see, Pippa, that is if the doctor

is finished . . .'

'I'm finished.' There was the slightest sigh in Glen's voice as he turned back to Rena and Davy again. What an odd position, Pippa thought, here was a lovely and a richly-endowed girl, yet neither of these two men— Rather grateful herself to get out of the tangle, even if only temporarily, Pippa walked beside Dom back to his office.

'What is it, Dom? More blessed events?' There were still unfulfilled dates on the calendar.

'No, Pippa, nothing immediately imminent. I just want to speak with you about the forthcoming show.'

'The Pony Gathering.'

'Actually it's more than that, it's a bit of everything, though I must admit the horses dominate it. There's the usual events, the usual judging, also a dog section, a cat division, and those delightful displays of jams and cakes competing for blue ribbons.'

'Is that what you wanted to tell me about, Dom?' she laughed.

'No, but you're entitled to enter,' he assured her. 'How are you on scones with wings?'

'They invariably crash,' she told him ruefully, 'my aunt did the cooking.'

'Well, perhaps the handiwork,' he smiled. 'Seriously, though, I'll be calling upon you to help out in some of the events.'

She nodded that she would, adding, 'But nothing fancy.'

'I did hope to put Suzy in the Steeple. Oh, it's a very restricted steeple,' he hastened to reassure her.

'Still too wild for me.'

'That's a pity. Suzy's a born hunter.'

They had reached the office by now, and he drew up a chair and handed Pippa a programme of events. They were very comprehensive. She noted, too, that the gathering was everything Dom had said. It went from flowers and produce, preserves and children's handwriting right through the usual gamut to finish up (after pigs, dogs, cats and cattle had been dealt with) at the real reason for the gathering: horses. There would be, Pippa read, the expected stalls and sideshows, coconut shies and wood chops. Even a merry-go-round was offering, Dom smiled, for the less heroic equestrian. He looked obliquely at Pippa as he said this, and, seeing his trend, she protested again that she would help him out in every other way but that she still didn't feel skilled enough for a steeple.

'Minor steeple.'

'It's still a jump. What about this event? And this? I'll even try this one.'

The morning of the gathering dawned blue and gold. It gave an early promise to grow into one of those flawless, brilliant days that the mild Southern Highlands so often puts on. Already there was a breeze with a pleasantly exciting edge to it that would flutter all the ribbons and flags. It would also tatter the tossed lolly wrappers and peanut shells, Uncle Preston said typically as Pippa said good-bye to him, but he had a smile about him for all his acid words . . . a satisfied smile that Pippa was to remember later.

Childlike, Davy was almost hugging himself with delight. Feeling the old magic of all-fairs-wherever-they-be-herself, Pippa held the little hand in hers and squeezed it as they passed through the turnstile.

The pony events were not programmed until after lunch, so Pippa and Davy did the rounds of the mouth-watering cake marquee, the mysterious fortune-teller, the fascinating fat lady, the frustrating Aunt Sally. Pippa was just heading for the handicraft, having bribed Davy who was not so keen on this with a cornet of spun sugar, when her small brother glimpsed something . . . or somebody as Pippa soon discovered . . . and darted away.

As she might have known the attraction was Crag Crag, even more wonderful to a wide-eyed small boy today in his black singlet, white pants, white boots and *standing by an axe*.

'Davy, come back!' she called urgently.

Crag, waiting beside a block of wood as were five others in the small arena, smiled at her and assured her, 'It's all right, the scrubber won't come to any harm. I'll send him off at Seconds Out, for I reckon he's my second. Are you, scrubber?'

'Oh, yes, Crag. What do I do, Crag?'

'You can pick up those few chips around my block, see to it that my sweat rag is ready.'

'Davy—' feared Pippa.

'He's all right,' Crag assured her again.

'But when you start chopping . . . you are going to, aren't you?'

'Reckon that's what I'm here for. Don't worry, Pippa, there's no danger, the stewards will put round a cordon, and anyway, woodmen place their chops.'

'But you're not a woodman.'

'No,' he agreed, 'but I do a bit up top, and it's on harder stuff than this.' He looked down at his log.

Pippa restrained herself from crying out 'Davy' again when her brother busily dusted the axe. The little boy was blissful, he fussed around Crag like a mother hen, but for all his excitement when the stewards called 'Seconds Out', he went at once at a nod from Crag to Pippa's side.

The adjudicator warned, 'Three seconds, gentlemen. One. Two . . .' Then the chop began.

Crag was slow off the mark and when he did start he

seemed to have a stolid pace. There was none of the quicksilver of the other competitors, the effortless rhythm, he just lumbered along.

'Crag,' Davy was calling, 'Crag!' And all at once Pippa heard herself calling it, too.

Then something happened. The lumbering pace changed to a swinging cut. Instead of standing upright, Crag now almost crouched over the log. By the time he reversed he had passed two of the other five and his chips were flying fast.

'Crag!' called Davy.

'Crag,' called Pippa. 'Crag . . . Crag!'

For a breath of a second, so infinitesimal it must have been imagination, the man looked up and across at Pippa, then at once the great chunks of wood were rising, the racing axe was flailing through the air as though wielded by a machine and not a man.

Then he was through.

Even had he not jumped apart to prove it, everyone would have known by Davy's shouts of joy that he had won. – Pippa's, too, only she was not aware of them.

But she was aware of Crag coming across with a trophy and putting it in Davy's hands, of his saying, 'Thanks, scrubber, I reckon the way you shouted for me it was you who won it.'

But looking at Davy's sister.

They had lunch together in the tea pavilion, Davy refusing to be parted from the large silver cup and having difficulty in managing his lemonade and sandwiches with its gleaming bulk enclosed in one protective arm.

After the break the gymkhana began. Pippa left Davy with Crag and took up her duties for Dom Hardy. A sheepdog trial, a tent-pegging, a camp draft were staged, then the races began.

Pippa won a red ribbon and two yellow ones for Dom's

stable in age classes, but once again refused the steeple. He smiled and took it philosophically, but she felt he was disappointed.

She went out to see if Davy was still with Crag, and after much searching found the pair of them leaning over the course railing and shouting encouragement to Rena. Rena was with the other steeple entrants at the starting post. *On Suzy.*

'What's Rena doing—' Pippa began, but the pistol stopped her query. The chase had begun.

Right from the beginning Rena left the others well behind. She rode faultlessly. She also rode contemptuously, and Pippa glanced up at Dom who now had joined them by the fence, and saw his tightened lips.

Her cousin won with ease. She was off the mount and handing him carelessly to Dom, when Pippa, remembering her strapper duties, came hurrying across.

'No falling off this time,' she heard Rena say in a hard bitter voice, 'no mistakes and no reckless words to be corrected by Mr. Hardy.'

'Rena—' Pippa heard Dom say tensely back. 'Rena—'

What would have happened then? Pippa was to wonder this afterwards. Would Dom have gone on from that tense 'Rena—' . . . would he have—

But she was not to know, for through the loudspeaker someone else called for Rena, called: 'Wanted at the office urgently, Miss Franklin. Miss Franklin, please.'

It was Crag who came up to Pippa to say quietly: 'Go with her.'

'But—'

'Go, Pippa,' Crag repeated. He assured her: 'I've got the scrubber.'

By the time Pippa reached the office, Rena had been told.

Told that a message had come from Uplands. Her father had died.

CHAPTER FIVE

THERE could be no doubt about Rena's grief. Pippa, who often had felt herself instinctively withdrawing from her cousin because of her apparent callous lack of relationship with her father, now saw that it all had been a façade, that the bond had been so tight that it had needed no word, no gesture, no daughterly embellishment.

Hours after the gymkhana announcement, and after the exhausting floods of tears had been released, Rena had sat up in the bed in which Pippa had placed her and said woodenly, 'We were one, Pippa; now he's gone I'm not whole any more, it's an amputation.'

Pippa, murmuring the usual consolations, was stopped imperatively by Rena's impatient hand on her arm.

'*One*,' she repeated. 'I'm as selfish as he was. We both thought only of ourselves.'

'You're wrong, Rena, Uncle Preston thought all the time of you.'

'Then he was thinking of himself, for we were the same. And now . . .' Again the tears flowed.

Pippa felt those tears could do more for her cousin than she could, and went out quietly. She was relieved that Crag had taken Davy to stop at Ku. Uplands was no place just now for the child, not with Rena's grief so evident. – Not with the close association of death.

Death. She stood in the garden and thought about it . . . and Davy. She was sad for Uncle Preston. For all his brusque ways, the occasionally awful things he had said, she had liked him. But Uncle Preston had not been a little boy who had only known a handful of springs. Tears stung at her, and she was crying softly and brokenly when Dom Hardy found her.

He put his arm around her and guided her to the barn; he seemed to know instinctively the needed thing to do. In the barn they spent some time on Silk and Satin, and Dom told her how he expected the other blessed events at any moment. It was good therapy, and she soon was talking back with him. Then suddenly, without any warning, he broke into their exchange with a terse: 'How is she?'

'Rena?'

'Yes.'

'Taking it hard.'

'I expected that.'

'I didn't.' Pippa had found by this time that she could be frank with Dom. 'I thought—'

'That's Rena,' he nodded. 'But it's all a veneer, Pippa, and under that skin . . .' He stopped abruptly to catch a quick breath. From the look in his face there was pain in him.

'Dom . . .' Pippa began, but Dom was on the stock again, talking briskly, and she knew she could not break in.

Doctor Burt had not been out to Uplands since his last attention on Preston Franklin, but sedatives had arrived for Rena, and the nurse had stayed on for a further period.

A message had come for Pippa from Crag that he was keeping Davy with him, and she was grateful about that, for the funeral had been set for the following day.

After it was over and the girls back in the house again, Pippa carried tea to the sun-room and sat with her cousin. She had previously steeled herself to say: 'What now, Rena?' for after all she had to know her future. She had Davy to think of.

'Daddy,' Rena shrugged, 'always said there was no

money.' She gave a little disbelieving laugh. 'That would be typical of Preston Franklin, my parent was always cautious. However, I don't believe it. There may have been a moderate recession, but there would still be a fair amount. Also there's this house.' She glanced around her.

'Yes, I don't think you need worry about finance, Rena.' Pippa meant that. For all his statements to the contrary, she had never taken seriously Uncle Preston's plaints of impending disaster, only his standards of disaster.

'It will make me free,' said Rena, much in the same manner as she had spoken once before, 'free to leave here, leave the Highlands.' She took out her cigarettes and lit up.

When she spoke next she seemed to be addressing the blue weave of smoke . . . anyway, she did not meet Pippa's glance.

'I won't be dependent on anyone else to get me away. Not Crag. Not Glen. – By the way' . . . a brief laugh . . . 'that last fell through. I think you know, Pippa.'

'Doctor Burt?'

'Yes. In a very discreet way our young doctor began referring to this former love of his.'

'Jennifer.'

'Yes. Quite a touching little story. Young students together. No words ever spoken but the feeling there.' Now Rena was back to form, her sharp astringent form.

Uncomfortably, Pippa inserted, 'I don't think you were really hurt, Rena.'

Rena narrowed her eyes on her cousin and said, 'And why should you think that?'

'No reason, except—'

'Except?' Rena demanded.

'Except I don't believe you ever loved him.'

'Very intuitive, aren't you? Well' . . . a deliberate yawn . . . 'you were right. He was attractive, of course, but Glen to me was primarily escape, escape from here. Oh, I know you think I could have gone whenever I liked, and I did go for periods, but because of Daddy I had to come back. And Preston Franklin' . . . she had the habit of calling her father by his full name . . . 'for all his regrets at having left Sydney, was still for some reason very much against returning again, from leaving here.'

'Probably his state of health, his age,' suggested Pippa.

'Perhaps.' A shrug. 'All I know is he wouldn't go. So I was tied down, too. But now . . .' She exhaled, and once more gave that little scornful laugh.

'Where will you go, Rena?' – Where will *we* go, was more what Pippa wanted to cry out, where can I take Davy?

'Here . . . there . . . who knows? Oh, you're worrying about the boy, aren't you? Don't fret, I won't see you stuck. As a matter of fact I wouldn't be surprised if Daddy hasn't seen to that in the will. Did I tell you it's to be read almost at once? In the morning, in fact.'

'No, Rena, you didn't.'

'It appears Mr. Callow, our solicitor, is anxious to start the proceedings at once. Rather surprising. Usually the wheels of the law grind painfully slow, or so I've been told. Though probably he's guessed my burning anxiety.' Another little laugh. 'Anxiety to leave.'

Rena got up and went to the window, looked out on the rolling, green, almost parklike qualities of the Highlands terrain, at the ordered perfection of it, then cried, 'Oh, to leave here! To leave here. How I hate the place!'

Yet when she turned back a moment later her eyes were dull and her lips set.

Rena seeming to have control of her grief now, as soon as lunch was over Pippa walked through the planting to Ku to visit Davy.

But when she got there, there was no sign of her brother.

'Mustering,' grinned Crag Crag, who opened the door to her, 'if you can call our small handful a mob. But the scrubber rushed the opportunity to bring the five of them back from the west paddock. He reckoned it would be good practice for later on.'

'Should he?' worried Pippa, making the mustering her first concern. 'Should you have let him?'

'He wanted to,' said the brown man, 'WANTED. I reckoned it would have done him more harm not allowing that want.'

'Perhaps.' Pippa thought of the guarded existence Davy had had in England and how it had done nothing for him. If Crag wished to work on the principle that since it had done no good this could do no worse, then she supposed she could let him. With a sigh she dismissed that concern to take out a second one.

'You shouldn't let him think like you do,' she remonstrated.

'About practising mustering for later on?'

Later on. She found she could not answer that for the rising lump in her throat, for the hopeless knowledge that Davy would never muster anywhere, but she did manage to murmur, 'About visiting you at Falling Star, because a visit is what you sounded like, and of course, we won't be going.'

He was packing his pipe, taking his usual time over it.

'I'd like to talk to you about it,' he said when he had done.

'If it's minding Davy for me up there until things are

99

finished here, thank you for the offer, and thank you at the same time for all you've done already in minding him, but no.'

'It wasn't that,' he said rather indistinctly, the pipe in a corner of his mouth.

She did not ask him what it was then, for there would be no need to mind Davy; anyway, quite soon, the legal matters would be wound up and she would take over again herself. She told Crag what Rena had said about the will reading. She proffered Rena's guess that there might be a little windfall for Uncle Preston's niece. 'That certainly would be wonderful,' she admitted, 'at least it would get us back to England.'

'And the scrubber miss his second spring?'

'Well, we can't stay here,' she pointed out. 'Rena intends getting rid of the house ... or rather I gathered that.'

'*Whose* house?' A smoke weave must have spiralled up at him, for he had narrowed his eyes on her.

'Hers, of course,' Pippa said irritably, 'Rena's.'

'I see.' Still the narrowed eyes. 'And this will reading, when is it?'

'Tomorrow.'

'I'd go if I were you, Pippa.'

'Oh, no,' she said sensitively. 'It would seem – seem – well, as though I was grasping at anything that Uncle might have left me.'

He smiled a little crookedly at her. 'Left to you, eh? No, that's not what I meant, girl. You just go – for Rena.'

'For Rena?' she asked, puzzled.

'For Rena,' he nodded.

'But—'

'And Pippa—' He paused.

'Yes?'

'Come back here after it's over and let me show you a way out.'

'A way out? Really, you do say the oddest things. — How long will Davy be?'

'It depends on how the muster goes.' He lost his serious air and grinned again. He stood up, impelled her upward with him. 'Come and we'll see how our young stockman is doing.'

Davy had completed the chore and was sitting, cowboy-wise, on the fence circling the corral, and regarding his 'muster' the while he chewed on a stem of bittersweet, held much in the manner that Crag held his pipe. Crag . . . Crag . . . what a hero he had made of that man! Uneasily Pippa thought of the wrench it would be when the two friends had to part, yet part they must. Uncle Preston was dead and Rena would be leaving Uplands, her cousins leaving as well. Besides this Crag had spoken many times on how he had outstayed himself here at Ku and how Falling Star needed him. Yes, it could not be long now.

Davy's smile at seeing his sister was quickly wiped off as a thought occurred to him. He said fearfully, 'You didn't come to take me back, did you, Pippa?'

'Not yet, darling, but soon, of course.'

Davy only listened to the first part. He said importantly to the brown man, 'I had a little trouble at the gate, but otherwise all went well. I reckon I'll be of real help to you up at—'

'Davy!' Pippa inserted sharply, but just as sharply Crag came in:

'You didn't drive home that bottom bolt quite enough, scrubber, you always want to make sure of these things,' then, as Davy hurried across to the gate to fix it, he said in a low tone to Pippa: 'No.'

She knew he was remonstrating with her for cutting

into Davy's dreams and she retorted bitterly, 'He mustn't build up like this.'

'Giving in that you could be right about that, though I still won't go along with it, at least wait for a while, girl.'

'Wait? For what?'

He was attending to his eternal pipe. 'Wait for the will,' he said.

'It won't make any difference. Even if Uncle Preston has ... if what Rena said is true ... if there *is* something, I won't be spending it on taking Davy up to—'

'All the same, *wait*,' he said. 'And Pippa, go with her to the reading. She'll need you, I think.'

'How do you come to think these things?' she asked curiously and a little tauntingly. 'Do you have some special knowledge?'

'Only of what *I* would have done had I been Preston Franklin,' he replied cryptically.

She looked at him a long moment, not understanding. But she did not feel like pursuing the subject so instead she called good-bye to Davy. Only that he looked so ecstatically happy, and Davy's happiness must always come first, she might have resented her brother's casual wave in return.

As she walked back through the planting to Uplands she wondered why Crag had asked her to be with Rena tomorrow. She could not go, of course, unless Rena asked her, then if she did ask, *should* she? After all, it was strictly Rena's affair.

But when Rena suggested it that night, she heard herself agreeing to accompany her cousin, and she was angry because it seemed that, like Davy, she was being directed by Crag Crag, and one in the family was enough.

But when Mr. Callow untied the Last Will and Testament of Preston Franklin next morning and read quietly and unemotionally in a dry solicitor voice, she was glad she was with Rena if only to sit there silently beside her. – How, she wondered, had Crag Crag known?

For Rena inherited nothing, yet not because the Franklin estate had dwindled down to that extent *but because she was excluded*.

Mr. Callow put down the papers at last.

'Of course,' he said, 'we will dispute this will.'

'There would not be the slightest doubt,' Mr. Callow went on precisely, 'that your late father's last testament would be proclaimed null and void. The time factor alone between its alteration and his passing would assure that. But even failing this, though I repeat that I have no doubt as to the outcome of an appeal, the appropriate authorities would insist on a re-distribution, and you, as his sole surviving—'

'No!' Rena came in sharply and emphatically. 'No.' She had sat silent until then.

'You are thinking,' interpreted Mr. Callow sympathetically, 'that we would be contesting it on the grounds of your father's mental state at the time of his altering it. You do not want that. I assure you, Miss Franklin, that such a step was not in my mind. It certainly offers a sure way out, but I would have to admit that on the day Mr. Franklin called me to Uplands to attend to this' ... he tapped the sheaf of papers ... 'that he was more alert than I have ever known him. I did attempt to reason with him. After all, what he wanted was quite preposterous. But never have I seen Preston Franklin so adamant, so certain of himself. His income had been receding for some years. Undoubtedly he spoke to you about that?'

'Yes.'

'But there would still have been a comfortable sum for

you, and with the house—'

'Yes. The house.' Rena looked directly at the solicitor. 'To whom was it – sold?'

He hesitated. 'Not sold, Miss Franklin.'

'Then – then given?' But before the solicitor could tell her, Rena said, 'Hardy?'

'Yes.'

'And the rest of Father's goods and chattels and money? To Hardy, too?'

'Yes.'

'Does he know yet?'

'No. I thought it better to tell you first, get you over the initial shock. Of course there won't be any trouble. I know . . . we all know Domrey. All this is going to upset him much more than it upsets you. He'll be more than anxious to have things fixed up as they should be and as soon as possible. As a matter of fact I've been thinking over that mental state again, Miss Franklin. Although to my mind your father had never been more mentally stable, doesn't that prove instability when an only and beloved child is deprived? What I mean to say is—'

'No!' Rena protested again. But this time she even banged the table with her slender white hand to drive home her refusal.

'How much is there?' she asked after a rather startled pause. 'I mean how much – for me?'

Mr. Callow glanced down to his desk. He looked unhappy. 'As I said, the income had plummeted for quite some time.'

'How much?'

'Then without the house,' continued the solicitor, 'and without the grounds—'

'I'm asking you how much?'

A pause. Then: 'Actually only anything in your own name.'

'That's all?'

'Yes.'

'I see.' Rena sat very still. Her face was expressionless.

'Of course,' Mr. Callow hastened to repeat himself, 'it's all too ridiculous to take seriously.'

'My father's last will and testament, Mr. Callow!' Rena rose, and after a moment's hesitation, Pippa rose, too.

Mr. Callow got up.

'You will get in touch with me, Miss Franklin,' he appealed. 'You will go home now and recover from this initial shock.'

'Whose home?' Rena answered, and Pippa remembered Crag asking her the same thing.

'My dear girl, there will be a way out, a way suitable for all concerned. Domrey Hardy—'

'Are you coming, Pippa?' Already Rena was at the door and pushing it open. With a nod to the solicitor she ran down the building steps to her car. 'At least,' she said, opening it up, 'this is mine, it's in my name. The other one, Father's, will be – *his*.'

'Rena—'

'Please, Pippa, not now.'

But Pippa could not contain herself. 'It's so unlike Uncle Preston,' she disbelieved.

'How little you knew him. It's Father exactly. In the same position I probably would have done the same myself.'

'What position?'

But Rena would not answer that.

'Don't you see what he was trying to do?' she said presently. 'Cunning old fox. Cunning old man. Only that old man won't win after all. How far can I get away from here, from Tombonda, on the sale of this car, would you say?'

'Not far,' judged Pippa reluctantly. 'It's not new, and these days—'

But Rena was not listening to her. She was repeating to herself '... he knew ... Father knew ... but he won't win ... I—'

'Rena,' cut in Pippa a little desperately, for all at once she was thinking of Davy, 'what can you do?'

Rena took her eyes off the road a moment to look fully at her cousin. 'You really mean what can you do, don't you? I'm sorry, Pippa, sorry to have built you up like that, sorry to have mentioned a bequest, but I really did think ...' She laughed wryly. 'How wrong I was!'

'It doesn't matter about the bequest. I only want to know where I stand.'

'Nowhere, like I do. I'm sorry, Pippa' ... she said again ... 'but I won't be able to help you at all. You can see how I'm placed myself. I advise you to get the boy, go to Sydney and find a job. There's a surplus of employment there, and you're quite a smart girl.'

'I see,' said Pippa hollowly. Then she asked: 'And you?'

'Don't you worry about me.' Rena's eyes were narrowed. 'I think I may have a solution. And it doesn't include any will-disputing moves, either, or any interviews with the inheritor.' She laughed shortly.

When she drew the car up at the door she just left it there, and ran, without another word for her cousin, into the house.

Pippa did not follow her. What could she say to Rena? Besides, she shivered, she had worries now of her own.

Instinctively she found herself walking across to Ku. Go to Sydney. Find a job. Rena had advised that, and it seemed the only course. But what if Davy were really ill ... *when* he was really ill ...

She had not realized she had arrived at the planting

until a hand reached out from one of the pines.

Crag looked down.

He did not take the hand away even after she had let him lead her to a tumbled log, instead he left it there to help her steady herself, and yet, she knew with surprise, I have never felt steadier in my life, even though I don't know what I'm going to do with that life, with Davy's little life, how I'm going to get through all this, still, holding on to Crag, I feel steady.

After several moments he took his hand away and reached for his pipe. He packed and lit it. Then he said: 'You know?'

'The will?'

'Yes.'

'Then I know. But' . . . curiously . . . 'how did you?'

'I told you, Pippa, it was what I would have done.'

'But why? *Why?*'

He looked at her in wonder. 'You haven't worked that out yet? No' . . . a shake of his head . . . 'you haven't. Well, it doesn't matter just now. What matters is *us.*'

'Us?' she asked, bewildered.

'You. The Scrubber.' A pause. 'Me.'

'I don't understand.'

'I told you I had a way out, remember, and I reckon you're needing it.'

'I could,' she replied desperately, 'write to Aunt Helen to get us back to England again.' She was remembering the small house, the week-to-week existence, she was knowing how distressed Aunt Helen would be to write back that raising the fares would be beyond her means.

He must have heard her doubt, for he did not even consider the thought.

He said bluntly, without any preamble: 'This is the way out, girl. I said it before on the train coming down to Tombonda, but you thought I was joking . . . or showing a damn nerve.

'Well, I was showing a nerve, perhaps, but never joking. I knew what I was asking and I know now.

'Will you marry me, Pippa?'

There was very little wind today, barely enough to stir the pine tops into a sibilant whisper. No ocean in the planting this time, thought Pippa abstractedly, no sound of the sea. The deep leaves had drawn a veil around them. Within that veil she sat and looked at Crag, but understanding what she had just heard. She said so.

'Marriage,' he told her almost gruffly, 'the ceremony or contract by which a man and woman become husband and wife.'

'Yes . . . but why?'

'I could give the usual reason, I suppose,' he said offhandedly. 'Love, isn't it?'

'Yes, but you don't . . . I don't . . .'

'No.' He came in before she could finish it. 'We don't, do we?' He looked at her so long she had to turn her glance away.

'No, we don't,' he confirmed at last. 'But I've heard, and I've read, of other reasons, and they've worked out in the end.'

'Worked out?' she said dully, for it was dull, she thought.

'One of my reasons is the scrubber,' Crag offered. 'In fact he's the only reason apart from—' He stopped abruptly. After a pause he went on, 'He can't be pushed around, Pippa, and you know it.'

'Oh, yes, I know it,' she said bitterly, 'but what can I do? We have to get out. Rena has practically said so. What *can* I do, Crag?'

'I told you,' was his reply.

'But I . . . but you . . .'

'You said that before and I agreed with you that we

don't. But what I offer still makes sense, girl, in fact it's the only thing that does make sense. For all of us.'

'All of us?'

'Davy, who would break his heart if you took him away, and you know it.'

'Yes' . . . a little angrily . . . 'I know it. You should never have let the association between you build up to this.'

'Well,' he shrugged, 'it has. Then me, Pippa, I want the boy. I want him very much.'

'That instant family?'

'Yes . . . yet just for Davy himself as well. I love the little scrubber. Finally, you.'

'Yes. Where do I come in, why is it the only thing for me?'

'Because what makes Davy happy must make you contented, because you're dedicated to Davy, because Davy—'

'But what about *me*?' She was surprised at the sudden note in her voice. She was surprised at what she had said.

He had leaned nearer to her, and instinctively she drew back.

'Well, what about you, Pippa?' he asked softly.

'I . . . I . . .'

'Yes, girl?'

'I . . . You're right, of course. It's only Davy who matters.' She spoke calmly, and it was difficult with such a sudden fast beating heart. 'But, Crag,' she added, 'does it have to be – marriage?'

'What else?'

'Well, I could go as your housekeeper,' she suggested.

'Not up there. It's a funny thing, Pippa' . . . he was attending his pipe now . . . 'it's a primitive corner all right, but not in that. Also, the way I feel about the scrubber it just wouldn't work. No, girl, that boy has to belong.'

'But you'd be saddling yourself, can't you see that?'

'I reckon if a horse is saddled the right way he's just as happy and a deal more secure than running free. I've actually seen it, Pippa, I've seen it up there.'

'Up there,' she said thoughtfully. 'I can't believe it's formal as you say, I can't believe I could not go merely as your housekeeper.'

'I have one already and she's not leaving,' he replied calmly. 'Besides that, there's the trip up. You see we'd be going overland. Camping out.'

'Camping out? But Davy—'

'Would thrive on it. I'm sure of that. I know he would benefit from those outback nights.'

'It still doesn't comprise a real reason for you to – to saddle yourself,' she said.

'One tent,' he answered levelly, 'you, the scrubber and me. It's a long way up, and you don't clutter yourself with gear.'

She had reddened, but she still held out.

'You would be cluttering yourself, Crag, can't you see that? – a sick boy, his sister.'

'My son,' he corrected soberly, 'my wife.'

'Oh, Crag, stop it! I – I can't be your wife.'

'If you're meaning what I think you're meaning I'll take you on those conditions as well,' he said quietly.

She flushed even more vividly, understanding him, then shook her head.

'I'm not a child,' she said gravely. 'I realize that complying to a certain state means more than living as – well, as I lived before.'

'I just told you if you want to make conditions, I'll accept you on them.'

'And keep to the conditions after the acceptance?'

110

He did not answer for a long moment, then he said, 'I don't know, Pippa. I feel like saying "Until you say", but—' He made a gesture with his big shoulders.

'Why did you make the offer in the first place?' she demanded.

'Because, dammit, I want to marry you,' he came back, 'because I want to have the scrubber with me, because that housekeeping thing of yours would be no go. Now are you answered?'

'No.'

'Right, you're not answered, but will you agree?'

Drearily she said, 'What else is there? What else?'

'Does that mean yes?'

'Yes.'

'Then say it, girl!'

'I just said it.'

'Say it with something in it,' he demanded.

She thought of Davy and what this would mean to him. She repeated, '*Yes.*'

He leaned right forward now and he kissed her lips. She simply stopped there in the caress, and he released her and said, 'He's a nice little scrubber, but does he have to stand between?'

'What do you mean, Crag?'

He gave a dismissive shrug, then told her he would like to get away immediately.

'We can get married tomorrow, Pippa,' he announced.

'Tomorrow?' She was taken aback. 'That soon?'

'It's got to be soon. I have to get back to Falling Star before it falls down.'

'You could go on and we could come later.'

'I told you I wanted Davy to have this camping experience.'

'Then you and Davy . . .'

'*Us*, Pippa. Look, girl, can't you see what Rena will try next? No' . . . a little sigh . . . 'you don't see it, do you, you never did. Never mind, it won't matter once we get away. But we can't do that until you're Mrs. Crag, so I've told the local minister—'

'*What?*'

'Oh, yes, and Davy, too. He's tickled pink.'

'You told Davy?' She could hardly believe him. 'How could you tell him when you didn't know?'

'I told him,' he repeated. 'I reckoned he'd like to be there when it was done. I reckoned you'd want that.'

'I would want that, but – but – tomorrow,' she said incredulously again.

'Tomorrow, Pippa,' he nodded.

A silence descended. It stopped so long that Pippa found herself searching for something to break it.

She could find nothing . . . and into the void came his soft: 'Want to back out, Pippa?' then her own: 'No.'

'Right then, we're being married. In the town at ten in the morning. After that we push off.'

'Rena—' she began.

'You can tell her if you like, but it might be hard to find her. I saw her leave Uplands just before I came into the planting. She'll probably be gone for some time, I'd reckon, while she thinks things over.'

'Then I can't tell her,' realized Pippa, half relieved, half uncertain.

'No.'

'Then I . . . then we just leave?'

'A little matter of a ceremony first,' he reminded her wryly.

'It's – unbelievable,' she said wonderingly.

'For me as well,' he said quietly.

'Then, Crag, why are you—'

'No, Pippa, not again. Ten tomorrow. And if you're not

there—'

'Yes?'

But he did not tell her. He just touched her shoulder briefly, then turned away. The next moment in the thickness of the trees he was gone.

Back again at Uplands, Pippa found that what Crag had said was correct. Rena had left.

Mrs. Mallory, the housekeeper, and the only resident servant since the rest of the domestic staff came in daily, told Pippa that Miss Rena had come in, walked around restlessly, then, when she had asked her could she get her something, help her in any way, had replied, 'Yes, Mallie, throw some things in a bag for me, I'm going away for a while to think.'

'Then,' reported Mrs. Mallory to Pippa, 'she said an odd thing, she said "I don't suppose I'll be thrown out straight off".'

Briefly, Pippa enlightened her, after all she had to know some time.

'That explains her paying up the daily girls,' nodded Mrs. Mallory, 'telling me to take a break and she'd see me again when she returned.'

The housekeeper did not look very concerned for herself, and when Pippa timidly asked if leaving Uplands would inconvenience her, she smiled and said, 'I don't think it will come to that.'

'But, Mrs. Mallory, the will—'

'Oh, yes, the will. But I've known Miss Rena since she was a child.' A little smile. 'I've also known Mr. Hardy a few years.'

Pippa searched the housekeeper's face for a sign of what she was thinking, but Mrs. Mallory was not giving anything away.

'I would certainly like that break,' she said. 'Carter

113

could caretake for a week or so.' She looked hopefully at Pippa.

'Then why not?'

'I couldn't leave you, miss.'

'But I will be going myself tomorrow. I'm ... I'm ...' Pippa tried to frame the words: 'I'm being married.' They wouldn't come, though. It all seemed untrue. Surely it was untrue.

Fortunately Mrs. Mallory did not notice her awkwardness. She said eagerly, 'It's my sister, she's not at all well, and I'd like the opportunity of visiting her.'

'Then do so. Go now,' Pippa urged warmly.

'It would make a difference if I could get tonight's train. You see, my sister lives in a small town to which there's only a night connection. You'd be quite all right, Miss Bromley, Carter would be here. By the way, Miss Rena left a note.' The woman handed it to Pippa.

As Mrs. Mallory bustled out to gather her few things together, Pippa opened the envelope. The several lines were written hastily, and backed up the housekeeper's statement that Rena had left in a hurry.

'Sorry it's turned out like this, Pippa, but you know the reason. You're on your own feet now, as I am. Rena.'

She put the letter back and went in to see if she could assist Mrs. Mallory. 'Perhaps I could drive you to the station,' she offered.

'Miss Rena took her car.'

'The other car.'

'Carter had to follow her with it down to Mr. Hardy's office. I don't know why.'

But Pippa knew. And she could see Rena storming out of her own car, throwing down the keys of the car Carter had driven, throwing them at Dom and saying: 'Here it is. After all, it's yours.'

'Perhaps I could borrow the car from Mr. Hardy—' she

began.

'He's gone, too. He went soon after she did. But don't worry about a car, Miss Bromley, the bus goes into town to catch the train. Are you sure, miss, that you'll be all right?'

'Quite sure. Carter will be here, remember. Also, I can ring Mr. Crag. He . . . we . . .'

But Mrs. Mallory was anxious to go, so Pippa did not say it after all. She walked with the housekeeper to the gate and waited with her until the bus came.

On her way back she detoured around the barns and stables, but Dom was still absent. Carter, whom she met on her way back to the house, said he had left in a hurry . . . everyone was in a hurry . . . that Mr. Hardy had only paused long enough to tell Carter what to do.

'What if there's a birth?' she asked the man.

'He saw to that,' Carter assured her. 'No events for a week, miss.'

'I'll fix tea for us,' Pippa offered, but Carter said not to bother, he was going to a meeting in the village, and would eat in a friend's place.

'But don't be worried, Miss Bromley, I won't be late.'

'I'm not nervous,' Pippa assured him, and she went into the house and up to the bare room she had been allotted when she first came here, the room with the window that looked out on the incinerator and mulch heap.

She could have had any room she liked now, she thought without much interest. She wandered out into the hall, wondering what would become of the house. When the bell suddenly pealed, it startled her, and for a few moments she forgot to answer it, accustomed as she was to the staff attending to that.

The second peal awakened her, and she ran down the stairs. She wondered if it was Rena back again . . . Doctor Burt . . . Crag. But the head showing through the glass door was only a little head, and eagerly Pippa opened up and clasped Davy so tight in her arms, he promptly wriggled free.

'Sorry, darling,' she said.

He rubbed some of her crushes off, and announced, 'Crag sent me to sleep here tonight.' He looked at her anxiously. 'I have to ask something.'

'Yes, Davy?'

'I have to ask this.' Davy took an important breath, then said distinctly: 'Still agreed on it, mate?'

'Crag told you?'

'Yes.' The anxious look deepening.

'Agreed,' said Pippa, and at once the little face altered. Never, *never* had Pippa seen such sunshine in her small brother. She would not have credited he could be so glad. It fairly bubbled out of him, he could not contain himself, and somewhere in her, Pippa, too, knew a song. It's worth it, she thought, for Davy.

They had tea together in the kitchen, though very little was eaten. Davy looked about to burst ... and Pippa, though she prepared a dish, only played with the food when it was done.

'Crag said that.' Her brother frowned at her plate.

'You're as bad yourself,' she smiled.

'But one thing, you're to go to bed early.'

'Crag said that, too?'

'Yes, Pippa.'

'Well, I will. We both will.'

They did. Arm in arm they went to Davy's room, the beautifully appointed room that Rena had had arranged for him.

Davy went into his little bed, and Pippa lay down on the day bed ... where, to her surprise when she awakened in the morning, she actually went to sleep at once. She had thought she would lie awake, especially when tomorrow ...

But she slept. It was a long restful sleep. She opened her eyes to Davy handing her a not-too-hot cup of tea by its presence of leaves but looking so proud of himself that she drank it and declared it perfect.

He sat on the day bed beside her.

'Where's your wedding dress, Pippa?'

'Oh, darling, wedding dresses are for brides, I mean brides who are having big weddings and will be written up in the paper.'

'Then what are you wearing?'

'Oh, my brown, I suppose ... or my grey wool.'

'Oh, Pippa!'

'But, darling ...'

'Brides don't wear those things, they wear – they wear—'

'Veils. But it's different, Davy. Can't you see, darling, that I—'

'I didn't mean veils ezackly, I – I meant a colour not grey or brown. And I meant flowers, Pippa' ... eagerly ... 'flowers to carry. There's lots of flowers in the garden. I'm sure we could pick them. The gardener told me it was good to pick them sometimes.'

'Oh, yes, we could pick them, but—'

'Then let's, Pippa.'

What could she say? What could she say to that little eager face? Thank goodness it was a climate in which seasons made little difference and flowers were always available. Pulling on her dressing-gown, she went out with Davy and gathered enough white marguerites and early violets to form a posy. She tied them with blue ribbon to please the little boy, and after her shower she put on a short blue frock that toned with the violet and white, then tied a blue band round her hair.

'Pippa, you're a bride!' Davy beamed.

'You're a bride.'

Crag said it when she opened the door at ten minutes to ten at his ring.

'I did it for Davy,' she said quickly. 'I did it because—'

'Don't spoil it,' he said simply, and came right in. 'Got a buttonhole for me?'

She looked at him incredulously, and he nodded.

'The scrubber, too,' he said.

There were carnations in the garden, and she plucked two. While she fixed them into buttonhole order, Crag packed their suitcases into the waggon. The waggon was pulling a trailer, she noticed, and the trailer was packed high with camping gear. Already Davy was capering around the gear, but he came running back to be buttonholed.

'It's all so absurd,' Pippa began to complain of the carnation in the little boy's lapel, but she didn't get it out, for all at once it didn't seem absurd, it seemed – right. It was Davy's bliss, she supposed, but it was right.

She had meant to write a brief note to Rena, telling her what she had done, where she had gone.

It was only when she was entering the church that she remembered she had not done so. She told herself she must get Crag to drive her back to do it before they left on their— Before they left. Heavens, she had nearly thought honeymoon. She gave a nervous half-laugh.

Then she stifled the laugh and looked at the minister who had come to meet and to guide them. She heard him say to the three of them, Crag, Davy, herself . . . and to a cleaner, a gardener and someone brought in from the street:

'Dearly beloved, we are gathered together here in the sight of God and in the face of this congregation, to join together this man and this woman in Holy Matrimony.'

It was too late to go back. In that moment she realized it. But with the realization came another realization, a realization so big, so bewildering, that for a moment she swayed, and Crag put out a hand to steady her.

She did not want to go back. *She wanted this.*

She heard 'man and wife' . . . she felt Crag's lips brushing hers. She felt Davy's younger lips. She felt the press of the minister's hand.

It was not until they were miles from the Southern Highlands that she recalled again the letter she had *not* written to Rena. She told Crag and he shrugged, 'Too late now, Mrs. C.'

Mrs. C. She was Mrs. C.

Beside her Davy chuckled delightedly and experimented, 'Pippa C. Mrs. C.' Then in a satisfied voice he said: 'My sister, Mrs. C.'

He was still smiling over it when he fell asleep somewhere on the road to Orange . . . they were heading inland and hoping to make Bourke that night.

Pippa removed the carnation which he had refused to take from his lapel, and pressed his little head to her shoulder. The carnation was wilted and crushed and she went to throw it away . . . and then she didn't. Instead she put it in her bag.

'Mine, too.' Crag took out his and handed it to her, and for a moment their eyes met.

Then he turned his attention on the road again. By nightfall they reached Bourke.

CHAPTER SIX

'Bourke isn't just a western town,' Crag said as they left the main street, 'it's a last stand before the hinterland sets in. Songs have been sung about it, verses written. Everyone speaks of "Out at the back-o'-Bourke".'

'How far back are we going, Crag?' Davy, who had wakened up, asked eagerly.

'As back as Falling-Star finally, scrubber, but right now only a mile back to the river where I reckon we'll make camp.'

An uncertainty enveloped Pippa. She had enjoyed her journey, finding the country much more as she had imagined Australia, not the second England the green Highlands had proved.

But making camp meant her first night as a wife. What had the man beside her said? One tent. You, the scrubber and me.

If Pippa was uncertain, though, Davy was rapturous. He was out of the waggon as soon as they reached the camping ground, helping Crag choose a suitable site, making ponderous agreements as to drainage should it rain . . . rain with a sky of flawless satin! . . . shelter should it blow . . . with not even a breath to stir the starlit leaves of the trees by which they would pitch the tent! *One* tent.

Crag decided on the most suitable spot, then set Davy to gather fuel and tinder. From now on that would be his duty, Crag informed him, until they reached Falling Star.

Pippa's duty, he said next, would be to start the tucker. Pippa nodded, and began laying the chops on the grid he had set out, but at once she was told to wait for the embers, since cooking over that flame would smoke the meat. Again Pippa nodded.

While Davy gathered the fuel, then threw it on ... Pippa was a little nervous about that, but Crag appeared to have confidence in the boy, so she must, too ... and while she waited, Crag pitched the tent and unrolled the sleeping bags. Then he came back to the fire and gave Pippa her first lesson in damper.

'I can make soda bread,' she said a little stiffly, 'which is the same.'

'No soda in this,' he instructed. 'Ashes.'

'Ashes!'

'Potash is a form of rising.' He took some from the spent end of the fire. 'You take your flour, salt and a handful of ashes and some water. Then you knead.' He did so. He told her to put the chops on the grid now and to stand by to turn them, then he finished his kneading and pushed the damper well in, saying it would be awaiting them for their breakfast.

They ate under a deep blue cloth of sky, the stars glittering with a brilliance never seen on the coast, Crag claimed.

Then, replete and drowsy, they all agreed on bed. While Crag built up the fire for the night, Pippa undressed the little boy down to his singlet and underpants and slipped him into the bag.

'God bless,' she kissed.

'Am I next?' Crag drawled as she came outside again. He was sitting near the tent flap and smoking his eternal pipe.

'I'll say God bless to you,' she promised lightly.

'Also tuck me in the bag?'

She flushed in the darkness, and reminded him, 'You'd be more of a job than Davy.'

He did not comment on that, he tended his pipe, and she stared out at the velvet darkness beyond the fire's flickering beams. A little noise that rose above the soft stir of the bush and the ripple of the river alerted her, but Crag assured her it was only a pheasant on the forage.

'He says "puss-puss",' he told her. 'Listen.'

Soon afterwards there was another bush noise that Crag said would be a wood pigeon.

'He calls "move-over-dear".' A laugh. 'Not much good in a sleeping bag, would you say, Mrs. C.?'

Davy gave a little possum snore, and Pippa went rather thankfully in to see to him . . . and to slip into her own niche.

She was drifting off when Crag finally came to his sleeping bag. He was so quiet she might not have known, except that he came across to her and kissed her cheek.

'Good night, Mrs. C.'

Now wide awake and staring into the darkness where he must be but she couldn't see him, Pippa answered a little indistinctly, 'God bless.'

The next morning the damper was taken from the white embers, its casing sliced off to reveal a perfect soda . . . no, potash, remembered Pippa . . . loaf that was deliciously warm enough to send the butter that Crag knifed generously over it into golden runnels.

'Mmm!' said Davy, eating more than Pippa had ever seen him eat. His little chin dripped runnels of gold.

Crag brewed tea, throwing the leaves into the boiling water, rotating the billy bush-style, and they drank and listened to the river and the sound of the awakening bush.

They set off again after Crag had carefully doused the fire, instructing Davy meanwhile how very important this was. Then he cleaned up the site to make it attractive for the next campers, telling Davy about this, too. Pippa saw

122

Davy nodding as he absorbed every word.

Now they went west, the bush road as straight as a gun barrel, and the names rolled from Crag's tongue . . . Milparinka, Tibooburra, Wittabrinna, Wompah. On the rim of Carya-punda Swamp they crossed the Queensland border.

Camp that night was by an overflow, and the sounds of the water birds enchanted Pippa as she helped Davy gather the fuel, which, because the trees had become sparse, was not so easy to find as at Back-o'-Bourke. Crag had told her to delay the meal until he went up to a station he knew. But, the fire started and thriving, Pippa could not resist trying a damper herself. Davy looked a little dubiously at the rather darkish result and asked his sister was she sure she had used white ashes.

'Yes.' Indignantly.

'Then it must be your hands.'

'It'll be all right. You'll see in the morning.' She shoved the damper in, Davy still looking dubious.

But at that moment the waggon came back, and Crag jumped out and held up three huge steaks. 'Also,' he rejoiced, 'station bread.' He exhibited a crusty loaf.

'I've already put in a damper,' Pippa informed him loftily.

'Good for you. But just in case . . .'

Pippa tossed her head at that 'just in case'.

There was also fresh milk for Davy, and a bottle of home preserves. By the time of the billy routine that finished off the meal three people were well fed and three heads were nodding.

Pippa was first up in the morning, and she went stealthily to the spent fire. She poked around . . . and poked around. There was no damper.

Crag came to the flap of the tent, let her search for a while, then drawled, 'Were you looking for a cricket ball, by any chance?'

'No, of course not, I was looking for a—' She saw the laughter in his face, and stopped. After a few moments of private wrath, she accused, 'That's not funny!'

'Neither was the ball, brick, what-have-you.'

'It was soda . . . I mean potash bread.'

'Leave out the bread,' he advised with a grin, 'for that's all there was, a ball of baked ash. Knowing small boys, and how they love to tease, I removed the evidence, Mrs. C.'

'I'm not!' she cried angrily, for she really had looked forward to surprising him with that damper.

'No.' His voice cut in quietly but all the more intensive because of its quietness. 'No, you're not, are you?'

She flushed vividly, suddenly aware of his bright eyes on her. 'I meant I'm Mrs. Crag, not that ridiculous Mrs. C.'

There was a pause. In the silence Pippa could hear Davy stirring. She knew she should go into the tent and help the little boy out of his bag, for he had the knack of tangling himself up. But somehow she could not pass Crag in that narrow space he had left her.

The silence grew. Even Davy did not break it again, so he must have gone back to sleep.

Then Crag broke it. He said: 'I wasn't meaning that.' He still looked at her, until, with an effort, she brushed past him into the tent.

Davy remembered the damper. Munching on a steak sandwich, he related the damper to Crag, and how Pippa had either used black ashes or her hands had given it a funny colour.

'Didn't turn out funny, though,' said Crag. 'Sorry I didn't leave you any, scrubber, but I was so hungry when I woke up last night—'

'You ate it all?' Davy did not look so much regretful as

124

incredulous, incredulous that anyone could have demolished that brick. He dropped the subject, though, for which Pippa knew she should be grateful to Crag. She was not. All the same she tossed him a cold appreciation of his lie.

'Needn't have been a lie,' he grinned. 'I was up last night, listening to the frog song down in the Overflow, looking up at the stars.'

All at once she pictured it . . . the velvet night, the star shadows, the bright moon, the crooning whispers and the soft rustling of the bush.

She wished she had been there, too.

'Why don't you, Pippa? Why don't you come?' He said it as though she had spoken her thoughts aloud. She jumped to her feet, aware of her scarlet cheeks, and began getting ready for the road again.

'Tomorrow,' Crag told Davy, 'you'll be wearing a fly veil.'

'Why, Crag?'

'For flies, of course. They're not everywhere Inside, but they are where we'll be passing through. Bush flies.'

'How will we eat, Crag? Through the holes?'

'If you intend eating only currants, yes, scrubber, but I think you can sneak in a mouthful here and there, then at night they'll be gone, they don't care about fire.'

'Where will we be?'

'Latitude twenty, I'd say.'

'What does that mean, Crag?' Pippa heard Davy's little voice as her brother followed his idol down to the water to get replenishment for the radiator. She heard Crag's patient answer. He was good father-material, she thought, and with that thought came a regret for him that so far that had been denied.

So far. . . . She stopped what she was doing. Although she had said to the man who was now her husband: 'I'm

125

not a child. I realize that complying to a certain state means more than living as I lived before,' she had never really thought about it. Now she thought.

'All aboard!' called Crag, and they were on their way again.

Each day, each moment of the day, the country changed. They were in the Inside now, that strange, unpredictable hinterland where for hundreds of miles there was nothing but red sand and gibber, saltpans, claypans, dry inland seas, but where at times, without warning, a blossoming burst on you, a verdure so intense that it hurt the eyes, flowers of unbelievable size and the tenderest of hues.

When Pippa called out that the paradise she suddenly looked out on must be a mirage, Crag shook his head, then told her that out here mirages came in different wrappings from the usual mirages . . . for instance drivers of trailers saw opposite trailers drawn up on the wrong side of the road, often they swerved to avoid them coming at them.

'Fatigue?' asked Pippa.

Crag shrugged. 'Perhaps . . . or a sort of second vision, a reflection. Look at that sign.' He pointed to a 'Beware of road trains 140 feet long'. Beside it a warning: 'No water for 900 miles.'

'Have we enough?'

'I know the wurlies around here – a wurlie is an old aboriginal watering hole. Also if you can teach yourself the plastic trick to trap moisture you won't parch. This is it . . .'

Davy was breathing down his neck in intrigue, and Pippa realized she was doing almost the same. This strange fascinating desert!

The red ochre days continued, the lupin-blue ridges that at night turned indigo, purple and scarlet. They passed a buffalo herd being headed in by buffalo hunters wearing ten-gallon hats against a blazing sun. These beasts were to be shipped to Singapore to work, and strangely it was from Singapore originally that they had come to work here. They passed camels, donkeys, packs of dingoes, flocks of galahs, graceful brolgas.

Now the nights were wine-dark until the moon came up, but before that Crag always made camp.

'Two fingers above the horizon,' he told Davy, 'is enough travelling for the day.' He held his big hand sidewise, extending two fingers.

'Your fingers or mine, Crag?' asked Davy.

'I see what you mean, scrubber. We'll make it yours this time and camp here.' As he drew up the waggon, he said: 'This is the last night's camp, folk.'

'What?' Pippa turned in surprise to him, but only Pippa, so Davy must have known already, but then there was little of this trip and this country that that young fellow did not know.

'Tomorrow,' nodded Crag, 'is Falling Star.'

It was with an odd feeling of the end of something in her life, almost the final turning of a page denoting a book is finished, that Pippa prepared the meal that night.

Davy was in high spirits, gathering tinder and fuel with nervous energy, anticipating what tomorrow would bring.

What *would* tomorrow bring? Pippa stared at the fire gathering embers much more quickly surely than it generally gathered them, forming white ashes for the damper ... she was expert on that now ... making the end of a day come faster. – And the beginning of a night.

She was silent as she ate that evening, silent later as she tucked Davy into his bag. She stopped with him long after her 'God bless', long after his little possum snores

127

told her that he slept. At length she knew she could stop no longer, yet still she lingered. There was a pulse and a throb in her that she had never known before. It was with an effort that she lifted the flap of the tent and went outside.

Crag was sitting out of the beam of the fire, for it was warm up here, no need to hug the glowing embers. She could just see his big dark outline against a tree.

He saw her, though. He got up. 'I was waiting for you,' he called . . . and as though impelled there she went across.

For a moment they stood looking at each other, then he took her in his arms, and she did not resist.

The navy blue night encompassed them. The stars. A silver of moon. Somewhere the pheasant cried out its 'Puss-puss', the wood pigeon began its 'Move-over-dear'. He . . . Crag . . . had smiled that that would be hard in a sleeping bag.

But they were not in sleeping bags now, they were on soft earth, and a tree leaned over.

'Good night, Mrs. Crag,' Crag called as he got into his sleeping bag in the tent, but she pretended oblivion at once, and did not answer.

For I am, she knew now. I am Mrs. Crag, not Mrs. C.

I am Crag's wife.

Every moment of that final day brought Pippa a mounting excitement. Always she had thought of her stay at Falling Star as something temporary, merely a waiting until Davy . . .

Never had she thought of the place which they would reach at sundown . . . Crag, veering north-west now, had just reported that . . . as home. It wasn't, either. It was

128

just a pause for her, a pause only, and yet . . .

She looked out on the nothingness either side, an astonishing nothingness, for the longer you gazed at it the more features . . . and *beauty* . . . it achieved, and wished she could lose this foolish concept of journey's end. For Yantumara could never be her journey's end. It was the scrubber that man loved . . . there, she was calling him that herself now . . . and because of that love he had married her. Just to have Davy. Last night . . . her cheeks flamed . . . had only been part of the biological pattern of life. Life went on. People went on. Children. What if— The sudden thought caught her breath. Oh, no, it wouldn't happen: Yet what if it did? She gave the man at her side an oblique glance. How had she thought of him? As good father-material. What if . . .

When the sun was right above them, Crag pulled up for lunch. While Davy examined one of the giant anthills that were part of the scene now, Crag, boiling a billy so quickly with dry tinder he almost could have pulled on an electric switch, said wryly: 'Relax, Pippa.'

'Relax?' She gave a start, then looked at him in question.

'There are eight rooms at Falling Star.' He threw on more tinder. 'Five of them bedrooms. We' . . . a deliberate pause . . . 'will only be using two.'

'Two?' she queried.

'The scrubber and I in one so I can watch him and you can stop wearing yourself out, another for you. No' . . . as she went to intervene . . . 'I know what you're going to say. You're going to tell me like you did before that complying to a certain state . . . stop me if I use the wrong words . . . means more than living as you lived before.'

'Crag,' she said awkwardly, 'I want to be fair.'

'Fair?' He repeated the word incredulously. He almost seemed to try out its taste. 'Fair?'

'Crag, I . . . I . . .'

'Look, Pippa.' He looked up at her from his squatting position, the tinder dangling from his big hand. 'Look, girl, last night didn't establish anything. I mean there's no ties tied. I mean—'

'Yes, Crag, what do you mean?'

'That it was nothing. *Now* relax.'

Relax. Pippa turned away.

Davy had run back from the anthills full of questions. The man answered him as to their magnetic properties as he scattered the tea-leaves in the bubbling water, then rotated the billy.

'Not much for tucker,' he regretted, 'but tonight will be better. I telephoned Mrs. Cassidy at the last station.'

'Who is Mrs. Cassidy?' Pippa asked.

'My housekeeper, and my father's before me. That's why you couldn't have taken over that role, girl.'

'Won't Mrs. Cassidy feel it's odd that we . . . I mean . . .' She glanced towards Davy, but he was still pondering over the anthills.

'She's had scrubbers of her own,' said Crag, 'and she'll accept that a man sometimes needs a man's attention. Anyway' . . . he poured three teas . . . 'she lives in her own cottage.'

'A cottage as well as the homestead?'

'It's practically a little town. Most of the Inside places have to be that. They form their own world. When you're hundreds of miles from a store you start your own store. That applies to amusements, too. For instance, you show your own movies.'

'Do you, Crag?' asked Davy enchanted, forgetting the anthills.

'Sure do, scrubber. You have your own church, your own sick bay, all the things an ordinary town would have.'

'Doctor?' said Pippa in a low voice.

He understood her concern. 'No, I don't take over that side, unless of course it's an emergency until the F.D. can get in.'

'F.D.?'

'Flying Doctor. Though I do dole out physic when needed to the pics.'

'Piccaninnies.'

'Yes. The scrubber won't lack young friends, Pippa.' At her frown he said stoutly, 'They're lovely youngsters, Davy will do himself proud.'

'Of course,' Pippa assured him, 'it was the lack of a medico that was concerning me. I mean if suddenly ...' Her glance went to Davy.

'Then just as quick as down south we get aid. Quicker, I'd reckon, there's no traffic in the sky, so that the F.D. or F.A.—'

'F.A.?' asked Pippa now.

'Flying Ambulance, ready to take a patient to the nearest base hospital, or, if more than that is needed, even down to Sydney or Melbourne. I tell you, girl, you've no worries.'

'No,' she said, relieved.

During the afternoon's ride some occasional green crept into the red earth and rocks, and Crag said that around here was cotton country.

'There's water, you see, something a cotton stand must have.'

'Haven't you water?'

'Cattle amount. Cotton needs more.' He had pulled up the waggon for her to see the plants at nearer range. She found the shrubs in bloom very pretty, even bridal.

'Why not when we have a bride here?' he teased. 'Along the track is the ginnery. I'll take you there one day.'

131

Soon the green cut out and the mulga and spinifex began again, the bare bones of rocks. They circled an emu's nest so as not to disturb the mother. Later on there was another detour around a taboo ground, a place, Crag explained, where the natives believed ancestors walked.

Davy did not sleep during the long warm afternoon, his eyes were wide.

'What will happen, Crag,' he asked, 'if the sun gets down to two fingers and we're still not at Falling Star?'

'I reckon we'd push on, scrubber. I know the track like the back of my hand. Only it's not going to happen. See that hill?'

By this both Davy and Pippa had begun really to see hills in Crag's 'hills'. At first they had laughed at them, refusing to admit even a slight rise when he had pointed out Mount Westward ... Purple Mountain ... Gully Peak ... The Ramparts ... But now they had adjusted their ideas ... and their vision ... and they both called eagerly, 'Yes.'

'Beyond that is Falling Star. In half a finger more, Davy, you'll be looking at your home.'

'Oh!' Davy breathed, and he judged the westering sun by his little digit held sidewise. Presently he called, 'The sun has moved that half finger, Crag.'

'And Yantumara awaits.'

'Where? I can't see. . . . Oh, yes.'

Pippa, too, had focused the setting. With Davy she sat silent while the waggon gathered speed on familiar ground and the distant cluster of buildings became more distinct.

'It's a township,' Pippa called.

'Not really,' Crag grinned.

'But all those buildings—'

'The land has been good to the Crags, and that includes those who lived on our land, so we've given back

what we can. Those cottages' ... he waved his hand ...
'replace the humpies of my grandfather's day. That shed
is an amenities hall, that small building our little hospital.
There's Mrs. Cassidy's happy home. Next door is the
book-keeper, and then there's a dormitory for the stockmen. And that's—'

Davy finished for him in a reverent voice: 'Falling
Star.'

'Yantumara,' nodded Crag. He had slackened speed so
that he could gaze, too, at his home.

Pippa saw that Ku, as he had told her, had copied its
pattern, there was the same sprawling design at Ku, the
same wide verandahs. But the setting here, she smiled to
herself, was very different. No cool country lushness at
Yantumara, no singing pines, just the bare hot hinterland. Yet there was a tree ... a rather strange specimen.

'It's a baobob,' said Crag, starting off again to finish the
last short lap, 'a bottle tree. Folk have been known actually to live in that wide trunk, but we're not going to.
Stand aside, scrubber.' He had halted now and lifted
them both out. 'This is something I'm told has to be
done.'

As he approached her Pippa saw what he intended to
do, and she said half in vexation and half in laughter,
'Oh, don't be silly, Crag.'

'Don't you be silly. I couldn't do it before, I couldn't
carry you over the threshold of a tent.' As he spoke he
lifted her in his arms and bore her through the open door,
Davy dancing delightedly at his heels, an audience of
little dark people ... and quite a few not so little ... at the
foot of the verandah. Also some ten-gallon hat men,
stockmen probably, a man with a ledger under his arm,
he would be the book-keeper, a woman in an apron, she
would be Mrs. Cassidy. Others.

'Oh, put me down,' Pippa implored.

He did . . . in a room that at once enchanted Pippa. It was large, with a cool cemented floor that had been painted green and polished to a high gloss. The blinds were rattan, the furniture bamboo, everything was for coolness, except the fireplace where fires would never be lit, and there, very effectively, either Mrs. Cassidy or the girls had arranged dried feathers of long grass.

Crag, watching her closely and seeing her approval, remarked of the fireplace, 'I told you that my great-greats only thought in terms of so many rooms and as many chimneys.'

'I like it,' she assured him.

Davy was scampering around the house, discovering it all for himself, occasionally letting out squeals of joy.

'There's a sea outside, Pippa. Look through the window!'

'Lagoon,' called Crag. 'We've had some wet. It mightn't be there next month.'

'There's a windmill and a corral.'

'We usually say pen, scrubber. Pippa, meet Cass, the best dab sponge hand Up Top. Cass, this is—'

'I'm glad to meet your wife, Crag,' the older woman greeted Pippa warmly. 'Your mother would have loved to have seen this day.'

Your wife. All through the tea that Mrs. Cassidy insisted on serving at once, even though the main meal could not be far away, Pippa kept on hearing those two words. Your wife.

The tea over, Mrs. Cassidy now insisted on running across to her own place while Pippa got her bearings. She would be back to serve the dinner, she said.

There was a sensitiveness in this back-country woman, Pippa saw, and she warmed to her. She wanted to say: 'Don't go. It doesn't matter. You see – this is a different

134

marriage.'

Then Crag was taking her along to her room, showing her the larger room he would share with Davy.

'Tonight we'll go through things, medical things concerning the scrubber,' he said, 'you'll tell me what to watch for in Davy.'

'He's my responsibility,' protested Pippa.

He patted her shoulder. 'Why don't you flake out until dinner? Incidentally Mrs. Cass always does the cooking. Up till now I've eaten with the men, and I thought it might interest Davy if we continued doing so. Suit you?'

'Of course. Unless—'

'Yes?'

'Unless you feel I should form a family table. I mean—'

'You mean you at one end, me at the other, the scrubber in between? Compliance to a certain state?'

'Oh, Crag!' she said almost tearfully.

At once he was contrite. He touched her head gently, said, 'Rest now,' and left.

But after he had gone she sat broodingly at the window, not looking at the new fresh things that at first had captured her attention, thinking wretchedly instead of this big warm house, and what this house should be. — What this house wasn't.

It should be filled with love ... and the children who come from that love. Of course there was the love of Davy, but for how long? How much more borrowed time?

She stared through the window but did not see the faintly mauve-grey grass that turned iridescent every time the small breeze teased at its blades, she did not see the glittering lagoon. When a bell went for dinner ... she supposed it would be dinner, for no one would 'dress' here

. . . she had only time to dab her eyes before Crag knocked and called 'Tucker!'

If he noticed pink rims he said nothing, but he did appeal before he opened the dining-room door an anxious: 'They're looking forward to you, Pippa, you're the only woman, bar Mrs. Cass, whom they see every day, for five hundred miles.'

'You're asking me to smile.' She did smile.

'Thanks, girl.' He turned the handle and pushed the door.

There was one long table with benches each side, and everyone sat there. That is they did until she entered, then they rose while Crag introduced them all to her.

'Barney, Snowy, Harry, Nobby,' said Crag. 'Boys, the Missus.'

Four leather-dark faces creased into smiles, and the eyes, deep in the creases from years in the sun, disappeared.

'Rupey, our bookie.' Rupert took off his glasses and bowed.

'Tim and Tom, two helpful jackeroos,' put in one of a pair of fresh-faced boys.

'Hopeful of stopping on considering the mistakes they've made while I've been away,' growled Crag, and the other half of the pair retorted that it could be hopeful of getting out of here, but his voice did not back up what he said.

There were others, sundry helpers, Pippa judged, and they all smiled appreciatively at her, so much so that tomorrow she resolved to wear a pretty dress and have bright eyes.

Davy's eyes, however, were positively glistening. Not from the company, she soon found out, and not from the festive board, but from the audience at the window. There was literally a score of little dark heads and double that of pansy eyes staring at Davy. Davy, who had known few contemporaries because of his restricted existence, looked back at them in fascination.

At last he could bear it no longer, and he tugged at Crag.

'Crag, where do they eat?'

'In their own houses, of course, scrubber, like you're eating . . . or I expect you to start soon.' He picked up Davy's knife and fork to prompt him. 'Only,' Crag continued, 'mainly their mums make one big fire and cook the rib bones there together.'

'Rib bones?'

'Over a eucalyptus fire there's nothing better.'

'Oh.' Davy looked with disappointment at his own tasteful plate.

'Look,' said Crag, 'if you lick that clean, tomorrow night you can have rib bones down there.'

Pippa gave a little gasp, and Crag said, 'Won't do any harm, in fact a power of good. I grew up on meals like that.'

'But Davy's different,' she said in a low voice. 'You shouldn't tell him things that will leave him disappointed.'

'Rib bones never disappointed anyone.'

'You know I didn't mean that,' she said angrily.

'Smile,' he advised. 'Only woman, save Cass, for five hundred miles, remember.'

Pippa, feeling more like kicking his shins, smiled.

Davy, prompted by Crag's promise, reassured by the shy welcomes on the little brown faces at the window, ate his meal, listening with fascination to the station talk of herds, horse-breaks, overlanding . . . places called strange names like The Overtake, Big Dry, Come And Get It.

It appeared that a horse-break was going on this week. The wild horses had been rounded up last month and

137

now there was the job of breaking them in. The mares had been done, said one of the stockmen in a soft voice that rather surprised Pippa for a man in such a tough position, and they had been nervous but easy enough, but the stallions had been a challenge.

'Especially,' came in the stockman Harry in an equally soft tone, 'that older feller we haven't got round to yet. He promises to be a bad 'un.'

Mrs. Cass brought out plum duff . . . she was certainly a great cook . . . then all took their plates and scraped them and placed them in a dishwasher and poured their tea from a huge brown pot.

The little pansy-eyed people had faded away from the window – no doubt, explained Pippa to Davy, they had gone to bed. On hearing this, Davy, too, agreed on bed, and Pippa took him along to the room he was to share with Crag.

'It will be funny,' said the now experienced Davy, 'sleeping under a roof.'

'You liked the tent better, darling?' Pippa was fixing a pillow.

'Oh, no,' Davy assured her, 'I like it here, it's my home.'

My home. He said it with such faith and assurance, Pippa's eyes pricked. How long a home?

'I feel like crying for joy, too, Pip.' Davy, mistaking her tears, smiled it up at her. He said proudly, proud of himself, 'You can go now. I don't need you to sit with me while I go to sleep, not any more.' As she rose obediently and went to the door, he called, 'Pippa, you'll tell him, won't you?'

'Tell whom, darling? Tell what?'

'Tell your husband about me not needing you to sit with me.'

'Yes, I will, Davy.'

'And Pippa—'

'Yes, Davy?'

'Tell him I think that very soon I won't want anyone ever at all. Will you tell him?'

'Yes, Davy.' She went slowly out. No one ever at all. Davy had said it with pride, he had always been sharply conscious of his dependence. But she had not heard it with pride but misery, because there soon would be . . . no one ever at all.

No more springs. Doctor Harries had told her that, and already that last spring was three months gone.

She found her way to the big room where she expected, by its lights, Crag would be awaiting her. The stockmen, the book-keeper, jackeroos and general helpers had departed to their own quarters. Mrs. Cassidy's kitchen light was out, so she must have left, too.

Pippa knocked on the door, then entered the cool domain. Crag got up from the bamboo rocker he was relaxing in and insisted she take it.

'No,' he said as she objected to shifting him out, 'I like seeing a woman rock, it looks more in keeping than a man rocking.'

'I think a man is more in keeping,' she argued, 'a man sitting on a porch smoking his pipe and looking back through the years.'

'Do I seem that old to you?' he grinned.

'No, it's just how I see a man and a rocker.'

'Shall I tell you how I see a woman and a rocker? I see her there with a baby and singing lullabies.'

'I suppose your mother rocked you here,' said Pippa a little stiffly, 'sang you lullabies.' Before he could elaborate, she prompted, 'You wanted to talk to me about Davy.'

'Yes.' He waited to light his pipe.

As he did so, Pippa remarked on the stockmen and how

impressed she had been that such big tough fellows could speak in such gentle, controlled voices.

He put down his pipe at that and laughed till the tears came down his cheeks.

'Barney, Snowy, Harry, Nobby,' he guffawed. 'Gentle, controlled voices! Wait till I tell the jackeroos.'

'I don't see anything funny.'

'You'll hear it, though, when I take you out to see a muster. Of course the fellers' voices are gentle and controlled, they're saving them for the next time they're cracking a whip and digging in the spurs as they take off after a trouble-maker. But' . . . seeing that Pippa was still unamused . . . 'it's nice of you to tag them "gentle and controlled".'

'Don't you like your staff?'

'Like them?' He looked at her amazed.

'You don't sound as though you do. Though perhaps' . . . coolly . . . 'you dislike anything gentle and controlled.'

He did not answer for quite a while. Then he said in a rather husky voice: 'It's not always easy to be that. Gentle and controlled.' He had got up and gone to the window. She saw that the knuckles of the hands on the sill were strained and white. 'Not easy,' he said again.

There was a long pause. Feeling uncomfortable, yet not understanding why, Pippa reminded him what they had come together to talk about. He nodded and came back to sit beside her, and then quietly but firmly he drew from her every detail she could give him concerning Davy. The first grave signs in a small child, the attention he had been given since, what each doctor of the many doctors had reported. Finally Doctor Burt.

'Glen Burt repeated what I had previously learned, but he said that every day new reading was coming in concerning Davy's trouble. He said—'

'Yes, Pippa?'

'That sometimes in spite of facts, in spite of all a doctor knows, it doesn't always happen as a doctor believes. But' . . . a break now in Pippa's voice . . . 'how long can a little boy wait?'

Several times during the long questioning Crag got up and made tea. Then he would come back and ask for more. But finally the questions stopped, and they sat silent in a room that Pippa realized with drowsy surprise was fast becoming lighter. They had talked all night.

Crag had got to his feet again, but this time not for tea. Leaning over, he gathered her up and carried her to her room. 'At least,' he said, 'you'll get an hour before early cuppa. – Though a fine watchdog I made for our scrubber.'

'You had to understand everything,' she defended for him, and knew it was the first defence she had made for Crag.

'Yes,' he agreed, 'and it was better to talk the night out than sit and think.'

She looked quickly at him, and he went on.

'*Think*,' he said, 'like you were thinking this afternoon, Pippa. Sitting at a window and thinking about this house.'

'How could you know—' she blurted, her cheeks burning. Then she stopped and looked away.

But he answered her unfinished question. He said, 'Because *I* was sitting at a window, too, thinking of what a house should be, but isn't. Grieving for a house. So it was better to talk out tonight, wasn't it? Though' . . . putting her down on the bed . . . 'it will be different . . . when a house *is*.'

CHAPTER SEVEN

WHEN a house *is*.

Pippa slept at last with those four words ringing in her mind. When a house is not a place of rooms but a place of love, she interpreted, but how could he ask love of her when the only love he offered was for her brother? Apart from Davy any woman could have stood where she stood. He had told her that first day on the train that time too soon ran out for life as life should be lived. Rena had set him back ... probably others ... so now it had finally come to Pippa Bromley. No. Pippa Crag.

'Missus,' said a soft voice, 'Missus,' and Pippa opened her eyes to a smiling girl with white teeth and coffee skin. 'Missus, you bin sleep long time. Missus Cass she sent me with cup of tea.'

Pippa started to explain that she had been asleep only a short time, but found she felt so refreshed that it was unnecessary. She smiled at the girl and said, 'Thank you—' with a question in her voice. The girl responded, 'Rosie.'

'It's very good of you, Rosie.' She took the tea.

'I'm kitchen girl,' beamed Rosie. 'I help Missus Cass. Your piccaninny 'e bin gone down with our pics.'

'Davy is up?'

'Dav-ee name belonga him? Yes, Missus. Your piccaninny, Missus?'

'My brother.'

'Oh.' Rosie looked sympathetic. 'Never mind, you have teetartaboo soon.'

'Teetartaboo?'

'Baby,' smiled Rosie. 'You and Boss have plenty babies.'

With pride she told Pippa, 'I have four.'

'Four!' She only looked a girl, though probably she had married in her early teens.

Pippa got up, gave her cup to Rosie, put on her dressing-gown and found the bathroom. The water ran very hot for a while and she remembered last night that Crag had told her there was no need for any heating system up here, the main concern was to run water cold. But eventually it gushed cooler and then quite cool. She finished off the shower with the cool and came back to her room braced and refreshed. She put on a simple shift, buckled up sandals, combed her hair and etched in a hint of lipstick, then went along to the kitchen.

Mrs. Cassidy was busy with more meat than Pippa had seen outside a butcher's shop.

'Up here we all kill our own, of course,' she told Pippa. 'Ben, he's our butcher, has just brought in today's meat to be dealt with.'

'All beef?'

'No lamb or mutton here, dear, it's steak, steak, steak.'

As Pippa gazed fascinated at the intimidating quantities of undercut, topside, chuck, sirloin and liver, Mrs. Cassidy said soothingly, 'Don't worry about it, you won't be called upon to deal with it. Unless' ... a quick inquiring glance at Pippa ... 'you want to. Crag's mother always left it to me, so naturally I thought you'd be the same. But I'm sure, Mrs. Crag, that if you wish—'

'I don't wish. I prefer things to go on as they went before. And I'm Pippa, Mrs. Cassidy.'

'Cass or Cassy will do nicely,' beamed the housekeeper, relieved to learn she still retained her position of kitchen boss. 'I like this work. You could say I was brought up to it. My mother was a station cook and used to bring me along with her. Old Mrs. Crag used to spend all her time

143

on the piccaninnies, then her daughter-in-law, Crag's mother, did the same after her.'

Pippa nodded, but did not comment. *This* Crag woman won't, she thought hopelessly, because she won't be here long enough, only as long as Davy... Her throat contracted. She said a little huskily, 'I'd like to help in that way, too, but I have my brother, and unhappily—' Her voice trailed off.

The next moment she was surprised by two warm arms around her. 'There, lovie, it's going to be all right. I know all about it, Crag told me, so don't worry yourself trying to tell me now. And don't think as you've been thinking, either. Miracles happen. They happen every day.'

'I know, but can one happen soon enough?'

'I see what you mean. Well, let me tell you something: this is the land of lots o' time ... songs have been written about that. So I reckon young Davy will have lots o' time, too, and while he's having it those miracles will catch up.'

'Oh, Mrs. Cassidy ... Cassy!' Tears were splashing down Pippa's cheeks, but they were happy tears. Already she felt almost cheerful.

'Sit down and get that breakfast into you, girl. That's one rule at Falling Star: a big breakfast. On a station like this, with mobs and herds always on the move in or out, you always make certain of at least the first meal of the day.'

'But that's big enough for three meals!' gasped Pippa at the sight of her laden plate, for it was surely the biggest steak she had ever seen.

'The boy got it into him,' pooh-poohed the housekeeper.

'Davy did?' Pippa looked incredulous. 'He's never eaten a proper breakfast in his life.'

'He did this time. Look, if you don't wrap yourself

around it, as Crag always says, I'll put another piece on.'

Laughing . . . and hungrier than she had believed she was, especially after the first bite of the plate-sized steak . . . Pippa proceeded to 'wrap herself around it'.

As she ate she watched Mrs. Cassidy with respect. The housekeeper was dealing with an almost incredible amount of meat.

'Because of our climate we have to cook as much as possible at once, Pippa,' she explained of the big roasts and rolls she was tucking into the vast oven, 'then pack as much as we can into the freezer, and salt all that's suitable for salting. Salt beef is for the boys when they're out with the herds. That, and damper, and black tea, is all they'll look at when they're overlanding. When they come in it's a different matter. They like a few fancy things then, even enjoy a slice of cake.' Mrs. Cassidy laughed and floured another large joint.

Pippa asked if she could help at least with the dishes, but was told that that was the kitchen girl's job, that Rosie might be hurt to see Young Missus doing what she should be doing.

'You'll soon find your niche,' Mrs. Cassidy assured her, 'this place is big enough to supply niches for all the world, I sometimes think. I often wonder why they made the Inside so big.' As Pippa wandered outside she called, 'Tea's in half an hour.'

Tea! After all that steak! Laughing, Pippa went down to look for Davy.

She found him playing with the piccaninnies in a shady hollow, and he at once remonstrated, 'You should wear a hat, Pippa, there's ultra-violent rays, didn't you know?'

'Violet, darling.' – Crag's tuition, she thought. – 'I'll wear one next time. But' . . . giving him the opportunity that he obviously awaited . . . 'the piccaninnies don't wear

145

hats.'

'It's because of their skin which has more protective pigs.' Davy must have been conscious that he was not exactly right, for he said hurriedly, 'I've been in with the book-keeper. There's a lot to do in Falling Star for a book-keeper. He has to check all the bills, and you should see the kitchen bill, but the book-keeper says that's mainly because orders are always for three months.'

'Yes, I expect you get through a lot of food in three months.'

'But not candles,' disbelieved Davy. 'Me and the bookie—'

'The book-keeper and I.'

'Yes, us – well, we were surprised at a thousand candles.'

'A thousand candles?' Pippa was surprised herself. She said foolishly that they had their own electric plant here. Even if they hadn't they wouldn't need a thousand candles.

'A thousand candles,' Davy informed her, 'is eight-four dozen take away eight. Me and the bookie . . . I mean the book-keeper and I, us, we added it up, and we were very surprised. As the bookie . . . the book-keeper says you'd think Crag would have ordered eighty-four dozen, or so many pounds, not a thousand candles.'

'Yes,' Pippa said absently. She was thinking of that first time she had gone to Ku and how Crag had told her of his father's and mother's life together. He had said, she recalled, that it was a thousand candles.

'Crag wouldn't mean it seriously, Davy.'

'Well, he shouldn't order it. The bookie . . . the book-keeper is a very busy man, so I'll ask Crag if he really wants—'

'*No*, Davy!' – Why was she going on like this? she thought helplessly; it was obviously a silly error in the order, and anyway to forbid a child was only to rouse a child's curiosity, and she did not want anything more said about candles. Fortunately, however, Davy had lost interest. He took her arm and carefully introduced her to all his playmates. There was Harold-Jimmy, Joey, Bobby, Trevor, Dougie, Paulie, Gary.

'No girls?'

'They're playing houses,' said Davy with the disgust expected from boys. – So children were the same the world over.

All the gang were in for lunch, as it was called, but it could have been dinner, for it ran to three large courses, soup, beef, of course, a big boiled pudding.

Pippa enjoyed the company of the stockmen again, with their 'distance' eyes, their rather old-world courtesy, their odour of ancient leather. The jackeroos, more her age, amused her with their competition in shirts and elastic-sided boots, their smart talk ... though she noticed that the last was kept to a minimum when Crag was around.

She had thought that Davy had forgotten the candles, but, a piece of potato poised aloft, he said, 'Crag, did you really mean a thousand candles on that grocery list to be brought out from town?'

'Davy!' remonstrated Pippa, and was annoyed at herself; it would have been better to have let the little boy have his say.

'Me and the bookie ... I mean the book-keeper and I ... we thought it was a lot of candles.'

'It is a lot, scrubber, but a thousand is the order.' As he spoke Crag was looking at Pippa, and she felt the pink mounting her cheeks.

Davy noticed the pink and reported, 'She never wore a hat. You'd better speak to your wife, Crag.'

'Reckon I will, scrubber, but at the proper time. Get

147

yourself around that spotted dog—'

'Spotted dog?'

'Now you're like Cass, she makes me say sultana pudding, but get yourself around it all the same, because after lunch you and Pippa are going out to watch a muster.'

'Oh, Crag!'

Pippa said nothing. She could scarcely refuse in front of all these men even if she wanted to, and she didn't want to, she wanted to be with Davy ... and she, too, wanted to see a muster.

They drove out in a different jeep, an extremely battered jeep, but evidently mechanically perfect, for it had no trouble with the bumps and rocks with which Crag confronted it. On a hill ... not really a hill, barely an incline, but now Pippa was seeing contours in the same way as the Insiders, Crag drew up the jeep for them to watch. The men and dogs were on the job, keeping the herd in a bunch, and Pippa noted the drovers sitting apparently relaxed in the saddle but actually sharp and alert.

'Mustering is funny,' said Crag by their side, 'sometimes I could drive you bang down the middle and nothing happen, another time it only needs the rattle of a stirrup. You never know when you're going to have a rush.' At Pippa's inquiring look he explained, 'A panic. A stampede.'

Even as he spoke, the mob began swinging. Pippa, who had been standing away from the jeep, turned sharply, and in doing so tripped and grazed her leg against the jeep wheel.

'It's nothing,' she said, embarrassed, as Crag immediately picked her up and put her into the back seat, lifting the injured leg to examine it. 'It's only a scratch.'

'Had your tetanus shots, Pippa?'

148

'Oh, for goodness' sake,' she laughed, 'it's barely touched.'

'But the jeep's old and rusty,' he fussed.

'Look,' she said, 'you only get tetanus in a deep wound. Don't be absurd, Crag.'

'All right,' he agreed, 'but at least we'll give you the earth treatment.'

She watched amazed as he made a poultice of water from the flask and some of the red earth not polluted by the wheels of jeeps or hooves of herds, then placed it on her leg.

'It's absolutely sterile,' he said, 'so not to worry.'

'It's an old aboriginal cure, Missus,' assured one of the stockmen, 'and I've seen wonderful results.'

'We don't recommend it, of course,' Crag went on, 'civilization has made it harder and harder to find the really sterile stuff. But if you're caught away from home, like we are, it's a good thing to remember.'

'Would it cure me?' asked Davy, standing and watching with interest.

There was silence. Then Crag bent over and made another poultice, a small one, and placed it carefully on Davy's small brow.

'Reckon so, scrubber,' he said. 'Well, folk, had enough?'

They saw camels on the way back, brumby ones whose ancestors had been brought in by the Afghans years ago. They were being herded by several cowboys ... Davy said it should be camelboys ... and seeing that the boy and Pippa were interested, Crag drove the jeep across the desert to where the camels were tethered.

The horsemen explained that a demand had opened up for camels, but that they had to be taught first to lead. Apart from the camel sales the men were hoping the station owners would pay them a premium for taking the camels away from their property, for it was well-known that they ate the precious scrub, knocked down fences and upset the waterholes.

Crag smoked his pipe as he listened, agreed as a station owner that they had a point there, but offered instead of a premium to buy a camel.

A broken-in, rather mild-looking fellow was brought forward, and Pippa was given the job of holding the tow rope as they led him back to Falling Star.

Here Davy had his first camel ride, and did quite well. Not so well Pippa, who did not care for the lunges forward, and when the animal dropped forward on its knees to let her off was so unprepared for the jolt that she somersaulted over its head. Davy adored that.

Crag taught Davy to say 'Hooshta' to get the camel started, then they left him adoring the camel, along with all the piccaninnies, and went inside.

'It's been a good day, Crag,' Pippa appreciated shyly.

'Tomorrow we'll go down to where I've enclosed the brumbies we caught last month. The stallions are due to be broken in, though most of the mares are finished.'

'You won't involve Davy in this?' said Pippa nervously.

'Oh, no,' he assured her, 'horse-breaking takes years of learning. Though I've no doubt that one day the scrubber—'

'Crag . . . please!' She turned away.

'It could be true,' he said stubbornly. 'I mean you don't *know*, Pippa.'

'The doctors knew.'

'But they also admitted that miracles can happen. How do you know that today a miracle didn't happen?'

'That poultice of red earth? Oh, Crag!'

'I really meant how do you know that somewhere

someone didn't discover what we want discovered. But'
... poking at his pipe ... 'that red earth will do for a
miracle right now, Pippa. You know what? The young
'un believes in it, he asked me was it all right to wash it off
now that it had cured him. He has belief, and that's a cure
in itself.'

She nodded, unable to reply.

The next day, as promised, Crag drove them down to
the horse-break. The brumbies were enclosed in a well-
grassed saucer of land by the lagoon, that is well-grassed
by Inside standards. The lagoon at present was nicely
filled, and insects were weaving flight patterns over it,
frogs croaking a raucous chorus.

The jeep rimmed the shore until it reached the enclosure. Already the jackeroos and several of the stockmen
were there, and one of the jacks was cutting out the
ponies selected for the break, comprising a mare which
had been put back from the former break because she was
touchy and the first of the stallions.

The other jack started the break with the touchy mare,
unsatisfactorily in the beginning, the same, the jack
called to Crag, as last time, and then, on Crag's advice,
using a more gentle approach, and soon achieving
success.

'She only needed sympathy,' said Crag to Pippa.
'Mares most often are like that, we don't have much
trouble with them.' He was eyeing a stallion thoughtfully.
'With good handling and good sense, stallions are no
great worry, either, but I don't know about that fellow
there. He's all of seven or eight years, I'd say, and wild
stallions of that age get set in their ways.'

'He's pretty, Crag,' said Davy, and Pippa agreed with
her brother. The stallion was a bright bay with a cream
forehead and cream feet. But his eyes were unfriendly ...
even more than that, thought Pippa, they smouldered.

151

Crag approached him quietly, standing in front of him with a noose wide open, no pretext at all. Pippa had the idea that Crag felt as she did, that it would be no use trying to deceive this fellow. Crag dropped the loop over him, and beside her Pippa heard Davy draw in a deep breath.

The stallion did not protest. He even waited while Crag opened and shut the gate, and after that he walked quietly for several circles with Crag, then repeated his docile waiting when Crag returned him to the enclosure.

'You've done it, Crag, you've done it!' called Davy excitedly when Crag came back to their side. 'You've got him round. He likes you.'

Crag attended his pipe. He was thoughtful.

'Well, haven't you, Crag?' asked Davy impatiently.

'The trouble is, I don't know, scrubber, I don't know at all. I think I'll be watching that fellow. He's much too quiet for my liking. I feel he's looking me over. It isn't normal for a stallion like he is not to fight the rope.' Crag turned to Pippa and instructed in a low voice: 'You'll keep the scrubber away.'

'Of course.' She added in her turn: 'And you'll keep the piccaninnies off.'

'What made you say that?' They were walking back to the jeep now. 'What brought the little fry into it?'

'Cass was telling me how your mother and her mother took over that part of the station. I'd like to, too.' She paused. 'While I'm here.'

'You needn't have added that,' he reproached, 'you're here for ever.' At her quick look he reminded her, 'It doesn't matter how short a time is, it still is for ever. I think I told you that.'

'You told me for Davy.'

'Then it's for you, too.' He had started the jeep and

they were rimming the lagoon again towards home. 'What the heck . . .' he began.

She saw he was looking at a plane that must have come in during their absence, but, in the noise of hooves, had not been heard. It now sat in the middle of the row of upturned white plastic buckets that marked the run-in.

'Doug wasn't expected till next week,' he puzzled. 'Someone must have chartered him across.'

Pippa did not take much notice. She knew no one here, so felt it would be no concern of hers.

But as the jeep approached the homestead, a figure emerged from the house to stand on the wide verandah, and Pippa's heart lurched. She did know the passenger. It was her concern.

Rena waited there.

It was Crag who spoke first after they had alighted from the jeep and climbed the four shallow steps to where Rena stood and smiled brightly at them.

'Well,' he greeted drily, 'of all the people I wondered about Doug flying in, the last I thought of was you.' He kissed her cheek.

'Now, darling, none of that,' she laughed back, kissing him on the mouth, 'you've been expecting me for a year.'

'You took your time.'

'But the end is the same.'

'No, Rena, it's not. You see—'

'Pippa, how brown you are,' interrupted Rena. 'I hope you don't mind, I've put myself in your room. I've lots to tell you, so I thought we'd be girls together.'

'There are plenty of rooms,' came in Crag, 'if you'd let us know—'

'I didn't let you know because I wanted to surprise you.'

153

'You did.'

'A pleasant surprise? Darling, don't fuss. Two rooms are quite enough. Two boys. Two girls. What else? Talking of boys, where's my other laddie, my Davy? I must see him.' She turned round, evidently having seen Davy dart down to the piccaninnies, and she ran lightly towards him, calling his name. He turned and ran to her. Everyone would have to run to Rena today, never had she looked lovelier.

Pippa stood very still waiting for Crag to speak. When he didn't, she darted a quick look at him and was surprised at his thoughtful expression, thoughtful as his own eyes followed Rena.

'Crag . . .' Pippa breathed.

'Look here, Pippa—' But Crag was not to say it. One of the jacks came galloping up from the horse-break to tell the boss that a native stockman, Bobby, had been hoof-grazed by the bay stallion while he tried to put on a saddle and blindfold.

Rena at once was out of Crag's mind. 'The fool! I didn't want that done. I wanted him watched for a while. How badly hurt is Bobby? No, never mind, I'll ring A.A., anyway.' He turned on his heel and hurried in to pick up the telephone.

Pippa half attended to him and half attended to Rena. Her arm around Davy, she was coming up to the house.

'Air Ambulance?' she heard Crag call. 'I think I have a case for you. Crazy sort of stallion and a too-eager boy. Reckon he might need hospitalization . . . some shots, anyway, so if you're out this way . . . That soon? Good.' The telephone went down.

Now it was Pippa's turn to forget Rena. She watched fascinated as a precise routine took over. The tabletop truck was brought out and a mattress put on it, and the truck . . . with Crag . . . was driven down to the horse-

154

break. Anticipating what would be needed next, Pippa went inside and gathered up blankets and pillows, and was waiting with them when Crag, sitting beside the prone patient at the back of the truck now, came up to the house.

He took a look at the blankets, and commended, 'Good girl, that's what I came for. Hop on, Pippa, and see how it's all done.'

'Is Bobby very bad?'

'He has a heck of a shock. That stallion was kidding them, pretending to play ball with them, then suddenly the boyo turned on the lightning. I think the bay could be a wrong 'un.'

'Do you have many?'

'No, and even when we do we can generally do something about it, but not when they're this feller's age. Here comes A.A. now. It's lucky we have plenty of space at Star, the A.A. is a bigger craft than the one the Flying Doc whizzes around in.'

By this time the plane was down, and two nurses climbing out, behind them two men, the pilot and the doctor. Pippa had a quick glimpse of resuscitators and oxygen apparatus before she was introduced to Doctor Todd, Nurse Brown, Sister Snell and the Captain.

'Mrs. Crag,' Crag said.

Bobby, the pain catching him quite severely now, was administered a shot, then the mattress was transferred to a light stretcher on wheels, a ramp put down and the patient edged in. There was the beat of engines again, the loud acceleration, then the few tree tops the station possessed moved in a sudden current of air, and the mercy flight was on its way.

'Will Bobby be all right?' asked Pippa.

'He'll be fine. A lot of his fineness, mark you, will be his importance. He would never have been up in a craft before. I try to take the boys up from time to time, but the trouble is there's not much time, and a lot of boys.'

'You have your own plane?'

'Surely,' he smiled.

For a while Pippa had forgotten Rena, but now, bumping back again, she remembered, and she knew she must speak with Crag. But somehow the words wouldn't come. She heard herself asking instead how the ambulance operated, heard him replying that all the Up Toppers paid a fee into it, and it was the best money they ever spent.

By now, the tabletop was nearing the house, but Rena did not meet them on the verandah this time, and when a bevy of men pounced on Crag to learn about Bobby, Pippa turned and went up the steps, down the hall to her room.

Their room. For another bed had been brought in. On it, surrounded by her clothes, sat Rena.

She looked up as Pippa came in, and spoke first.

'How is the stockman?' she asked, and took out, shook and hung up a blouse.

'He'll be all right.' Pippa knew that her cousin had not inquired out of concern but had merely used Bobby for the opener for whatever it was she had to say. For there were things to say. She had indicated that when she had laughed at Pippa on the verandah and told her: 'Girls together.'

'Tiresome of us,' continued Rena calmly, 'to have that episode staged just when we're itching to chatter.'

'It must be more tiresome for Bobby. It could have been disastrous. That stallion . . .' Pippa gave a little shiver.

'Nonsense.' Rena spoke airily. 'A horse can be managed if you go about it the right way. I'm sure I could go down now—'

'Rena, *don't!*' Pippa's voice was sharp. 'He's wild, he's

156

quite set in his ways. Crag said he could be a wrong one.'

'Yes, Crag.' Rena ran her tongue round her lips.

So it was to begin.

The older girl took out a frock now. She put it carefully on a hanger. She had a lot of clothes as though she intended to – stay.

'Well,' Rena demanded at length, 'aren't you wanting to hear about your dear cousin? For that's what I've come about, to get you up to date. That ... and something else.

'But first' ... briskly ... 'my present position. Well, Pippa, it's exactly as before.'

'I didn't expect it to be changed this quickly,' admitted Pippa. 'I mean legal things take time.'

'They take longer when they're not even begun. Yes, that's true. Mr. Callow hasn't filed any papers for me, and on my instruction will not do so.'

'You said this at the will-reading, but I thought you might have changed your mind, Rena. For you're entitled to everything, there would be no trouble, as your solicitor pointed out. I'm quite sure that when Uncle Preston made the new will he had your ultimate protest in mind.'

'Oh, yes, he would,' agreed Rena contemptuously, 'he would see me going cap in hand ... isn't that a ridiculous phrase these days? ... to Domrey Hardy. That certainly would be in Father's thoughts. Only it wasn't, and it isn't, and it never will be in mine. When I raced out from Uplands, Pippa, it was to give myself a thinking space, though I knew even then that I would never appeal. However, I made myself consider, and I reached the same decision. *And*' ... coming back from the wardrobe, where, typical of Rena, she had taken three-quarters of the space ... '*I came to another decision.*'

She waited for Pippa to ask it, but something cold had settled in Pippa, and she could not speak. She just sat there frozen, somehow knowing what Rena was going to say, wishing she could stop her.

When it became patent that she was not going to ask, Rena smiled slightly and began to speak.

'You heard poor Crag just now with his reproachful "You took your time." I did, I'm afraid. I've been a real trial to that darling man. For he's crazy about me, you know. Always has been. Always will. But' . . . quietly now, watchfully . . . 'he was also set on a family life, someone to bring up on Falling Star, someone to take over the station when he, like his father grew too old, grew old. And that's *why*, Pippa dear, he . . . well . . .' She gave a careless. shrug. 'Oh, I'm not blaming you, darling,' she began again. 'I mean how could you tell how I felt? I've never been the emotional kind.'

'Felt? *You* felt?'

'Yes.'

'For – for—'

'For Crag.' Rena nodded. 'Yes, I loved Crag. I always have. It's always been Crag really, Pippa.'

'But, Rena, it hasn't . . . it hasn't.' Pippa heard the shrill break in her voice but did not care. 'It hasn't. You know it hasn't.'

'Oh, darling, don't get carried away. You'll be quite all right. Crag's nothing if not generous – why, you'll have more than you would have ever had from Father or me.'

There was a pause . . . for Pippa an incredulous pause . . . then Rena calmly resumed.

'You must have seen Crag's face when I confronted him just now. You must have seen his eyes following me. It's always been like this, but I . . . yes, I admit it . . . I've treated him abominably. I played with Glen Burt. I—'

'Did you play with Domrey Hardy?' Pippa could not have said why she inserted that.

At once a change came over Rena. She went a grey-white. 'I never played with him. I – I loathe him.' She stopped talking for quite a while and went and stood by the window.

Minutes ticked by. Pippa thought: All this is a dream. It's too impossible. Surely Rena must know that Crag and I ... that we ... In a little village like Tombonda she must have heard—

Rena was coming back from the window.

'I'll never return to the Highlands,' she stated definitely.

'But *Crag* returns to Ku.'

Rena winced, then said, 'He'll dispose of Ku.'

'He loves it.'

Her cousin looked narrowly at her, then she said clearly, 'He loves me.'

'Rena ... Rena, this is going too far. There is something you must know. You can't know it or you wouldn't be talking like this.'

'Oh, yes.' Rena was lighting a cigarette now, exhaling idly. 'I did hear some fancy tales about you.'

'About *us*. About Crag as well as me. You see, we were – we were—'

She stopped incredulously as Rena went into peals of laughter. 'Darling, don't tell me that absurd rumour was true?'

'It was ... it was. If you want proof—'

'Want proof?' The laughter had left Rena. She was cold and hard as she often was. 'Haven't I proof here?' She looked around her.

'What do you mean, Rena?'

'This room,' Rena indicated the four walls, the space between the walls. 'This room, darling, *I* will be sharing with you. Girls together, remember? Do you think Crag of all people would stand for that? I know Crag very well. I've known him for years. He's never halfway. He's all man. Why, he wouldn't put up with his "wife" ' ... a small laugh ... 'next door to him any more than he would abide that stallion down there beating him.'

'Then you're wrong. He's come to a decision about the stallion. He says he's no good.' – Oh, why was she talking about irrelevant things like this? Pippa wondered blankly.

Rena was laughing softly, confidently. 'I'll soon change his mind about that, too, though, being Crag, I don't believe it will need any changing. However, it was the similarity I really meant, the no half-measures. For that's Crag. He goes the entire way.'

There was a pause, then:

'Darling, I did hear about that caper of yours, and I sympathize with you – after all, you had your brother to think of, and after all, Crag is something of a catch. But I'm afraid I didn't take it very seriously. I mean I did admit it could happen, and as you now tell me, and I do believe you, Pippa, you needn't produce any marriage lines, it has. But not' ... with an undertone now ... 'as I intend to take notice of. When I saw his room – and your room this afternoon, I'm afraid I *smiled*, Pippa. Crag would never accept that sort of wife. I think he went overboard for Davy, he always had a strong paternal streak, and I think because of that—

'But don't worry, Pippa. Everything will be all right, dear. I promise you I'll encourage Crag right to the hilt in any generosity he decides for you. But' ... thinly ... 'please don't give me that "marriage", because there never has been. *Has there*?' Rena waited a smiling moment, then went on.

'And now,' she said sweetly, 'away from intimacies.

Here's something you'll really want to hear. Before I came up I was in touch with Glen Burt. Oh, it was quite friendly. He's extremely nice once he isn't pursuing me.'

'Has he married Jennifer?'

Rena did not bother to reply to that. 'He said to tell you that a virus has been isolated in America, and that it's being worked on. That it could have reference to Davy.'

'Rena, stop. *Stop*!' Pippa got to her feet. She felt she was going mad. Not waiting for Rena's reaction, she ran to the door, turned the handle, closed the door behind her. Ran down the hall.

Once away from the house she raced blindly, unaware, uncaring where her feet took her. It was only when fatigue caught her up that she stopped, and fell, exhausted, to the ground.

CHAPTER EIGHT

SHE must have undergone a period of unconsciousness, or at least a blankness, for when Pippa opened her eyes the sun that had been well aloft was tottering on the edge of the horizon; even as she looked at it, it tipped right over, and where everything had been an antique gold, violet crept in, instead.

She was thankful that she had lain in a dwindling heat, for she had heard what the fierce rays of an Australian hinterland sun could do. But instead of feeling dehydrated, possibly alienated, all she was aware of was a great tiredness, natural enough after that foolish run. For it had been foolish, she realized that; she could have imperilled the lives of others who would have come out looking for her as well as destroy herself. She might even ... hearing the engine of a small plane, probably Crag's plane ... have imperilled someone now.

She got to her feet, ready to wave the moment she saw the craft overhead. But the plane did not come into sight, so it must have taken the opposite direction.

Biting her lips at the trouble she had caused, she looked around her. She had not anticipated any problem of direction, for although she had run blindly she considered she had not run all that long; the heat and her emotion would have seen to that. But although the terrain was flat as ever, she could see no distant buildings. She could not even glimpse the glitter of the lagoon. She forced herself to consider from which direction that beat of the plane engine had seemed to come, for that would be the field with the upturned white plastic buckets, and once she found it, she was near enough to home.

Home? She felt around that word sensitively, and knew with bitterness that she should have said homestead. If she were Mrs. Crag of Yantumara it should be home, but was she Mrs. Crag? Oh, yes, she had a marriage certificate, but was she Mrs. Crag? She remembered Rena's smiling face as she had said: 'Don't give me that "marriage", there never has been.' She had said '. . . not as you'd notice, and not as I intend to take notice of.' She had said: 'Crag would never accept that kind of wife.'

What kind of wife? What kind of marriage? Why hadn't she answered Rena when Rena had challenged tauntingly: 'Because there never has been. *Has there?*' Had it only been because of Davy that she had come wildly out here or had it been because she had nothing to answer to Rena? Only that night of which Crag had said:

'It's nothing. No ties tied. Relax.'

But had he not assured that, would she have remained there with Rena, would she have answered her: 'Yes, there has.' Would she have said that?

Pippa stood very still . . . and knew she would.

For she loved him. She was aware of it in that moment, aware that somewhere deep down in her she had known but not recognized it all along. She loved Crag, but to him it was 'no ties tied' . . . 'nothing' . . . 'relax'. Worse than that, Rena had come and now she stood between Crag and Rena, a pitiful little barrier, only there because a man had been drawn to a child.

Oh, Crag, she thought, what am I to do?

She had not realized she had called it aloud until a matter-of-fact small voice said, 'Crag's up in his plane with Ludy, Pippa, taking her into Minta Base Hospital to see Bobby. Bobby is Ludy's husband. Why did you come out here?'

It was Davy, hand-in-hand with a small brown boy he

163

introduced as Brucie.

'Brucie Indian-scouted after you,' Davy informed her next, 'only it wouldn't be Indian, would it? He's showed me how.'

'Oh, darling!' In her relief to get away from her torment, if only temporarily, Pippa hugged her brother, and for the first time she could remember he struggled free. At times he had wriggled uncomfortably, but mostly he had accepted caresses. Now he said quite gruffly, 'You don't do that, Pippa, not in front of name belonga Brucie.' He was picking up pidgin quickly.

'Sorry,' Pippa apologized, recognizing his new status. 'Well, I suppose we'd better start walking, it's getting quite dark.'

'Falling Star is only over there.' Davy waved nonchalantly. 'Just past the hill.' Pippa smiled ruefully. She had forgotten these infinitesimal inclines that could blot out all that lay beyond.

'Can I have tea with Brucie?' Davy was asking.

Pippa was not sure about that, not sure if the rations down the gully could include an extra, so she got round it by suggesting that Brucie had tea with them. 'I think Cassy will find room.'

'Plenty of room,' nodded Davy. 'The table will be empty. The stockmen are out, Crag's gone, and so has Rena.'

'Rena gone?'

'With Crag,' said Davy. 'Come on, Pippa, Brucie's hungry.' He waited, though, for Brucie to make the first indicative move, for in spite of his scouting tuition he was really as uncertain as Pippa which direction to take.

Brucie knew, though, and stepped out unfalteringly, whereupon Davy stepped out, too.

It was only Pippa who stumbled, and that was not because of any doubt of her direction, not with a scout like

164

Brucie. It was because of tears in her eyes.

So Rena had gone. With Crag.

She never would have found her way back without the scout. Pippa realized this as she trudged along behind Brucie and Davy, she acknowledged fully the mystery of this red terrain where, only half a mile from a point, that point was no longer visible or even familiar. She wondered how Brucie, even though it was his country, went so unfalteringly. Everything around her seemed exactly the same, so how could Brucie tell?

'The wind on the sand,' instructed Davy importantly when she said this, 'the way that tree bends.' The sand was all as red and all as rippled, and the tree was another mulga, and to Pippa it bent the same as all mulgas. She determined, unless by some miracle she achieved Brucie's scouting powers, never to run out like that again.

Back at the house she was relieved to find that her absence had not been noticed, or anyway, noted. Mrs. Cassidy must have thought she was in her room, or . . . a wince that Pippa despised herself for . . . even seeing the plane off. Quickly she proffered, 'I've been looking around Falling Star, Cassy.' Davy had not come in with her, so she was able to ask casually, 'Did I hear Crag's plane go out?'

Mrs. Cassidy looked up. 'Yes.' A pause. '*She* went with him.'

'Miss Franklin?'

'Yes.'

Another pause. Then: 'What's she here for, Pippa?'

'I . . . well, there was a message concerning Davy.'

'There are always letters,' said Mrs. Cassidy. 'There are phones.' She tossed her head.

'This was personal,' said Pippa. Well, Davy was personal, he was hers, because of him she was here at Yantumara, because of him she had married Crag. – Or that had been what she had thought.

Mrs. Cassidy did not pursue the subject of Rena, whom obviously she did not like. 'You look tired, dear. Did you walk too far?'

'No, not too far. The boys came after me. Davy wanted to have tea with Brucie tonight, but I thought if you didn't mind Brucie could have tea with us.'

'I don't mind, but probably Brucie will,' smiled Mrs. Cassidy. 'It's as Crag said, there's nothing like rib bones cooked over eucalyptus leaves.'

'Can I help you, seeing we have an extra?'

'You can supervise Rosie setting the table if you like, she has a habit of putting the knives and forks back to front.'

As Pippa corrected the knives and forks, she asked Cassy: 'Is Bobby any worse?'

'Oh, no, but Minta rang to say he would be better with someone by him. "Patients' relations" is a very big factor in hinterland hospitals. When I was growing up it was father, mother, sisters, brothers, uncles, aunts, then cousins, second cousins, right down the list. If you didn't allow them around the patient just pined to death. But it's getting different, and so long as Bobby has his wife he'll be all right.' With a sympathetic look at Pippa that made Pippa want to glance the other way, Mrs. Cassidy added, 'Miss Franklin would have been taken along just for Ludy, dear. Mostly the men are very thrilled to fly, but the women are a little apprehensive, and need a companion. If you'd been here I'm sure—'

'Yes,' said Pippa, but *she* was not sure. Not sure that if she had been there it would still not have been Rena accompanying Crag.

Brucie, as Cassy had said, was not over-impressed with the meat course, but certainly impressed with the ice-cream that Cassy gave the little boys instead of the adults' caramel rice.

After the dishes had been put in the dishwater, Pippa went and sat on the big verandah with the book-keeper and those of the stockmen and jackeroos not out with the herds. It was a velvet night, as velvet as only hinterland nights could be, she decided, an exaggerated gold moon, stars so big you felt you could pluck them down. It was not the sort of night to sit alone ... yes, alone, even with seven men. It was a night for one man.

She wanted to ask how long Crag would be away, but the words would not come. She waited until it was time to call Davy to bed, then after she had bathed him, heard his prayers, something that Crag had taken over from her, she, too, went to bed. Rena's things were strewn all around the room. It didn't seem Pippa's own room any more. But then it wasn't, it was their room. Girls together, Rena had smilingly said.

With a little sigh she tidied up some of the things that had tumbled from Rena's bags, scarves, blouses, the beautiful negligées she had always had ... and a photo in a leather case. Only a small photo. Able to be fitted ... as it was ... in the fold of a handkerchief. Pippa looked down on it and smiled as she saw the rather crafty yet likeable face of naughty old Uncle Preston, Rena's father. Then her glance fell on the other side of the case. Dom. Domrey Hardy. What was the overseer, whom Rena despised so heartily, doing there?

She closed the folder, freed the bed in case Rena did come in late, though she knew that an aircraft could never put down here at night without a flare, then clicked out the light.

She did not go to sleep for a long time. Although she knew that Rena ... and Crag could not come, she could not help herself from listening for them. But at last in the

167

small hours, sleep took over, and she was still asleep when Rosie brought in her tea.

Her first glance went to the bed, but it was still un-occupied. Well, she had known that.

Then Rosie said, 'You look for Miss, Missus, she not home all night. Boss, too.'

'I expect that.' Pippa accepted the tea.

'Yes, but those two,' went on Rosie, 'they come back all right, but not here.' She gave some actions. 'They have trouble with no gas for that plane, so they put it down in Western Field and stay in the stockies' hut.'

'How – how do you know this?' Pippa held tightly to her tea.

'Our Billy, him going past that hut when Boss tells him to get someone to bring gas for plane to get back. Bobby's all right, Billy says, and Ludy is stopping with him. You bin like more tea?'

'No, thank you, Rosie, I'll get up.'

When she went down to the kitchen, Cassy repeated Rosie's story.

'Evidently Crag wanted to get home yesterday and left as soon as he had deposited Ludy with Bobby at the hospital. But he mustn't have checked as he always checks, either that or the engine was amiss, for they had to come down at Western Field while it was still light. Billy was going past rounding up some stragglers, and Crag in-structed him to get fuel out today. Why don't you go along, dear?'

'No. No, I don't think so. I – I thought I would have a morning with the mothers and the piccaninnies.' She hadn't thought so, not for this morning, anyway, though she had intended to do it one day, and she knew she could not bring herself to go out there.

She heard the jeep put off later with its succour but did not look up. – Also she did not let herself think of last

168

night. She thought of another night outside a tent, a navy blue night with a sliver of moon. Somewhere a pheasant, somewhere a wood pigeon. Soft earth and a tree leaning over. It all seemed unreal now. Perhaps it had never been.

Then she thought of Rena, Rena so lovely that any man's head would be turned, and especially a man who had loved her once. And loved her still? 'If you're coming, Pippa,' Davy reminded reproachfully by her side.

'I'm coming, darling.'

Down in the gully, no actual gully, really, just a slight indentation and probably indented like that by many feet passing over it for many years, for Cassy had told Pippa that for as long as she could recall meetings had been held there, it had been a discussion place, the gins were shy at first, but still friendly. The piccaninnies, however, having heard all about her from Davy, flocked around at once, and their mothers, following up to scold them, remained instead, and soon all the women were talking together.

Children predominated the conversation, of course, didn't children always? ... and Pippa heard how Mary's Elizabeth was three and the eldest four and how last year Janey's Gary had got ruddy fever ... scarlatina, Pippa decided ... and passed it around the camp. Janey was very proud of that achievement.

The pics got tired of the conversation and wandered off, but their mothers remained to talk eagerly with Pippa. Like all women, they were keen on dressing up, even though it was true that right now they wore very little. 'But,' they giggled, 'when that hairy feller comes we buy very good cloes, Missus, you'll see when Mr Walker calls.'

One of the jackeroos had joined the group to call Pippa up for tea, and he explained, 'We call the Afghan

169

hawker ... yes, he has long hair and a beard, hence he's the hairy feller ... Mr. Walker because his own name is quite a mouthful. There's not many of these unique characters left now. Once they were the only Up Top itinerant salesmen. I doubt if you'll find anything maddeningly exciting in Mr. Walker's bags, but the gins adore his beads, scarves and baubles.'

After morning tea, Pippa returned to the gully again, and on an invitation from the women went into their houses. She decided that as far as health went, they were very well catered for. The homestead kept a close eye on their general condition and a specially close eye on any possibility of leprosy, once a danger out here. Also, a Government glaucoma team called every year.

But education, she thought, was sadly lacking. Over lunch later the men who had been left behind for their rest periods said that Crag was trying to contend with this by correspondence, only it was difficult to find someone to superintend the lessons. One of the stockmen asked Pippa if she had written yet for Davy's enrolment. 'It's a good system,' he said, adding modestly that it was the only instruction he had had, whereupon the others at the table laughed uproariously and advised Pippa to have nothing to do with it.

'Seriously, though,' they added when the laughter had died down, 'Snow's right, it does teach the kids, and you need have no fear that the young 'un is missing anything by not going to school.'

Davy had never been to school, either she or Aunt Helen had taught him everything he knew, so Pippa knew it would be no miss. But a sudden thought came to her that here could be the niche she needed. She could superintend the lessons, Davy's and the pics'. Perhaps Crag could even allot a little schoolhouse from the many buildings. She would be like his mother and his grandmother, she thought, she would be a true countrywoman. She felt enthusiasm bubbling through her ... then hollowly came the realization that it would be no good. What was the use of thinking of schoolrooms when before anything could eventuate she would be gone? What was the use of thinking about lessons for Davy when—

She did not go back to the gully that afternoon.

The day wore on. She would have thought that Crag and Rena would have been in by now, but the jackeroo informed her that it was a fair run out by jeep so they could not be expected until late afternoon. When late afternoon grew into night she found herself listening so hard that her ears throbbed. She did not want her evening meal, but she forced it down, hoping that Cassy and the men did not notice her preoccupation.

'Cessna must be playing up, so Crag's coming in by the jeep,' decided Snowy. 'But don't you fret, Mrs. C., you'll have your man back tonight.'

She tried to smile back at Snowy's kindly face, but it was a hard try. Mrs. C. That was Crag's tag for her. But *your man*. That was not, and never had been, and never could be, a tag for him.

She did the usual after-dinner things, she sat for a while on the verandah with the others, then she called Davy from the gully, bathed and bedded him. What a much more independent little boy he was becoming, she thought. He took over most of the washing himself, and told her after she had tucked him in that she needn't leave on a light. He even did not ask as much about his idol Crag. So a little boy was growing up.

But ... achingly ... a little boy couldn't. He had only now one Australian spring.

She went to bed herself and could not have said at what time she heard the jeep coming in. It was Rena and Crag at last, she knew it by their voices that carried distinctly through the quiet night. They were on the verandah, and she heard Crag say: 'Impulse, Rena, impulse, that's all it was. How else can I drive it home to you . . . how can I make you see it that way . . see how it's bringing chaos to the heart?'

'But, Crag . . .' She did not hear Rena's answer and she did not want to.

So already Davy was an impulse to be regretted . . . or was it what Crag had done because of Davy that was the regret? The chaos to a heart?

It was much later that Rena came in. Even in her numbness, Pippa was aware of the length of time that had passed. . . .

When Pippa went along for breakfast the next morning, Rena, already the mistress, it seemed, having ordered Rosie to bring her breakfast to her bed, it was to learn that Crag had left very early. He had taken Davy and Brucie with him. They had gone, Cassy reported, to run down some scrubber steers that Crag had seen coming back from Western Field.

Pippa did not notice that she waved aside her usual concern for Davy, especially when his activities included running down scrubbers . . . what had he reported to her? you do it in full gallop, leap from the horse, flick it by its tail and pin it to the ground . . . to ask instead if there had been anything amiss with the plane.

'Yes, so they left it there and came back in the jeep. Mind you, though' . . . a smile . . . 'it was out of gas as well. If you ask me, Pippa, your man was so anxious to get home to you he forgot his usual check.'

Yes . . . but he did not forget to linger on a verandah and say: 'Impulse, Rena . . . you must see it that way . . . see how it's bringing chaos to the heart.'

But it was no use going over things like this. So long as

172

she remained here she must occupy herself. Either that, or she could bear it no longer, and she had to, for Davy. So as soon as the meal was finished she went down to the book-keeper's office and asked Rupey for as much unwanted paper as he could spare. He found her a generous armful, then, when he learned that she intended starting off those of the pics who would sit still long enough on some elementary lessons, found pencils, too.

'There's manuals here,' he smiled, 'probably left over from Crag's young days, so not the latest methods, but at least they'd give you a pointer.'

Pippa thanked him and went off, calling back to him when he advised her not to be disappointed at her first attempt an assurance that she would not.

She had expected, with the book-keeper, that the pics would be bored with any attempt she made, that they would scribble over the paper, but to her delight they listened intently when she started them off, their pansy eyes big and grave, their little pencil marks on the paper thin and delicate.

It was there that Crag, having finished rounding up the scrubber steers and come home again, found her, and for a while he stood looking down on her.

'The hillside's dew-pearled,' he said softly.

'There's no hillsides here,' said Davy practically, 'unless you mean what we call the hills but are really only inclines.' He added indignantly as Crag smiled, 'You told me so yourself.'

'I was just wondering where a poet had gone,' said Crag, thinking of a little boy on a train who had told him that Pippa had been called that because she had been born at seven and had hillside eyes. 'You're a different scrubber now, Davy.'

'Of course I am, because I'm better. Ever since you poulticed me I've been cured. You said it made you

173

better, and it did.'

'Then you're better,' agreed Crag.

He went over to Davy's sister. 'Well, Teacher?' he smiled.

'It is well,' she answered with shining enthusiasm in the green eyes he had been watching. 'These children are wonderful. If they can do that just sitting around me on the ground, imagine what they'd do in a proper feller school.'

Crag burst into laughter, Pippa, after some surprise at herself and the pidgin that, as with Davy, had crept in, laughing with him, then the pics and Davy at the madness of old people.

Rena joined them to ask about the mirth, and the mothers, never far behind their children, looked admiringly at the beautiful new miss with the lovely clothes.

'I'm afraid you've spoiled them for Mr. Walker,' smiled Pippa to her cousin as they went up the hill again, but Rena's smile back as Pippa explained about the Afghan hawker did not reach her eyes.

The old restlessness was on her. Pippa recognized it at once. How often had she seen that look on Rena at Uplands? That strange unrest. That unhappiness. Why was Rena unsettled like this?

For a moment she wondered longingly if her cousin's preoccupation was because of something that Crag had said to her ... But no, not with an answer such as he had given her last night. Again she heard that: 'Impulse ... you must see it ... see how it's bringing chaos to the heart.'

'Crag.' Rena's cool voice cut into Pippa's pain. 'Crag, when are you taking me down to the horse-break?'

'Now, if you like.' He stopped to light his pipe.

'In a *frock*?'

'What did you expect to wear?'

'Jodhpurs at least,' she flung.

He took the pipe out of his mouth and looked seriously at her. 'What for, Rena? There'll be no riding down there.'

'Oh, Crag, don't be an old fuddy, I know as much about horses as you.'

'Southern Highland horses,' he agreed, 'but these are vastly different, Rena.'

'Oh, I know they've run wild,' she said impatiently, 'but I've handled horses that have been in the field all the year.'

'These have been in the scrub, Rena, all their lives. Most of them have never seen a man, never felt a rein.'

'I can look after myself.' She tossed her head.

'Perhaps, but you're not doing it down there.'

'We'll see about that.'

Quite obviously she was irritated, on edge. Pippa sensed, though she did not comprehend, Rena's urgent need to expend herself ... to escape from something that was enclosing her. Puzzled, Pippa glanced up to see how Crag was reacting.

He was reacting calmly ... but intentionally. 'Yes, we will see,' he nodded firmly. After a moment he offered equably, 'I'll get a pony up for you this afternoon.'

'Not a pony, Crag.' Rena's voice was shrill. 'What do you think I am, a week-end rider? I want a horse. I want that stallion I've been hearing about.'

'*No one* is going to try him any more. You know now, from going into Minta, what happened to Bobby.'

'Bobby's hands might not have been right. I have excellent hands for a strong-willed horse. Dom ... I mean I've often been told so.'

'I imagine you have been, Rena, but this is not just a strong-willed horse, this is a wrong 'un. What I should do

175

in these circumstances is very obvious, but what I'm going to do, being a fool I suppose, is take that feller right back to where he belongs.'

'To the scrub?'

'Yes.'

'But that's a terrible waste of a horse like that. He's a handsome thing.'

Sharply Crag said, 'Have you seen him, then?'

'Oh, yes, I had a quick look after breakfast.' She smiled at him, but Crag did not smile back.

'I'm not pleased with you, Rena,' he stated. 'The horse is unpredictable.'

'But then,' she came in, 'so are most things.'

'Rena, I'm not joking.'

'Neither am I.'

'You're not to go down to the horse-break unless I say and unless I'm with you.' He waited. 'Understand?'

'Very well.' She capitulated so completely and so unexpectedly that Pippa looked at her in surprise.

'Very well, darling,' she said again, and she leaned up and touched his cheek.

Uncomfortable at the closeness that Rena deliberately had established between herself and Crag, both physically as she stood in front of him and in the endearment she used, Pippa murmured an excuse and hurried ahead.

Through the bathroom window she could see Rena and Crag walking up together, Rena now being demure and submissive as she kept close to Crag's side. What is she doing, Pippa thought wretchedly, and why is she doing it? I still don't believe she really loves, or has ever loved, Crag, so why is she going on like this? – But she didn't ask herself how *Crag* felt, for she already knew; she had heard. She had heard – '. . . impulse . . . see it this way . . . chaos to the heart.'

176

The meal was an ordeal. Trying to appear normal. Trying to join the conversation. Trying even to eat. That last was very important, for several times Crag's keen eyes estimated her inroads on her laden plate, and he looked stern. Just how did he consider her, she wondered bleakly, simply as another child to be told what to do?

She heard the men at the table ... there was a full complement for the meal, for there was to be a strenuous afternoon programme and they were stoking up ... discussing the stallion again. Snowy had had an experience once like this and he suggested gelding the wild one, if it could be achieved, because often it availed a character change, and that feller certainly needed one, but Crag said no, the horse would go free, he was to be left alone, not touched. He was taboo.

He nodded this gravely to Rena, and she nodded docilely back.

And perhaps ... Pippa was to think this later ... her cousin really meant that agreement, perhaps if what subsequently happened that afternoon had not happened, Rena would have rested on her laurels, for laurels they must be, thought Pippa bitterly, hearing once more those words of Crag's to Rena last night.

But, the meal over and the men gone, and following Rena to hear more fully from her Glen Burt's report on Davy, the report she had interrupted before because she had been unable to listen any longer, the station telephone suddenly pealed, and Mrs. Cassidy came into the hall and picked it up.

From the moment it rang there was something electric in the air. Pippa could not have put a finger on it ... only a finger on Rena, who suddenly stood very still and looked white and strained. Her cousin could not possibly know, as she herself could not know, the identity of the caller, but she stood there *and she knew*. Pippa could tell

177

she knew.

Cassy listened for a while, then said, 'Yes, I'll write that down.' Then she put the phone back.

'Rena, I want to discuss Davy and what Glen Burt told you,' Pippa began.

'Why didn't she read the message out?' Rena said stonily.

'It wasn't for us. It would be for Crag. Rena—'

'Why did she have to be so secretive?'

'She wasn't being secretive, it just wasn't our business. Rena—'

But Rena turned impatiently on her. 'I told you what he said,' she cried irritably. 'Now I'm going down to that horse.'

'Crag told you not to.'

'I know. Pippa, I *know*. But I have to do something. Can't you see that?'

'No.' Pippa looked back at her. Then she cried, 'Rena ... Rena!'

For Rena was running out of the room and down the steps.

She still had on her frock, so at least she would not try anything foolish, but, remembering Crag's injunction not even to be near the horse, Pippa went after her.

Halfway there, she turned back cautiously to check up on Davy, for she knew that Crag would want him ... as she did, too ... well away from the break. But she glimpsed her brother through the office window sitting at the desk with Rupie, probably checking the station accounts again, another job he had quaintly taken upon himself. She also saw that the piccaninnies were playing safely in the gully, so all, away from the break, was well.

When she got down to the enclosure, it seemed at first that it was deserted, then she noted that the recently broken mares and stallions were cropping quietly in one

178

corral, the ones yet to be dealt with in another pen. But there was no sign of the bay stallion. She would have turned away, thinking that Rena had come and then gone in the belief that Crag already had done what he had said he would do, release the wrong one.

Then she heard the small noise from the barn that adjoined the inner enclosure. She went towards it, keeping well outside the fence, climbed the few rungs and peered in. It was dark after the sunlight, and for a while Pippa could not focus. Then she outlined the shape of two stalls. In one of them, crouched as far as she could from the intervening half-way wall, was Rena, and she was staring with fear ... Rena afraid! ... at the horse on the other side. It was the wild one. Evidently the men had got a rope over him and manoeuvred him inside.

He seemed quiet enough, but he was looking back at Rena, and even from where she watched Pippa could see the fiery red in his eyes, the red in his flaring nostrils. She could see that Rena could not move.

'I'll get help,' she said softly but clearly. Rena dared not answer back.

Pippa climbed quietly down and ran swiftly up to the homestead. As she raced she remembered sickeningly that Crag and all the men had gone out.

She was standing on the lower step of the verandah, wondering whether to summon Rupie, wondering what she could do, when she saw the private mail and hire waggon bumping along the station flat. It was not mail day, but never had the mail-man ... and the man sitting beside him ... been more welcome. Pippa was unaware that she was crying with relief.

Mrs. Cassidy had come out by now to greet the visitor, and she said, not noticing Pippa's anxiety, 'That was fast, if you like. A message to say you're coming and you're here!'

'The F.D. was going out to Crossroads, so I took my passenger that far. I brought him the rest.' The driver pocketed the fee the passenger handed him and said, 'Thanks, Mr. Hardy.'

Hardy. Domrey Hardy. Dom. For a moment Pippa heard again the phone call that had electrified Rena, she saw Rena's strained face. It had been Dom . . . *and Rena had known.* She had sensed, in the way people do sense when they are close, that— But Rena and Dom— *close?*

It didn't matter now, though, only a girl in danger mattered. She was running to the overseer, shouting his name, shouting incoherent things, yet they must not have been entirely incoherent, for Domrey Hardy began running with her. Running down to the break.

When they reached it, he pushed Pippa back firmly, then he mounted the fence. He peered in.

'Rena,' he said at last very quietly, 'it's me. It's Dom.'

Rena did not reply.

'The horse is no good,' he said next. 'The moment you turn it's going to knock down that wall, then strike. You know that, don't you? The only thing is for me to divert it as you scramble out. Do you follow me?'

It was several minutes before Rena spoke, then she said without any sign of the panic she must be undergoing, 'Since when have you told me about horses, Hardy?'

'Rena, don't be a damn fool.'

'I've ridden worse ones than these,' came the reply.

'Well, you're not riding this one now. Do as I say. When I divert the stallion, you—'

'I won't.'

'Then you won't come out alive.'

'Would that worry you?' Her voice came clear and contemptuous.

'It would be two deaths, and you must know it. With-

180

out you I ... Rena, I'm moving in now. Are you ready?'

'I'm stopping here.'

'Then the only thing for me to do is handle the horse myself.'

'You think you're capable?' Rena jeered.

'Oh, Dom, don't listen,' Pippa said urgently, for she had seen the man stiffen. She put out her hand to stop him, but he brushed it, though without anger, aside.

He said bitterly, seeing the danger, 'If it has to be this way ...' and he moved over the fence towards the stallion's stall.

What happened then happened so fast and so terrifyingly that Pippa felt it was like the frenzied flicking of a movie camera suddenly gone crazy.

Hardly had Dom moved forward than the stallion came at him like a hurricane, teeth bared, ears flattened, hooves raised high. As Rena screamed, Dom fell down and rolled over, rolled just in front of where the hooves struck, rolled again and again only a fraction of an inch from each cruel strike.

Now he was on his feet and jumping for the snubbing post, but it was clear that the stallion would get him before that.

Pippa stood sick and useless, seeing it all in those unrelated flicks again ... and then she heard the welcome swing of a rope, the scared mares in the next enclosure whinnying and galloping wildly round the fence, then the rope descending and pulling the stallion up.

It would not hold him for long, though ... the haltering rope had not succeeded in doing that ... so Crag, for it was Crag, wasted no time. He yelled for Pippa to stand clear, then he opened the gate and let the stallion out. One moment the horse was there, the next it was gone. Pippa did not watch where, she had turned to Dom

Hardy and Rena.

Dom was lying unconscious on the floor of the stall, and Rena . . . Rena was kneeling by his side . . . lifting his head on to her lap. She was crying, 'Dom! Dom! Oh, darling!'

The tears were streaming down her cheeks.

CHAPTER NINE

THE Flying Doctor had come and gone. He had examined Dom and reported no need for Air Ambulance to take him into Minta Base, not even a need to bring out a nurse. There was no concussion, no breaks or strains. By some miracle, or by some remarkable adroitness, Dom had missed those savagely flailing hooves. All he was suffering was a reaction from the horrifying minutes that had nearly cost him his life.

After they had taken Dom up to the homestead on an improvised stretcher, Rena by his side and holding his hand, then eased him into a bed, Pippa and Crag had stood on the other side of the bed to Rena, and in silence the three had waited . . . had watched the grey face.

But slowly the colour had begun to creep back, and by the time the F.D. flew in, Dom was breathing normally again. Yet when his eyes had looked up, Pippa had known that it was only Rena whom he saw, and when the F.D. said it was safe for the patient to be left so long as someone remained at hand to attend him if needed, there was no question who the attendant must be.

Pippa went out behind the two men and watched them as Crag nodded the doctor into the jeep then got behind the wheel. As the pair drove across the strip to where the doctor's Auster waited, she thought again of that anxiety in Rena's voice when she had knelt beside Dom . . . then Rena coming up from the break by Dom's side, Dom's hand tenderly in hers. Later, Dom's eyes as consciousness had returned, those eager eyes only aware of Rena.

What had happened once between those two? What would happen now? Most of all, when it did, what of

Crag?

She stood on the verandah a long time just staring into distance. Where was the wrong one now? she wondered. She hoped the stallion had regained his old haunts, for somehow she could feel no anger against him, and she was glad that Crag had set him free.

Mrs. Cassidy came out with tea, and must have been thinking of the horse, too, for she said, 'Let's hope he doesn't pass his meanness on to any of next year's foals, or if he does that they're not caught in the round-up. Those sort are always dangerous.'

'Next year's foals?'

'It's spring,' reminded Mrs. Cassidy, 'and in spring ...' She smiled at Pippa. When they had finished she took up the emptied cups and went back to the kitchen. But Pippa stopped on the verandah.

Spring. It couldn't be. It mustn't be! She looked around her in alarm, searching for it. There was nothing to proclaim it, not like it had been proclaimed in the springs she had known in England. She remembered Aunt Helen's garden ... snowdrops, narcissi, blunt buds on trees burgeoning into miracles of petals, honey bees laden with sweet largesse. *That* was spring, not this barrenness, and yet, she recalled indignantly from Crag: 'It's the most spring in all the world.'

How could he have cheated them like this, even for the love of a small boy for whom he had taken a fancy? A small boy, she thought dully, who was now only an 'impulse', an impulse that, on Rena's arrival, had brought 'chaos to the heart'.

No, there was no spring here.

Yet ... 'September is the first of spring,' Davy had sung, and if Cass was right about the season, then this was that spring she had left England for. It was Davy's final spring. She had borrowed Australian spring for him, but

184

she could never borrow again, there would be no second chance. Ten months, Doctor Harries had said. So this — this nothingness was all that Davy would have.

She could not see the scene before her for angry tears, but one thing she must see, and that was a calendar. Running down the steps, she crossed to the book-keeper's office. There at least she should find the date.

Once more Davy was helping Rupie to check the accounts; he took these self-appointed jobs very seriously. He did not look up as she came in. She crossed to a wall almanac, where it was another self-appointed job of her small brother's to cancel each spent day. As she stood there she heard the Auster leaving, and knew that Crag would be waiting out there in the field, his wide hat tilted over his eyes against the glare, watching for the F.D. to hide himself in that vast inverted blue bowl. She came back to the calendar and saw that the last cancelling was August the thirty-first. If she had harboured any disbelief the piles of accounts on the desk would have been witness to the end of the month. So it *was* the first of spring.

She turned desperately away, but Rupie called, 'Did you want anything, Mrs. Crag?'

What would he say, she thought dully, if I answered that I want time, I must have more time for Davy, can you bring some time out of your stock cupboard, Rupie, the way you brought out Crag's old school manuals?

'I see you haven't cancelled Crag's thousand candles,' tut-tutted Davy busily, checking a long list, still unaware of his sister. 'Did you speak to him about his mistake?'

'Yes, but he said it wasn't a mistake. He said he wanted a thousand candles and there seemed no other way.' Rupie scratched his head in bewilderment, whereupon Davy did the same.

'Perhaps it's for a party,' suggested Davy.

'Some party!'

'Some party,' copied Davy. 'Now, what about all this rice?' He looked disapprovingly at the list, no doubt seeing many rice puddings, which he disliked. Instinctive laughter bubbled up in Pippa . . . but at once it died down again. Time, she was thinking painfully, is running out. She turned away.

She did not know she was running herself until she ran into Crag. He had come back from the field, but the jeep was still on the drive, and when they collided, he wheeled her swiftly to the waggon, and the next moment they were bumping down to the gate.

'Crag,' she said bitterly, 'why did you tell me – tell us—'

'Sorry, Pippa, let me be first. Because I have to show you something. It must have happened yesterday.' He was drawing up the jeep now, sweeping her out and down to one of their few little gullies. She had never noticed this small scoop before, and she cried out in pleasure at its tiny saucer of water, and there in the middle of the water actually one pink lily, now past its prime, almost drooped down . . . but it had bloomed.

'Spring,' said Crag proudly, 'was yesterday. Now what did you want to say, Pippa? Pippa. Pippa – Oh, my little love . . .'

For Pippa was crying, crying brokenly. It seemed bitterly unfair to her that this was the last offering for Davy. 'You told me . . . you told us . . .' Then abruptly her words were trailing off in a wonder instead of a resentment. *Had* Crag just said: 'My little love'?

She looked up at him, looked extractingly. So he, too, had caught that glance between Dom and Rena, and now that he was out of the running, out of a lovely girl's heart, he was trying for a second-best.

'Don't cry, tell me, Pippa,' Crag was urging.

'This isn't spring,' she answered, coming back to Davy, 'only one withered flower. So Davy has had his last spring after all.' She looked at him with accusation as though he had done it himself.

'I'm sorry that it's all we have to offer,' he admitted humbly.

'But you said it was the most spring in all the world.'

'It was once . . . five years ago,' he recalled. 'There were carpets of flowers, forests of grass. This place occasionally does miracles like that. Who knows, Pippa, there may be another bursting another year.'

'You said there was the most spring—' she repeated doggedly.

'I also said "sometimes",' he sighed. As she still looked at him in anger, he went on, 'If it's not next year we'll have to wait for the year after . . . then the year after that But while we're waiting . . . the *three* of us, Pippa . . . the doctors will be finding something for Davy. Rena has told me what Glen Burt said . . . what could come from this new breakthrough.'

'But it has to be now, not then, otherwise—'

'Don't you believe that. I put a poultice on him, remember?'

'Oh, don't be foolish, Crag.'

'Don't *you* be, Pippa. The scrubber believed in that poultice, and I do, too. I really mean I believe in his belief, so we'll keep him believing, and we'll keep him waiting for spring. And we'll keep this' . . . he plucked out the lily . . . 'just between us.'

'But it takes more than that,' she said dully, 'it takes more than belief and a poultice.'

'Then I have it for you. The F.D. has been looking Davy over regularly . . . you didn't know that, did you? The last time he did he said: "This boy is coming back to us so fast I can't keep up." '

'Oh, Crag, he didn't say that. Doctors don't.'

'All right then, he said "Pulse ... temperature ... breathing ... metabolism." He said the rest. After which he said "I'm amazed." Yes, Pippa, that's true.'

She stood dumbly, knowing she mustn't believe it, though yearning to. Then she whispered, 'Crag, it can't last.'

'It has to last till spring. *One* spring. And I reckon Falling Star can keep on putting that back until the scrubber's good and ready. Look what we've done this time.' He threw the tired lily away.

She watched it flutter to the scoop of water, float there. 'Did the F.D. really say—'

'What a disbeliever you are! Do you want to ring him for yourself? You shouldn't need to, Pippa, you have your own two eyes.'

Yes, she had her eyes, and they had seen Davy's eyes, brighter and bluer than they had ever been. She had seen his little body, browner, firmer, stronger. She had seen ...

But could – *could* Davy wait?

Crag's arms were around her ... she had not noticed them slip there ... and he whispered, reading her as he always did: 'He'll wait, wife.'

She stiffened in the arms at that, remembering the 'second-best', and she said bleakly, 'I have to talk to you about that.'

'I have to talk to you about it myself, Mrs. Crag. Do you remember when we first started this fool arrangement—' Fool arrangement. So he was going to ask for a release.

'Yes,' she said.

'Do you remember the terms we made and how they could be broken?'

'Yes,' she said again.

'I made no firm promise ... I left that much open ... but I also said that until you said...' He looked at her and waited, but she did not speak.

After he had waited for a long while and she still did not speak he sighed, 'Just as well I left that loophole, Pippa, because I'm not wasting any more time. You're Mrs. Crag, and that's the way it's to be. Do you hear?'

'I hear, but I can't believe you. Not with "impulse" ... "see it this way" ... "chaos to the heart." ' As he looked back uncomprehending, she called angrily, 'Oh, Crag, can't you understand, I *heard*. I heard you and Rena talking on the verandah that night. – Crag?'

For Crag was laughing at her, saying, 'Oh, *that*!'

'That,' he went on, 'was for Rena. That was what impulse, Rena's impulse and Dom's impulse, had done to two people. It had brought chaos to the heart.'

'Then it wasn't *your* impulse of loving Davy?'

'Loving the scrubber was never that.'

'It wasn't *your* impulse of accepting me as well?'

'Pippa, in one minute I'll—'

'But I have to know, Crag. I have to know about Rena. You love her.'

'No,' Crag said.

'Then you loved her?'

'No,' he said again.

'You asked her to marry you.'

'In a way. It was after my father died ... I was returning to Falling Star, and I thought how I would like a son, too ... But you know all that. Perhaps I might never have come to it, asking her, I mean, had Rena not asked first. That's rotten of me, I know, but it's the truth. You must have seen yourself how it was afterwards with Glen Burt.'

She had seen it, so she could not deny it. She asked

helplessly: 'Why, Crag, *why* was she like that?'

'Because she was running away. Because pride, which was more predominant in Rena than I've ever seen it in anyone, stood in her way.'

'Running?'

'From Dom. She loved Dom. She loved him from the first moment she saw him . . . over in England, I think it was. Because she was Rena and spoiled rotten . . . yes, she was spoiled rotten, Pippa . . . she had to "buy" him at once, or at least have her father "buy" him for her. Old Franklin was willing enough. He liked Dom.' Crag took out his pipe. 'Who wouldn't?'

Pippa murmured, 'Go on.'

'So they purchased the Highlands estate and made Dom the overseer.' Crag tapped the tobacco. 'With an end in view. But Hardy was as proud as Rena was. He loved her as much as she loved him, but he could accept no charity, and he wouldn't be bought. So—'

'So, Crag?'

'A man's stubborn pride stopped him asking what she waited for him to ask, and when Rena asked instead—'

'How do you know this?'

'I know,' said Crag, 'because I was there. I didn't think much about it then . . . I didn't think much about it afterwards. But it came to me at last that for a girl who had rushed me . . . yes, Pippa, *rushed* me . . . Rena was not following up that rush. I asked myself why, and I came up with this: It was because she didn't really want me and never had. She only wanted out from Uplands, away from Hardy. Because Hardy had said something that Rena had never experienced before. It was NO.'

'No to what?'

'No to Daddy's estate. No to all that Daddy's money could buy.'

'But, Crag, how can you say all this?'

'I heard it. I told you, Pippa. Rena had just suffered a fall from her hack ... Bunting, I remember. It was following one of her usual spats with Hardy about riding. It seems those two will always be horse-involved. I was riding with them. But it was Hardy who picked her up, and it was to Dom that she looked and said: "This is how it will be, won't it?" and he looked back at her and shook his head.

'It meant little to me then, but later, when she attached herself to me ... then attached herself to Glen Burt, I knew she was running away from something. Oh, this pride!' Crag shrugged his big shoulders.

'Yes, but Dom had it, too,' Pippa said loyally, loyal to Rena.

'But he put it aside when he came up here after her. And for that we have to thank old Franklin. If he hadn't altered his will like he did ... I often wonder, though, adoring Rena so much, that he—'

'I think,' said Pippa, 'I can explain that.' She told him of that last afternoon in Uncle Preston's sick-room, and how she had spoken of Dom as stubborn, proud and determined. How, later, when she had asked Uncle Preston was there anything he wanted, he had answered: 'You've given it to me.'

'So he clinched it by that will,' mused Crag. 'He knew that Dom would never agree to that will in a thousand years, so he kept an ember red and a fire alight. Though I think, Pippa, it could still have gone on and on but for the stallion. You know what, I'm glad about that wrong 'un, Bobby and all. After all, Bobby's no worse, in fact he's having a whale of a time in Minta, so we can say the wild feller saved Rena and Dom that thousand years,' he laughed.

Pippa said thoughtfully, 'You're fond of that number, aren't you? In fact Rupie and Davy intend questioning you about it again. You wrote it down in an order. A thousand candles.'

'Put into gross they wouldn't sound so crazy,' Crag admitted whimsically. 'I'm sorry I've worried our two bookies.'

'Rupie was not so worried as puzzled. He reported that you'd said you'd always wanted them and there was no other way.'

'Sometimes I thought so, Pippa,' Crag said sadly. 'I thought that was only for people like my parents. – Do you remember?'

'Their love was a thousand candles,' Pippa remembered. She waited for him to go on.

'I knew the first light of a candle that day in the train to Tombonda. Ever since then they've been lighting up, one by one. But sometimes some went out' . . . he blew his cheeks, then puffed . . . 'you turned away.'

'You turned away yourself,' she came back hotly. 'You said "no ties tied" . . . "nothing" . . . "relax".'

'And every syllable seared me, killed me. But what else could I do, knowing—'

'Knowing, Crag?'

'That the scrubber had been between us. Oh, I loved him, Pippa, but—'

'But you're wrong,' she said quietly. 'Davy wasn't there. – Oh, Crag, are you quite mad?'

For the brown man was actually counting up . . . holding her tightly to him as he did so . . . skipping hundreds; he must be to reach 999 so soon.

'One thousand, Pippa. A thousand candles.'

She believed it. There was light everywhere.

THE MUTUAL LOOK

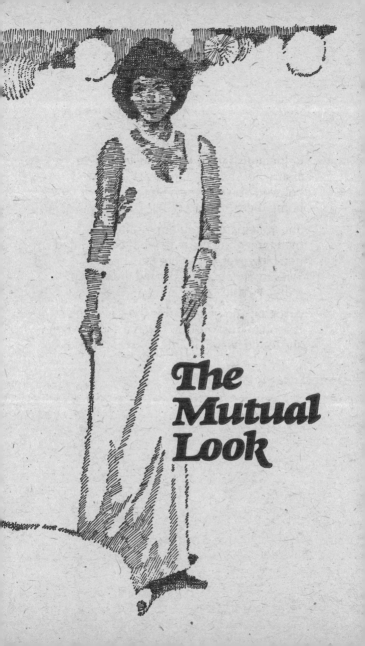

The
Mutual
Look

Reluctantly Jane went to Australia—to assure her retired employer that their beloved horses were adapting to their new home there.

She anticipated problems—after all, it meant meeting the man who'd once jilted her. However, it was her new boss, William Bower, who proved the source of her troubles.

Arrogant and overbearing, he gave Jane no reason to trust him. So it was a shock when she found herself falling in love with him....

CHAPTER ONE

THERE was something the matter with Rusty.

Jane was turning this over in her mind as she crossed the final meadow that led to the Little Down Stables. 'Rusty,' she found herself adding ruefully, such a flippant name for the owner of a serious stud. Yet right from the beginning her employer had insisted on that. 'Never call me Mr. Russell,' he had instructed his girl strapper when he had first signed her on five years ago, 'call me Rusty. I had it at school, and it stuck.'

'Yes, Mr.—er—Rusty,' Jane remembered agreeing a little awkwardly on that initial occasion, for to her Rusty had sounded more like one of his chestnuts. 'I'm Jane Sidney. Jane.' She had smiled and put out her hand.

'Welcome to Little Down, Jane.' Mr. Russell had sealed the new union with a press down of his old, gnarled hand on hers.

Yes, old even then, Jane frowned now, pushing the meadow's kissing gate to the yard that led to the outbuildings. She, Jane, had been just eighteen. How old had Rusty been? She smiled affectionately as she closed the gate behind her, then walked on.

Jane's parents, and she had been thankful for this, had been tolerant over her decision to make horses her career. They themselves had tried herbs, seedlings, bonsai trees, then finally finished up growing coffee in Kenya. Jane's brother followed a honey flow. 'You could say,' her mother had laughed, 'that we're outdoor-obsessed.'

Jane felt she had done well at Little Down, and Rusty never had complained. But this last month she had noticed him giving her sidelong looks, she had heard him clearing his throat as people do when they are going to say something important. His health? she had wondered. Health often diminishes as the years accrue. Or was he selling out? Whatever it was she hoped he would not wait too long to tell her. She would have to make plans for her future, strap somewhere else ... or go out to Kenya ... or join her brother David. She was twenty-three, unmarried, not even engaged. Not now. For a moment her lip quivered, but she did not permit any thoughts on *that*. Only on Rusty. What ticked with old Rusty? .

The stud was out of Guildford, one of those breathtakingly lovely settings that Surrey does with such heartwarming frequency. A creek at the end of the rough acre, now three fields behind her, was noisy with running water, trees behind the creek bent back against the sky as they took the wind and so spared Little Down, and, since it was autumn, damson, cigar-leaf and gold were changing the hills from their summer bruise-blue. I love it, thought Jane, and I'll hate to go, but there's something about Rusty, something to do with me, and I must know.

She was outside the neat barns of Little Down now, approving, as she always did, Rusty's meticulous arrangement. It was a small stud, the only help beside herself several casuals, but it was perfectly set and perfectly maintained. It also produced, Jane thought proudly, perfect animals.

On Rusty's orders she had just put Simeon in the western section. It was higher there, and Simeon could look down on the fillies in the smaller field, for Rusty believed in courtship as well as marriage. They had been his actual words. What an adorable old man he was, and how she would hate it if——

She stepped inside the first stable and saw that Alex Russell was there before her, there intentionally by the determined set of his now stooped shoulders. So she was to know at last. 'Sit down, young Jane.' The old man indicated one of the two stools, taking the other himself. He nodded satisfaction at her equipment, all in good clean order, the arrangement of girths, stirrup leathers, buckle guards. 'You're a rare strapper,' he awarded.

'You're a rare boss,' she awarded back.

'But' . . . Rusty paused sensitively . . . 'not for long.'

So, thought Jane, here it comes.

'I hoped you'd find out,' Rusty said unhappily. 'I hoped to be spared the telling.'

'Of what?'

'That new motorway, Jane,' he said in a rush.

But Jane found she could not answer in a rush. She said slowly, painfully, 'Oh, Rusty, no!'

She had known about the motorway, everyone around here had, but not the actual location. Nor when. But at this moment Rusty was telling her silently, telling her with sad eyes that here, *right here at Little Down*, was the actual location, and the time close at hand.

'I've had my notice to quit, Jane.' Rusty found words at last.

'Any hope of a stay of procedure?'

'This is the final notice, girl—it's been going on all this year.'

'And you never told me? You carried your burden around by yourself?'

'No need to make two people miserable. Only one, now, as it happens, I have come to terms with it. And no one miserable at all if what I plan comes off . . . If you'll only agree.'

'What, Rusty?' Jane asked.

'It seems at eighty-four I'm due for the resting paddock, anyway. Now' . . . a laugh . . . 'you know my age, Jane. I guess you always wondered.'

'I did,' Jane admitted, 'but not as much as I'm wondering now how a man like you will ever rest.'

'I wondered myself until a month ago when an old friend, and a contemporary from ancient stable days, wrote from Kentucky for me to join him there. I know I'd like that, Jane, soft rain and limestone for a man's last years.'

'Rusty, rain and limestone are for good horses.'

'What's good enough for a horse is good enough for me. The letter lifted me up again. I'm not fretting any more. Only' ... a careful pause ... 'about you.'

'Darling, I'm not eighty-four.'

'I know exactly how old you are. I have it on your contract. On your record I have other information, Jane, I have the written report that you're the best stablehand, male or female, a man could ever ask.'

'Thank you.' Jane's cheeks, always Surrey-scarlet, now positively flamed with pride.

'Well,' said Alex Russell briskly, 'enough of the blue ribbons, you can't eat ribbons. As you must gather, Jane, because of the motorway I can't sell out.'

'Not the actual stud,' Jane agreed, 'but the stock? The boys? The girls?' They had always called them that between them; they were, Rusty often had remarked, a pair of softies.

'Yes,' the old man nodded, 'and I intend to, Jane.' A pause. 'But not all.'

'Which ones not?'

'The gems, of course,' Rusty said. He had always called their specials the gems.

'Gretel, San Marco, Ruthven,' nodded Jane.

'Also our couple of D's,' added Rusty, 'Dotsy and Devil May Care.'

'You're leaving out the best D.'

'Oh, come now, girl!'

'I mean it, Rusty, you couldn't exclude Dandy.'

Rusty sighed, shrugged his defeat, then corrected, 'Dotsy, Devil May Care and Dandy.'

Jane smiled gratefully at him. 'What happens to them? Over to Kentucky to the soft rain and limestone?' She smothered an ache at the thought of losing Dandy, but after all, if Rusty was with her boy ...

Rusty looked hard at her and said: 'Over to Australia, Jane.'

Jane winced.

There was a silence in the stable, all the horses were out, the only small noise a little breeze worrying at a splinter of straw. 'Now, Jane girl,' Rusty remonstrated, and there was a concerned note in his voice.

'It's all right, I'm over that,' Jane assured him.

'Are you though? Are you ... well, look here, Jane, are you over it enough to—well, to go there, too?'

'Go where?' Jane stared at him stupidly.

'New South Wales.'

'Why should I ever go there?'

'Because that's where the gems are going, over to New South Wales, Australia, to become part of my nephew's concern.'

'Then I'm sorry about that.' Jane's voice was cold. 'Not about your nephew, I don't know your nephew, but——'

'But Australia,' finished Rusty for her. 'And all because of one man.'

'Well, that's one woman's reaction. This woman's.'

'You're foolish, Jane.'

Jane did not answer.

'You're foolish,' Alex Russell went on, 'because you'll be throwing away a job.'

'I can always get employment.'

'Throwing away a better job,' Rusty said, 'superior employment.' A pause, then: 'Plus one-fifth.'

'What, Rusty?' Again Jane said that.

'I'm sending the gems to Australia, Jane. Three of them leave next week, three later, the first three getting into their quarantine stride 'while you' ... a pause and then a correction ... 'while the second contingent begin their journey.'

'I'm glad you altered that,' Jane said.

'But must I? Think it over, girl. At least' ... appealingly ... 'hear me out now.'

Jane opened her mouth, closed it again. The old man began to speak.

'William Bower is my sole relative. My sister Alice is dead now, and had only the one child.'

'Bower,' Jane said tightly. 'Not the Bower who had the stud called Bowers in the south of New South Wales?'

'Had and has,' Rusty answered uneasily. He added hopefully, 'Studs must have been in the blood.'

But Jane was not to be diverted. '*That* Bower,' she dismissed.

'Jane——'

'Oh, I know I'm mad to go on like this, I know I'm unfair, but any man who employed a man like—like Rodden proved, well—well, he must be the same himself.'

'It doesn't follow, Jane.

'I think it does. You, for instance. Would you employ me if I was—if I—if——'

'I won't be employing anyone soon,' Alex Russell said factually. 'And that's what's worrying me, Jane, I'm worrying about you.'

'I told you, I'm twenty-three and able.'

'That helps you, girl, but it doesn't help me. I'm fond of you, Jane, so fond I just can't let you go without—well, doing something.'

'That's unnecessary.' Jane's voice was stiff ... stiff from emotion as well as pride. Dear kind Rusty, she was thinking.

'If it was necessary I wouldn't be begging you to do this.'

'To go to Australia?'

'Also to accept that one-fifth,' Rusty reminded her.

'I don't understand what you're saying. All I understand is you want me to go out there, there of all places, and not only there but to Rodden's particular corner.'

'Perhaps not,' suggested Rusty reasonably. 'I mean it needn't be any more. Young vets change their corners continually. They strive for a place of their own, especially ambitious blokes like Rodden Gair was.'

'You're still asking me to go?'

'Yes, I am asking that. Why not?'

'Why not? Why not?' Jane barely prevented a little sob.

At once the old hand covered hers. Alex Russell let his rest there a while, then he said fairly: 'Yes, why not. It doesn't make William, my nephew the same breed.'

'But you don't know, do you, you don't *know* your nephew.'

'No,' agreed Jane's employer, 'I don't, but after all he's my blood.'

'Part,' she reminded him. 'But' ... taking pity on his concerned old face ... 'I'll still hear you out.'

'Thanks for that at least, girl.' Rusty gave a wry grin and started off again.

'I've written to Chad Ramsay telling him I'll join him,' he said, 'finish my days in the soft rain and limestone of Kentucky like a good horse. The family strain in me urges me to give what's left over to my own breed, Jane. I expect you can understand that.'

'Of course.'

'But not entirely, there's a certain filly I can't get out of my mind, and never will.'

'Dotsy.'

'You and your Dotsy! All of your D's. No, it's Jane Sidney, of course. Girl, I can't let you go like this.'

'I told you——'

'And I'm telling you I want you to have one-fifth of my gems. The telling fifth? Who knows?'

'How do you mean?'

'If a man holds four-fifth of something, mustn't the other fifth be the one in control? Mustn't it, girl?'

'I think you're not sure of your nephew,' Jane suggested.

'As near sure as my memory of my sister can make me,' Rusty defended. 'Alice was fine. No, it's not that—well, not entirely that, it's the gems as well. They need you, Jane. Can you say no now?'

'No,' Jane said to show him.

'No to Gretel, San Marco, Ruthven?'

'To Dotsy and Devil May Care, too.'

'Ah—but to Dandy?'

'Dandy,' Jane said, and she felt herself biting her lip.

'See!' Alex Russell pounced triumphantly. 'See, Jane?'

Right from his shaky beginning Dandy had been different from the rest. When he had stumbled up from the turf, the vet, Rusty and Jane frankly had been doubtful.

'No gem here,' Bob Westleigh had regretted of the shivering morsel to his client. 'Well, Rusty, you can't have it every time.'

'Does look more like a bit of junk jewellery than a gem,' Rusty had agreed ... and Jane had started to agree, too, then stopped. Dandy had been looking up at her with soft pleading eyes, and she had looked back. The mutual look, Rusty had called it later.

'I always know where there's a mutual look that it will be all right.'

'What is a mutual look?' she had asked.

'Just something between the two of you and you two only. You looked at that fellow, and knew, didn't you? He looked at you, and knew.'

'Knew he could be something?'

'Knew you could make it come true. Well, it will be quite a job, Jane, he's not very prepossessing, but he's yours to do with what you can.'

It had been a challenge, and Jane had taken it up. She had spent more hours on Dandy than she had spent on any other horse. Not just grooming but careful manipulation, tireless massage, the exercising, when Dandy was ready for it, meticulously planned, assiduously carried out. No horse was ever brushed more, polished more, cosseted more. She remembered Rodden saying when he had come to England from Bowers, Australia, to complete a course, and had called, at William Bower's request, to Little Down to meet Bower's uncle, and, as it had happened, Bower's uncle's girl strapper: 'Silk sheets, Janey?' She had remembered laughing back at Rodden, not thinking he was serious.

She hadn't laughed later.

'Dandy?' Rusty was dangling now. 'Look, Jane,' as Jane

did not answer, 'I feel pretty sure of William. I have his photo. Would you like to see it?'

'No.'

'There's a look about him.'

'A mutual one?'

'That takes two people.

'Oh, Rusty, don't go on like this. At least' ... angrily ... 'talk sense.'

'Right,' Rusty said. He probed in his pocket and brought out some papers. 'First contingent,' he told Jane, 'leaving Thursday week. You've just time for your jabs and your what-have-yous, girl.'

'You mean,' she interpreted, 'five weeks out by sea, fly back again, do it all a second time?' She knew that over twelve thousand miles by air would entail a strain on the horse, and that Rusty would never agree to that.

But—— 'No,' Rusty said. 'Half of each—half air, half water. I reckon it would be the best way for the gems. I plan on them flying Boeing to Singapore and then catching their breath during a week or so at sea to Sydney. Does that make good sense?'

It made good horse sense, everything that Rusty had done concerning Little Down always had made sense, but——

'Nice for them,' Jane said.

'And you?'

'Oh, Rusty!'

'Oh, Jane,' the old man said back.

There was silence a while, then Rusty spoke.

'I'm happy in the thought of Kentucky ... couldn't really be happier. I'm happy about William, too. After all, he's Alice's child. But when a man has spent nearly all his life perfecting something, he can't let it go without some backward glance. Jane girl, can't you see that you are that for me, or I hope you will be.'

'The backward glance?'

'Yes. You'd write to me, write personally about the boys

and girls, not—well, not like a stranger would write, even though he's the same blood. I wouldn't feel the amputation, in other words. Now do you understand?'

'Yes, Rusty, but don't you understand how I feel?'

'Not entirely. That Rodden Gair——'

That Rodden Gair. Suddenly stifled, Jane got up from the stool and went to the stable door. Rodden, she was thinking. Rod.

It had been a day rather like this when she had first met him, a shining kind of day. He had come down from London to have lunch with Rusty, pass on his boss's and Rusty's nephew's good wishes, and afterwards had strolled out of the Little Down house.

Into Jane's heart.

Tall, blue-eyed, charming, he had won her at once ... and it had been obvious, and flattering, what she had done to him.

Within two weeks they had been engaged. Everything had been whirlwind, magic, romantic, the quick exuberant way a girl wants such things. Rodden was no laggard lover, he had planned marriage the moment they hit Sydney, which, he had said, would be the beginning of next month.

'Oh no, Rod, Melinda foals next month, only in the middle of it, so we'll have to wait a week or so.'

'Darling, you're not serious?'

'I wouldn't be over any of the others, they're normal breeders, but Melinda——'

'Wants you to hold her hoof?'

'Roddy!'

'Janey,' he mocked.

'Rod, I'm in earnest.'

'And I, Jane, have never been more earnest in all my life. Putting a mare before me, the very idea!' He had made a jest of it, but unmistakably there had been no laughter there.

'But I'm not, Rodden. I'll marry you right now. This very moment.'

'Only it happens I don't want it like that. I want a ceremony back home, all the glamour and fuss and——'

'You really mean the hand-outs?' He had told her several times about the Bower generosity when any of its members married.

'Perhaps I do,' Rodden had said unabashed.

Jane had been silent a while, she remembered, then she had pleaded: 'You don't have to leave at that time, you could wait an extra week.'

'I'm going at the date I just said. With you.'

'Rodden, I know I sound unreasonable——'

'You do.'

'But this time it means a lot to Melinda. She's been unlucky before, and Bob Westleigh believes——'

'Spare me from a sentimental vet! I've looked the mare over and she's as strong as the proverbial horse.' Rod had laughed at his wit.

'Only,' Jane had inserted quietly, 'she's not.'

'Then she's expendable, my dear Jane, and old Russell should see to it. You can't run a stud on redundant stock. We don't.'

She had noted that 'we', but not commented on it. 'You have to be sensible, I agree,' she said, 'but surely affection——'

'Can't come into business, Jane. Good lord, what have I here and not known it before? A pony high priestess?'

'I am not!' she snapped.

'I've seen dog women,' Rodden had gone on, 'soppy sentimental females drooling over Fido or Rover or Prince, but I've never encountered the horse variety yet.'

'Rodden, I like horses. You must yourself or you wouldn't have followed your career.'

'It's a sound career, and, I hope, in time a rich one, but never if sob stories fill the page instead of figures.'

'Profitable ones, of course.'

'Of course.'

They had stood looking at each other, neither giving

207

ground. If only Rodden had said: 'Darling, I see your point, so see mine, come with me when I say, I need you,' she would have agreed.

But Rodden's lip had stuck out, he had said instead, 'Pony high priestess. All right, stop and hold Melinda's hoof.'

And he had turned and gone.

She hadn't believed it. She had his ring on her finger, his promise in her heart. She loved him, he loved her.

But a week later a letter had come from William Bower, Rusty's Australian nephew, thanking his uncle for the good wishes his vet had brought back with him from Surrey. And that had been all.

Another week and no letter. A month. Two. Jane had boxed the ring and sent it over. Still no communication. At the end of six months she had known it was the end. Such a silly thing to put Finish to it. And yet——

'Is the door shut, girl?' Rusty had asked once; tactfully the old man had requested no details.

'Yes, Rusty,' she had said.

'Then don't fret. I'm not. You two—well, you had no mutual look.'

'Oh, Rusty, you are a fool!'

'Fool's Gold, that's what I'm calling Golden Girl's foal. Like it?'

Slowly but progressively, and eventually without pain though still with a little bitterness, Jane had emerged from her abyss.

Now, she thought, gazing out of the stable door, it could all happen again, if she went.

'It's a long time ago,' Rusty was intoning, 'he'll be in some smart business of his own, that young fellow.' The old man had guessed her thoughts. 'Anyway, what does it matter, Jane?'

'No matter. It's dead.' She said it truly. 'It's just that it makes me wonder about your William Bower.'

'Look at his photo.'

'No.'

'All right, don't look, then, but don't see him with Gair's face until you come face to face with him.'

'Which I won't be doing. No, Rusty, I'm sorry. If you want to—well, reward me, why can't it be without going out there, without giving me a share of the gems? One gem would do,' she said intensely.

'Yes—Dandy. But what would a scrap like you do with Dandy? Especially now that we know——'

'Yes?'

But Rusty had not continued with that. 'Horses cost money, Jane,' he said, 'a deal of money, you should appreciate that. William has enough, I believe, some from his parents, most from his own initiative. If Dandy is to have the best, it's to be out there.'

'Very well' ... a sigh ... 'consign Dandy, too.'

'With you?'

'No, Rusty. It will hurt me terribly, but I would get over it.'

'I wouldn't,' the old man said sadly. 'I'd feel cut off completely from my fellows knowing you weren't there ... well, until they were acclimatized, anyway.'

Jane pricked her ears at that. 'Till they became acclimatized ... then it need only be temporary?'

'I'd like it to be longer, but I haven't made that stipulation.'

'Rusty, just what stipulations have you made?'

He brightened at that, evidently seeing a gleam of hope, and, folding his arms, looked across at her, still standing at the door.

'The stipulations are that to earn that share you must go out and work with our two consignments. When you judge them as properly settled in, when William judges them as that as well, if you like you can sell out your dividend.'

'Oh, I'd do that all right,' she promised.

'Then you'll go, Jane?'

'I haven't said so.'

'If you don't go, then what will you do?'

'Another job ... I told you ... the parents ... or follow the honey with David. He writes that honey is very lucrative.'

'And be happy while you're doing this?'

'Of course.' Her voice was too enthusiastic, and she knew he would pick it up.

He did. 'Transparent Jane,' he said, 'you'd be miserable away from horses, you're a real——'

'Pony high priestess?' she said sharply.

'That Gair!' Rusty fumed. 'He certainly did a bad job.'

'Well, it's done.'

'I don't think so. Not entirely. You know what I think?'

'What, Rusty?'

'I think Dandy will win this argument, that you'll go because of him.'

'No!' Jane declared.

'Then I believe I'll win, that you'll go because of me.'

She had turned right back from the door now and she looked fondly down on the old man.

'You're not really so happy being put out to grass,' she insinuated gently, 'even Kentucky blue grass.'

'No, but I could be nearly happy knowing that Gretel, San Marco, Ruthven——'

'Dotsy, Devil May Care——'

'Dandy,' they both said together.

Rusty finished, 'Were in my girl's hands.'

'Only till I bow out,' she stipulated.

'Yes.'

'And if I can't stand it I can waive that fifth and leave on my own accord?'

'Yes.'

'Then——'

'Then, Jane?'

'I'll do it.'

'Thursday week the first contingent, twelve days to go out by air and ship, two days to fly back and to start it all again. I'll be waving you away on the fifteenth of June, Jane, and should welcome you home the beginning of the next month prior to you going off again.'

'Then Kentucky for you?'

'And Australia for you. Write often, Jane.'

Jane said a little chokily, 'Yes, Boss.'

CHAPTER TWO

ALMOST at once, or so it seemed to a saddened Jane (and no doubt Rusty) the jack hammers began. Men invaded Little Down with all varieties of destructive machines, men looking like invaders from other planets in their yellow safety gear and steel helmets. Bulldozers lumbered in, semi-trailers, salvage lorries, and as they advanced, the stud ceased functioning.

The lesser lights were dealt with first, among them Toby, who had loved apples and actually pulled them from trees, Minnie, who once had bitten a rather pompous VIP visiting Little Down and who still wore a smile of wicked remembrance, Melinda, because of whom Rodden had departed, along with Melinda's several offspring, for one good thing had come out of that episode: Melinda had beaten her birth hoodoo and was now the perfect mare.

Each farewell wrenched Jane. She wondered what Rodden Gair would have had to say about that. She wondered if mindlessness was an Australian trait. If so, what would William Bower have thought?

Because Rusty had been in the habit of sending Jane abroad fairly regularly to pick up some colt or deliver some pony, her shots were up to date. All she had to do was pack and collect her tickets. While collecting, she changed the class from First to Tourist. Dear Rusty, how typical of him to cosset her! Well, he need never know that she had altered her travelling standard, and she was sure he could do with the extra cash.

Saying goodbye was not so hard; she would be back in little more than a fortnight. The thought of saying goodbye the next time, though, made Jane feel bleak.

She, Gretel, San Marco and Ruthven left duly from Gatwick, the mare and two geldings by air freighter, Jane minutes after them by a regular line. The plan was to rest the girl and boys at a Singapore stable owned by an old customer of Rusty's. A day would be sufficient, and a day would fit in admirably with the departure of the *Southern Princess* for Sydney.

The flight to Singapore proved comfortable and uneventful. One quick check of the four-legged travellers assured Jane that Gretel, San Marco and Ruthven had fared just as well.

She had a pleasant stopover in Singapore, doing the usual things ... Bushy Hill, Change Alley, selecting a length of Thai brocade to be made into a cheongsam in one day and delivered to her *Southern Princess* cabin.

It was there when she boarded, and, to her delight, a perfect fit. About to change back, she decided she had better check up on her precious cargo; she had left full instructions for the boarding of the mare and geldings, but she had not actually seen them on the ship. Running along the narrow passage of her tourist class deck, she giggled to herself at her unworkmanlike gear. She must be the oddest pony high priestess ... she never forgot that from Rodden ... in the world.

No one saw her, however, and she gained the appropriate deck without attracting any stares. She slipped past several boxes of unenthusiastic canine travellers, stopped to cheer up a disapproving white cat on a leash, then found the girl and the boys. Well, they were there all right, but not, she saw at once, very happy.

She checked their tethering—it was not too tight—she saw to water, availability of movement, light, several other necessary details. It was while she was attendding to a small leg cut that Ruthven must have suffered in transit that she noticed a foot among the hooves. A man's foot. A long, expensive-looking shoe in dark tan leather. Dark tan socks above it. The end of a dark brown trouser leg.

She looked up.

The horses' berth was exclusively their own, this was

213

something she had not changed when she had changed her standard of travel. Which made this man an intruder.

'Did you want something?' she asked sharply.

'No.' That was all he said.

'Then I must ask you to leave.'

'Not before I ask you to tie those horses in the other direction ... that is if it's your job.'

'It is.'

'I'm surprised. Since when have strappers worn brocade?'

'It's a cheongsam I bought in——' Jane stopped in annoyance, annoyed at herself. What did it have to do with this man? 'You're trespassing,' she said instead.

'I'm leaving at once. I merely stopped to look at the ship's arrangement, see what quarters they offered.'

'If you've seen, will you please go?' she demanded.

'Not before you change that tethering.'

'Why should I?'

'Because,' he fairly burst out, 'the beasts are uncomfortable. For heaven's sake, can't you see that?'

Jane looked and saw that obviously they were, though why they should be she did not know.

'We're *sailing*, in case that fact hasn't reached you,' the man said, 'and the way they're tied, they're getting more than they should of the not inconsiderable swell. But perhaps pony high priestesses' ... pony high priestesses? ... 'are unaware that a horse can be seasick. I assure you they can be quite dangerously so, dangerous because they don't possess the therapy of being able to retch.'

She knew all that, Rusty had instructed her, but she still could not find words to defend herself. *Pony high priestess*, he had said.

And then something was pushing aside Jane's wonder, her resentment. The ship was certainly moving, indeed, down here, moving quite unpleasantly. To her utter dismay and to the ruin of her new cheongsam, *Jane* was now being sick. Thoroughly sick. At once the man tossed across an overall,

214

and while she pulled it on he moved over to her, then propelled her to the door.

'I'll change them around for you,' he said briefly. He
took time to look her up and down. 'I don't know whether
that stuff cleans,' he added, 'but if it doesn't you can discard the soil and use the rest as rags. You always want rags.'

She hated him for that, hated him for seeing her sick, for
commenting on her now poor bedraggled little cheongsam,
in short she simply hated him. Leaving the girl and boys in
his hands, something a really responsible strapper would
never do, ill or not, Jane ran back to her berth.

Once away from the horses' quarters she felt much better. She regained her cabin, was relieved to find it empty,
undressed, wrapped up the cheongsam distastefully and put
it aside for disposal whenever convenient, then showered
and put on fresh clothes.

The chance to throw away the offending garment came at
afternoon tea time. Instead of obeying the gong as the rest of
the tourist class appeared to be doing, Jane hurried back to
her cabin and picked up her parcel, regretting as she did so
that her economy on account of Rusty had deprived her of a
porthole; a porthole would have been very convenient just
now.

When she went up on deck it was to apparent emptiness.
She lost no time in hurrying to a strategic position ... only
to be beaten to the chosen spot in a very unnerving fashion.
Two figures ... in her confusion at first Jane did not see
they were children ... had run forward and before her horrified eyes were toppling over a figure. She could not see
any details, but she sensed hair hanging down, a hat of sorts
on top of the hair.

'Stop at once ... what have you done ... Steward!
Purser! Cap——' The last she uttered to the accompani-
ment of peals of laughter. Looking down to the sea she saw
an old mop riding the waves.

'You little fiends!' She realized now that the pair were
quite young.

215

As they still doubled up in mirth, she threw away her own evidence, then, relieved on two counts, one that murder had not been done, two that she had rid herself of the wretched cheongsam, Jane joined the laughter. She and David had staged larks like this, and anyway, she liked children.

They seemed a little surprised at her participation, and looked at her with interest. Jane found herself looking back at them with equal interest. Twins undoubtedly, male and female version, but like as proverbial two peas.

'Robert and Roberta,' they introduced themselves.

'Jane,' said Jane.

'Where are the rest of the people?' they asked.

'Afternoon tea. Don't you pair like cakes?'

'We're First,' they said unenthusiastically, 'and the only kids in First this trip. It's awful in First, just like a morgue. In Tourist you have a ball. Are you having a ball?'

'I only boarded at Singapore.'

'So did we, but we sailed up. It was just as bad then. Why can't Father William book Tourist instead?'

That had been Roberta, identical with Robert as to basin-cropped hair, sloppy joe, shorts and sandals, but slightly smaller and finer in build.

'Because,' explained Robert, 'there are nine hundred Tourists but only a hundred Firsts, so Father William reckons there's all that less for us to drive mad.'

'Do you drive people mad?' Jane asked.

'Yes,' they said factually, 'we're indirigibles.'

'Do you mean individuals or incorrigibles?'

They could not remember, but they were agreed that it was something bad.

'We have a bad name,' Roberta said.

'That's true, and it's probably deserved.' This was Robert, more articulate than his twin. 'You see, we're unsettled. Our mother is doing a course in Paris, so Father William has to have us until we can go on to school. He's not very happy.'

216

'But,' came in Roberta, 'he's going to be unhappier still.' They both went into peals of laughter again.

'Show her,' Roberta urged Robert.

'She could tell.'

'No, she's all right. She laughed about the body. Besides, she won't see Father William down here in Tourist, so she can't tell.' Roberta looked at Jane. 'You wouldn't tell, anyway, would you?'

'I would tell about a real body, anything like that.'

'It isn't, it's a passport—Father William's passport. We've put a photo over his photo. Wait till he has to show it!' They doubled up again.

On Roberta's prompting, Robert took out the passport. 'It's all right,' he reassured an alarmed Jane, 'I take good care of it. Look.' He showed her the usual document, only where the likeness should be, a likeness ... if such a likeness could be like to anything ... of something else.

'It's an artist's impression of the Yeti, the Abominable Snowman,' Robert said proudly.

Jane tried to look severe, but the dripping whiskers and long black teeth undid her. Again she laughed.

'See,' the pair rejoiced, 'she's one of us. Why aren't you in First?'

'The usual reason,' Jane said, wiping her eyes. 'And after this' ... looking at the passport now being carefully returned to Robert's pocket ... 'I can't say I want to better myself. You two are——'

'Robert! Roberta!' The summons came from a deck above, the deck of the more exclusive section of the ship. It was a man's authoritative voice. Jane had no time to see the caller, but she did see the reaction of the children. They might be individuals or incorrigibles, but, as far as that voice was concerned, they were disciplined.

'Blimey,' they said together, and turned and obeyed their summons without another word.

The episode had cheered Jane. Giggling over the Abominable Snowman, she went down to look at her girl and boys again, much more suitably clad this time, she thought, wondering if she would encounter that man again. She supposed she would have to thank him. That would be hard. It could never be easy apologizing to someone who had seen you being most unglamorously ill. However, there was no one about, the stable occupants looked fit and settled, so Jane came out again. As she crossed to her deck to relax in the sun, she saw the twins on the deck above her. They caught sight of her and waved enthusiastically, and Jane waved back. If she encountered them again, she thought, she must ask why they said Father William of their parent, that parent who had the care of them while their mother did some course in Paris, and who was not very happy over it, or so they had said. Jane found a chair, turned over the pages of a magazine ... Slept.

She saw the twins fairly frequently in the shipboard days that followed. Whenever they could escape to Tourist, they did so, and after a charity concert in the First Saloon open to all who cared to donate, Jane did not blame the small people. Luxury to children could never take the place of companionship, contemporary companionship, and the only people she saw in First were distinctly mature. Across the room she glimpsed the man who had trespassed into the stable berth during her primary check there. She was not surprised to find him here, not someone with an autocratic look like he wore. If he noticed her, he made no sign. Jane gave her attention to the music ... yet not entirely as before. Oddly uncomfortable, she was glad when it was time to return to the stern.

Whenever they could the twins would sneak down and look longingly at the pool.

'You have a pool of your own,' Jane reminded them. 'A much better pool.'

'Inside, in case the poor old dears get sunburned,' sneered Roberta.

'Anyway, no one goes in, except Father William, so

218

where's the fun?' Robert looked jealously at a boy ducking a girl.

'Why do you call him that? Father William?' Jane asked curiously.

'William's his name, and once he said he'd kick Robert downstairs.' It was Roberta, and she reported it in a suitably scandalized voice, but Jane gave a tolerant smile and asked: 'What had Robert done?'

'Nothing at all. Only put a bucket of water where Father William would tread into it, but he didn't,' said Robert.

'Then no wonder he was angry. I would have been, too. Why do you do such things?'

'Childish exuberance,' they both proffered together, and when Jane refused to accept that, they defended, 'Our mother says so, anyway.'

'It's plain naughtiness,' Jane scolded. To change the subject she said: 'Lewis Carroll wrote *Father William*. Did you know he wrote *Alice in Wonderland* as well?'

'Oh, I like Alice. Remember the part where she finds the little cake with EAT ME in currants?' It was Roberta.

'Yes, and that part——' took up Robert.

Jane knew, and participated. When they had to leave they said wistfully, 'You're fun, Jane.'

She did not see the twins for several days, in fact they had left Malaysia behind and when sailing down the west coast of Australia to Fremantle before the pair descended on her again.

'We've been in bad trouble,' they sighed.

'What did you do?'

'You saw it.'

'Not the photo?'

'Yes. Father William had to take it when he went ashore at Djakarta. We were to go with him in the afternoon for a tour.' A sigh. 'We never went.'

Jane tried hard to keep a straight face. She could imagine the effect of the Abominable Snowman looking up through his dripping whiskers to the officer at Passport Control.

'You awful children!' she said ... then broke down.

The Australian Bight, several days later, lived up to its reputation and proved quite rough. Jane spent most of her time with Gretel, San Marco and Ruthven. They plainly did not care for the motion, but they weathered it fairly well. Jane did not care for it, either, not down there, but she weathered it, too.

Then Adelaide was taking them into its calmer waters, and after Adelaide, Port Phillip Bay, fortunately in a benevolent mood, and soon they were steaming up the New South Wales coast. They came into Sydney on a bright blue and gold day, journey's end for Jane's girl and boys, but not yet for Jane herself.

She looked to the upper First-Class deck in the hope of seeing the twins, saying goodbye to them, for she had become very fond of the naughty little pair. They were not in sight, but the autocrat was. He returned Jane's look with an equal look, and that, shrugged Jane, was putting it in precisely the right words.

She did not encounter the children again, even if she had she would not have found the time to talk with them. Until she left Kingsford Smith Terminal for the U.K. once more, she had not a minute to spare. She settled the horses in quarantine, stopped with them as long as she was permitted, then spent the rest of her hours to her departure wondering whether she should ring up Rusty's nephew ... she had looked at a map and seen that the place was too far away for a casual visit ... then gave the thought away and took in a few city highlights instead. In no time she was aboard a Jumbo and speeding home. Home, she mused. I must get out of saying that. I don't know how long it will take once all the boys and girls get to Bowers for them to settle, but I should think it would be a fair part of a year.

This time it was hard to part from Rusty, they both made light of it, but there were sudden breaks in the laughter, and Rusty's hand holding hers was tight.

'Keep me posted, Jane.'

'Everything, Rusty ... including Dotsy's colt or filly if we mate her out there, for I feel she should begin, don't you?'

Rusty mumbled something indecipherable, and Jane put the mumble down to distress. He was distressed, the poor old dear. 'They tell me there's no grass like Kentucky blue,' she cheered him as they left.

Again she went over the previous programme ... checked the three D's, Dotsy, Devil May Care and Dandy at Singapore ... saw to their embarkation this time to the *Ariadne*.

The second sea trip began. Right from the start it was much more pleasant, the company was more her own age and outlook, and, though she still missed the twins, there was John.

She liked John Rivers at once. In the way people pair up in ships, she found herself pairing instinctively with the young man. They took shore excursions together, John altered his table in the dining saloon to be with her.

After a strenuous deck tennis bout one day, John said: 'I know all about you *now*, but nothing about you *yesterday*, and what's more important, nothing about you *tomorrow*.'

'That's easy,' she laughed. 'I was a strapper ... the same as I am now, and incidentally, John, Devil May Care is looking quite devilish again.' The horse had been slightly off colour.

'And tomorrow?' John smiled; he had a pleasant boyish smile.

'Strapper, or stablehand, once more. Place called Plateau in New South Wales. Would you——' She had started to ask 'Would you know it?' but saw at once that he did. He was beaming at her, crinkling his nice bramble-brown eyes in pleasure.

'Of course I know it. In fact I'm only some twenty miles away in the valley. We'll be neighbours, Jane.'

Jane crinkled her own eyes back. She felt as pleased as he obviously did. 'It's going to make it much easier,' she appreciated, 'knowing you're there.'

'For me, it's going to make it——' But John reddened and did not finish.

A little embarrassed, Jane said, 'Tell me about this place.'

'You mean you don't know anything about where you're going?'

'I don't.'

'Then,' he smiled, 'I'll tell you. You're going to perhaps the loveliest corner in the world.'

'That's local pride.'

'I expect so, but it's still a glorious spot. It's in the south ... can get quite cool in winter ... beautiful timber as well as good pickings for hops.'

'Which are you, John, trees or hops?'

'Some of both, and doing nicely, thank you, though never, of course, as well as the Baron of Bowers.'

'Why do you call him that?'

'He looks a proud devil, though I'm assured he's quite a decent guy. Severe, perhaps, but then you have to be when your commodity is livestock—I mean, Jane, I love trees, but they're still not flesh and blood.'

'And hops, do you love hops?'

They both laughed at that, then John went on to tell her more about the place.

'The district is called Urara, which is aboriginal for Far Away. I suppose it was far away once, but these days of air travel——'

'There's facility for landing, then?'

'At Plateau, private only. That's where Bowers is situated. I'm down the valley, so I take the official coastal route if I fly. But I won't be flying this time, I'll be trucking it, and I hope you'll come with me.'

'By truck?'

'Yes, Jane. Too lowly?'

'It's just wonderful,' Jane enthused. 'In that way I'll see the country.'

'Then that's fine,' John smiled.

222

The days sped fast, the weather was kind, the horses never looked back, and in no time the red roofs of Sydney were looming up again.

'You'll have to give me a day to settle Dotsy, Devil May Care and Dandy,' Jane stipulated to John Rivers.

'I'll wait a year if you say so,' John said deliberately.

She did not answer that, but she was not unpleased.

But Jane spent no day settling her trio. The moment the *Ariadne* berthed, a figure she would have recalled, had she been on deck to watch, joined the ship, joined it in that confident manner confident men always do. But Jane was not there.

She was putting last things into her case when the message came over the loudspeaker.

'Wanted at once at the Purser's Office: Miss Sidney. Wanted at once by Mr. Bower: Miss Sidney.'

Jane was halfway there before that 'at once' struck her, and then she fumed. She had barely arrived, she was not in anyone's employment yet, how dared he . . .

She came to the office, then stopped short. It could be only coincidence, but there appeared to be no one else here, apart from the uniformed purser, than——

'Miss Sidney, I presume.'

He wore country corduroys this time, a rather wide-brimmed hat, but there was no mistaking the identity of that man who had tossed her an overall in the *Southern Princess*, who had impelled her outside to be sick.

'Mr. Bower?' Jane asked faintly.

He said: 'Yes.'

'Are you packed?' William Bower inquired briskly.

Jane nodded.

'Good, then. I'm hoping I can get you a quick passage through Customs.' But his tone did not evince mere hope, it evinced haughty confidence. 'Then we can make a prompt start.'

'Start to where?'

'To Bowers, of course.'

'Urara.'

'I see you know the name.'

'John told me.' Jane added, 'John Rivers.' As there was no comment, she added again: 'He knows you.'

'A lot of people in the game do.'

'He's not in the game, if you mean the stud game. He grows hops and raises timber in Urara.'

'Interesting.' He said it in an uninterested voice. 'He'd be in the valley, then. Bowers is on the plateau, which very originally' ... he did not accompany it with a smile ... 'is called Plateau.'

'And the stud is called after you, of course.'

'A mere coincidence. I really named it after the bower-birds that are there.'

'Still there? Hasn't the activity of stables moved them on?'

'Bower-birds don't move on, they simply make a bower and then commute there from their nest. Sometimes it goes on for their lifetime. You said you were ready?'

'No. That is ... I mean there's John.'

'Yes, you mentioned him.' William Bower waited.

'I'd said I would travel down with him.'

'To Urara?'

'Yes.'

'Why the devil would you say that?' He glared at her.

'Why shouldn't I?' She glared back.

'Because during my employment of you——'

'You're forgetting that I'm in a slightly different category from the usual employee.'

'Ah, I'd expected this.' William Bower pushed the wider-brimmed hat than usual, a hat he had not taken off yet, to the back of his head. 'My uncle couldn't have made a more idiotic arrangement if he'd tried.'

'I have no doubt that he did try,' she said coldly.

'On your persuasion?'

'If you're referring to that one-fifth——'

'What else?'

'I had nothing to do with it.'

'But plenty to do with it now,' he suggested.

'No. I mean——' She stopped. How could she say to this unapproachable man that the final and *telling* point of Rusty's 'idiotic arrangement', as William Bower expressed it, had been the loving fact of Rusty himself?

'I think you might be under some misapprehension, Miss Sidney.' The man was packing a pipe and lighting it. 'You have that one-fifth all right, for what it's worth, but it's more bonus than status. I really mean to say that it comes *because* of your employment under a new boss, not *with* it. In short, employment and not a directive capacity.'

'Bonus.' Jane repeated his word.

'That's what I said.'

'But' ... a pause from Jane now ... 'still—a telling bonus?'

'You have one-fifth of the stock that have come from U.K. Note that, please, the U.K. fellows only. Taking in their consignment costs, their quarantine costs, a million and one other costs, at present that one-fifth means nothing at all—indeed, you're well in debt. But my uncle must have considered all this, for he added the stipulation of your employment. Under me. You are employed right now, and the steep way charges soar in this country you should be glad of this. So' ... a shrug ... 'start earning your money.'

Jane had flushed vividly. 'I didn't intend not to. I meant to settle the new lot, check up on the old, then——'

'And then jaunt down with Rivers? No need for any of that. I've seen to the first three fellows, made arrangements for the next three, so we can get away at once.' He added, 'By air.'

'John is going by road.'

'Unless he flies to Ribberton on the coast, the only other way, there's no rail there.'

She was disappointed, she had looked forward to seeing the country down to Urara. She knew John would be disappointed, too.

'Have you booked for me?' she asked hopefully, hopeful that he might not have done so, might try now and be unsuccessful.

'I fly my own craft,' he said shortly.

'Then' ... inadequately ... 'at least I must tell John.'

'Oh yes, certainly tell him.' Before she could move, he moved to the desk, and the next moment Jane heard: 'Wanted at the Purser's Office, Mr. Rivers.'

What an autocrat this man was! Yet ... seeing John already down the passage ... what a successful one!

But when the valley man joined them, Bowers treated him amiably. They talked together for a while on Urara. William Bowers asked him if he would like an air lift down.

'There's room,' he assured him, 'it's a specially constructed craft in case I ever have to fly up a patient, and I don't think' ... a grin ... 'you're bulkier than a horse.'

'That's kind of you, but I have my own transport.' For a moment John looked wistfully at Jane. 'I brought the lorry up to Sydney, then left it here because I knew I would need it on my return. I made quite a few machinery purchases in Singapore.'

'Then we'll leave you. Please call in to Bowers should you feel like it. I know we have rather different interests' ... the slightest of pauses and the slightest of glances at Jane ... 'but you may find it a diversion.'

'Thank you, I will come. Goodbye, Jane.'

'Goodbye, John.' Jane did not put out her hand, she just smiled ... though she felt more like pulling a wry face.

As William Bowers had said, customs was soon dealt with, so evidently the 'Baron' had influence. They emerged from the wharf and Bowers hailed a taxi. 'Stock quarantine,' he directed the driver.

Jane looked at him in surprise. 'I thought we were leaving for Bowers immediately.'

'Immediately after you check your bunch.'

'I thought you checked them.'

226

'Only my four-fifths of them.' He said it coolly, but the fact that he was giving her the opportunity to see Gretel, San Marco and Ruthven before she went south impelled Jane to thank him.

For a moment he looked at her without the lift of one sardonic eyebrow, a habit, she had noticed, of his whenever he had something pertinent to say, which seemed most often. 'Like them, don't you?'

'Oh yes.'

'Is that—good?'

'How do you mean, Mr. Bower?'

'I mean' ... he said deliberately as he repacked his pipe ... 'Rodden Gair.'

'Oh——' Jane exclaimed. 'He's still with you?' she asked presently.

'No.'

'Then can—can we *not* talk about it?'

'It would bore me if you did,' he replied, and made no further exchange. After a while he indicated: 'Here is Sydney quarantine, sea view and all. I think you'll find your boys and girls are quite happy in their temporary quarters. Why are you looking at me like that?'

'Boys and girls. Rusty and I always said that.'

He did not reply, but she saw that he reddened.

'How long will Gretel, San Marco and Ruthven be?' she inquired.

'They've nearly finished their term. This next lot——'

'Why, they're here already!' Jane explained in surprise and delight. Now she would be able to say 'Goodbye, it won't be long' to Dandy. 'You certainly get things done, Mr. Bower.'

'I need to, when they get done to me.' He opened the door for her and she stepped out. She felt like answering him in his own coin, but at least he had availed her Dandy. She went across to where a float was discharging a load of three, touched two satin heads in turn ... and nuzzled a grey one. Dandy's.

The man waited for her. At last Jane turned and said, 'Thank you, I'll come now.'

He nodded and they returned to the taxi. They did not drive to Kingsford Smith where Jane had boarded a Jumbo back to England but to Bankstown where the private craft put down.

Waiting in a corner of the field was a light plane that William Bower claimed as his, a neat but capacious Cessna, custom-built, he told her. 'Made for my special needs, Miss Sidney. Climb in.'

Jane obeyed. They took off smoothly, circled the field, then set off in what he called out was a south-south-west direction. 'We don't cross the Divide,' he went on, 'only land on it when we reach Plateau on the plateau.'

They were passing over countryside now, their craft travelling in shadow on the green-gold fields beneath. Bush followed, olive-green terrain, but lit up here and there by warm yellow that the man beside her told Jane was wattle. To the right, he indicated the mountains of the Great Dividing Range, jutting pinnacles straining upwards, yet evidently not so lofty as many mountains rate, for every peak wore a crown of trees. Fascinated, Jane looked down, traced streams beneath that ended in silvery ribbons of waterfalls, traced clearings where some hardy soul had carved out a farm. Then, without any warning, a wide pasture, a golden summit that spread out lushly on four sides but was stopped by cliff edges on each of the sides, looked back at her, an oasis of neat paddocks, of perfectly symmetrical buildings imposed on the paddocks, everything as clear-cut and disciplined as in a child's farmyard set. 'Urara Plateau,' the pilot called. Then he added with pride: 'Bowers.'

No wonder he was proud, Jane thought unwillingly but honestly as she got down on a field as neatly clipped as a suburban lawn. No old thistle here, tousled bramble, sloe, just immaculately shaven grass.

A jeep was coming out for them; on its side was inscribed 'Bowers', then a bower-bird, rather the shape of a Bird of Paradise, Jane thought, imposed.

'Is he like that?' she asked of the sign.

'Yes, he's a relative of the Paradise chap. You'll see him. Hi there, Jake.' The jeep had pulled up. 'This is Jake, Miss Sidney.'

Jane smiled and the man grinned back. The bags were stowed and the jeep started the run to the model buildings she had looked down on from the Cessna.

Often, Jane thought a little spitefully, things look better from a distance, so perhaps the stud...

No, it was perfect, quite perfect, Rusty should have seen it. She said it aloud.

'I'd have liked the old man to have come out, but he had different ideas.' A small pause. 'What was Little Down like?'

'Beautiful, but not in this way. We were small.' She saw him noticing that 'we' and tightening his lips.

'*I*...' a slight emphasis ... 'am large, as you will soon see. The quarters, please, Jake. Miss Sidney will want to settle in, she can tour later.' The jeep came to a halt in front of a large red-brick building. 'It's laid out in motel style,' William Bower informed her, 'and is serviced, Miss Sidney, so don't waste any time on domestic chores. You'll find the women's quarters are to the right, the men's to the left. Separated,' the man added, 'by the canteen, an all-hours canteen, so no need to knock off to get in for a meal for fear it will go off. Jake will carry up your bags.'

Jake did carry them, and Jane followed Jake. She did not turn round to see what William Bower was doing, she knew he would still be sitting in the jeep watching her. But at the door curiosity overcame resolution, and she did turn to look.

The man looked back.

The motel, for it could have been that in layout, was two-storeyed. 'Twenty mod bedrooms,' Jake, carrying the bags and leading the way, told Jane, 'all singles, all with built-ins, television, own bath recesses.

'Then there's two big rec rooms and two laundries, though the room linen, of course, is done for Bower's boys.'

'And girls?' Jane had been wondering if there would be female strappers as well as herself.

'Girls, too, even the married couples, though they're not in the motel but in flats across the way. If you don't feel like going down for a cuppa, Miss Sidney, there's always provision in your room.' They had reached the room by now, a generous sixteen by sixteen with all that Jake had boasted, as well as a snack corner providing milk, sugar, tea, a packet of biscuits, a few tinned easy meals.

'He doesn't appear to have forgotten anything,' said Jane.

'Not him,' admired Jake.

'Where will I find the work roster?'

'Reckon you'll be written down on it?' Jake doubted. 'I'd rather gathered you weren't exactly the usual stable-hand.'

'I'm in Mr. Bower's employ,' said Jane factually. What had the Baron said to her? 'That fifth say is more bonus than status ... it becomes *because* of your employment, not *with* it.' Then: 'Employment and not a directive capacity.'

'Reckon I'll be down.' Jane adopted Jake's manner of speech. They grinned at each other.

When he had gone she looked around her. The room was very tasteful, she found. Instead of the mannish tans she rather expected in a strapper's quarters, male or female, everything leaned to a soft woodsy green. It made for a more feminine touch as well as suited the pleateau setting.

She went to the window and looked out. The view was magnificent. No mountains, for they were on the mountains, but rolling pasture as far as the eye could see, and that, Jane knew from her Cessna lookout, was where the cliffs, four sides of them, dipped down to four surrounding valleys.

She noted the immaculate lawn verges between each row

of buildings, a garden with tended plots and a shrubbery. Further to the right was a large single-storeyed house enclosed from the rest of the estate. *His* house, she thought. A rotary clothes line was idling round in the warm breeze. She saw some smallish jeans hanging from it, two pairs of them, two pullovers. Children's. So the Baron was a family man. She wondered, idly like that idle wind, about his wife.

Though she was tempted to brew some tea in the privacy of her own room, she knew that this was never a way to settle in. She brushed her hair, rubbed in a suggestion of lipstick, all the make-up she had needed in the crisp air of Surrey, then went down to the canteen. A cook in full equipment greeted her genially and asked her to name it.

'Just a cuppa,' she said, laughing. 'I know I could have fixed it myself, but I thought I'd look around.'

Harry . . . that was his name, he said . . . was anxious to show her around his quarters. He was proud of his freezer room, wall ovens, dishwashing machine.

'We run the meals on the hatch system,' he said, 'since although Mr. Bower has run to everything else, he hasn't run to waitresses. It's better, anyway, for folk to see what they're getting.' As he talked, Harry made a large pot of tea and joined her at one of the tables. He put down a plate of raisin scones.

'You think this kitchen's good, you should see the other,' he told Jane.

'The other . . . oh, you mean the Baron's? I mean Mr. Bower's?'

'No, Boss mostly eats with us.'

'But there's children.' Perhaps they were his housekeeper's family, Jane thought.

'Yes. Their mother's away for a spell. But he likes them to eat over there. Better for kids, you know.'

Jane did not know, she believed children should eat *en famille*, she believed family men should remain with their family. But before she could continue on the subject, Harry continued on the 'other' kitchen he had mentioned.

231

'Strictly secret, not the kitchen itself but what they make there, though I can tell you some of the ingredients I sent over.' Harry tabulated them. 'Powdered milk, glucose, rolled oats——'

'You·mean for the horses?'

'That's the reason this place functions,' Harry smiled. 'All this' ... he waved his arm around ... 'is just to keep folk happy doing the function. More tea?'

Jane said it had been a large cup, took it to the machine, thanked Harry and went back to her room.

As soon as the girls came in, she would introduce herself—they probably would be younger than she was; most girl strappers started in their teens and were married before they became seniors. She had been a little older than that herself when she had thought in such a way and maturity should have assured such a conclusion, but ... a shrug ... it hadn't come out as she had dreamed.

She went to the window again; the small clothes were off the line now. She was about to leave to place round some of her things when she glimpsed a figure rotating madly from the wire of the clothes-line, the idle wind being helped vigorously by a junior operator whirling it from the ground. Only two small people wearing identical basin crops that she knew of would do that, Jane thought eagerly, it was precisely the outrageous prank that a certain pair would embark on.

She leaned out, called, 'Robert ... Roberta!' but they did not hear her. She saw them leave the line, climb over their enclosing fence to the stud side, then disappear, undoubtedly on more mischief, for they were an incorrigible ... indirigible, they had said on the ship ... pair.

On the ship. He, the Baron, had been on the ship. So *he* was Father William, the voice they had obeyed so promptly. He was the parent of Robert and Roberta, yet she had never thought of placing them together. She doubted, though, if it would make things any easier for her—that man would be a disciplinarian with his staff as well as his children—but she had taken to the imps, and hurrying to the door she ran down the steps to catch up with them, wherever they had gone, enjoy a reunion.

It was on the last step down that Jane heard the shrill scream. She looked around her, trying to trace the source of the scream—a child's scream, and not, Jane judged, even keeping in mind the naughty traits of the impish duo a cry-wolf scream. Whichever of the twins had cried out had really meant the alarm. Meant it urgently.

'Robert, Roberta!' she called, hoping that the scream would come again, since not yet knowing the layout of the place she had no idea which way to turn. Though surely, she thought frantically, someone else in this vast settlement, this—well, this small town you could almost say, had heard. She looked back to the quarters. No one in sight. Perhaps Harry in the kitchen ... But there was no time to check. She remembered from Little Down how completely far away a person can be at even a hundred yards. Once one of the fillies had fallen and—— But not to waste time on thoughts now, she had to find the source of that one urgent cry, and at once.

Jane ran forward, looking left and right as she hurried, hoping desperately for someone, anyone. A strapper returning, a hand sweeping out a stable, a gardener, a handy man, anyone who could direct her to the possible source of a child's scream. Help her.

There was no one at all.

'Robert ... Roberta!' she shouted again. Surely they would reply, even if it was another scream. She listened for the scream, she waited for it. Prayed for it.

Now she was running between what seemed unending small buildings, machine rooms, fodder rooms, all the usual offices associated with a stud. Then there was a row of neat bungalows, the married quarters probably, she thought vaguely, surely someone, a wife, a resting hand, should be around.

No one.

Jane could not have said afterwards how long she would have run, to the end of the plateau, perhaps, even to a cliff edge to peer desperately (and stupidly, since the cry could not have penetrated from that far) over, had she not glimpsed, between the tight buildings, a sparkling patch of blue.

She ran some yards before the fact of that blue hit her. Blue! In a world of unrolling green! Blue in that circumstance must mean water, pool water. There was a pool, and the children had gone to it. That scream had been when one of them had fallen in. But there had been no scream after it. Could it mean that the other one had gone to help, and had——

She did not know how well the children swam, for that matter she did not know whether they swam at all. They had looked jealously down on the Tourist pool on the *Southern Princess*, but that had been because there had been fun going on, not because they envied the swimming it offered them, for had they wanted to swim they could have done it in their own quite superior First-Class pool.

Jane had retraced her steps to the patch between the buildings where she had glimpsed the blue now. It was still there, so it hadn't been a trick of her imagination, she had not been seeing the sky in reverse, and, turning her direction, she raced towards the shining rectangle, wondering fearfully why she could glimpse no sign of life there.

Then as she got nearer she saw that it was not the usual pool, but a pool that had been built exclusively for horses. For a moment Jane knew a fierce anger that the man could have seen to a pool for his horses before he had seen to his children. And *he* had said of her 'pony high priestess!' She saw that the reason nothing or nobody had been in sight was that the pool, because of its purpose, was much deeper than usual, that its walls were twice the rise, that the eventual capacity of the pool twice the expected amount, but that just now it was only semi-filled.

Because of this, the walls, the depth, the water amount, all making for concealment, Jane had to run right up to the

234

edge before she could check.

Yes, there they were. One face downward, the other trying to manipulate Roberta ... or was it Roberta trying to manipulate Robert? ... to an upward position again. The first twin must have entered from the shallow end, the ramp end, but like pools for people, horse pools evidently deepened as well, what was worse unmistakably deepened much more abruptly. Even though the pool was not yet filled, at the end where they struggled it was far too deep for a child.

It was too deep for these two. Even as Jane sized up the position, Roberta ... or Robert ... lost grasp of the other child, then went under as well.

CHAPTER THREE

AFTERWARDS Jane could not remember jumping in, she could not have said whether she ran to the ramp and waded out, or whether she leapt directly into the deeper end from the other side of the pool. All she remembered being aware of in retrospect was the sudden contact of water, then the feel of Robert's basin crop . . . for it was Robert face downward and Roberta who had screamed . . . as she turned the boy over. She did not remember pushing Roberta to the shallows, and, still holding tightly on to Robert, giving the girl a hearty breath-encouraging slap between her shoulders.

Then she had turned to the boy twin. She had wasted no time. Perhaps he had been under only briefly . . . that, anyway, was her desperate hope . . . perhaps Roberta's scream had resounded not on her brother's contact with the water but on his subsequent turning over into the water, but she still wasn't taking any chances. Bending across the child, she had begun breathing evenly into his mouth.

Vaguely she had heard Roberta sobbing beside her . . . thank heaven it had been the girl on the pool side and not in the water, for though boys act quicker, are more resourceful, a female screams, and without that alerting and summoning scream——

She had heard, still vaguely, Roberta's sobs turning to sniffly noises of apparent relief, heard her say: 'Father William, it's R-Robert.'

She had felt herself pushed aside, then, still knee-deep in the pool, she had watched William Bower cover Robert's entire face, not just his mouth but nose too, with his own large one. She had heard his deep breaths.

Within a minute, Robert said: 'Am I alive?'

'You don't deserve to be.'

236

'Why are you giving me the kiss of life?'

'There's many more things I'd sooner give you, young man!'

'Really——' Jane could not stand it any longer; this was no way to talk to a child who had just cheated death.

William Bower read the reason for her indignation. 'He was a long way off snuffing it,' he announced brutally. 'In fact he could have recovered quite nicely under your own much gentler administering.'

'I could, too,' regretted Robert, 'only I felt too tired, so I just stopped there. If I'd known you were taking over, Father William, I would have got better, though. Jane doesn't have bristly hairs on her lips like you.'

'I should hope not, it's not a female ambition. Can you get up now?'

'Yes.' Robert rose a little unsteadily, but he made it to the edge. 'I was leaning over and I fell in.' He must have decided an explanation was called for.

A quick look at William Bower's face told Jane that this was not enough, and, though he had the sense not to question the boy in his soaked state, he did slip in a warning.

'Run back now and get Teresa to put you into a hot bath.' A pause. 'I'll have more to say later.'

'Was that necessary?' Jane asked as the twins ran off.

'The hot bath?'

'You know what I mean.'

'You mean the reckoning. Yes, it is necessary.'

'But you could have waited till the shock wore off.'

'Never wait, drive the lesson home as soon as the thing happens. Shall I do that now with you?' He had narrowed his eyes on her.

'I have no lesson coming,' she retorted.

He considered this. 'No, you acted pretty slickly, Miss Sidney. My thanks for your resourcefulness.'

'Can I have any post-mortems afterwards,' she inserted shortly, 'the same as Robert? I'm wet and uncomfortable.'

'Run in at once. Soak. Shoot out your clothes to be

laundered. Then——'

'Then?'

'Come to my office for a recuperative brandy.'

'Tea will do.'

'Have what you like,' he shrugged. 'I'll be having brandy.'

'But still in the office?'

'I said so.'

'Where,' she asked, 'is the office?'

'In my house.'

'Where the children are?'

'Yes. Unfortunately.'

'Un——' Jane did not finish, she felt too disgusted.

She went back to her quarters, grateful that everyone still seemed out and that she did not have to explain her bedraggled appearance. She did not soak, but she did shower vigorously. When eventually she emerged, dressed, then crossed over to the house within the enclosure, she was rosy and scrubbed, her short hair had curls with damp-hanging ends.

Teresa ... she supposed it was Teresa ... was a smiling Italian, and she showed Jane into the office. A tray of tea awaited, but, as he had said, he was taking brandy.

'I have my meals at the motel, or big house,' he tossed. 'You could say this is my wet canteen.'

'Yes, Harry told me you ate over there. He said' ... the slightest of pauses ... 'the twins eat here.'

'Of course. Adult talk, particularly stud and stable talk, is not always for tender ears. Tender, did I say? That pair?' He gave a dry laugh.

She would have liked to have given him her opinion of family, but he did not wear a receptive expression and he did not follow up the subject.

'Will your clothes be all right after their dunking?' he asked. 'Any you have a doubt about report to the bookkeeper. He'll see to a recompense.'

'Thank you.'

'No, thank you for saving ... or at least making the gesture, for, thank heaven, it wasn't needed ... the kids' lives. Why the little devils went there is beyond me.'

'I would say it was a natural consequence. It's a warm dry day.'

'So you would forgive two brats going out of bounds to try themselves in a horse pool?'

'If they have no pool of their own, yes.'

'And why should I build a pool for them?'

'Why should you ...' she echoed aghast. Pony high priestess, indeed! This man put everything, even his chilren, second to horses. Though *his* reason, she added to add more fuel to her disgust, would be entirely monetary.

'I won't argue about that,' she said coldly.

'I had no intention of arguing,' he said more coldly back. Before she could make any rejoinder, he asked: 'Tea all right?'

'Thank you.'

He had lit his pipe and now the smoke wreaths were weaving upward.

'So you knew the children on the ship?'

'Yes, I met them. We became friendly.'

'Good God!' he disbelieved.

Angry, she retorted, 'I suppose that does seem unlikely to you.'

'Unlikely is the understatement of the year!'

A few minutes went past.

'How was it you came to rescue Robert?'

'I saw the children crossing from the house, recognized them, then went off after them. It was on the bottom step that I heard the scream.' She gave a remembering shiver. 'I'm glad it was Robert who fell in, if it had been Roberta he would have jumped first without screaming as she did. It's the girls who scream.' She became aware that he was looking at her with that one raised eyebrow, and she squirmed.

'So you raced to lend succour?'

239

'Not exactly, I didn't know where to go. No one was around to ask. But luckily I saw a glimpse of the pool between some buildings.'

'Yes. I think it's a good idea, don't you?' He said it quite seriously, she saw in anger. 'A race across a beach, then a plunge through breakers would be preferable for a horse,' he went on, oblivious of her reception, 'but failing that——' He attended his pipe, and she watched him mutinously.

He did not even notice. That was the maddening part. He unmistakably believed he was doing the right thing supplying his horses with a pool while his children, while they——

'So you haven't seen around the place yet?' he broke in.

'No.'

'Then finish your tea.' He made it sound like an invitation, but she heard an order there. However, she wanted to examine her place of employment at some time, so it might as well be now, and under the boss's guidance; at least a boss should know all the answers.

'I have finished.' She got up. As they reached the door she asked: 'How are the children?'

'In bed. Strangely enough they submitted without protest. Must have been tuckered out.'

Jane thought to herself, remembering the way they had obeyed his voice on the ship, that it had been him and not the weariness that had had the effect. She followed him out of the house and through the gate to the stud.

'First, the kitchen,' William Bower said, 'and what goes with it. Not the human roast beef variety ... possibly you've seen that already.'

'Only it was tea and scones,' she nodded.

'Here' ... they had reached a building, neat, immaculate like all the buildings ... 'the magic formulas are dreamed up.'

'Are they magic?'

He grinned. 'Nothing is really magic with horseflesh, but

you can have a jolly good try by adopting good diet additives.' He led her in, and she stood in disbelief at benches of chrome and tile.

'Why not?' He said it defensively, and she knew she should have anticipated that and not shown her surprise. This man was before all else a businessman. His business was horses, these concoctions being encased in pellets were to make the business bigger and better. All the same, such equipment ...

To divert his attention from the feelings she felt must show, she asked, 'What's in the formula?'

'Apart from glucose, iron, calcium, which probably you've guessed anyway, it's strictly secret.'

'What about my consignment when they arrive?'

'Your fifth of them,' he corrected.

'They're not to participate?'

'Of course they can participate, but it still doesn't give you the right to learn a formula. For all I know you could be a spy in the camp. Besides——'

'Besides?' she asked furiously.

His answer disarmed her. Anything else he might have said could not have spread oil like these words did.

'I don't know what you delved in at Surrey, Miss Sidney,' he replied sincerely, 'but certainly your fellows don't look in need of formulas.'

'We dealt in soft rain and soft air,' she nodded, suddenly almost unbelievably nostalgic. She had to turn away. To her surprise, for she had not expected understanding ... an understanding of this variety ... from a hard, tough horseman, he went, presumably to examine something, to the other end of the room. When he returned she had herself in control once more.

'I have my own resident nutritionist and pathologist,' he announced.

'Vet?' She was sorry the moment she asked that, it brought up the subject of Rodden Gair, but what she had been inquiring was whether the vet, too, was resident, or only in attendance.

'Everyone resident,' William Bower said, and made no other comment on the matter. He turned to the door again. 'Each stable,' he informed her as they walked out, 'has its own farrier's shop, its own automatic feed-mixing hopper. My silo holds some four thousand bushels of oats.'

'*Could* there be anything else?' she disbelieved as she walked on beside him; she frankly believed no stud could provide more.

'Hot and cold showers for the boys and girls.' He must have remembered what she had said on that last occasion when he had spoken of his stock as that, for he broke off quite abruptly. 'Covered walks,' he went on presently, 'that lead to the sand rolls.'

'I can't understand it,' Jane murmured.

'Can't understand indulging a horse?'

That was not what she had meant, she had been thinking of Rodden's scorn when she had elected to stay back at Little Down to see Melinda through her foaling, yet Rodden Gair, she thought, had come from this stud. It seemed odd that in spite of all the luxury, all the indulgences, this man's employee had raised his brows at a simple human kindness. It made it all the more positive to Jane that any balm given to any of the stock here at Bowers welled from one reason only: Money.

He was talking, so reluctantly she had to listen.

'It has to be like this.' He was excusing the indulgences. 'Australia is not a "natural" for horseflesh as are England, Ireland, America ... you can include New Zealand. We have to fight for what we achieve. Those others get it on a gold plate. Here's the clinic.'

'Vet variety, of course.'

'I naturally run a casualty for the staff, but then there's always transport available to fly them over to Fetherfell across the Divide, which runs a fine hospital, and in which I support a ward.'

'Of course.' Jane could not help that.

'We have a girl in here now ... I mean we have a filly,' he corrected himself quickly. 'Bessie has leg trouble.'

He went up to the pretty, chunky grey and Jane went, too, and fondled the satin head.

'However, we still follow the old rule of operating in an open paddock,' William Bower related. He laughed ruefully. 'You can put out thousands on a hospital, some more again on an X-ray machine, a sterilizing plant, but when it comes to a crisis...' He shrugged.

'It's usually like that.' In spite of herself, of her determination to stand aloof, Jane said it eagerly. Experiences came pouring out ... she and Rusty spending days in a row in the rough acre on Stately Lady, because, in spite of her name, that elegant chestnut had refused to foal anywhere else.

'Yes,' William Bower broke in just as eagerly, 'that's the way it goes. Sometimes I think that love is not cloud nine, as the song goes, but ten cold nights in a paddock.'

Love is ten cold nights in a paddock. It had been eleven, Jane remembered, because Stately Lady had been lazy, and the paddock had been a meadow, but——

Jane was unaware that she was looking up at the man, unaware that he was looking back at her.

Then ... abruptly ... she became aware. She looked away again.

'You've just about seen it all.' His voice came matter-of-factly, she could not have believed it was the same man who had broken in before: 'Sometimes I think that love is not cloud nine but ten cold nights in a paddock.'

He asked: 'Shall we go back? It's the only place actually to go, unless you drive out and go over a cliff.'

'But there must be roads to the valley.'

'Glorified tracks only.'

'But the timber down there has to get out.'

'Of course, but not by way of Plateau. No, the timbermen, hop-men, eucalyptus oil men ... yes, they go in for a mixed plate in the valley ... avail themselves of the road to the coast. You could say we're fairly isolated up here, we're the top of the tree, so to speak, no way to get out except to fly or climb down, and that's why we have to be self-sufficient.'

They had reached the centre point of the stud again, it almost could have been called a village square, Jane thought, for Bowers was large enough to be a small village.

'So you swim,' he broke in casually.

'Yes,' Jane said, a little surprised.

'And the kids don't.'

Now she was considerably surprised, surprised at a father not knowing that. However, she did not know really about the children herself. She had not found out on the ship, and she had not really found out here, either. All she had known when she had reached the horse pool's edge was that a child was in difficulties and that the other child had made it difficult for herself by trying to help.

'It could be,' she said, 'that Robert stunned himself in the fall.'

'I didn't see any evidence on him. I'll question him later, and if he and Roberta can't swim, then——' He was interrupted in what he was going to say by the bookkeeper coming over to discuss some matter. Jane was introduced to Stan Littleton, invited to call in to see how his side of the stud business functioned, then, as the men went off together, she turned back to the digs.

She had yet to meet the nutritionist, pathologist, probably a dozen grooms, a dozen exercising hands, and—the vet. She did not dwell on that.

A cantering behind her attracted her attention, and she turned to see two female strappers coming in from their duties. They could have been girls from Little Down had any girls beside herself served at Little Down, they could have been stablehands anywhere, with their fresh faces, bright eyes and wind-combed hair. They were young. Well, she had expected that. Only the unlucky in love reached her own age, Jane thought, without that confirming ring.

At that thought her eyes had dropped instinctively to the girl, Maureen...

Jane would have recognized that ring in any corner of the world. She expected there could be many aquamarines with silver filigree settings, but there is always something about your own ring...

Your own ring. What was she thinking about? She had sent the ring back to Rodden, it had not belonged to her any more.

And now, unless she was mistaken, Maureen wore it. Well, that made sense. Maureen was a very pretty girl, and Rodden, besides liking pretty girls, had worked here.

Jane accepted the girls' invitation to join them in a cup. She walked behind them to the canteen, answering their questions, asking questions of her own. But never the question she wanted to ask. It wasn't that there was any hurt left, she had accepted everything long ago, it was just that she wanted to *know*, for if you knew, then naturally you handled things better, and if Maureen was engaged to Rodden, even though he now worked away from here there could come a time when she, Jane, and Rodden met up again. So it must be well-handled, Jane thought.

She was trying to handle her cup without spilling any tea, and it was difficult because at the same time she was endeavouring to manipulate herself into a better ring-observing position ... *just to be sure* ... when the canteen telephone pealed.

Harry answered it and said, 'Yes, Boss.' He turned to the tables and called: 'Mr. Bower wants to see you, Miss Sidney.'

Jane did not move. The house was no further than an enclosed yard away, surely, even though he was the boss——

Harry finished: 'Over there.'

The topic of the Boss's call appeared concluded. The girls looked at her expectantly, then went on to something else. Everyone in the room looked quietly expectant ...

expectant of her immediate obedience. What an autocrat this fellow was! Again ... many times again ... Jane thought that.

But to sit on, to wait for him to come to her, and somewhere within her Jane accepted the fact that he wouldn't come, would only draw attention, something she did not want. Finishing her tea—at any rate she did that—Jane got up, nodded around, and left.

William Bower opened the door for her. Jane could hear dishes being clattered and presumed that Teresa was busy with nursery tea.

'I've found out that the brats can't swim,' he said, leading the way to the room where she had spoken with him earlier today. 'I examined Robert for any knock-out marks. No, he simply overbalanced, fell in, then couldn't right himself. A fine state of affairs.'

Fine, indeed! rankled Jane.

'So I asked him. He hated telling—went around it all ways before it came out.'

'That's natural,' Jane defended.

'Not being able to swim isn't. I intend to right it at once.'

'Where? The horse pool?'

'No.'

'There's another?'

'No, but there will be. I intend building one for the staff.'

For the staff! And yet when it came to his two children——

'However,' William Bower went on, 'that will take time ... months. Besides, even if it was fenced, grown-ups could still suffer from young trespassers, and no adult wants a youngster monkeying around.'

'So what do you do?'

'Down the valley we have the Urara River. There's a section of it that all of us residents have made safe and attractive. Thousands of tons of sand have been put down, old

246

logs removed. The shelf is very gradual. In fact you could say it's a real charmed stretch.'

'The children will learn there?'

He was lighting his pipe.

'That depends on you.'

'On me?'

'Depends on whether you'll teach them.'

'I'd love to teach them. I feel very strongly about children swimming. But I came here to work, remember, not to——'

'You have different ideas of work, then, than I have. To teach that pair an Australian crawl——'

'I believe dog-paddle will do as a start—after all, the purpose is to bring them to a pitch of saving their own lives, not winning a race.'

'Then will you?'

'My consignment——' she began.

'Won't be out for over a week.'

She looked at him levelly. 'If you're really saying I have nothing to do with Bowers, only to do with what Rusty is consigning to Bowers, say it.'

'One-fifth of it,' he put in.

'Are you saying that?'

'No. I'm asking you to teach the kids to swim. The same salary as if you were working on the horses.'

As she sat silent, he probed, 'What gives, Miss Sidney? I'm making a straightforward request of you. Does everything I say have to be met with suspicion?'

'I wasn't suspecting, I was disbelieving.'

'Isn't it the same?'

'Not that. I was disbelieving that a parent couldn't see to such a basic thing for a child as swimming.'

'Yes,' he agreed coolly. 'But then they're exceptional parents.'

She looked at him in more disbelief, disbelieving now that a man could not only hold such an opinion of himself, but openly flaunt it.

'I'm not asking for any excuses' ... *he* wouldn't, Jane seethed ... 'but when you have two exceptional people, you can't expect the niceties of ordinary parents.'

'Since when has preservation been a "nicety"?' she flashed.

'Yes, that was the wrong word,' he conceded. 'What I really meant to say was that Gareth has always been preoccupied with his gift, while my cousin-in-law——'

'Your cousin-in-law?' Jane broke in.

He raised that brow again. 'Isn't there such?' he shrugged.

'You mean—the wife of your cousin?'

'My cousin Gareth's wife Dorothy.' William Bower paused a moment, his eyes raking Jane's face. 'Owners,' he informed her drily, 'of the brats.'

CHAPTER FOUR

JANE sat silent, wishing desperately she could think of something to say, something to divert his amused attention from her flag-red cheeks and her obvious air of guilt. For she *had* been guilty without inquiring first of putting these children down as his, any naughtiness they flaunted as his fault.

But it was no use. Her mother had always laughed over Jane's air of guilt, she had said her daughter was an open book. Now the man opposite was reading the open book and smiling lopsidedly at her discomfiture.

'You thought——' he said, then laughed.

'Why not?' Words came at last, only not the off-putting words Jane had searched for. She had wanted to close the subject, or at least change it, but now she was continuing it instead. 'You had them in your care,' she accused indignantly, 'they called you Father William.'

'My name is William. In case you've forgotten, it's William Bower.'

'I hadn't forgotten. But why Father William?'

'You should have asked them that yourself.'

'I did,' she recalled unwillingly. She recalled, too, the answer. Roberta's answer. ' "William's his name," the girl twin had reported, "and once he said he'd kick Robert down the stairs." ' Jane also recalled, this time from Robert, that a bucket of water had been strategically placed.

So Father William was not their paternal parent but their second cousin. Jane worked out the relationship laboriously.

'Lewis Carroll,' she heard herself murmuring aloud.

'From the sound of him once as beggared by kids as I am,' William Bower inserted.

'I wouldn't say that.'

249

'Miss Sidney, you're not being asked to say anything.'

'Only do something.'

'Yes, teach them to swim . . . only we're not finished with Father William yet, are we? Let's get the thing straight.'

'You mean your guardianship of your second cousins?'

'Is that how it goes?' he asked admiringly. 'No, I didn't mean exactly that, I meant your fool conclusion.'

'I don't think it was foolish. You had them with you on the ship.'

'Where evidently you didn't associate the three of us as belonging.'

'And you have them now.' She ignored the interruption. 'Surely anyone would conclude then that you were their parent.'

He was leaning across the desk to her. He did not speak for several moments, and every moment built up a curious nervousness in Jane. She could not have said why, but it was all she could do not to get up and run out of the room. He could be very frightening, this Father William of the children's, no wonder they obeyed him on the double.

'Look at me,' he ordered at last, but Jane looked anywhere but at him, 'look at me, then tell me if that is the sort of arrangement you think *I* would have in my married life.'

'I don't know what arrangement you'd have. I don't even know if you're married.'

'Then I'm not. Also I would have things very differently. My youngsters would be with me, and so, by heaven, would my wife.'

'Why are you telling me this?' she asked.

'Because you have the presumption to associate me with a position like this.'

'Is it that important?'

'You appeared to think so before.'

'I meant,' she corrected herself, 'is it that important that I should be told so forcibly?'

That stopped him a moment. Then he said in a rather surprised voice: 'Yes . . . yes, it is.'

He was staring at her. She felt it. It had to be feeling, for she was not looking back at him. She found she could not look.

'What kind of talents have the children's parents?' she tried to divert.

He permitted diversion. He said, 'They paint. Dorothy does portraits, Gareth landscapes. They're both good. And that's not just someone who doesn't know art but knows what he likes talking, critics who do know are agreed that the two Courtneys——'

'Courtneys?' she echoed.

'You've heard of them?'

'Of course. I think most people have.' Dorothy Courtney with her exquisite child studies, Gareth Courtney with his vigorous canvases had reached the European scene as well as the scene in Australia.

'Then I'm to look for talent in the children?' Jane said with enthusiasm.

'No.' She glanced inquiringly at him. 'Not essentially. They're adopted children. You might remember I said the owners, not the parents, of the brats. There were none forthcoming of their own, so they adopted this pair. Gareth, my father's sister's child, and his wife Dorothy felt in their absorbing life that they must give out as well as take in.'

'That was good of them.'

'As well as gifted, they're good people. This branch of the family' ... he made a gesture to himself ... 'must rely on the goodness, I'm afraid, for I have no talent.'

'The stud?' she asked in all seriousness, for to her way of thinking a stud was much more than the usual occupation.

'Only requires a pair of strong hands.'

She did not comment. She was thinking suddenly and sharply of his 'love is ten cold nights in a paddock', and the quiet manner in which it had touched her.

'It must be hard for the children having their father and mother away,' Jane said a little breathlessly, afraid she might voice those other thoughts.

251

'It's the first time it's happened, though Gareth and Dorothy sometimes go solo. I suppose,' he had the grace to submit, 'I should keep their talents in mind when I say it wouldn't happen to me.'

So he was on to that again, that masterful head-of-the-family act.

'But then,' he went on, 'I would never choose an artist.'

'No,' she agreed, incensed, 'you would consider all things beforehand—as in a stud.'

'Of course. Surely, as a strapper, as someone among horseflesh, you're not examining me on that? You must have learned from my uncle the necessity of acquiring desired qualities in a brood mare, the opposite desired qualities in the sire. For instance, a long-backed mare should be crossed with a heavy-ribbed stallion, and——'

'I was speaking,' Jane broke in, 'of you, not your business.'

'Then I, too,' he said coolly, 'would know what would be advisable for me to take on, what wouldn't be.'

'Don't you mean whom?' Jane corrected.

'I told you I was without talent,' he came back, 'as well as being unartistic, my grammar shows holes. I'm no man of words.'

Yet—love is ten cold nights in a paddock, Jane thought.

'No,' William Bower went on, 'my type would need a more basic mate than an artist.'

'A dairymaid, perhaps,' Jane said flippantly.

'Admirable. A country girl would be a very advisable choice. Only' ... a pause ... 'never a stud variety.'

She had not been looking at him, intentionally not looking at him. But now ... angrily ... she did. He stared intentionally back at her, and for some reason she thought of old Rusty and his 'mutual look'. This look was the very opposite to that. She waited.

'Rodden Gair,' William Bower reminded her in a low voice.

'What about him?'

'You tossed him, didn't you?'

'No, I——'

'Oh, we all know you put it in fancy words, but you showed Rodden where to go.'

'Is that what he said?'

'He didn't say anything. He just came back, and a month later a ring came back. I expect he should be grateful at least for that.'

'You've only half the truth. I was coming, but Melinda——'

'You threw him over,' he said factually.

'All right, if you want it like that.'

'How did *you* want it?' he came in. 'As dedication? As work first? "I want to come," the pony high priestess intones, "but——"' William Bower laughed scornfully. 'So,' he concluded, 'no female strapper for me.'

'And yet you're devoted to your work,' she baited.

He reddened slightly. 'It's just that to me. Just work.'

'But work close to your heart,' she suggested. 'The "girls" and the "boys".' She quoted him, not caring if he reddened properly now from the embarrassment he had shown before. He was a very male male, she thought. '"Love is ten cold nights in a paddock,"' she added triumphantly.

'Trust a female to store that up!' he came in acidly.

'I didn't store it, the words struck a chord in me, because once I'd spent ten plus one. Her name was Stately Lady.'

'Not Melinda?' he said like a whiplash.

'You store up things, too, don't you, Mr. Bower.'

There was a pause, a long one.

Then: 'In a stud, the nearest to you is the vet,' William Bower said quietly. 'Rodden was my vet. When he returned from England he was a broken man.' He tapped at his pipe.

Jane looked at him helplessly. There were many things she could have said, but she could see he had closed himself up; you cannot explain to a shut door. She wondered what Rodden had told him, but she did not wonder about Rodden's attitude; he always had been a master of attitudes, she knew that now.

'I sent him away,' William Bower announced factually. When she did not question him, he explained, 'Married staff here move into the flats.'

'Yes, I saw them.'

'One was to have been for Rodden and his English wife. I couldn't have him staying on here to pass each day by what might have been his haven.'

The falseness of Rodden infuriated Jane. She took it out on William Bower. She said deliberately, 'When do the violins play?'

'You're a very cold, collected, calculating young woman, Miss Sidney. You stayed behind in Surrey because to leave might have endangered the hand-out you anticipated eventually from my uncle.'

Rodden had been long before that, she had never anticipated anything, Rusty's gift had been a complete surprise, but all at once Jane felt too tired to fight back.

'Yes,' she said recklessly, 'I did just that. I'm sorry about Rodden. Evidently he suffers more in retrospect; he wasn't what I call a broken man when he left me. Also he appears to have recovered. Maureen is wearing my—wearing a similar ring to the one I returned.'

'Rodden is vetting at one of my smaller satellite studs over at Fetherfell, across the Divide. On my advice he took out his flying licence, and I've provided him with a small plane, so he can visit Maureen as any ordinary suburban man can visit his fiancée.'

'Maureen is that, then?'

'She is.'

'That's very nice,' Jane said. 'Now can we return to what you wanted to see me about?'

'The swimming,' he nodded, allowing the closing of the subject. 'Pending the release of your first consignment in several weeks, instead of making ordinary strapping your way of earning your keep, you can keep an eye on the twins.'

'Will the parents agree to that?'

'They'll be very pleased,' he assured her. 'They don't usually both leave home together, but this time Dorothy was asked to do a course in Paris, and Gareth was finishing a client's order in Singapore. I took the kids across to see their father for a break for all of us. Only' ... feelingly ... 'it wasn't. I never considered Paris except as too unsuitable for nippers like them. But' ... feelingly again ... 'Paris couldn't have been worse for me.'

'Nor for them. They were bored up in First.'

'There were fewer people to drive mad in First,' he said back. 'School had been arranged, but it fell through, or at least the school the parents wanted. So there was nothing for it than to be inflicted. If you can ease that infliction for several weeks...'

'You dislike children, don't you?' She looked at him pityingly.

'As a matter of fact in my unguarded moments I like them.'

'Why must moments be guarded?'

'Because of people like you,' he said at once, 'people ready to pounce, ready to remember and relate back.'

'Boys and girls,' she recited slyly, 'ten cold nights in a paddock. I promise you I'll remember just as well when you're unguarded over Robert and Roberta.'

'Only them?' he asked unexpectedly.

She looked at him in surprise, but whatever had impelled him to speak like that had left him. He looked back, and except that there were steps on the verandah outside the look would have gone on, that odd uncalculated look...

Someone knocked, and, at William Bower's call, came in.

'Miss Sidney, this is my present Bowers vet. Tim Harris. Tim, Jane Sidney.'

Jane turned to a stocky but well-proportioned young man

255

eyeing her with unconcealed approval. The hand that took hers was strong and friendly, and she grasped his back in the same manner. He seemed nice, she thought.

'It's Sovereign Gold,' Tim said to his boss, 'that old chronic hoof condition is playing up again.'

William Bower turned to Jane. 'Sovereign Gold has good connections. I had hopes of the colt proving himself as a top-class stayer this year. He's galloped brilliantly on occasions, but failed just as frequently.'

'It sounds rather like it might be pedal-ostitis,' said Jane, remembering an instance at Little Down, and the inflammation of the pedal bone that one of their boys had suffered.

Tim was looking appreciatively at Jane. 'You're so right. As soon as there's pressure on the hoof, Sovereign is in severe pain. We've taken more X-rays. Perhaps you'd like to see them, Miss Sidney, see Sovereign.'

'Oh, I would!' Jane stood up.

She followed the vet to the door, rather relieved to be finished with Bower, but before she reached the verandah William Bower's voice stopped her.

'You left this, Miss Sidney.'

'Excuse me,' Jane returned.

The man was standing at the table. He did not offer anything, and she realized he only had called her back to say something.

'He's even more vulnerable than Gair,' he said coolly.

She followed his trend, and flushed with indignation, but before she could speak, Bower went on.

'I wouldn't want Tim hurt, too. And you do rather gather vet scalps, don't you?' An unsmiling smile.

'Yes, Mr. Bower,' she said, 'they're my favourite scalps.'

'No boss's scalps?'

'I've only had one boss, and he was elderly.'

'You must try a younger variety.'

'And be scalped myself?'

'Miss Sidney, you read my thoughts.' He nodded carlessly as she turned to join Tim again.

But he did come to the door to call out to his vet.

'The lady has had a long day, Tim, a rather eventful day. Don't keep her too long.' As with everything that Willam Bower said, it sounded a suggestion but was really an order. Tim did not seem to mind being ordered, however. He promised to look after Jane, and they went off.

Sovereign Gold was in the paddock where the trouble had taken him. Jane examined the pedal bone and confided a few things that Rusty had done to Silver Bell. Rusty had been no vet, but he had had a lot of experience ... and a lot of success. Tim listened attentively, and Jane recalled how Rodden had smiled thinly and patronizingly over the old man's wisdoms. Tim was entirely different. She liked him, too, liked his friendly approach, liked his manliness. But ... stepping back a pace, and Tim looking up questioningly, and a little disappointed ... she must watch her step with William Bower's eyes on her.

'I'm sorry, Tim, but it's been a long day.' It had been a very long day, she could hardly credit it was only one day. But then they had berthed in the early a.m., and flying made minutes of miles.

At once Tim was apologizing, taking her over to her digs.

Jane went up the stairs at once, deciding to skip dinner, even though she wanted to meet the rest of the stud. She passed Maureen in the corridor, and the girl flashed her a bright smile. She can't know, Jane thought. I hope she doesn't know in the future. There's always a tension, a distrust in a situation like this. The thing to do is not to meet Rodden because Rodden is the only way Maureen can find out. I don't think William Bower would tell her, he sounded quite fond of Maureen. She seems a very reasonable child, too, but no girl wants another girl's ring.

She showered ... the second time since she had come to Bowers she shrugged under the spray ... came out, got into a gown and made a cup of tea.

She didn't finish it, though, she was too weary. She

hoped she was not too over-tired to sleep. At first sleep did elude her, and then she was drifting. She was saying: 'Love is ten cold nights in a paddock,' then changing it to eleven in a meadow.

An English meadow. With Rusty. Not an Australian paddock with cold, efficient, estimating, enigmatic William Bower.

'Father William,' she mumbled. And slipped off.

It was bright daylight when she opened her eyes. She wondered drowsily what had aroused her at this particular moment, she felt there had been a little noise somewhere. Something attracted her attention at the window, and she saw it was a sheet of paper with badly printed letters: HURRY UP.

She smiled, but wiped the smile off as she crossed to the window and saw the twins on the roof top above her dangling down the sign. Luckily, she thought, feeling with William on this occasion, the roof was a flat type.

'Hurry up!' They repeated their printed message.

'You shouldn't be there!' she shouted.

'We wouldn't if you were up.'

'You're taking us down the valley,' said Roberta.

'Father William says so,' called Robert.

'You're bad children, you could be killed!' she scolded.

'Everyone can be killed. The window could drop down on your head.'

'Robert could drop on it,' Roberta said admiringly, admiring her brother's greater daring in leaning over.

Quickly Jane stepped back, and at the same time saw the note. That was what must have awakened her, the sound of the note being pushed under the door. She took it up.

'Dear Miss Sidney, Apropos our discussion [apropos! So he was not entirely adverse to words!] in the garages you'll find a small car for your use. Ask Donnelly. I have no doubt that a stablehand can drive a car as well as ride a horse. If not, we must think of something else. Please be careful, I have every wish to return both minors in a sound state. Careful for yourself as well, though I doubt if I need remind you of this, as you would know, as I do, that a forfeited fifth share would only benefit me, which should be sufficient incentive for you not to take risks. There's only one track, so you can't lose the way. Harry will pack a hamper. Don't forget towels. Have a bearable day.

W. Bower.'

She put the letter down, dressed as quickly as she could between crossing to the window to see if the twins were still intact, then she ran down the stairs to the canteen, collected a hamper that William Bower must have ordered, and emerged to find the children waiting for her.

'We thought you'd never come. Did you bring your swimming togs?'

'Yes. Did you?'

Their skips and whoops proclaimed that they had. The three of them crossed to the garages.

Donnelly, also prepared, had a manoeuvrable small car awaiting them. Jane found the gears familiar, and within minutes the trio were on a track that Donnelly indicated.

It ran, a narrow earth ribbon, through the lush green swathe of the plateau until the rolling paddocks ended, then it descended cautiously, for caution was needed down the steep cliffside, past peaks, gorges, sudden deep gulches, great isolated rocks, splaying waterfalls into a valley. Between keeping her attention strictly on the track, Jane darted brief looks ahead, and saw, in the distance, that paddocks fanned out once again from the valley towards the coast, mostly cleared paddocks for cultivation, but in the dent of every small rise in them blue-smudged shadows from the overlooking mountains in the unfolding golden-green of the grass.

'It's beautiful!' Jane had stopped the car.

'The pool,' came an impatient duet from the back seat. With a little sigh, Jane reduced another gear and started carefully down once more.

She would have loved to have known the trees. When she asked the twins they said, 'Gums, of course.'

'Not all of them. Some of these are quite different.'

'Red gum, silver gum, scribbley. There's billions,' they tossed. They were obviously anxious to get to their goal.

There was no trouble in finding the pool. Rounding a bend at the bottom of the cliff, a grassy bank under willows with a wide golden sand frontage ... the gift of the Urara residents, Jane remembered from William Bower ... greeted them.

It was a charming spot; the residents could not have chosen better. The water idled by in a gentle pace that would never alarm new swimmers, but it moved sufficiently to keep it clear and singing, in fact the only addition to its shine and sparkle was a floating leaf.

Also, a man, swimming now towards Jane, lifting his hand in delighted greeting.

It was John, and, just as delighted, Jane raised her arm and waved back.

'Who is he?' asked Roberta, but she did not wait for an answer. Robert had beaten her in, so there was no time for Jane's explanation.

Jane herself wasted no time as well. William Bower had said that the shelf of the rivulet was a safe and gradual one, but the sparkle of the water was enticing, the children obviously unafraid, so she must be extra careful. She was grateful to John that he caught the purpose and did not hinder her with any talk until the first lesson was over, and the children, a little tired, were launching bark boats from the bank.

They had done exceptionally well, they were fluid children, agile, fit. They would be naturals, Jane thought.

'Perhaps,' said Robert, 'our real mother and father were Olympic swimmers and we've taken after them.' So the twins had been told the truth, Jane gleaned, and evidently, by their contented faces, told in a wise way.

'We were chosen, you know, Jane,' Roberta added casually.

That had been after they had emerged on Jane's insistence almost waterlogged from the stream. Now they lazily launched boats and Jane could turn and greet John.

'I didn't expect you.'

'I told you I was a Uraran.'

'Yes, but it was only yesterday we left the ship.' It seemed impossible to Jane it was only that, so much seemed to have happened.

'You thought it would take me longer,' he nodded. 'I didn't waste any time. Also, I'm just arriving now.'

'You haven't been home, then?'

'No. I always carry trunks for the times when I pass this spot—it's a lovely place, isn't it?'

'It's beautiful.' She told him William Bower's plans for the teaching of the children.

'That's wonderful. I'll be seeing you, then.'

'How far away are you?' she asked.

'You passed it,' he told her.

'I'm sure we didn't pass a house.'

'Like to bet on it?' he grinned. 'Call the kids and we'll go there for lunch'

'I have a hamper.'

'Then you can eat from it if you want to be independent. However' ... the twins, having finished their launching, returning ... 'I make rare Johnny cakes.'

'Johnny cakes!' They took it up in a delighted chorus.

'Why not?' John laughed. 'My name is John.' He turned to Jane. 'I'll take one, you take the other. Follow me.'

Jane hesitated, at once the thought of William Bower crossing her mind, but the first lesson had been successfully concluded, the children were eager to go a d ... With a smile she took Robert and got into the small car.

They retraced only a few hundred yards, then turned into

a side track making its own canyon as it wound through thick trees. From his several yards ahead of her, John called of the trees: 'Blackwoods. Sassafras. Mahogany.'

'*Not* all gums,' Jane told Robert.

There were small musk trees and tree ferns, too, fallen logs from dead trees covered with lichen, mosses and old man's beard. In fact there was so much overgrowth and undergrowth that there seemed no room for anything but leaves.

But there was room for a house, Jane found, negotiating a bend after John had, a low, oiled-timber one, looking as at home as though, like the trees encircling it, it had grown there, too.

Delighted, Jane got out. It was a lovely place, built to fit in with the woods, with John's hopfields further along the valley, with the eucalyptus distillery he was telling her he also had, though it was tucked away in a fold of the hill, he said, behind the house. 'I have to include all the variations I can, Jane, these times competition is tough.'

He was making the Johnny cakes, for the twins wou'd give him no peace, he said ruefully, until he produced the promised batch.

'Me, too,' smiled Jane, looking at John's frothing mixture. 'Why,' she asked, 'such a big house?'

'I've always intended it for a family house.' John looked up from his mixing at Jane.

'I hope you have your family, John,' she said.

The Johnny cakes were wonderful, there was not a crumb left. There was also no room in the twins for Harry's offerings. Jane wondered if Harry might tell William Bower about that.

After the meal, John took them down to his timber section, and Jane stood sadly with him by some of the bigger trees marked for cutting.

'Yes, I feel the same,' John nodded, sensing her mood, 'but that's life, Jane. Come and see a brighter side ... at least it goes to provide a brighter life.'

'The hops?'

'Yes.'

It was not a large hop garden, just more bread and butter, John told her, on his plate. Some of the fellows in the district had gone in entirely for hops, he said, and when the picking was on, the valley was worth visiting. New Australians came in as well as the old ones, and the variations in the cooking, and, at night, in the dancing, was exciting.

'We'll come,' promised the twins.

'To pick, too?' asked John. 'Being a small grower I don't hire hands as the others have to do, and I'd be glad of help.' He showed the children and Jane how he had provided vast networks of strung wires for the hops, supported by a forest of poles. 'Self-grown poles,' he boasted.

'Now come and examine the third home-grown product, the distillery. Tell me if you see a difference in the trees, Jane.'

They were certainly gums again, but instead of Robert's 'billions' of varieties, there seemed only one type.

'It happens,' John said when she told him this. 'Sometimes a valley of blue gum builds up a stronghold and won't let anything else in. It doesn't happen frequently, and that's where I'm lucky.'

'Why, John? Don't you like the other gums?' This valley of John's was all blue gum.

'An identical valley of trees makes for a good eucalyptus yield. I'm getting twenty gallons a week from this little acreage, Jane. You could say the oil is the jam on my bread.'

He told her his simple but effective method of piping off and condensing. As he spoke he rolled leaves in his hard workman's hands, and sniffed them, and Jane did the same. They smiled across at each other.

The children had come with them, but must have got bored with the technical explanation and sauntered off. When they did not return in the next ten minutes, Jane started to fuss.

'No need for worry,' insisted John comfortingly, 'though it looks a formidable wood they can't go far where we stand now.'

'The Australian bush——' Jane feared.

'Should be treated with respect, I'll give in, but right here it's a corner, and they can't get out unless they climb out, and I hardly think' ... looking up at the ramparts ... 'they'll do that. I'll give them a cooee ... that means come here, did you know? ... and they'll be bounding back.'

But they didn't bound back. At the end of another five minutes John repeated his assurance of safety, to which Jane replied: 'Perhaps, but I hardly like returning the twins late on my first day.'

He agreed with her on that, and gave another summons, louder than before, following it with: 'Come out, you two, or no more Johnny cakes!'

They came bounding down a track, full of apologies.

'The man in the bush kept us,' panted Roberta.

'Kept you, you mean,' corrected Robert. He added, 'He wanted to sculp her.'

'Scalp should be more like it,' John scolded mildly. 'Don't worry, Jane, I know the old fellow. He comes here now and then ... it's an abandoned woodman's humpy round the next valley and free for all ... to live with nature. Quite harmless.'

'Not so old,' said Roberta, but Jane took no notice of her ... then. She was bustling the children to the car.

'We must get up to the plateau at once.'

Although the climb was steep, the little car took it well. The moment they were on the flat, Jane accelerated to home.

She was garaging the car when Donnelly came across.

'No troubles?' he asked.

'No, everything went wonderfully.'

'Wish I could say that about the stud.' Like all the employees, even though Les Donnelly was a mechanical and not a horse man, the horses played a very big part in his life.

'Anything wrong?'

'The old mare Wendy is foaling. She must be all of twenty-one years.'

'That's advanced,' nodded Jane, then, seeing the concern on Donnelly's face, 'But lots of mares do it successfully.'

'Reckon it's the mare and not the newcomer that's concerning the boss. He loves that old girl.'

'I wonder' ... Jane hesitated ... 'I wonder if I could go across. I haven't got a degree or anything like that, but I have had experience.'

'I reckon that would be real fine, miss,' Donnelly said eagerly. 'As I said, we all love Wendy. Hop in the jeep and I'll take you to the western paddock. That's where the old girl is.'

Forgetting the hamper she had not removed yet but had intended to, glad that she had dropped the children at the house, Jane got into the jeep.

The western paddock was a quarter of a mile away. 'Wendy always foaled here,' Donnelly related. He stopped the jeep by the fence, and Jane got out, climbed some bars, then walked quietly to the small group of men gathered round the foaling Wendy.

William Bower glanced up at her as she came, and had she not known that cool man now she would have said that there was a flicker of gratefulness at her approach. As for Tim, the vet, there was no mere flicker, there was a welcoming smile.

The smile was soon wiped away, though.

'Wendy's no good,' Tim said.

The next ten minutes were a bigger nightmare than Jane ever had with Rusty back at Little Down. For there they had never lost a mother, only horses in general, since horses have their life span, too, and must go on. But never, Jane recalled, a mare in foal.

But now they lost Wendy. The foal was born, an impetuous filly whose robust fight to enter the world, plus Wendy's advanced years, certainly caused Wendy's death.

But although the mare was haemorrhaging, she lived long enough to give the little girl the first vital feed. Most foals, Jane knew, die without that initial suckling of colostrum, which contains the maternal anti-bodies to protect the baby from disease.

Then Wendy died. She was twenty-one, she had the credit of many children, some of them quite famous, she had enjoyed a full life ... but Jane understood when William Bower pushed his hands, not needed any longer, into his coat pocket and turned and walked away.

Impetuously she ran after him. 'Mr. Bower——'

He wheeled round.

'I'm sorry,' she said.

'She was old,' he replied shortly, but she understood it was only a cover-up.

'I'll watch the foal,' she offered.

'Yes, do that.' He got into his car and went back to the stud. Jane went to the wobbly, spindly-legged little girl, gazing around her with astonished eyes. She wiped her, then said: 'Nine ounces of vegetable extract, dried skim milk, calcium, edible oil, dextrose and glucose was our Little Down formula, failing, of course, a foster-mother.'

'Which we don't have,' said Tim.

'Then if I feed her hourly on that?'

'It will be wonderful,' the vet accepted. He covered Wendy and sighed: 'Green pastures, old girl.'

A float was coming out and Jane took the foal with her into the box. Tim came, too.

'Boss is upset,' he said. 'A man has to be when it's a thing like this.'

But when Jane emerged from the stables after making arrangements with Tim which feeding hours would be hers and which his, William Bower was waiting outside the door for her, and the tone of his voice as he asked her to come across to his office was no longer the tone of a distressed man. In fact he seemed in full control of whatever position he ... and presumably Jane, since he had come for her ... found themselves. All his sentimentality was gone, he was hard and cool again.

'Tim and I have come to an agreement regarding the night feeding of the foal,' Jane began. 'During the day we thought the other girls——' She stopped at a dismissive movement of his big hands. 'What is it, Mr. Bower?' she asked.

'You recall our talk yesterday?'

'Very well.'

'I asked you to waive your strapping duties for a while, didn't I, and instead concentrate on the kids.'

'Yes, you did. Then' ... believing she saw what he was after ... 'you don't want me to take over Wendy's Pride—we called her that pending——'

'I *wanted*' ... he made a point of the past tense ... 'you to take over the twins.'

'And you don't want it now?' she asked.

'I don't know. I do know I want an explanation first.'

'Of what?'

'Your late arrival back from the valley. That was one heck of a long day, Miss Sidney.'

'Yes, it was, but I can explain.'

'Explain, too, an unopened hamper? Harry was quite upset about it. Felt he hadn't made it attractive enough. He came and asked me. In case you don't know, just as with an army, a stud marches ... should I say canters?' ... an unamused laugh ... 'on its stomach. In any concern a cook always stands top in importance, even over the boss, and Harry is a very good cook. I wouldn't care to lose him.' He waited. 'Through you.'

'I'll speak to Harry,' she offered.

'Telling him what? That the three of you were on a diet? That you purchased goodies from the shop that isn't there?'

'No,' said Jane honestly, 'that we had Johnny cakes with John.'

267

He looked at her a long incredulous moment. 'Are they the words of a song? Johnny cakes with John?'

'No, of course not,' she answered sharply, feeling somehow caught-out, and she shouldn't, for really there had been nothing. But still she had the stupid sensation that she had inveigled something, that she had deceived.

'Tell me, please.' His voice was dry.

'When we reached the beach, John was swimming there,' she began.

'Prearranged?'

'Certainly not. He was on his way to his house—he says he always stops for a swim.'

'That adds up. It's attractive. All the same——'

'All the same what, Mr. Bower?'

'All the same it all makes a tall story.'

'I'm sorry I can't shorten it for you.'

'Then,' he shrugged, 'I expect I'll have to accept it as the truth.'

Before she could answer that, tell him, as she fully intended to, that he could do what he liked with the story, he came in: 'So that's why you were late. You dallied at John's.'

'No. But John did show us the timber, the hops, the eucalyptus distillery, but the children going away as they did——' Too late she realized she had said too much. She closed her mouth, but knew it could not finish there.

'They went *where*?' he asked.

'They got bored with the distillery and went away.'

'*Where?*' Again he emphasized it.

'Away—I told you. Through the woods.'

'My God!' he exclaimed.

'It was, and is, all right. John's place backs into a mountain, there's no possibility of being lost.'

'But they were, I gather? You said they were late in coming back.'

'No. They met this man.' Again Jane stopped, knowing she had said too much.

'What man?'

'John knows him. A harmless old fellow.' As she said it Jane remembered Roberta's 'Not so old', but again did not dwell on it. 'He comes at times and lives with nature. I think' ... remembering Robert this time ... 'he's some sort of sculptor.'

'So eventually you rounded them up and returned here?'

'Yes. Mr. Donnelly told me about Wendy, and...' Her voice trailed off.

A minute went by in silence. It was a long minute. Then William Bower said: 'I thank you, anyway, for that, Miss Sidney.'

She nodded, and the silence started again.

'How did the kids go?' He broke the quiet. Evidently he had accepted her explanation, she thought, but how typical of the man not to admit it.

'Good. They're very applicable. Robert more than Roberta.'

'It's good to learn that the male sometimes leads,' he said drily. 'You believe then they both can be taught?'

'I'm sure of it. Robert is practically swimming already. Roberta——'

'Better follow suit. I've had word from the quarantine that the first contingent will be ready next week. Once they arrive you'll begin the duties you came here for.'

Jane said, 'Of course.'

'So if you can teach the children within five days——'

'I know I can.'

'Then' ... a narrow smile ... 'I'll forgive today's Johnny cakes.'

Jane said consideringly, 'I don't know whether it's your prerogative to forgive them or not.'

'In my employment time, it is.'

'And—out of employment time?'

'You mean before nine and after five? But a stablehand always should be available for emergencies, didn't you know that, or were the Little Down rules different, Miss Sidney?'

'The same. But I did have complete days off.'

'As you will have here.'

'And then, Mr. Bowers?'

'And then? Oh, of course, you mean is it my prerogative then?'

'I know it's not.'

'Then why do you ask me.'

'I didn't, I——' Suddenly Jane felt this was all too much, and she turned away.

But she turned back to ask: 'Was that all, Mr. Bower?'

'All, Miss Sidney.'

'Am I still to teach the children?'

'Still to teach them, Miss Sidney.'

'In five days?'

'Five days.'

'Good evening, Mr. Bower.'

'Good evening, Miss Sidney.'

Going into the big house, Jane passed Maureen sitting on the steps and polishing her boots. She was a pretty girl at any time, but she looked particularly pretty now, bent over the leather as she brushed assiduously, her long thick nut-brown hair touching her pink cheeks. No wonder Rodden——

'I'm not generally this funny, Jane,' she smiled, 'but my fellow's coming. That sounds like the hit parade, doesn't it? My Fellow's Coming.'

The second song in an hour. Johnny cakes with John had been the other.

'He's flying over,' Maureen went on. 'He's at Fetherfell across the Divide. Mr. Bower lets him have his second Cessna so he can flip over to see me. Oh, horrors!' She began removing boot polish from her ring. 'I shouldn't wear it when I'm working,' she grimaced, 'but it's very pretty, isn't it? It was bought in England.' She put her hand up to Jane.

Jane pretended to examine it ... well, she thought, what else could she do? She could scarcely say, 'I know it already, Maureen, you see it was my ring.'

She said: 'Yes, very pretty.'

As she left the girl she told her, 'Thank you for showing it to me,' but she really meant thank you for telling me Rodden is coming.

For when he arrives, she was thinking, I won't be here.

Her duties were over for twenty-four hours, except that self-appointed duty she had insisted Tim accept from her for the alternate feeding of Wendy's Pride. But she felt confident she could slip out unnoticed when she did that. Anyway, the small plane would not fly at night; Rodden either would be inside the house with his fiancée, or back at Fetherfell again.

She felt unhappy over her subterfuge with Maureen. She meant no deceit, she felt very attracted to the young strapper, but what else was there? She had to live with these girls. She wanted to live with them *amicably*. But no two women on earth, Jane thought, could live really amicably when one of them wore the other's ring. Then Kate, she considered, contemporary in age to Maureen, once ... or if ... she ever knew the truth, undoubtedly would support her friend. It was all very distasteful, but ... again ... what else was there?

She went down to the library that Bowers provided for all its hands and chose some books. Her first feed was at eleven, and she did not intend to sleep before that in case she really slept. Not ... tolerantly ... that Tim would criticize, he was no big boss.

The books she chose dealt with hop-growing and training a swimming champion. She smiled at her instinctive choice, then, hearing a craft circling over the house, from the sound of it a light craft, she wasted no time in taking the books upstairs.

She estimated that Maureen would ride out on the jeep to collect Rodden. Being lovers ... strange how that had no

271

effect on her at all ... they would take their time to come in again. So Jane went down to the canteen at once for her evening meal. She met the nutritionist, several more of the hands, which was what she had wanted to do, but resisted their appeals, for in a male establishment like a stud it was almost an S.O.S., to stay on for some record playing.

She went upstairs again, lay down and read. She heard a light plane take off again just at last light, and knew that Rodden had left.

At ten she got up, put on her overalls, then went down the steps and out of the house. Across to the stud kitchen. She knew now where everything was, and she set to making Wendy's Pride's bottle with the same efficiency that she had made Turtle Dove's, Billy Boy's, Bella's ... half a dozen other's in her old strapper days. Back at Little Down, Rusty had always boasted that she was a dab hand on a bottle. 'We might even make a mother of you one day,' he had forecast. Jane smiled ruefully at that.

She had just finished warming it, and was testing it on the back of her hand, when the light in the kitchen went out. The plant was a local one, power had to be self-supplied up here, so either for conservation it was switched off at a certain hour ... she must remember next time to bring a lantern ... or it had failed.

Then a hand was gripping her shoulders, turning her round. But the hand did not stop her from crying out, a mouth did. A mouth pressed on hers.

In the small light from an outside lamp ... so nothing had failed, the darkness, like the mouth, had been deliberate ... Jane saw the outlines of a face—a man's face.

'Rodden!' she cried.

She pulled herself away. It was not so hard; evidently Rodden ... she knew a disgust ... had expected her co-operation, her participation, not her distaste, for he had not steeled his grip.

'Hi, what's this?' he demanded laughingly of her withdrawal. 'Going to play hard to get?'

'I'm not here to be "got" at all!'

'Oh, come off it, Janey, as soon as Bill Bower told me—very tactfully, of course, mindful of sparing me any more distress' ... a short laugh ... 'that you were coming out here, I knew what was in the wind.'

'If you were thinking——'

'I was.'

'Then you couldn't have been more wrong. I wouldn't come after you, Rodden, if——' She paused, not wanting to use old clichés but finding that this one filled her needs—'... if you were the last man on earth!'

'But you came,' he persisted.

'To look after the stock Rusty was sending out. Rusty was good enough to give me a share of them.'

'Yes, I heard about that,' Rodden said with interest. 'A fifth or something, wasn't it?'

'A fifth.'

'Anyway,' Rodden resumed, 'it was as good an excuse as any.'

'For what?'

'Janey, you used not to waste time like this,' he sighed.

'For what, Rodden?'

'Us, my dear girl. You've come to your senses, as I did, the moment I got back here.'

'The moment before or after Maureen?'

'Ah' ... evidently quite pleased that Jane had found out that she had not been indispensable ... 'I expected that.' As she did not comment, he went on, 'I can explain that.'

'I'm not interested,' she snapped.

'You see, darling, you were there but Maureen was here, and that, to a man, is the all-important factor.'

'Rodden, I'm not interested.'

'But Maureen is a wily witch, if she could have managed it she would have had it all down in writing, but the next best evidence was something on her finger. I didn't mind, there's more rings—and more girls—in the world, particularly one girl. You, Jane.'

273

'Rodden, can't you understand, I'm not interested in you.' But Jane knew she could not pretend uninterest in Maureen.

'Why have you built her up like this?'—'My fellow's coming,' Maureen, fresh young Maureen had carolled.

'Don't make a bête noir out of me—it takes two, remember.'

He was one of the most unpleasant men she ever had encountered. How on earth had she——

There were steps on the path that led to the stud kitchen. The light was still out, so it made Rodden's escape easy. Feeling absurdly heavy-hearted, though the heaviness, she knew, was for Maureen, Jane switched on the light just in time to catch William Bower turning the corner of the nearest building, then coming across to where she now stood at the door.

At the same time she saw that Rodden had left.

CHAPTER FIVE

WILLIAM BOWER looked at the feeding bottle Jane still held in her hand. 'You don't have to do this, Miss Sidney.'

'It's all right,' she insisted.

'You're not paid for it.'

'I'm doing it because I want to, Mr. Bower, because——'

'Love is ten cold nights in a paddock?'

'Wendy's Pride is in a cosy stable and it's a beautiful night.'

'Well,' he said, 'so long as Tim didn't ask you to.'

'Tim had to be persuaded to let me help out. He'll do the midnight and small hours and then I'll come on again at dawn.'

'Oh, no, you won't!'

'But the foal at this stage must have hourly feeds,' she protested.

'And will have, but not with you at the holding end of the bottle.'

'Tim has to have some rest—he told me that Persian Daughter is ready for her foaling at any moment and he believes it could be twins.'

'Yes, he has his hands full, and I wouldn't want him to forgo those few hours' sleep, but *you* are not doing it for him, Miss Sidney.'

'Why? I mean why apart from it not being my job at this moment?'

'Because,' he said frankly, 'you look done in.'

'Done in?'

'You look' . . . he searched for a word . . . 'concerned.'

Concerned . . . she was more than concerned, she was terribly worried for Maureen. For a mad moment she felt like telling this man, asking for his advice. Then she remembered how concerned he had been in his turn—but for Rodden. You could say if there were sides, that William Bower was on Rodden's.

She said nothing, and after waiting a moment, perhaps for an explanation, but Jane could not tell from that enigmatical face, he said, 'Is the bottle ready, then?'

'I think I'd better warm it again, it might have got cold.'

'It couldn't have. I've only been here several minutes and you were coming out of the door.'

'All the same,' she evaded, and turning to the stove she quickly fixed it up to the desired temperature again. When she turned, he was still there. When she left the kitchen and went down to the stable, he went with her. Well, it was his filly, his stable, his stud.

There is nothing so appealing in the world, Jane thought a few minutes later, than a foal. Already Wendy's Pride had lost her wobble, but her not-quite-certain-yet spindle legs still could not judge distances, and when she came to meet Jane ... or the bottle, more probably ... she did it with that lovable awkwardness of all new young things. Jane gave her a taste of the goodies by putting her finger in the bottle and then in the filly's mouth. After which Wendy's Pride sucked deliciously. A little guidance, a lot of patience and a steady allotment of encouragement, pats and assurances, and Wendy's Pride soon was enjoying a good meal.

Jane had forgotten William Bower. Her preoccupation with the soft pansy-eyed thing so desperately dependent on her pushed everything else aside. It was almost with a start that she focused the man again.

'I'd forgotten about you,' she admitted a little foolishly.

He did not reply. *His* preoccupation had not been with the filly foal, so he had done no forgetting. He had stood watching her. It was with an effort, though he did not let her see it, that he took his glance away.

'Now back to the house,' he said a little gruffly. 'I'll see Tim and tell him I'll do your shifts. For that matter Rod-

den could do them—he flew in this evening and he's stopping the night. Bill Walsh, my pathologist, fortunately also
a pilot, is taking the opportunity to see Fetherfell's bright
lights.' He laughed—but cut short the laugh to ask
sharply: 'Do you always flinch when you hear his name?'

'I don't know Mr. Walsh.'

'I didn't mean Bill, I meant Gair. Do you always flinch?'

'I didn't,' she protested.

'I assure you that you flinched. You better take a hold of
yourself, Miss Sidney—if you flinch at his name, how will
you be face to face?'

'I'll return the bottle to the kitchen and go to bed,' Jane
said.

'*I'll* return it,' William Bower altered. 'Think over what
I just asked you before you slip off to sleep tonight. I don't
want you to lie awake, like an employer I want my
money's worth from my employee, but some time or later
you're going to meet up with Gair, and it's best to know
ahead how you intend to handle that occasion. Because' ...
a pause now, a warning one? ... 'he's betrothed.'—Betrothed, thought Jane a little hysterically. What a ridiculously old-fashioned word for a modern, sophisticated
man!—'He's Maureen's now, and I wouldn't like any
broken hearts to mend on this stud as well as our inevitable
broken fetlocks and the rest.'

'But the human casualties are flown out, aren't they?'

'You know what I mean.'

'Yes, I do. But I don't think there'll be anything to
mend.'

'I'd like your promise about that.'

'Mr. Bower, I'm tired,' Jane sighed.

'Your promise, Miss Sidney.'

'I promise, I promise, I promise! Will that do?'

'One would have done,' he asnswered, 'but said from the
heart.'

'You're intolerable!' she flashed.

'You know what to do then?'

She followed his meaning. She asked coolly: 'How much would my one-fifth return me?'

'I'll tally it up, let you know in the morning.'

'Then I'll sleep on *that*.'

'As well as the other,' was his final advice. He stood back, let her pass him, then hurry up to the house. She had the fear that Rodden might not have returned to Maureen, that he might have been waiting behind some bush to see, and talk to, her again. She ran. She was breathless by the time she got to her room.

There she stood a long while at the window, thinking ... trying to find a solution.

She still had not reached any decision, when, suddenly recalling Bower's '... like any employer I want my money's worth,' she made at least one decision, and went to bed.

Jane made friends with Harry the next morning, apologizing over the untouched hamper, telling him how John had taken them to his house for hot cakes.

'Were they good cakes?' asked Harry jealously, and Jane grabbed her chance.

'Good, but nothing like your raisin scones, Harry.'

'I've put some into today's tuck, Miss Sidney, along with a slab of my cut-and-come-again. Lots of large places like Bowers, and certainly all projects, buy in big squares of sawdust instead of making their own cakes in their own kitchens. That's my name for it, sawdust, for that's what the tack tastes like. But not me. There's nothing like home-made, I say.'

'I say, too,' appeased Jane. 'Thank you, Harry, there won't be a crumb of this left.' She really intended that. No wandering off with John today.

As it happened, John did not come, but he left a message, Indian scout fashion, at the base of a tree.

The twins were enthralled tracking it down, and Jane thought what good father material John Rivers was for thinking of this. As far as she could see William Bower made no effort at all. He was a born bachelor. And yet, her thoughts ran on, he had looked furiously across his desk at her and called: 'My youngsters would be with me, and so, by heaven, would my wife.'—So sometimes . . .

'Here it is!' yelled Robert, who had first discovered the arrows on the ground and the mysterious 5 which meant, as all small boys know, 5 more paces. 'It's a letter,' he thrilled, 'for you, Jane.'

Jane smiled, took and read it. 'It's for all of us,' she announced. She read to her wide-eyed audience:

> *'Congratulations, Secret Three,*
> *At finding this beneath a tree.'*

This was a block of chocolate.

> *'I cannot join you, more's the sorrow,*
> *Let's hope for better things tomorrow.'*

'He's beaut,' awarded Robert.

'Jane's not,' pouted Roberta, seeing Jane take the chocolate firmly from them.

'It's strictly for swimmers,' bribed Jane. 'First one to do three strokes without my finger under their chin gets a block.'

Roberta won. She actually swam first. But Jane considered she would not advance very quickly from that level. On the other hand, Robert, like all boys seeing more danger, though slower to strike out, struck further and faster once he started. However, by hamper time they both could account for themselves for several yards, so Jane voted it a successful morning.

They ate every crumb from the hamper, as Jane had promised Harry, then the chocolate was split up, and the three lay back on the bank. It was unusual for Robert and Roberta not to be on their feet at once, exploring, discovering, but tracking the chocolate and, then earning the right to eat the chocolate had evidently exhausted them. The sun filtered down through the trees, the sand was a warm soft bed, the stream was a lullaby, and the two youngsters slept.

Jane dozed, too, but not as deeply as the twins, for she heard the jeep. She leaned up on an elbow to see William Bower sauntering across to the beach. As he came nearer she indicated the children, then put her finger to her lips.

He nodded, and she got quietly up and joined him.

'They look as though they're resting on their laurels,' he said.

'They are. Roberta did four strokes, Robert did six.'

'Excellent. I said five days, but I didn't expect——'

'In five days they'll be swimming the creek. Did you come down to see how they were progressing?'

'You didn't let me finish, Miss Sidney. I said five days, but I didn't expect you wouldn't have half that time. I've had a message from quarantine to get our first contingent out. I can't ignore it, room at Q is very precious. So we'll have to go up tomorrow.'

'And I'll start my real work.'

'I reckon you've been doing that here.' He said it sincerely.

Jane flushed with pleasure, she did feel satisfied with her results.

'I wouldn't like them to slip back, though,' she said regretfully.

'They won't. There's Maureen and Kate to fall back on. Maureen, for obvious reasons, has her attention across the Divide and not down the valley, but Kate would be quite keen, I think. She's a good swimmer, and would, I feel sure, like to carry on where you leave off.'

'Then that's fine,' said Jane. 'Can we collect the horses in a day?'

'Good lord, no, it will take three full days. One to get up there, two and three to get back. You can't eat up the miles with three horses trailing behind you as you can with only two aboard.'

'I see. So' ... a slight pause ... 'we have to stop overnight.'

'Two nights. One is Sydney, one night on the way back.' He was looking in the children's direction with interest. 'Harry did you well for lunch, I see.'

She noticed that he was eyeing the chocolate wrapper, which was a bright blue.

'I didn't mean to leave it there,' she assured him.

'Nor' ... a throaty laugh ... 'did someone else.'

'Someone else?'

'Don't move, Miss Sidney, but someone is about to take up that wrapper.'

'There's no chocolate left.'

'He doesn't want chocolate, in fact he wouldn't know what to do with it. He just wants blue.'

'Wants what?'

'Hush!' William Bower pointed, and, enchanted as the children had been with John's game, Jane watched.

It was a shining, blue-black bird what William was indicating, a glossy fellow with strikingly blue eyes. He did not appear to pay any attention to them, but, William said quietly, he would know they were there, he would have looked them over to see if they offered anything blue. For blue, Jane's boss informed her, was the bower-bird's obsession. He pointed out the almost *compelled* way the bird was approaching the chocolate wrapper, as though he *must* have that flash of blue.

'Mind your blue eyes, Miss Sidney,' he advised.

Because of the bird's absolute absorption they could speak to each other quite freely.

'Is it after this particular bird you named Bowers?' asked Jane.

'Actually, no, this is a more rare specimen, it's the Satin Bower-Bird, ours on the plateau is a more common variety. But I did call the place Bowers for the birds as well as for myself. I told you that.—Look, there he goes now.' The bird, having darted down and lifted the wrapper, flew off.

'Do you know what,' said William, as excited as a boy, 'I reckon his bower is in that thicket of bushes. It will be away from his nest—they commute from nest to bower. Shall we look for it?'

'Will he mind?'

'Perhaps we can leave him something.' He glanced at the blue ribbon with which Jane had tied back her damp hair.

She removed it and handed it to him, her still-wet honey strands falling to her shoulders. She followed him into the thicket.

They found the bower at once. The bird had flattened down the grass to make room for his treasures, and the little square opened up as they parted the growth.

It was like looking into a tiny Eastern market, except that instead of many colours, all the purloined things were blue. Blue flowers. A blue river pebble. A discarded blue pen. Actually a blue dart that must have been taken from some camp and been rather awkward to carry. The new blue chocolate wrapper.

'It's wonderful!' Jane looked with delight on the flexible twigs with their ends stacked against each other, making a clear passage beneath the interwoven sticks to the previous spot.

'He may be returning with a heavy load,' said William, 'we'll not impede him.'

They stepped back. By the time they reached the river again, the twins were awake, and had to demonstrate their new art. Jane had intended to ask her employer to show the children the bower, but in their swimming pride, and her own pride for having helped achieve it, she forgot.

They went up to the plateau again, Roberta with William, Robert with Jane. As Jane went into the big house she met Maureen. The girl looked heavy-eyed today, all the sparkle of yesterday had left her. There was no 'My Fellow's Coming'. Kate was with her, and she loitered back when Maureen went off.

'Lovers' tiffs,' Kate sighed. 'I'm never going in for anything like that.'

'Sometimes it goes for you,' warned Jane.

'Well, it doesn't attract me. I think I'll settle for a borrowed family. Did Mr. Bower tell you I'll be taking over the twins and their swimming when you can't make it?'

'Yes. Thank you, Kate.'

'It'll be a change,' appreciated Kate. 'I've always loved the valley. I'm not a natural with horses, not like a strapper should be, I just took it on because I simply couldn't work at a desk and this was all that seemed offering. Well, I'll go and see to Maurie now. She and Rodden must have had a few words, because she never went out to the strip to wave him off again.'

'He's gone, then?'

'Oh yes.' Kate ran off, and, at a more leisurely pace, and in a much more relaxed state of mind, since Rodden Gair was no longer at Bowers, Jane followed.

The next morning, directly after breakfast, Jane and Willam left for Sydney. The three-horse float had been attached to the biggest of the Bower cars, and while the boss issued his stud orders for the next few days, Jane examined the float. Like all the Bower equipment it was ultra-modern and very functional. It also looked extremely comfortable. It was padded against bumps, roomy enough to let the passengers move away from each other, and weather-sound. Gretel, San Marco and Ruthven should enjoy a good trip down.

She waited beside the car and presently her employer joined her.

'Did you want to drive?' he asked.

'No.'

'You're entitled to, Miss Sidney. 'We're going after part of your possessions, so you have every right to see we arrive there safely to make the claim.'

'I believe we'll arrive safer in your hands—I don't know the road, remember.'

'It's a highway, once we get out of the valley.'

'How do we get out?' she asked.

283

'The track you take to the pool ... incidentally, the trio have already left! ... then along the flats to the coast. It's not as easy with this big car as with the jeep or mini, but you'll call it simple after you climb up from the valley again towing a parcel of horses. Oh, well' ... releasing the brake ... 'it makes us more exclusive up on top.'

They conversed idly until they had left the plateau and descended the valley, but once they had left the river, the children already there swimming with Kate and waving gaily as they passed, Jane turned her attention to the scenery, for this, for her, was new country. It was timber-land for a while, with occasional hop breaks, acres of apples, then gradually the lessening hills fanned out and down to softly-rolling fields that ran right to the sea. Mostly they were pea fields, their clean bright green contrasting with the bluest ocean Jane had ever seen. The sand was a warm gold, a contrast, Jane's driver told her, to the north coast, where the sands were creamy pale.

William Bower told Jane a lot of things on that trip, snippets of history, facets of natural life, all the outdoor things Jane always had loved, and all told in that robust manner that only an outdoor man who loves them, too, can tell. He showed her that he could be very charming as well as interesting and informative. Lunch at a restaurant over-looking a small south coast harbour became an event, not just a necessary restorative en route.

It was only when the coffee came that he struck the first discordant note.

'You asked me what your share would be worth, Miss Sidney.'

'Yes.' Jane was looking out at a cornflower blue sea and at the moment couldn't have cared less.

'I've been going through these two consignments, reducing them to the dollar state.'

'Yes,' Jane said again.

'It's not easy to give an accurate figure, one never knows with horseflesh if one has a champ or a miss.'

284

This time Jane murmured 'No', still looking at the sea.

'Gretel could prove a likely brood mare. Has she foaled much?'

'Once only. Quite successfully. A fine little girl ... I mean a filly.'

'I see.' His face did not alter at Jane's slip. He had taken out a notebook and he put down some figures.

'San Marco,' he said presently, 'I know already. According to racing news I've had sent out from England the fellow has a few country wins to his credit.'

'Yes, San Marco can sprint.'

'There's no reason why he shouldn't do it here.'

'He likes soft going,' warned Jane.

'I think you're trying to tell me he's a country horse—but *your* kind of country.'

'I was. I didn't mean any disparagement, I think I would love the country here. But not San Marco.'

'That's all right,' William Bower assured her, 'because, believe it or not, we can provide as gentle a terrain as your Surrey or Kent. And what's more, all with regular meets. In which case we can jot you down a nice figure for San Marco as well. Now how about Ruthven?'

'Not proved yet, but Rusty—but your uncle was very hopeful about him, he has excellent connections.'

'Then I'll strike an average figure for Ruthven.' William Bower did so.

He took out his pipe, called for more coffee, then said: 'That brings us to the second consignment.'

'The three D's.'

'Three D's ... oh yes, of course.'

For a few moments he attended to the ritual of packing, tapping and lighting, then he began.

'First of all, Dotsy...' He looked rather narrowly at Jane, though it could have been the smoke, she thought. 'We'll leave her last,' he said. 'Now, Devil May Care.'

'A winner,' came in Jane enthusiastically. She spoke proudly of how a young jockey at one of their northern meetings had called in delight as he had raced Devil May Care to first past the post the day before his marriage: 'You've just given me my wedding present, you fine boy!'

'He's tough, too,' she praised, 'and not at all temperamental. I think Devil could even win one of your red earth races.' As he jotted this down, Jane apologized a little uncomfortably, 'I seem to be saying all good things. I hope you don't think it's to—well——'

'To pop up the price? No, I don't think that. Anyway' ... an oblique look ... 'Dandy would bring the price down. Miss Sidney' ... before Jane could indignantly interrupt ... 'why in tarnation did my uncle consign Dandy?'

'Dandy's a darling!' she exploded. 'Dandy ... why, Dandy——'

'All right then, you love Dandy. Things like that happen. I believe it's what they call a mutual look—— And why are *you* looking at me like that?'

'Because—well, Rusty used to say that. He said if there's a mutual look it will be all right.'

A silence had come between them. Jane, embarrassed, kept her eyes to her cup.

'Did my uncle explain that phenomenon?' William Bower broke the silence.

'He said,' Jane said a little unevenly, 'it was something between the two of you and you two only.'

'I see. Do you know where it comes from?'

'The—look?'

'Yes.'

'No, I don't.'

'A man called John Keble wrote it. He said:

> *"Sweet is the smile of home, the mutual look,*
> *When hearts are of each other sure."* '

'I see,' said Jane.

He nodded. There was another silence. Then:

'But why in tarnation, why in Betsy, did he send Dandy?' the man exploded. 'The boy—I mean the horse

286

has nothing. Oh, you've prettied him up. I've no doubt you've spent more hours on him than you have on yourself. All very nice, Miss Sidney, but when I jot Dandy down on the statement the profit goes down as well.'

There were so many rejoinders rising up in Jane. she could find voice for none of them. At last she almost croaked: 'All right then, get on to Dotsy. You said you'd deal with her last.'

'Can you take it?' he asked carefully.

'Take what?'

'What I'm going to tell you ... and what I think you don't know.'

Now Jane did look at William Bower. But she did not speak.

'I think ... mind you, I saw her only briefly in Sydney ... she's having a foal.'

'She is not!'

'And how would you know?'

'I'd know like I do with any of my girls, I mean—'

'Skip that. Keep on with how you'd know.'

'Well, she's agile.'

'She's early yet.'

'Slim.'

'The same reply to that.'

'I—I've watched her.'

'You'd want eyes at the back of your head. Look' ... a little more kindly ... 'I could be wrong. Anyway, we'll leave it for Tim and the experts. When Rodden's over, I'll ask him.'

It was just too much. Jane got up and left him to settle the bill. When he came out she was sitting in the car waiting to resume the journey.

He got in beside her.

'Not to be upset, Miss Sidney,' he tossed, 'it happens all the time. You can't cheat nature. Not' ... getting once more into the coastal road traffic ... 'after there's been a mutual look.'

287

'Can we just have the final figures without any comments?' Jane asked a few miles further on; it had taken her all that time to compose herself.

'Yes. The comment merely was made to prepare you for the lower sum you must be prepared to accept because of Dandy, who would line no pockets, also because of Dotsy, condition uncertain but suspected, and sire unknown.'

'I still don't believe you.'

'You may be right at that, it's not always easy to tell.'

'Also, if it's true, Rusty would know.'

'Then we must write and ask him, mustn't we?' He said it fatuously, knowing, she thought resentfully, that it would irritate her. 'The amount I've jotted down comes to . . .' He told her a sum that positively rocked Jane. Never would she have put the value so high.

'One fifth of it would be——' he went on.

She disbelieved him for several minutes. It couldn't be that much! She couldn't be that rich. He must simply want to be rid of her.

'Mr. Bower,' she broke in indignantly, 'there's no need for bribery, no call for you to try to buy me out. If I wanted to go, I'd go, but not all the money in the world would hurry me.' She stuck out her bottom lip and finished, 'And *won't* hurry me!'

'I'm stating a correct sum, Australian-wise,' he said flatly. 'Perhaps you would get less in England where there's plenty offering, but out here where the top class commodity is more rare, you can almost name your own reward. So' . . . negotiating a bend . . . 'you don't want to leave yet?'

'I want to last out until the two contingents are settled, and I know that that's what Rusty wants.'

'All right then, we'll drop it. It was your idea, anyway, for me to give you a figure.'

'You've given it. Thank you.' Jane turned her head from him to look outside. They were still in the country, but closer settled country now. The space between the villages was considerably less. In half an hour the small towns seemed to have merged on each other to form an endless city.

'Yes, we're in Sydney,' Bower said when she commented on this, 'the outskirts now, but we'll make the hotel in a quarter of an hour.'

'What about the horses?'

'They can wait till tomorrow. But it will be an early tomorrow; we'll be taking off at daylight, and making it an easy trip.' He ran into a snarl of city traffic and did not speak again until they arrived and a porter collected the car to garage it, and, at Bower's indication, Jane followed another porter upstairs.

She was not tired, for it had been an easy transit; tomorrow with that 'we'll be taking off at daylight' of his, and the day after, should prove more strenuous journeys. She knew that William Bower had been hinting that she should rest tonight, and that any hint from Bower was tantamount to an order, but she had not seen Sydney before, only passed through it, and this fact as well as the rather exciting fact that she stood for more money than she had thought (even with the debits of Dotsy and Dandy, or so Bower said) made it impossible for Jane to stand still now. After she had showered and changed, she went to gaze down from the window to the city traffic below, at the canyons of streets between towering buildings, at a snippet of harbour that a slat of space separating two skyscrapers awarded her, and then, irresistibly, she turned and went down.

Inner Sydney was not such a big city, she found, since regional shopping and suburban spending had taken away from it, but the squares she did cover were exciting and comprehensive. Besides every London line she had loved, there was a subtle Eastern influence here, also the charm of flimsier, more tropical wear.

The fact that she stood for more money even though she did not have it in hand, made Jane more reckless than usual. She splurged on a pure silk blouse, a phial of brown boronia perfume and a wind-up jolly swagman who sang 'Waltzing Matilda' in a squeaky voice. Rusty would smile over him, she thought.

When she emerged from the souvenir shop, Jane knew she was lost. It did not bother her, for her hotel was a popular one and she could always ask ... but what did bother her was William Bower walking towards her. She determined not to let him know she had not marked the way she had come.

'So you've decided to sell out your fifth after all.' He was eyeing her purchases.

'I do have some money of my own,' she answered coolly.

'Finished now?'

'Yes.'

'Where to next?'

She thought hard. She wanted to see the quay and the Opera House. But she also wanted first to deposit her purchases. She took a chance and said: 'Oh, I'm just looking around,' and went down a side street.

He let her go, and it rather surprised Jane. He wouldn't want her company, she knew that, but it did appear to amuse him to have her by him for baiting purposes.

She hastened her steps ... then stopped, annoyed. It was a blind street. She turned back and found William Bower waiting for her, a grin on his face.

'Lost, aren't you?'

'No, of course not. I mean ... that is ...'

'Lost. Why won't you women note little details such as first turn to the left, second to the right? This way.' He barely touched her elbow with cool fingertips.

'Where are we going?'

'Where were *you*, apart from that looking around?'

'Well, I have these things—but I did think the harbour——'

She had barely got the words out than he had her in a store again, buying a carrier bag. Together they put in the parcels, then they took a bus to the quay. The Manly hydrofoil was ready to leave.

'It's a good way to see things,' said William Bower, helping Jane on.

Jane loved that harbour trip, loved the sails of the Opera House poised ready, one would think, for flight, loved the red roofs of the houses, the endless unfolding of little bitten-in bays all with their own golden beaches.

They had tea at Manly after walking to the ocean side, one long wave-kissed stretch of sand.

'You like the sea?' William asked as Jane poured.

'Yes. Only——'

He raised his brows in inquiry.

'Only I like "inside" the best,' she admitted, 'I like meadows, brooks, villages.'

'How do you judge paddocks, creeks, towns? As rather a bit too much, even though you say you like the "inside"? As too raw?'

'No,' she said, 'not at all.'

'Then does that mean you like our "inside" as well?'

'It's very beautiful,' she said sincerely.

'You'll see a different aspect of it tomorrow. We'll take the non-toll roads home for better scenery as well as less trammelled traffic.'

'After we get the fellows,' she said with anticipation; she had not thought she could look forward so much to seeing her contingent.

'Of course. That's our purpose.'

They left soon after that, returning this time by ferry.

'Want to see any more of Sydney?' Bower asked.

'Am I allowed?'

'I never said you weren't.'

'Then your words, Mr. Bower, emerge differently.'

'I'm glad you told me. I must watch myself when I say something I mean, otherwise you won't believe it. You never answered as to what you wanted to do.'

'The hotel,' Jane said, and got into the taxi he called over.

The next morning her summons to get up came with coffee. The maid told Jane that Mr. Bower said just coffee would do as they would breakfast afterwards on the road. Jane wasted no time and was downstairs almost on Bower's heels.

'Good girl,' he nodded.

They went direct to the quarantine, and there Jane went straight to the three D's, to talk to them, assure them it wouldn't be long now, to fondle Dotsy, pat Devil May Care, run her fingers round Dandy's soft ears. Dear, dear Dandy. And he, the great Bower, said the horse had nothing. Perhaps, in all honesty, Dandy hadn't, not if you put it down in figures, but he did have, Jane knew lovingly, a girl's heart. He had had it right from the beginning, ever since they had exchanged that mutual look.

'These three are staring daggers at you.' William Bower strolled across. 'Do you always play favourites?'

'They'll have me all the time now, but the D's won't, not for three more weeks.' She touched each D in turn. 'Be good,' she smiled.

Even after he had left the city traffic snarl behind them, William Bower drove moderately over the minor roads he had chosen. They took the Blue Mountains route, riding into soft blue air that changed to green at closer quarters, because that air, Bower told Jane, was coloured by distance from the wind turning over the eucalyptus leaves.

Then, the range conquered, they turned south once more. They lunched from a picnic hamper that the hotel had packed, and William Bower took out the horses and exercised them. Resuming south again, Jane noted fewer and fewer motels and inns, which was only to be expected, she thought, on a secondary road. She asked William where they would put up that night.

'A place called Iroola. It's comfortable and I can paddock the fellows. Not many motels or inns these days can accommodate horses as well.'

'That will be good for them,' Jane appreciated.

The travelled through the warm afternoon. Occasionally Jane napped. Then, at an ejaculation from the man beside her, she opened her eyes ... and gasped. It was now near elf light, the sun had gone down almost an hour, but instead of a last apricot flush, a first hint of dark pansy, the sky in front of them was charcoal, with, here and there, a streak of vicious red.

'Fire,' William Bower said. Even as they watched a dark smudge began spreading ominously, the blurred beginnings of a smoke pall to take over.

All the time William Bower kept driving, and thinking of bush fires of which she had read there were many in Australia, Jane asked shouldn't they stop.

'No. Never go back. Anyway, it's localized. It's no fire of nature.'

'How can you tell?'

'The shape of the pall. It could almost be an atomic explosion, couldn't it? No, it'll be a homestead.' he added, 'Poor devils.'

They drove for another half hour. It had become quite dark now, and Jane was concerned for herself as well as the horses. Where on earth on this dark smoky road were they to lodge?

As though he read her thoughts, Bower said: 'Iroola. I told you. Only a few minutes to go now.'

They did the last mile in silence. Jane knew that William Bower had grown as concerned as she was by the times he poked his head out of the window to try to pierce the gloom without the intervention of glass, by the occasions he sniffed deeply and estimatingly.

'It's close,' he said at last.

'The fire?'

'Yes.'

'Close—to us?'

'To the hotel.'

'You mean——'

'I mean I believe the hotel *is* the blaze. I only hope——'

293

She knew what he hoped, and she hoped with him.

Turning a corner, they both saw their hopes were in vain. All that remained of what once had been an inn was a smouldering ruin. Only a small annexe remained intact. Bower turned the car and float into a side track, drove some safe hundred yards, then told Jane to wait there.

He was a long time gone. Jane got out and talked to the horses, who seemed supremely unaffected, thank heaven, by it all, then she turned eagerly as she heard steps through the bush.

It was her boss again, and he gave her a reassuring smile.

'Bad ... but could be much worse. Not one life lost. The place is a shambles, but I have no doubt the Donnisons would be well insured. Mrs. Donnison is as cool as the proverbial cucumber ... how do you women do it? ... she even rang up Yanni for me—Yanni's further down—and got us a room.' He darted Jane the quickest of glances.

Only when they were on the road again did Jane recall that look. It came at the same time as she heard in retrospect that '... got us a room.'

Us. Not you. Not me. And a room. Not rooms.

She opened her mouth. She shut it again. She moistened her lips.

'Yanni coming up,' said William Bower presently, 'no doubt the horses will be pleased.'

'No doubt.' Heavens, Jane thought, that was almost a croak.

William was going slowly now, it could be that they were almost at the place ... a very small place, Jane saw, straining her eyes through the darkness ... or it could be——

'It's this way, Miss Sidney,' William Bower was saying.

'Yes?'

'In England do you have family units?'

'In hotels, you mean?'

'This is a motel.'

'I don't know. I mean——'

'Perhaps I'd better tell you what I mean, then. A family

unit is—well, for a family. It's larger than the usual accommodation. Generally quite a dormitory of beds. Well, to put it briefly that's all they have left. To put it more briefly still' ... a pause ... 'we have it.'

'We?' she echoed.

'We,' he said. And drove up to the door.

Mecahanically Jane helped him with Gretel, San Marco and Ruthven. She did the automatic strapping things that should be done to an animal which had been cooped up, even if it was in a roomy, comfortable box, for some hours. She fed, watered, brushed, massaged, soothed. Not that they needed soothing, they were perfectly calm and well adjusted.

Not like I feel, Jane thought.

At last she went to the room. A glance around the car-filled courtyard had assured her that it was in all truth a last offering, the motel was small, and, probably because of the fire at Iroola, now taxed to its limit.

The unit proved large, as William Bower had said it would be. There was a shower recess and its own kitchen. There were at least six beds.

'We could put quads in here as well.' William was standing at the door and looking across the room at Jane.

Suddenly Jane knew she had to say something ... Anything at all would do. But what she could *not* do was to stay silent. And meet his eyes.

She began to chatter. Shocked at her nervous babble yet somehow unable to stop herself, she agreed: 'Yes, we could put up a whole family, couldn't we? Which bed for you? I'll take this. I'll shower and then you can. I'll ... you'll ... we'll ...'

At last she found she could stop, and she did.

He was still looking at her, but differently now.

'Don't waste your breath,' he advised. 'But do have that shower.'

'I——'

'The shower, Miss Sidney.'

His eyes compelled her, she didn't want to go, she wanted to calm herself, to be matter-of-fact, sensible, practical, a woman of the world, a girl of today, not the—well, the near-hysterical ninny she was being now. But she went.

When she came out again from the bathroom, he wasn't there. Jane got into her selected bed and shut her eyes. Around ten o'clock, she judged, the motel electric plant cut out, and the light she had left on for him switched off.

She listened for him, but did not hear him. She listened ... listened ... Then she was opening her eyes to the first pale buttering of piccaninny daylight ... and at once turning those eyes to the rest of the dormitory beds. They were all still closed up. No one had slept there.

Jane dressed rapidly and went out to the courtyard. The car was where it had been last night, and the float beside a shed that they had been given for a shelter for the horses.

She went to the barn and looked in. Gretel, San Marco and Ruthven looked back, and San Marco whickered. She glanced around, but saw nothing—and nobody—else. Then that must mean that the motel had found William Bower a room after all. She was glad about that, but felt he could have come back and told her.

As she came out of the barn she had a feeling that someone was watching her. She hesitated, then looked to the car ... and saw that it was William Bower. As she looked back, he yawned, stretched and heaved his big person from the back seat.

'Sleep well?' he asked her.

'Yes.' Jane hesitated. 'Did you?'

'No. Ever try a fitted box?'

'You needn't have slept there, Mr. Bower.'

'I know,' he nodded. Then he mimicked cruelly: 'Which bed for you? I'll have this one. I'll shower and then you can.'

'What,' broke in Jane in anger, 'did you want me to say?'

He regarded her with cool estimation. 'Ever consider trying the truth?'

'You must have read it even though I didn't say it,' she flung, 'by coming out here.'

'I came out here because I preferred out here, because I have no time for humbug. Why in heaven couldn't you have said: "Bower, I will not sleep in a family unit if you're there, I know it's the only thing offering, but it's not for me." Why did you try to slide out like you did?'

'I didn't, I——'

'You floundered and dithered and generally made me sick, Miss Sidney. Either you wanted me *not* there or you wanted me *there*, but you were too "nice", too "polite"— and too damn puerile to say it!'

'Then I'll say it this time,' said Jane. '*I did not want you there*. As for the other possibility, that——'

'Wanting me to remain?'

'As far as that's concerned, I'm now *not* too nice, too polite, too puerile to tell you that that would be the very last wish I could ever make, Mr. Bower!'

'How soon' ... frozenly and finally ... 'before we push off?'

CHAPTER SIX

AT mid-afternoon, when they reached the Urara valley,
Jane leaned out to wave to Maureen and the twins, who
again were swimming in the creek, but William Bower did
not stop, presumably since he had a tricky run in front of
him to gain the plateau, but more probably, Jane thought
feelingly, because he was still in that filthy mood.

They had barely spoken since they had left last night's
hotel. They had eaten lunch in near-silence at a roadside
teahouse, then resumed the return journey just as silently.
The man did not even acknowledge the children as they
crossed over the small bridge. He made it seem as though
driving the float on this final lap needed all his attention,
and perhaps it did, but all the same . . .

It was so unfair of him, Jane's mind ran on resentfully.
Perhaps she *had* babbled too much, been a fatuous little
fool, but the unit had taken her by surprise. He had. She
saw now that she had marked something that was really
nothing at all by dithering over it, but good heavens, not
everybody was as cool, as certain of themselves, as supremely composed as he was.

If she could have explained now, she would have, but she
still had no words, and . . . a surreptitious glance at her
driver . . . no reception.

As they ascended, in all fairness Jane had to excuse William Bower's absorption. The hairpin bends, the tortuous
curves were all in a day's work to her mini model, but for
a big car towing a float it was a hard, hazardous trip. But at
last they were on the top and travelling the last miles to the
stud.

William Bower drove up to the stables. 'I'll get a couple
of the boys to help me unload them,' he tossed, 'settle them
in. You can knock off.'

'No, thank you.'

'That was not a consideration, Miss Sidney, it was an order. You've had a long day.'

'So have you. And I' ... getting a word in at last ... 'at least had the benefit of a good night's rest.'

'I didn't. But I'm still signing you off.'

'I'm not going. After all, I'm a partner, not an employee in this.'

He looked thunderous a moment, but he must have seen he would have to climb down.

'All right then, do the chores yourself. I'll send Andy and Bert along.'

'We don't need four for three horses.'

'I'll sign myself off. No need for everyone to be tired.'

About to retort, 'I'm not,' Jane left it at that.

After Andy and Bert had got Gretel, San Marco and Ruthven out and into their boxes, Jane still stayed on. She brushed them, cosseted them, watered them, fed them, extending each chore unnecessarily. She knew she was filling in time, but she had to work off her frustration.

It was dark when she came out at last. It was several hundred yards to the big house, and Jane looked across to the twinkling lights rather nervously. Had Rodden come again? Was he likely to step out at one of those shrubs? And yet it was what she really should strive for, another meeting, but this time with a definite understanding, with Rodden.

She forced herself to walk calmly, not hurry as she had before, to the house. But Rodden did not step out, and when she entered the building he was not there either.

After dinner she sat in the common room and listened to records. The men obviously enjoyed her company, particularly as tonight neither Kate nor Maureen were there. Kate, they reported with malicious glee, was child-worn; that should learn her, trying to get a family the easy way! Over Maureen, they were more serious. It was strange, Jane thought, how in a small community individual troubles became public cares. Maureen didn't look happy, they said, and for a while they looked unhappy themselves.

Feeling false, Jane made the suggestion of pre-wedding jitters.

'But Maureen's not being married for ages,' said the nutritionist.

Tim, the vet, added: 'She's a damn pretty girl, I can't understand what's holding Gair up.'

'I suppose after his last experience——' murmured someone.

'First I've heard of a man being a jiltee,' said someone else. 'Is jiltee a word?'

They argued amicably, and pleading weariness after a long day Jane went upstairs.

She regretted that at first when she reached her room. Maureen was sitting at the window.

'I'm sorry,' the girl said. 'I shouldn't have come in.' She shrugged. 'But I did.'

'That's all right, dear. I'm glad you're here. Tea?'

'No. That is ... All right, then.' A pause. 'Jane——'

Jane switched on the jug before she turned. She made herself do that.

'Yes, Maureen?'

'You're always so calm.'

'I think calmness is something a strapper acquires, you have to be calm with horses.'

'I'm a hand, too, but——' Again the girl was quiet a moment. 'Jane——'

'Yes, dear?'

'I can't ask Kate, she's younger than I am, only a few months, but—well—— Not that you're much older.'

'Almost five years, Maureen.'

'Is it five? It doesn't seem it, I mean not just in looks, but—well, in the *way* you look.'

'How do I look?'

'Not unhappy. Not ever. But then you haven't been in love, have you, Jane?'

'Love shouldn't make you look unhappy.' Jane hoped Maureen did not notice she had not answered her question.

'It does me. I know you can't help me, but Kate is quite hopeless. All she says are things against Rodden—she doesn't like him, never did—but it can't be all Rodden, can it, some of it must be me. My fault, I mean.'

'Some of what?'

'The change in him. The——' A pause, quite a long one now. 'Jane, I don't think Rodden wants to marry me.'

'But, dear, you have his ring,' Jane heard herself say, and was a little shocked at her duplicity.

'His ring ... or someone else's? I think that sometimes. I don't know why. Jane ... Jane, what's gone wrong? Oh, I know you can't say, you wouldn't anyway, you're too sweet. But I just had to blurt all this out to someone, not to young Kate who would only say "Ditch him". I—I won't have that tea after all. Thank you, Jane.'

She was gone before Jane could protest.

Jane did not have tea, either. She went and sat where Maureen had sat, by the window. Most of the lights had been switched off before she went to bed.

A few days from a stud made a big difference. Jane had found that out in Little Down. She supposed it was nature; nature never stood still. In the short period she had been away, Persian Princess had foaled. She had come through wonderfully, Tim reported to Jane, for a mother of twins. Maureen, he added very warmly, had been a marvellous help. But the little fellows, a colt and filly, seemed to be slipping back. Tim asked Jane to attend and see what she thought.

Jane had had no experience in this. Rusty had had a twin birth, but it had been the mother who had looked ill, though eventually she had recovered. This mother, Persian Princess, obviously was in perfect condition. But the two foals ... Maureen, kneeling by them, looked up at Jane and shook her head sadly.

The girls between them 'specialed' the foals all that day. Jane thought several times of her own three, and whether they were feeling strange and abandoned, but she put the thought aside. At least they were fit and had each other. These poor small mites . . .

If nothing else, the watching of the foals diverted Maureen, but seeing the end in sight Jane wondered whether she would have been better without such diversion, for it would be harder now.

It was. When the foals died late in the afternoon, Maureen broke up in a quite unprofessional manner. There were floods of tears. The girl was near-hysterical. Tim came forward and took the distraught Maureen in his kindly arms. Jane hesitated, wondering if she should offer her comfort, too, but decided to leave it at that.

She went out to the stable.

William Bower was crossing to it, and to spare Maureen, though Jane had a suspicion that Maureen would have got off lighter than she, Jane, would have in the same circumstances, Jane went forward.

'The foals died,' she said.

He nodded. 'I expected it. Bad luck. But better for the poor little atoms to go now if there was something gravely amiss.'

'I believe there was,' said Jane.

'We'll have Tim do a post,' William decided. 'It may have been that two births upset the result for Princess where one would have been a routine affair, or it may be that she just isn't a breeder.'

Still Tim and Maureen did not emerge. 'I was going to see Persian Princess,' Jane said to give Maureen more time to compose herself.

'To break the sad news.' William was lighting his pipe and his smoke-narrowed eyes baited Jane.

She looked at him coldly. 'She may be very uncomfortable; Tim said there was enough milk for two.'

'I'm sorry,' he offered at once. He really did seem

ashamed of himself. 'I didn't mean to needle you, not on a thing like that. The Princess does have a lot of milk. But I believe we can fix that. Rodden lost a mare while we were away over at the Fetherfell stud' ... he frowned and was quiet a moment ... 'and is badly in need of a foster for the orphan.' They had turned into Princess's box now.

The mare did look at a loss, and Jane said: 'I think what you suggested would be wise, I believe you should make her a foster.'

'We'll go over tomorrow, then, I'll take the Cessna and we'll bring the orphan back.' He touched the silky nose. He looked worried, Jane considered, and she felt she understood. Running a stud, she remembered from Rusty, could bring many worries, though she hardly had believed that this self-sufficient, efficient man ...

Her silence must have started something. 'I lost another one today.' Bower's voice actually shook slightly.

Jane remained silent.

'Cam was an old friend,' he said presently, 'quite ancient. I expect a man is a fool to——' He shrugged.

'He died?'

'I had him put down. He was crippled with rheumatism, I couldn't see him suffer another season.'

Jane nodded.

'Well, that's the way it goes.' William Bower broke the small silence. 'How are your three?'

'I really haven't had time to look into that.'

'You should, you know. Anything apart from them is just employment to you, not personal property.'

'One-fifth of,' she reminded him.

He ignored that. 'See to your own interests,' he advised briskly. 'Don't consider anyone else.'

Jane wondered if her sympathy because of his departed mate that had been trembling quite apparently on her lips had caused his sudden brusqueness. Possibly this withdrawn man had resented her intrusion. She stiffened herself. 'Always think of Number One,' she interpreted. 'Yourself first.'

'Exactly,' he nodded. Then he nodded to Jane and went back to the house.

The next day they flew over to Fetherfell. Scarcely were they up than they were descending again, gradually lowering to the green slopes of the tablelands, that stretched, William Bower called out to Jane, right to the plains, and then, given time, to Australia's red centre. But at Fetherfell it was green and rolling, not red, and, coming after the sudden and dramatic abyss that separated it from Plateau, very peaceful as it looked back and up at them. It was a comfortable-sized hamlet, William also called, a hospital, several streets of shops and a railway station. Jane, woman-like, was a little regretful she would not be seeing the shops, but she had to accept that fact as William flew the Cessna across the town, then put the plane down in a wide paddock strategically marked for take-offs and landings by white up-turned plastic buckets. They must be at the satellite stud. Shortly after their arrival a jeep came out. Rodden drove it, and Jane stiffened herself, not because it was Rodden she was about to encounter a second time, but because on this occasion she would have an observer. And of all observers, William Bower.

She pitied herself as the jeep drew up. It was two against one, she thought childishly, for William Bower's sympathies were entirely with Gair. She stood and waited.

Then she was sensing a rather strained atmosphere between the two men. Rodden greeted his employer as an employee would, but there was a challenge there. William was almost terse.

They got into the jeep. They went at once to the stables, and while Jane fussed over the small orphan, the men went out to the yard. It was soon afterwards that she heard William's raised voice.

'Two of them! Good lord, Rodden!'

'It happens.' Rodden's voice was lower, but still clear to Jane's ears.

'Is that all your explanation?' demanded Bower. 'That it happens?'

'I'll make my report, of course, but I'm not Mother Nature, or Father, either, sir.' The sir was almost flung at William, thought Jane. 'Also I don't play Fate and pull strings as to who survives and who doesn't.'

'But two in as many days!'

'It happens,' Rodden repeated.

'I suppose I'll have to accept that, but I'll still study your report.'

'In professional terms or for laymen?'

'I don't want your impudence, Gair.'

'I don't want it, either, but it appears to me that you're questioning my skill.'

'No. I know your skill. But I could question your management.'

'And are you questioning it now?'

'Look, we'll leave it this time. Persian Princess lost her twins.'

'Then in a way this misfortune is opportune.'

'Misfortune is never opportune, don't ever try to rationalize that it is. But because I haven't time, I'll close the subject here. Miss Sidney——'

Jane, who had moved to the door of the barn for better listening, gave a guilty start, then went out.

'Mr. Gair has just broken the news that we have two foals to succour, not one, that two mares went down. This means that both foals will have to go over to Bowers, and it means also that there'll be no room in the larger Cessna for you. Mr. Gair will return you in the smaller craft.'

'Yes, Mr. Bower,' Jane said.

Rodden led the way to the second orphan, then the two tiny foals were carried to the jeep, after which Rodden drove William Bower and his cargo out to the waiting craft. With minutes the Cessna was taxiing off, then turning into Plateau's direction again. Jane saw Rodden coming back. He was in a bad temper, which at least diverted his atten-

305

tion from Jane, even though the effect would only be temporary.

'Glenda was too old,' Rodden said angrily. 'What did he expect me to do? Perform a miracle? These laymen!'

Jane had heard that said to Rusty, and it was Rusty she defended when she answered, 'Sometimes experience is a better thing than an instruction in a book.'

'Oh, so we're all for the boss now, are we?'

'No. But I can see his point. What happened?'

'They both died foaling, that's all. As I said, it happens.'

It did happen, knew Jane, but not generally so frequently. She thought of old Cam, who had had to be put down, of the twin foals who had died, and now, on top of these losses, the added losses of two mares. She explained it to Rodden.

'When do I cry?' he said.

'Rodden!'

'Sorry, my beautiful, I do say the wrong thing, don't I? I should have remembered.'

She knew what he meant, he was referring to the Little Down Melinda incident, and she put in quickly: 'That's all over.'

'The ashes are not white yet,' Rodden reminded her.

'They are for me.'

'I don't believe you, Janey.'

'Besides,' said Jane, 'there's Maureen.'

'Yes. There's Maureen,' Rodden said slowly, thoughtfully. Then: 'Thank you, Jane.'

She looked at him in surprise, surprise that he had accepted her reminder so calmly. She felt she had never known Rodden.

'Well,' he shrugged, 'we'd better get going. How do you feel entrusting your life this time to me?'

'Presumably you can fly,' said Jane.

'I can.'

The smaller craft was garaged in a hangar on the field. It was very light and only needed help from a stablehand to wheel it on to the path. At Rodden's nod, Jane climbed in, then Rodden climbed after her. The engine whirred, the small machine went forward, and they nosed into the air.

Coming across, it had seemed to Jane that barely had she looked down on the valley beneath Plateau than she had been looking down on the tablelands of Fetherfell, but evidently, perhaps because of its smaller size, this craft must take longer than those few minutes, for already they had been up for a lengthier period, and the stud still was not in sight.

Peering over, a little puzzled, Jane caught the different note in the engine. She glanced at Rodden, but he did not look back. She looked down again, and saw that they were approaching a clearing in a valley.

'Rodden, you're landing,' she called.

'Looks like it, doesn't it?'

'But why?'

'Fuel, lack of, is the usual accepted excuse,' he replied. 'I'll be reprimanded, no doubt, about that, but oh, what manna from heaven!'

'Rodden, what on earth are you talking about?'

'Shut up, Jane, there's no buckets to mark the way here.' All the same he landed, and landed perfectly. He was good, she had to admit. When the small plane finally stopped, he sat back and looked at Jane.

'Thank you, Jane darling,' he said.

'For what?'

'For saying that, for reminding me, "There's Maureen."'

'What do you mean, Rodden?'

'You may be a good strapper, Janey, but you're not good at catching on. I mean us, of course.'

'How, Rodden? Why?'

'How? By Maureen not caring about this little episode.' He slid ... or tried to slide ... an arm around Jane. 'Why? because it's you, Jane. It was. It is. It will be. Anyway' ... as Jane pulled right away now ... 'it's not Maureen.'

'How will this make a difference?' Jane was looking at

the isolation of the valley strip and feeling more hollow than she would have cared for Rodden to know.

'Darling, you shock me.' Rodden had taken out his cigarettes.

Flippantly . . . or she tried for flippancy . . . Jane yawned: 'All that went out years ago, Rod. You're being very naïve.'

He exhaled lazily. 'I admit that the scheme is a trifle old-fashioned.'

'It's antiquated!'

'But' . . . ignoring Jane . . . 'it still has its points. Maureen, for all her flaming youth, isn't so flaming after all. I'd even go as far as to say she's slightly Victorian, and that she won't like this.'

Jane stared at him in loathing. However had she felt anything for this man?

'Why can't you tell her outright?' she demanded.

'I could,' he said, 'with your support. If you would come with me and say——'

'I wouldn't.'

'Then' . . . a shrug . . . 'we have to adopt measures.'

'Don't include me.'

'Janey, the whole procedure is because of you,'

'You're crazed, Rodden, you must be! You know as well as I do that it's all over, why otherwise would I have sent you the ring?'

'In a fit of pique,' he suggested, 'because I wouldn't dance to your tune. Hushabye, Baby, wasn't it? Belinda's baby?'

'Melinda,' Jane said mechanically.

He ignored her correction. He said what she had expected him to say. 'You followed me out.'

'Rodden, I never followed you out! I came because——'

'Yes, you've said all that before. But the fact still remains, Janey, for everyone's . . . and Maureen's . . . consumption that we were once engaged, that we split up, that

I came home.' A deliberate pause. 'That now we're together again.'

'We are not!'

'Aren't you forgetting something?' He glanced significantly around him, and she followed his meaning. They *were* together, as together as two people in a lonely valley, miles away, she expected, from anything had to be.

'It makes no difference,' she said firmly.

'To you, perhaps, but—Maureen?'

'She's young, and the young are outgoing, not—not vulnerable in things like that any more.'

'Don't you believe it. How would you like your fiancé away all night in the bush with a beautiful girl?'

'I won't be away all night, Rodden.'

'Then you'll still clinch it, darling, for sure. If you're found scratched and bedraggled by running through the undergrowth from me, everyone will think the worst.'

'Of you, Rodden.'

'That will do nicely, thank you. My little Maureen, who is sweet, I'll admit, but as cloying as sugar, will be handing back your ring in flash.'

'It is *not* my ring!' she snapped.

'I agree with you there entirely, Jane, we'll start off anew, start another life with another stone. What will it be?' he smiled.

'Aren't you being rather reckless, jeopardizing, or trying to jeopardize, your career with the Bower stud like this?'

'I'm not just trying, Jane, and no, I don't think so. Bower and I are all washed up, anyway. Those damned mares——' He scowled. 'I can get a job anywhere, Jane,' he went on. 'With your little capital we two should——'

'My little capital is staying with me, Rodden.' She looked at him contemptuously. 'Is that the reason——'

'No. No, Jane. It's just as I said: it's you. *You.* Maureen has been bothering me for some time. The old, old story' ... a laugh ... 'she wants to proceed from the ring.'

'It's customary,' Jane observed.

'But it wasn't for you. You never pursued, did you? Not until now.'

'*Not* now, Rodden, please try to realize that.' She actually leaned across to him. '*Know it*, Rodden,' she advised.

Something must have penetrated, for Rodden sat quiet a while.

'You'll change,' he said presently, 'and at least it will get Maureen out of my hair.'

'If she learns.'

'Of course she will learn. Even by now Bower is allotting me another black mark for running out of fuel, and as you must know by now, that man never does things by halves. Undoubtedly the mechanic knows, and from the mechanic the next down, or the next across. Right across to the stables? I think you can say, Janey, that when we don't arrive by dusk, everyone will be aware.' A small pause. 'Including Maureen.'

'You're hateful!' she burst out.

'Yet efficient?' He had taken out another cigarette.

'I don't know.' Jane was narrowing her eyes to the further end of the clearing. There was no road from the small valley strip, but there must be a track of sorts, for a jeep was labouring up. She heard Rodden give an angry grunt.

'They're coming across,' Jane said unnecessarily, for she knew that Rodden would be equally aware of that.

She wondered who it could be ... some bushman who had seen them put down and suspected they were in trouble? Surely not William Bower himself, there would not have been time.

Then she heard shouting, and began to laugh. For, as opposed to Rodden's two of them, it appeared there were to be six of them. John drove the jeep. Kate sat beside him. Behind them both sat the twins.

'A ring from Bowers,' John called. 'Bill Bower reckoned you'd be putting down here, and he was right. He told me to bring out some gas for you to get back to Fetherfell,

Gair, but for us to fetch Jane.'

John helped Jane down, then, with a big white handkerchief, flagged Rodden out of the valley again. It was not so difficult, the craft was small and the cliffs banking down to the valley were in accommodating positions.

It was only when the plane had gone that Jane noticed that Rodden had *not* taken on any fuel. She hoped that John did not notice that the supply he had fetched out had not been touched. That if he did, later, he would not be sufficiently interested to tell William Bower. Yet did Bower need to be told?

'Bill reckoned you'd be putting down here,' John had said.

Just as he seemed to know everything, even the biological condition of Dotsy, it appeared that the great Bower had also known this.

But William Bower said nothing at all. All the way up to the stud, Kate driving the mini that had been parked in front of John's when they had emerged from the valley strip ... more Johnny cakes? Jane wondered briefly ... Jane had rehearsed her answers to Bower.

But there had been nothing to answer to. Neither had any of the innuendoes, subtleties and sarcasms she had anticipated been voiced.

'There's been a hitch in the fostering,' was what the stud boss said instead. 'It appears that the Princess isn't as well endowed as I thought, and can only provide for one orphan. However, as you already have a hand-feed job, Miss Sidney, Maureen will take over our second waif.'

Jane nodded ... and still waited. He was not the kind of man to let a thing like this pass.

But he did let it pass, and because the boss did, all the stud did, too. No doubt they had noticed and noted Gair's non-arrival after Bower—working almost on the landing paddock as they did they couldn't help being aware—and no doubt, too, they had noticed and noted Jane's arrival by car instead, but there was no question, no comment. Jane accepted it thankfully, she had been dreading the construction Maureen might put on the brief episode. As it was, it had been so brief that it became no episode at all. Jane liked Maureen, and she wanted no change in their friendly relations.

There was no change ... not apparently. Maureen asked Jane for her formula for feeding. She asked several other pertinent questions. It was as if nothing had happened. And yet ... Jane could not put a finger on it, she did not even know why she thought it, Maureen was as pleasant and as nice to know as ever, but somewhere there was a withdrawal. She could be imagining it, Jane told herself, but there was no outgoing any more from the younger girl to Jane. It was a pity. That night she had opened her bedroom door and found Maureen there had been a very precious moment, Jane knew in retrospect. A younger girl coming to an older one is always an intrinsic thing.

But it was not like that now. Maureen, though she sought Jane out, asked for advice, nodded agreement, thanked Jane, *all the time looked away*. Had she not found herself suddenly very busy, Jane could have fretted over that.

Her first consignment was now entirely in her care, and the seven weeks they had been out of training would take some catching up, Jane soon found. Gretel had put on weight and needed exercise to reduce that tub she had achieved; San Marco, who had won several country events in U.K. and had revelled in activity, had grown lazy, and Ruthven of the good connections was only showing outward signs of the bad sides of his families.

'You slackers are going to wake up,' Jane said sternly.

That week went as though it was a day. As soon as she was off Gretel, Jane was on San Marco, San finished she tackled Ruthven. They protested at first, they had become used to the *dolce vita*, but slowly they sniffed the old sweetness of dew-wet, herby-breathed morning paddocks (for meadow or paddock the sweetness was still the same) and the indolence they had got into dropped away. They be-

312

came Jane's fellows again.

She was exhausted every evening, and sometimes she nearly fell asleep over the feeding of Wendy's Pride, who was coming along very nicely, and making the second hand-fed orphan, Billy Boy, attended by Maureen, look very junior indeed. Jane wondered how the lucky foal who had won himself a mother and not an attendant with a feed bottle was faring, and went out to the east paddock where Persian Princess and Little Persia, as the adopted foal had been named, were domiciled.

When she reached the sliprail, she stood and laughed. Persian Princess was every inch a princess. Her mother had been a queen, Jane had learned, Queen of Persia, her sire something equally regal. The Princess moved haughtily, even when she cantered it was with royal dignity. But now a lot of the protocol was wiped out, wiped out by a rather shaggy, ridiculously spindly-legged, mischievous, distinctly plebeian bundle of colthood, name of Little Persia, rollicking by her side. They just didn't match, that pair, the top drawer mother, the bottom drawer baby, and when they ran together it was almost buffoonery. Jane laughed till the tears came to her eyes.

'And yet,' pointed out a voice at Jane's side, 'the Princess is as proud as Punch, or as proud, anyway, as if she had her own elegant offspring beside her, not the product of Scaramouche out of Ragamuffin.'

'Is that the baby's line?'

'Yes.' It was William Bower who had joined Jane.

'Little Persia wouldn't change mammas either,' Jane said, smiling at the odd couple. 'It's strange, when they're so unlike.'

'It must be that mutual look that did it,' he offered, "... when hearts are of each other sure." '

'I rather think it's a sure meal as far as Little Persia is concerned.'

'How factual we are today!' William looked at Jane more closely. 'Or is it weariness making you see only the

313

business side? I've been watching you, Miss Sidney, you really are working your fellows hard, aren't you? What's the incentive? Is it because they personally belong?'

'Only a fifth of them. No, not entirely. They were in shocking condition.'

'Were?'

'I believe they've improved.'

'I believe so, too. I was looking them over'—Jane fumed privately at that, but had to add in all fairness that he had every right to, he owned more of them than she did.

'Yes?' she asked.

'Gretel is losing her tub.' A sly pause. 'Easier to get rid of it, I would say, than Dotsy's.'

'*You* are saying that, Mr. Bower, I'm not. Not yet.'

'Have you written to my uncle asking him?'

'I will.'

He nodded, and resumed once more.

'San Marco looks fine. So does Ruthven. Which brings up a subject I would like to discuss.'

'Yes, Mr. Bower?'

'I'd like to try those two fellows out at a few meets. How does your one-fifth feel about that?'

'Four to one doesn't give me much scope to feel anything,' Jane said.

'That's a different story from what you boasted before, then your fifth had the final say. Seriously, though, would you have any objection?'

'Of course not. I want them to race. It's what Rusty bred them for.'

'There's a few provincials coming up, I'd like to try out their reaction.'

'How do you mean? They've both raced before.'

'Try their reactions to the various courses, which you'll soon see down here can be categorized as good, medium, then problem, or poor. I don't know how it is over in U.K., but in some of our more inferior backgrounds there are still some excellent prizes offering. Also, though the going is

314

rough, some horses actually like it rough.' William Bower looked at her.

'Yes, I believe Ruthven could be one,' mused Jane, 'though I don't know how rough.'

'We can try them out, gradually lessening the standard of fields. I may as well tell you now what I'm really after. I'd like finally to enter one, or the two, of them in the coming Farley Downs event.'

'Downs don't sound rugged to me,' she commented.

'Your downs mightn't, but these are in our red centre, and more sand and spinifex than turf.'

'Oh,' Jane said.

'Anyway, think it over while we do the preliminary trials. There's a meet on Friday at Lilyborne, down the coast, a very pretty, very green picnic race sort of place, that I'm sure you'll like as well as San Marco and Ruthven. It won't be so much different from your own plusher courses. After we get over Lilyborne we'll ... but one thing at a time, the next can wait.' He looked at her. 'Yes?'

'Yes,' Jane agreed.

As taking the horses down to Lilyborne would entail an entire day and an early start, Jane asked Maureen to take over the feeding of Wendy's Pride. Maureen already had the Fetherfell foal in her care, but she agreed at once ... yet still, Jane somehow felt, with that slight withdrawal.

'Maureen,' she wanted to say, 'what is it? Can't we sort this thing out?'

But almost as if she anticipated something, the younger strapper assured her: 'Don't worry, Jane,' and left Jane standing and watching her go. *And worrying.*

It was useless asking Kate, who was so enthralled in her twin-minding and valley excursions that Jane wondered how she would take to stabling again when the children's parents returned, so Jane just let it pass.

The take-off down to Lilyborne was to be very early, and it was still dark when Harry tapped on Jane's door and said that breakfast was ready.

Jane had it standing up. William was there and standing up as he ate already. Within ten minutes they were on the road. The journey down the valley, their only exit, because of the half light was negotiated very carefully, but by the time they reached the coast all the morning shadows had gone, and it was a shiny day full of sunny premonitions for a shiny afternoon.

They went down the south coast road, San Marco and Ruthven in open boxes so they could enjoy the morning as well. A soft explosion of little waves came up at them from the strings of yellow beaches beside the road, a musical scrabbling of surf-sifted pebbles. It was a beautiful ringing sort of day.

'I suppose we're mad,' laughed William Bower, in a ringing mood, too, Jane saw, 'apart from your exercising our two fellows are practically untrained.'

'They were trained at Little Down.'

'Untrained to our methods,' he explained. 'However, it will be experience, and, let's hope, a profitable one.'

It was. San Marco came in third in the race that Bower selected, and the newchum Ruthven actually shared a first.

'Now we can go down a grade,' said William on their way back, 'try a meeting with less of that English plush and lush.'

Jacumba, west this time, was selected, and here San Marco showed definite distaste for anything but green fields, but Ruthven frankly enjoyed himself, no place admittedly, but demonstrating a distinct lack of dismay over clumps of billy buttons and last year's thistle.

'The Downs now for Ruthven,' William decided. 'Agreed?'

There was no need for Jane to pretend to contemplate, she was as keen as Bower was.

'How long will that take?' she asked.

'Longer, of course. I'll have us flown, us comprising you, me, Ruthven, the previous day, then stay a day, then return the next day.'

'You won't pilot the plane yourself?'

'In a journey as far away as the Centre, no. I'll charter a larger craft, and just sit back.'

'Won't all that be expensive?'

'Thinking of your fifth, Miss Sidney?'

'I could be.'

'Then hope to recoup it all in the race that I have my eye on. Anyway, tallying up what the boys have already won you, you should break even, even if we lose.'

'That's all right,' Jane assured him, 'I'm well aware that in this business you have to take a risk.'

'. . . Only in this business?'

Something in his voice stopped Jane from answering him with a question of her own, a question as to what he meant by that question. Instead she asked when and where.

'Tuesday next. We'll leave early again and pick up the craft at Quinton.—By the way, Miss Sidney.'

'Yes, Mr. Bower?'

'These Centre meets are social as well as racing events. I'd pack something more than jodhpurs.'

She would have liked him to be more explicit, but he turned and went.

She asked Maureen that night. It was good to have something to ask the girl, Jane thought; the way things were now, Maureen growing progressively more and more withdrawn, apart from the feeding of the foal and the problems to be discussed, they never spoke with each other.

'Long dress,' Maureen said abruptly.

'I haven't brought one.'

'You can have mine. It's long and white.' Maureen's voice was more clipped than ever.

'That sounds like a wedding dress.'

'It was.'

'Maureen ... Maureen dear ...'

It was no use, the girl had left. When Jane went along to Maureen's room and tapped on the door, she was not answered.

They drove to Quinton the next morning, Ruthven looking regally pleased with himself riding along in a float intended for three. William Bower had taken the extra precaution of padding the box in case Ruthven in his solitary state bumped around over any rough patches, but he had still left Ruthven with a good viewing section. Jane was pleased about that; she had inherited from Rusty a firm belief in horses having an unrestricted view when they travelled.

They passed through the valley beneath eucalypts, black-woods and sassafras, waved to millmen milling big logs and piling pale hummocks of sawdust, called to the children from farms and hopfields hanging out mailbags for the mailman, then reached the coast with its soft burst of waves and washing pebbles again.

Quinton, much larger than the rural strips Jane had encountered so far, was not far distant. When they got to the field a moderate-sized freighter was awaiting them, with a crew of two, the second pilot doubling for a wireless navigator, a comfortable section for Ruthven and two easy seats for the passengers. The engines whirred, they taxied, rose above the coast and at once set off west.

They crossed the Divide, and for a while rural centres displayed their pattern of streets and parks fairly frequently, then the country cities disappeared, the flats flattened out even further, and salt pans, and clay pans, and eventually the desert took over. Jane stared down fascinated at red ochre sand, purple patches of Calamity Jane, or so William Bower told her, and outcrops of rocks taking on almost unbelievable colours.

'I only hope,' said William, 'that Ruthven is as impressed as you seem to be.'

'Oh,' breathed Jane, 'I really am.'

Several hours afterwards the engines changed their beat and Jane knew they must be ready to put down. She could see little to descend to, only a few scattered buildings, surrounded, as was everything here in the Centre it seemed, with endless space.

318

'Is this Farley Downs?'

'Yes. You mightn't think much of it commercially, but it's still the recognized hub for a thousand mile square. Also, it's the accepted social centre.' A slight laugh. 'Believe it or not, people will be attending this meet from even further than those thousand miles.'

'How do they get here?' she asked.

'By truck, jeep, 'rover, plane, whatever means they can rustle up. We won't be the only charter, either, you'll find a dozen of them flying in, some carrying as many as six horses. Then, of course, there'll be the sideshow men in caravans, the picture showman, Ahmed the Afghan, and the last, I think, of his breed in the west, with his covered waggon full of pretties.'

'What kind of pretties?'

'Dresses for milady. You didn't think,' William laughed, 'there were shops out here?'

'I thought there might be a vestibule in the hotel.' Jane was thinking of the very attractive shopping she had encountered in many hotels.

'No hotels here,' said William, 'only pubs.'

'Aren't they the same?'

'There is,' William Bower said cagily, 'a subtle difference, Miss Sidney. You'll see.'

'Are we booked into one?'

'There is only one. And no, we're not. Thank heaven.'

'But why? Then where are we to stop?'

'Why, because I, anyway, want some rest, and rest you can't expect when Centralians who haven't seen each other since last year meet up again. No, we're rooming at the Marriotts', old customers of mine. I sold them a winner two years ago, since when I'm an even more welcome guest. I say even more, for everyone is welcome in the west.'

When the plane put down, Jane could see why William Bower had been glad of the Marriotts. The landing paddock was practically in the town, if you could call one weathered timber hotel and one small post-office that, and already the town was humming.

'The hotel—pub has swinging doors!' delighted Jane.

'And a well-worn counter.' William watched her fascination at the ten-gallon hats with their owners underneath coming out of the dusty street with frothing glasses.

'You must try a beer,' he said, 'they have a very fine art of putting on big white collars to them here.' When she shook her head, he agreed, too, to wait.

'Until we celebrate our win,' he grinned.

They found a truck willing to take them out to the Marriott's.

'Ruthven?' Jane asked.

'Bob Marriott has a stable here in town and has agreed to put Ruthven with his fellows.'

It was not far out, William said, to the Marriotts'; they were lucky there, for most of the other entrants, unless they had secured a hotel room, which was unlikely as each room was pre-booked from the previous year, and even then never catered for less than seven or eight on beds, sofas, divans and what-have-you, would be up to a hundred miles away.

'And you think Plateau is isolated,' he finished.

'I've never said so.'

'No,' he agreed after some thought, 'you haven't. Actually, Miss Sidney, you don't say much at all.'

'Is it required?' she asked.

He pretended to be thinking. 'I can't recall it on the agreement,' he said at last.

The Marriotts had what William told Jane was a fairly typical Downs home. It was wide, one-storeyed, spread over what seemed an immense space, with green polished cement floors and coolness, a lot of bamboo and many bright rag mats. Mrs. Marriott, middle-aged and eager for female company, at once asked Jane about her dress for the hop.

'I should say the Race Ball,' she corrected, giggling.

'I haven't brought one.'

This caused Mrs. Marriott to cry out with disappointment and William Bower to say dourly: 'But I told you, Miss Sidney.'

'I know, but I hadn't one' ... for a moment Jane wondered what would have been the reaction if she had worn Maureen's wedding dress ... 'and there was nowhere in Plateau to buy anything.'

'Nor anywhere here,' said Mrs. Marriott. She added thoughtfully, 'Unless——'

'Unless I go in the afternoon dress that I did pack?'

'Oh no, dear, it has to be an occasion dress. A long one. You might find it hard to believe, but there won't be a woman at the dance who hasn't been planning her get-up all the year.' Her eyes met William's. 'I wonder——' she said.

'It's too late for David Jones, Marry,' discouraged William.

'But—— Ahmed?'

'Ahmed? Would he have anything for Miss Sidney?'

'It's not all bargain basement he carries, Bill, I've seen several things I wouldn't mind buying myself.'

'He's at the course, I expect.'

'Along with all the other itinerants.'

'We'll go now,' said William Bower, not asking Jane whether she wanted a new dress, for that matter whether she wanted to attend the ball.

There were plenty of cars at the Marriotts', belonging both to them and their staff, so getting back to Farley was no difficulty. Finding Ahmed proved more of a difficulty; already the outside of the ring was canvas city.

Jane looked around in fascination. Little Down had had its village fêtes, but never had she seen anything like this. There were trucks, jeeps, caravans, tents all huddled together, and beside them merry-go-rounds, hooplas and Aunt Sallys already snaring trade. There were balloon men. Pie pedlars. Hamburger Harrys. As a matter of fact there were five Hamburger Harrys, each Harry looking resentfully at the other.

'Tomorrow,' said William, 'you'll see signs Original Hamburger Harry.'

'On all of them?'

'Very probably. Here's Ahmed now.'

Ahmed had a covered waggon, and he had circled each side with his wares, mostly bright shifts and dangling baubles to wear with them.

At first Jane thought it was a waste of time, that there could be nothing here, then both she and William saw the long, fresh pink cotton number together, more simply made than the heavily beaded offerings beside it, in fact quite a possible dress, Jane had to admit.

'It's not Pierre Balmain,' said William.

'Nor, I expect, David Jones,' Jane smiled.

'Will it do?' he asked.

'So long as it doesn't offend you.'

'If it does, I'll only look the once,' he promised. He told the Afghan to wrap it up.

They did not come back into Farley that night, where, Mr. Marriott said, the swing doors would be swinging overtime. Instead they sat in the cool green room and talked Territorian. How interesting it all was, Jane thought, listening intently.

The next morning she put on the floral jersey she had brought and went into the big event. It was, she found, like nothing else on earth, it was completely, wildly, fascinatingly different, and she enjoyed every moment, even when William Bower said of her red ochre hair, for the stirred-up dust and covered that part of Jane as well as everywhere else, a laconic: 'I know now why my uncle signed you on as his strapper.' He nodded to her head. 'After a name like Rusty, how could he help it?'

'Rusty was short for Russell,' she reminded him.

'Yet probably a favourite colour with my uncle, too.'

'But I'm not red. Perhaps faintly inclined that way in a natural state, but still far from titian.'

'Who said such a nice thing of you as titian?'

'So long as it's a removable colour that's all that concerns me,' Jane said plaintively.

'It'll come out in the wash,' William assured her. 'Have you seen around?'

'I've bought six lucky tickets and been unlucky six times, had a cornet of fairy floss, a——'

'Had tea?'

'Not yet.'

'Come on, then.' He put the tips of his fingers under her elbow and led her to the tent, where great urns of strong brew awaited, toppling piles of corned beef sandwiches, wide wedges of sultana cake.

Jane was intrigued with the jockeys, already parading up and down, not the professionals who had flown up from the cities for the main events, but the local offerings for the minor races, wearing everything on their heads from ten-gallon hats to crash helmets, and instead of breeches had put on shorts, chaps, jeans, even in one instance waist-high wading boots.

William told Jane that Ruthven was down for the Downs Cup, the main event. 'Ambitious of me ... of *us*,' he corrected that at once. 'You've no idea of the aristocrats he'll have to meet.'

'It'll be experience at least,' said Jane.

'That's all I'd bet on if I were you,' Bower advised.

He was entirely wrong, as he said proudly, if regretfully, an hour later.

'Had I known that Ruthven had that in him ...'

For Ruthven was first away from the barrier, led all the way, came in an indisputable leader.

'I reckon that boy was born for the mulga,' William glowed. He looked at Jane, then grinned. 'But someone else was not. You're Eve in ochre, Miss Sidney. If you want to wear that pink creation tonight you'd better tone down your colouring a little. Shall we leave now to give you time to soak?'

'The Marriotts are still here,' she pointed out.

'I reckon we can run to a hiring. In fact' ... serious now ... 'between us at the very minute we could buy the taxi. Do you know what that stake was?'

'No.'

'Then take a breath.' He told her, and it was so incredible she stared open-mouthed at him.

'That's true. Now you know why I wanted a spinifex sprinter, the prizes to say the least were rewarding. If you'll close your mouth long enough to rattle off some arithmetic, Miss Sidney, you'll see that your fifth entitles you to——'

'I'm rich,' Jane said unbelievingly. 'Not exactly, but you are comfortably placed.' He looked at her sharply. 'It could make all the difference, couldn't it? You could step out of the show right now. With the extra sum I'd pay you for your now valuable share you really could be that rich woman.'

'No, thank you.'

'Going for more?'

She hesitated. She had been going to say, as she had said before, 'I'll wait for the D's first, see them settled.' But all at once she knew it was not just that, that it was—— She fastened her teeth on her bottom lip to stop her making an audible sound of discovery, for she had just discovered an entirely mad, an entirely impossible, incredible thing. She had discovered—and she would not believe it—that when it came to this man, to this great, overbearing, overwhelming, over-*everything* hunk of——

'I should say you're going for more,' he drawled.

No, Jane knew, I won't. I won't.

As soon as she got to the homestead she soaked, scrubbed, shampooed. When at last she emerged, the tub wore a bright red rim, but Jane was her usual colour. Perhaps a little pinker from her long immersion, but it suited the rosy cotton. She regarded herself in the mirror and thought she looked rather nice.

The Marriotts arrived, dressed, too, then they all left in

the biggest of the cars for the Farley social event of the year.

Jane was impressed with the appearance of the barn, which had received much more attention than sweeping and dusting. The local ladies had adorned it in trailing ferns, native ti and flowering vines. With paper lanterns and balloons it became as festive a hall as any city offering, and Jane went approvingly in behind the Marriotts ... then stopped.

At the other end of the barn was a replica of her pink cotton. She dodged behind Bob Marriott so as not to embarrass the wearer just as a third pink cotton danced by.

'Well,' remarked William Bower by her side, 'Ahmed at no time said it was an exclusive model. Want me to drive you back?'

'To change into what?' Jane sighed.

Mrs. Marriott broke eagerly in: 'Ever since last night I've been thinking, Jane.'

'Good for you,' said her husband admiringly.

'Be quiet! I've been thinking, Jane. You see, I saw you in your negligée last night. So many girls now are wearing them for social events as well as home relaxation, or so my fashion mags tell me. You *could*, you know.'

'Well, one thing,' admitted Jane ruefully, 'I can't wear this.' For a fourth Ahmed creation had appeared. Followed by another pink. Then another. Ahmed must have won himself a considerable discount for accepting an entire batch of pinks.

'Come on, then,' William Bower said.

Back at the homestead, Jane took a long searching look at the garment. It was, as Mrs. Marriott had said, very possible. Also, she had done this sort of thing before back home. That buttercup brocade, she recalled, she had worn it to——

'What do you think?' she asked William Bower, holding up the article.

'Put it on,' he said.

Jane did. It was deep cream and it fell softly in a straight line to her ankles. It had a deep décolleté and no sleeves, but she felt it did not have a nightie look. She added shoes, beaded bag and went out to the room along the polished green floor, her heels making little clicks.

He was standing by the french window, looking out on the night, and surely no nights, thought Jane, were more beautiful than Centre nights, with their overdone stars and their big ... melon-big ... moons.

'Well?' she asked.

He turned around.

He looked at her. And looked. It took such a long time that Jane found herself squirming, found herself wanting to cry out not 'Well?' but 'WELL!'

Then, still looking, but what sort of look it was, amused, unamused, mutual, Jane did not know, for she found she could not look back to find out, he said: 'I think its original purpose is best, Miss Sidney.'

'You mean——' Now Jane did look at him, looked angrily at first, and then——

'Yes, I mean that,' William said in a quiet voice.

CHAPTER SEVEN

BACK once more at Plateau, Jane found herself less work-harassed than before. San Marco had been passed on to appropriate hands for specialist preparation for the better class provincials, and eventually, Jane suspected, a forth-coming Southern cup; Ruthven, having shown his rugged preferences, was being further toughened up at another of the Bower satellite studs—one, William Bower told Jane, dealt in similar conditions to the conditions, or lack of, that the Downs had provided. This left only Gretel, later to be mated, in Jane's hands, so Jane had only one girl and one orphaned foal to attend. She knew that her leisure period would be brief, in fact only till next week when the three D's emerged from quarantine, so she took the oppor-tunity, seeing she was not even required for the twins, Kate still eagerly retaining that position, to explore her new surroundings.

She did it on Gretel, and the pair of them enjoyed the runs across the flats, and, upon occasion, the cautious (for Gretel was a stranger like Jane was) descents of the easier sections of the cliffs.

Several times Tim called upon Jane for veterinary assist-ance, since Jane was at present the sole Bower member literally not run off her feet. It was that period of the year (Down Under version) when a stud, always busy, becomes near-hectic.

There were seven top-class stallions ready for siring, and every day floats arrived from far distances, some even from interstate. Records had to be kept, and to make it more time-consuming, at Bowers the hopeful mares were agisted free until after their pregnancy tests. It all made for more work again.

On top of this, the yearling sales were being arranged.

They would not occur for some time yet, but Jane appreciated from her Surrey days that they took a lot of planning, a lot of pre-determination and pre-selection ... and a few tears. Or it had been tears of goodbye for her. For dear old Rusty, too, she had often suspected. It was strange, Jane pondered, that however much you disciplined yourself on what had to be, you could not successfully discipline your heart. She recalled, and still felt a pang, Little Down's sadness over their parting with Village Square, Eastern Night and Darcy.

She wondered if William Bower, too, experienced tugs. She knew that he would have scoffed at the idea, even possibly repeated that 'pony high priestess' of his and Gair's, but she had caught him out several times on 'boys' and 'girls' and 'fellows', on observed unrehearsed looks, and she was not sure he was the strict business man he tried to appear.

He certainly wasn't when he sought Jane out one evening.

'A sale tomorrow,' he said abruptly.

'I hope you do well.'

'Thank you.' There was a tinge of impatience in his voice at her formal reply.

'Did you require my help, Mr. Bower?' Jane asked, still formal.

'Yes. You're not doing anything special, are you?'

'Only exercising Gretel. Maureen seems to be coping as far as Tim is concerned.' Jane said that a trifle tetchily; she had been a little put out at the vet's obvious satisfaction with Maureen.

William Bower nodded disinterestedly. 'It's Fair Honey,' he said. But this time with interest.

'Oh yes.'

'You know her?'

Jane nodded. 'A pretty golden girl with a——'

'Yes, with a nasty-looking scar on her hip. Up till now Fair Honey has discouraged buyers with that hip, as soon as she goes into the sale ring and they see that scar they're frightened off.'

'How did the scar occur?'

'Honey cut the hip when she ran into a salt trough on a sheep property. It was before I got her.'

'Then you weren't frightened off.'

'I liked the girl at once. I mean the filly.'

Jane felt like adding: 'The mutual look?' but forbore. 'She's not that now, though, is she?' she said instead. 'Not a filly?'

'No. Fair Honey has had two very successful foalings. And that's what's concerning me.'

'Yes, Mr. Bower?'

'Because the catalogue hasn't been altered as I intended to alter it, Fair Honey is once more down for sale. Only this time her success as a mare could have leaked out, and there could be bids.'

'Can't she be withdrawn?'

'Too late. I've always made it a strict rule to stick to my programme.'

Jane nodded. 'Then what do you want me to do?'

'Bid, too,' he said.

'For myself or for you?'

'I wouldn't put you to that expense.'

'But if it wasn't such an expense?' Jane had had a thought.

He looked at her searchingly, but found nothing there. 'Just bid,' he advised.

'I still don't understand it; isn't the sale a yearling one?' Fair Honey was halfway now to two figures in age, Jane judged.

'The yearlings are months ahead. Even not being acclimatized yet you should know that. No, tomorrow's sales are just that. Sales,' he said gloomily.

'I'll bid,' Jane promised, taking pity on his gloom, remembering how she had felt on countless occasions. She added: 'If it's necessary.'

329

Again he gave her that curious look, found nothing once more, so left.

Jane went down to Fair Honey. She was an exceedingly pretty mare, and perhaps because of this received more attention than usual from the female strappers. Her coat was perfection, and Maureen ... or Kate? ... had worked on the scar until it was a very small flaw in the diamond.

But, said Jane to the mare, it's going to be a very discernible flaw, Honey.

It seemed strange to do things in reverse, to take the shine off instead of put it on, but that was what Jane worked at. She could not entirely diminish the gloss, as Honey was in excellent condition, but she did manage a discouraging lacklustre through untidy disarray to the shining gold coat. The scar showed out much more with the hair combed revealingly away from it. Jane even considered highlighting it by means of a cosmetic pencil, but she felt she could not cheat too much.

The next morning the country sounds of Bowers were punctuated in a way Jane recalled from Little Down. By raucous bid! By hammer! Always she had hated the blood sales, and she found she liked them no better now. But if the selling of Barbie, Mr. Six and Mahal upset her, barely knowing them, how much more upsetting must it be to William, who did? She would have liked to have flashed a sympathetic glance at him, but she was keeping an eye on Fair Honey, seeing that her scarred hip was in full view.

'And now, gentlemen, we offer Fair Honey, out of——'

Jane, taken by surprise, saw that she had not attended enough; she had let one of the grooms take Honey into the sale ring, and on her good side. She went to follow, but it was too late, the bidding actually had begun.

And such a beginning! It was a higher start even than Mahal had attracted, and everyone had had their eye on well-connected Mahal. Feeling a little sick, seeing her Farley Downs' profits vanishing for ever, for William Bower would never countenance this expense, Jane went higher.

The bidder—she could not see him—bid again. Jane bid.

All the attention was on her, standing as she did in the front row, and also, Jane knew from experience, because she was female, reasonably young, reasonably attractive.

Another bid from a retaliating Jane, and then, to her utter horror, even though it was doing what William Bower had asked of her, the acceptance from the auctioneer of that bid. An acceptance of three thousand five hundred dollars for a scarred mare.

Jane edged away from the ring and hurried towards the stables—just, as she had found years ago, as mothers find comfort in children, strappers find comfort in foals. She pushed the door of Wendy's Pride's box, and there, as well as Wendy's Pride, was William Bower. And he was laughing. Not just amused laughter but hilarious laughter.

'Your face!' he said, and laughed again.

'What's wrong with it?' Jane rubbed at her face with her handkerchief.

'Not now. Then. Then when you made that last bid and was accepted.'

'If you think it's funny——'

'I think it's side-splitting. Your poor worried little face!'

'It was a lot more money than I—than you intended,' Jane said unhappily. 'But what could I do? I did de-glamorize Honey.'

'The worst thing you could have done. If I'd known you had that in mind——'

'De-glamorization?'

'Is there such a word?' He laughed again. 'The moment I saw Fair Honey come in, saw her dusty coat, I knew all the wiseacres, and believe me most of them there today are that, would be wide-awake.'

'They were,' agreed Jane miserably, 'or at least one was. Does it matter much, Mr. Bower? Does it mean that you'll have to recompense your company for that very big bid I made?'

'No company,' William Bower informed her calmly, 'only yours truly in this concern ... except, of course, your fifth of the new lot.'

'Then?'

'No, it doesn't matter.' Again he laughed. 'Don't go fretting, Miss Sidney, all's well and all that, and it's brightened up what's usually a saddening affair.'

'Saying goodbye,' she nodded. She asked: 'Who was it bidding for Honey? Do you know him?'

'*You* don't know?'

'It was someone at the back.'

'And you didn't know?'

'Who was it, Mr. Bower?' For William Bower was moving out of the stable, yet not right out.

'Two thousand,' he called to show her. Then: 'Two thousand two hundred.'

Jane stared across at him. 'You,' she said.

'Yes.'

'But—but why?'

'The moment the mare came in I felt the interest; heard the stir, and no one reads a stir more clearly than a stud man. "What's this?" the atmosphere clearly said, "why is Bowers presenting a sale in an unpresentable manner? Watch it, it must be worthwhile." That' ... William gave a nod ... 'was what I received in the atmosphere.

'There were several very affluent buyers,' he resumed. 'You wouldn't know them, of course. I did. I decided the only way to put them off was to scotch the thing straight away.' Another bout of laughing. 'So, Miss Sidney, I did.'

'I was bidding against you!' Jane was not amused.

'Try to look at it this way,' Bower advised kindly, evidently taking pity on her, 'try to look at it as keeping out the big buyers.'

'All I can look at it is from the amused angle, the amusement, no doubt later, of all the stud.'

'Well, why not? It's not given to everyone to amuse.'

'You've made a fool of me, a clown!'

'A very nice clown,' he assured her. 'Also, it's not every clown can raise a laugh wearing his ordinary face.'

'Shall I paint it and get a bigger laugh?' she said bitterly.

'Just keep it its English pink and white, Miss Sidney,' William said.

'I——' began Jane, but it was all too much. Before a tear, which was fast welling over, fell on to Wendy's Pride's soft brow, she escaped. She heard his soft pursuing laugh, his assuring, 'Take it easy, no one will think twice about it,' as she shut the door behind her and went across to the big house.

At dinner that night she found out he was wrong with his assurance, though she had expected that, of course.

'Here comes Miss Moneybags,' greeted one of the boys.

'Can I put the fangs in for a loan, Miss Sidney? Something around two thou would do fine.'

'Beats me,' said Harry at the canteen door, 'how they didn't see it was the boss bidding, too.'

'He was right at the back and the attention, naturally' ... a flattering look which Jane in her present mood did not appreciate ... 'was on our girl.'

There was more delighted laughter, and Jane decided she might as well join in. After all, her purpose had been achieved. Fair Honey remained on at Bowers.

Only one person seemed unamused. Maureen did put on a smile so as not to be conspicuous, but there was no laughter there. It was because it entailed Jane, Jane knew. She knew also that she must have an understanding with Maureen.

The chance came when Maureen had to consult Jane concerning a new diet for the foal in her care, for Billy Boy had got beyond a mere bottle.

Jane had no doubt that Maureen had asked Tim first, and been referred to Jane, for there was a thinly-veiled reluctance in Maureen's voice as she told the senior strapper how Billy Boy was looking for something else.

Jane passed on her knowledge, knowledge learned in Little Down as well as Plateau. She advised Maureen to augment the new diet still with the daily bottle until Billy Boy wouldn't accept a bottle any more.

'You'll know when that time comes,' she smiled, and the absence of a smile on Maureen's face decided Jane that here and now was her time.

'Maureen.'

'Thank you. I'll see to that new diet at once.' The younger girl turned away.

'Maureen——' Jane repeated rather in defeat; how could you broach a subject to a back turned deliberately on you?

But—'Yes, Miss Sidney?' asked Maureen, and that 'Miss Sidney' did it. It gave Jane determination.

'You always called me Jane,' she said firmly.

'Yes, Miss Sidney?'

'Maureen, what's happened between us?'

'Was there anything?' Maureen had turned right back again. Her eyes and her face were hard. She had a pretty, gentle little face, and the change in her expression grieved Jane.

'Not strictly. I mean we weren't bosom pals, anything like that. For one thing, I was too old.'

Maureen said fairly, 'I've never thought of you in that way. I've thought of you the same as I think of Kate.'

'You're referring now to my age, of course.'

A pause, then Maureen said stonily: 'Of course.'

'If I've done anything to upset you, please believe it's been unintentional.'

Silence.

A little desperately, Jane went on: 'I'm referring now to that time when I flew back from Fetherfell with' ... a pause ... 'your fiancé.'

'He is not!'

'He was then.'

'I don't think he ever was. Not really. But please go on.'

'You don't mind me saying this?'

'No. In a way I think the thing should be cleared up, the same as you think.'

'Then I'll explain why I didn't come with Mr. Bower. There were two bereft foals, you see, instead of one.'

Maureen said impatiently, 'I know all that.'

'So,' persisted Jane, 'I came with Mr. Gair, and he ran out of fuel and we had to land in some valley.'

'I know all that, too.'

'Then,' said Jane a little helplessly, not knowing what else she could explain, 'you know everything.'

'Not quite. Oh, I know it's all over between Rodden and me ... that is if it ever was on. Sometimes ... most times ... I don't believe it was.'

'Maureen——'

'And the strange part is I can't feel unhappy over it.' The girl looked challengingly at Jane, challenging her to look back. Jane did, and saw that Maureen was telling the truth.

'Then, Maureen, why are you like this? We were friends, instinctive kind of friends. You came to me.'

'And you must have been laughing your head off!'

'I wasn't. I was trying to know what to say.'

'It should have been easy enough. Just four words.'

Jane looked up at Maureen.

'Four words concerning my ... *our* ... ring. Just "I wore that once."'

'Maureen——' How many futile times had she mumbled that, Jane thought in despair.

'I liked you, Jane. I liked you very much. I would never have gone to Kate, who's a dear but immature, but I did go to you. Rodden is over—I just told you. There's nothing there, and, as things have turned out' ... what things? Jane wondered a little stupidly, for she felt stupid with regret for a friendship lost ... 'I'm glad. But you were different. I looked up to you. I—came to you. Oh, Jane, you needn't have deceived me like that.'

'How could I have said "Yes, a lovely ring, Maureen, I should know, I chose it." How could I have warned you about Rodden? I mean, what happened between Rodden and me could have been entirely my own doing. I still don't know for sure, Maureen.'

'Well, you'll have plenty of time, because it's all over so far as I'm concerned.'

'It was over years ago with me. So why ... *why* must we perform post-mortems like this?'

'It was your deceit,' said Maureen stonily. 'I needed you. I never had an older sister. I can't remember my mother, nor any aunts. You were just what I wanted. But you let me show you my ... our ... ring, and you let me come to you for comfort.'

'Yes,' said Jane, 'and I'm sorry about that.'

A silence came between them. Jane had apologized. She could do no more. She knew that time alone would bring reason to Maureen, and that there was no use trying to force matters now.

'I'm glad, anyway,' she said inadequately, 'that we've aired the affair.'

Maureen looked away, possibly ashamed of herself, but wisely Jane did not pursue the matter.

'I'd try that diet on Billy Boy,' she told the younger strapper, 'it's working for Wendy's Pride.'

'Yes, I shall. Thank you.' Maureen left Jane.

It could have been much worse. Jane sensibly realized. Maureen could have made a scene. More important still she could have put down her end-of-the-affair with Rodden as Jane's fault, but it was no one's fault. Maureen had simply fallen *out* of love with him ... or had she only ever thought she had fallen in love? Recalling Maureen's frank eyes as she had said, 'And the strange thing is I can't feel unhappy over it,' Jane believed this could be true.

Very soothing for Maureen, she accepted, once the indignation of being deceived by Rodden's former fiancée wore off, but no solace for Jane.

Doing what she always had done in times of doubt, stress or simply needing comfort, had done in Little Down before Bowers, Jane went across to the stables to press her head against a silky shoulder, fondle a soft brow. It never failed. She decided to have a run out.

Gretel was the only offering, unless she borrowed one of Bower's boys or girls. However, the mare liked blowing cobwebs away as much as Jane did, though Gretel's were only stable cobwebs when she would have preferred a meadow ... I must say a paddock, Jane reminded herself ... and Jane's were much more involved.

Saddling up, sympathizing with Gretel's whicker of pleasure, the pair of them, a girl and mare, left the stud behind them for Plateau's inviting green flats.

Gretel, as usual enjoyed every moment. She had never been a pernickety mare, Jane thought appreciatively, she did not step with female fastidiousness as many mares did once away from familiar turf. Jane remembered riding her once around a chalk pit, imprudent, perhaps, but she had trusted Gretel not to tread on any crumbling edge. Not that there were edges on the flat ... not until you actually came to the edge. Jane glanced in that direction. She had taken Gretel down some of the more gradual cliff tracks and the pair of them had loved it. Well, why not again? She was in the mood for diversion and Gretel was dependable.

'All right, girl, we'll go exploring.' Jane turned the mare down a path that looked as negotiable as the ones she had explored before. She was careful about that, she had no intention of being reckless.

It proved a pretty way. It edged round outcrops of rocks and entanglements of trees. Some of the trees met each other high above them to form a green arch. Once horse and rider passed a little stream singing down the valley, and Jane found a scoop of water from which Gretel enjoyed a long drink. If she had practised what she had practised on her previous explorations, and that was to go so far but no further, nothing would have happened. She and Gretel would have returned refreshed—and minus a few cobwebs —to the stud.

But, about to retrace their way, something between the trees caught Jane's attention. It was well below them, so for caution's sake should have been resisted, but the huddle, or cluster, or closer settlement of something, Jane could not have said what, intrigued her so much she felt she could not climb up again until she found out what it was down there. Gretel's whicker of disapproval, too, should have put Jane off, for all horses have a tremendous sense of the unknown, but Jane chose to call Gretel lazy, and pulling on the rein she impelled the unwilling mare further along the track. Not, some minutes later, that you could call it a track any longer. Someone had been here, you could see that from the bent bushes, but it was not a path even in the faint way that the other paths had been, it was practically nothing.

Several times Jane lost even the bent bushes, but, peering between the trees, she could still glimpse the huddle. It was a kind of get-together of rough logs, she saw, probably a crude humpy, as she believed these bush shelters were called here. Yes ... peering closer ... it was a humpy, a shack, a shanty. It would be the place the twins had visited the day that John had taken her to the eucalyptus distillery and they had sauntered off. Well, she would do no visiting. She was about to turn the disapproving Gretel back to the track proper when she saw a figure coming out of the huddle, and, not wanting to be seen herself, she climbed down from Gretel.

She looked between the leaves of the trees. John had spoken of this occasional bush visitor as an old man, but this man definitely was not. Then Jane was recalling Roberta as saying also on that occasion: 'Not so old.' She wondered——

Deciding she had looked enough, Jane turned to see a fed-up Gretel disappearing through the bushes.

'You bad girl!' Jane gave pursuit.

She did not know how she lost sight of Gretel, one moment the mare was rounding a bend and the next moment, Jane having gained that bend, there was simply no mare there. Nor at the side. Nor behind her. Nor anywhere. Gretel it seemed had vanished into air.

Now Jane did what she knew, but temporarily forgot, a walker in a new territory must never do: she plunged into the bush without first marking herself by some bend of the track, some peculiarity of a tree. Within moments, within yards, from the path, she was lost.

She pushed through tanglewood to find a small stream running down the valley—the same rivulet she had met earlier, she wondered, where Gretel had found a scoop from which to drink?

Its waterbells tinkled louder further down the gorge, which meant it must hasten its pace to leap somewhere, probably it became quite precipitous, so Jane turned back. If she could climb a tree she might be able to pinpoint herself, even find that lean-to in the bush and make her way towards it, but all the trees around soared straight and sheer for many feet, and even then did not offer any accommodating branches until much nearer the top. They were essentially valley gums, and reaching up to the sun.

She walked on ... though stumbled would have been a better word. There was not the slightest semblance of any path now, in fact there was nothing at all but dark green undergrowth, sage green bush and trees, trees, trees.

She must not panic. That could be fatal, she knew, she could go around in circles, exhausting herself, confusing any rescuer ... if rescue came. She presumed that Gretel would find her way back as most horses did, but she was remembering, too, that Gretel was a new chum, as she was, and could take hours to do that. By then it would be dark, and any search would have to be delayed until the morning. The thought of spending the night in this unfamiliar bush dismayed Jane so much she forgot her determination to think and act calmly, and began pushing through the tanglewood again, this time with abandon.

A sharp scratch from some thorny bush pulled her up sternly. She took stock of herself. She was scratched, blistered, tired, and ... if she thought about it ... hungry. She had cut her knee, though she could not recall doing it, a twig had ripped her blouse, she had slightly but painfully turned an ankle. On top of everything she felt giddy, lightheaded, unreal. Also she felt afraid.

She found a smaller rock outcrop and sat down. It was hard to force herself to do it, every impulse in her urged her on ... and out. But on, she knew now, was not necessarily out, not the way she had gone so far. She tried to think rationally, plan reasonably, look around her and assess and consider. But every stir in the bush set her nerves pounding, and when a lizard came over the rock in search of sun she gave a little scream, jumped to her feet and ran wildly forward again.

Undergrowth stopped her once more, so she came back, but not to the outcrop and the lizard, for all that, too, had gone. Only the baffling tanglewood remained. I'm lost, hopelessly lost, Jane knew, and unable to think even now, she gave way to helpless little sobs.

After that she stumbled on, stumbled back, walked entirely without plan or reason. She was crying openly and she let herself do it. If I exhaust all that, she thought, I might be able to make some sense at last.

It happened that way. Utterly depleted and exhausted, she began walking in a more restrained manner, looking where she went instead of stumbling blindly through her tears. And it was then she saw the humpy once more, the small huddle between the trees. She saw the man she had seen previously ... or had she? This man seemed younger, taller, or was her imagination playing tricks with her? She had no opportunity to check up again, for the man went back into the shelter.

It didn't matter, anyway, she simply had to get down to

that shack and tell her story. All her prior distaste at meeting the hermit, for only a hermit would live like this in the bush, had left her now. She needed human contact, then a direction home.

She hurried down, always keeping the little clearing in sight. Then at last she was on it, sliding the final steep slope to the crude lean-to of bushes, roof of several iron sheets, sapling walls.

'Is anyone there?' she called breathlessly, and heard a movement in the humpy.

The man came to the door and Jane stared in disbelief.

It was Rodden.

Afterwards Jane knew she must have lost contact for a few moments. She could recall pitching forward, being caught in Rodden's arms, but then nothing more until she opened her eyes and found herself in the tiny dark hut. Still in Rodden's arms.

'This time I could make something of it, couldn't I?' Rodden's lips twisted in a crooked grin.

'No!' Jane said it definitely for all her weakness, and the man nodded.

'I know, Janey.' He released her and got up. 'There's nothing there. But at least' ... ruefully ... 'you needn't have scotched me with Maureen.' He had left her now to go to a Primus stove to pump it and put on some water to heat. She saw him take out lint, adhesive tape, scissors, a needle that he proceeded to sterilize.

'Are you going to mend me?' she asked.

'Yes. You don't deserve it, but I am.'

'I didn't do anything against you as regards Maureen, Rodden, it was entirely her own decision. Anyway, wasn't that what you wanted?'

'Only if I couldn't have you, Jane, and perhaps had I known——'

'Known what?'

'Known *for sure* that Maureen was to inherit a penny or

341

two come the age of twenty-five, because it was being mooted around. But I didn't know.' (Evidently, thought Jane, he did not know of her own improved financial state.)

She said in disgust: 'Rodden, you're nasty!'

'I have to be nasty. I had the misfortune of landing poor parents. Oh, they educated me, and I won scholarships, but a man needs more of a boost than that. I want my own business, Jane, I don't want always to kow-tow to a boss.'

'Is that really why you renewed your friendship with me? Because of what Rusty gave me?'

'Partly,' he admitted, 'though still something persisted from that first time. I was a fool, Jane, I wanted the hand-out that Bower gives all his employees on marriage at Plateau, quite a considerable one; no doubt he likes to play the benevolent squire. When you've had nothing all your life things like that count.'

'They do to you. They counted, anyway, more than I did.'

'Not really, but I didn't realize that until it was too late. I was attracted by Maureen, she's a pretty little thing, and that inheritance rumour was being mooted around even then.

'Then you came. My real love plus a positive income, not one falling due reputedly at twenty-five.'

'Rodden,' said Jane again, 'you're quite impossible.'

'But at least I'm honest.' The kettle had boiled and he was pouring the water into a bowl, adding some salt. He worked efficiently, but then he was a qualified vet. He came across to Jane with the bowl, a towel, the rest of the equipment.

'I've got OUT from Bower. I suppose you knew that?'

'How would I?'

'I imagined you might be chummy.'

'We're not.'

'Well, I have to go. Some other underling post, no doubt.'

'You were boss at Fetherfell,' she pointed out.

342

'Still an underling post. I want my own place, Jane, and that's why . . .' He did not finish. Instead he got busy on her injuries, and his touch was professional, gentle yet firm and very thorough. He let out blisters, applied tape, bathed, dabbed, dried, pressed, soothed.

'You're a good doctor, Rodden,' she observed.

'But a rotten vet?'

'You're not.'

'No,' he said ruefully, I'm not.' He looked at Jane. 'How come you're here?'

She had been about to ask him that for herself, but she answered briefly, telling him how she and Gretel had explored a new track, and how she had seen the humpy through the trees and dismounted to look closer.

'A man came out, but he wasn't you.'

'You're having delusions,' Rodden said lightly. 'The bush does that.'

'Then it was?' She supposed that could be, the humpy had been some distance away.

'It was I, Jane dear, only don't give me away.'

'Give you away?' she echoed.

'To the big boss. I'd sooner remain incognito when it comes to my retreat.'

'This is your retreat?'

'Why not?'

Why not, Jane thought, everyone should have somewhere secret to go, only . . . and she frowned a little . . . a retreat did not seem like Rodden.

'I'll get you up to the top now, Janey, if you feel you can make it. I'd brew some tea, only by leaving at once you could catch up on your mount.' He said it rather hurriedly, and Jane had the idea he wanted her out as much as she wanted it.

'Yes, I can make it,' she nodded.

She did . . . with Rodden's help. He knew a short-cut to the top, steep but accessible. And there, actually only cropping a few yards away, Gretel waited. She would not have waited after sundown, Jane knew, but the fact that she had waited at all sent Jane running forward to kiss the mare instead of scolding her, as she had intended, for running off.

'If you go at once you should escape any notice,' Rodden advised. 'When I came past there was general stud activity in the northern field, and that's the furthest away so the longest return to the house.' He paused. 'Don't forget, Jane.'

'The retreat?'

'Yes.'

'What do you do there, Rodden?'

'I could say paint, compose, write poetry,' he parried.

'You!' she said disbelievingly.

'Credit me with it, or not, at least keep it to yourself. I have patched you up, remember.'

'Yes, and thank you for that.'

'Thank you for everything, Jane.' He said it sincerely, or at least, Jane knew, with as much sincerity as he was capable of.

'Friends?' he asked as he helped her mount.

'Yes, Rodden.'

'And silence?' He nodded back to the valley.

'Yes, Rodden,' she promised hurriedly. She was anxious to get home before the others.

She did it, but barely. She bathed, did some more patching to herself, then saw to it at dinner, and afterwards, that she did not move around any more than was necessary, in case her injuries showed.

William Bower fortunately did not appear for the meal. She saw him only briefly afterwards, and in the more muted light of the hall.

'Good evening, Miss Sidney, you're looking pale. Was it the strain of the auction, do you think?'

Of course she was pale, she had put on a thicker make-up than she had ever worn before. She wondered if he saw that, if he saw the scratch that the powder was concealing.

—Or so she had hoped.

'I trust it passes over, whatever it is.' His tone was carefully casual. 'Because tomorrow it's on again.'

'An auction?'

'No, your collection of your second batch. You'll leave early as before. Take a few days.'

She was quiet. She was thinking of the numerous cuts and bruises as well as the facial scratch she had suffered, she might camouflage them from this man by night, but by day——

'I won't be going this time. Tim will accompany you.' He added: 'And Maureen.'

'For convention's sake,' she said flippantly ... also with relief, relief that she would not have Bower's sharp eyes on her tomorrow.

'Oh, I have no fears about *that*,' he reminded her, and she knew he was baiting her with that family unit episode. 'Five a.m., overnight bag, you know the drill,' he tossed. 'Also, can I advise less of what you have plastered on your face? It's a long trip and it can play the devil with a woman's make-up. And after all' ... a pause ... 'a scratch is still a scratch. Who did it, and why, Miss Sidney?'

'A bush, and because I ran into it,' she said in angry frustration. This man simply missed nothing at all!

'Well, it's you who's suffering,' he dismissed carelessly. 'Have fun.' Without another word, he went away.

She knew she had been let off lightly, if he had really wanted to know he would have persisted, and she might have had to tell him.

She went upstairs, tired after the day's happenings, inexplicably discouraged even though she had escaped quite well, all things considered.

Then she was realizing with a leap of her heart that she was collecting Dandy tomorrow. Dotsy and Devil May Care, too, but Dandy. Dandy.

Jane was smiling as she fell asleep.

CHAPTER EIGHT

TIM picked up the three D's quicker than William Bower had collected the first contingent. He spent less time on meals than the stud master had on Jane's first Sydney trip ... Jane recalled lunch and the long discussion on the value of Dandy, the condition of Dotsy ... which meant he could get the horses out of quarantine earlier, then have them ready for their journey home.

On the second day of the collection they followed the highway instead of the longer mountain road, and by dusk were back at Plateau. It had been a pleasant if uneventful journey. Several times Maureen had put out awkward feelers of friendship. If Tim had not been there, Jane would have said, 'Darling, it's all over, it was all the silliest thing, anyhow, but it's passed and now it is the past.'

As they crossed the little bridge they saw the twins racing each other over the creek. Kate was not with them, but with swimming efficiency like that they did not need her.

'Hop-picking festival next week,' Tim remarked. 'Ever been to one, Jane?'

'No.'

'It's something not to be missed, not here, anyway. Every nationality in the world, every tongue, every dance, every drink, every dish. It's a great show. John will want you to go.'

'I doubt it. I haven't seen him since *Kate* took over.' Jane emphasized Kate slyly.

'He'd be out of luck if he wanted to take Kate,' Tim laughed.

'Be quiet,' said Maureen sternly. She said evasively to Jane: 'We all go, it's tremendous fun.'

'It sounds it,' Jane nodded, wondering why Tim had been

346

silenced.

But Jane could not wonder about anything very much, she was too happy because of Dandy. Although the other pair had clearly recognized her, it had been Dandy who had greeted her. The tears had been streaming down Jane's cheeks as she had put her hands on each side of the satiny head and pressed her lips on the big brow.

She had had no time to consider Dotsy, whether what William Bower had said of her was right, or otherwise. However, she asked Tim on the way home, and he said he couldn't be sure, either.

'A vet?' she queried.

'That's right, Jane.'

'But you've been giving pregnancy tests to the mares who have been in for service.'

'Yes. We always do, for at that stage the tests are simple. But Dotsy, if she is, would be well on by now, and, strange though it seems, not so easy. For on the other hand she merely could be well on with plain avoirdupois ... as Gretel was. You have to take your time over an opinion at this stage.'

Jane questioned Dotsy herself that evening. Dotsy was a nutty brown, very glossy, and certainly showing a slight rotundity. But it needn't be pregnancy, as Tim had said, it might just be a tub, the same as with Gretel, that Dotsy had grown through idleness and overeating.

'Are you or aren't you, Dotsy?' Jane asked.

Dotsy whickered.

'Who was it?'

Dotsy, Jane could have sworn, winked.

'You're a shameless girl! I'll have to write to Rusty.'

'It's high time you did.' That was Jane's first indication that she had been talking aloud and that William Bower was standing at the door of Dotsy's box listening. 'I thought it had been written long ago, and that this was the answer.' He held up a letter with an American stamp.

Jane put down her working tools and came across to

347

claim it. About to slip it in her pocket for reading afterwards, she remembered that this man was Rusty's nephew, so opened it instead.

There was nothing that couldn't be shared. Rusty loved the part of America in which he found himself, he believed he would be happy there until it was time for him, too, to be put down.

He asked about the boys and girls, and, on second thoughts it appeared, his nephew.

'Nice of him,' broke in William drily.

'Most of all, you, Jane.' Jane read that aloud before she could check herself. 'Are you contented? Are you happy? Have you exchanged any mutual look?' Jane stopped, annoyed with herself, annoyed with old Rusty.

'Go on,' said William.

'That's all,' she said.

'Well, have you?'

'Have I what? No' ... impatiently ... 'don't bother to answer. It's all too silly. Anyway, it's no business of yours.'

'Agreed. But what is my business as your employer ... oh, yes, I'm that as well as co-director ... is that scratch, Miss Sidney. It's rather a deepish one. If you indicate the bush that did it I'll have it cut back.'

'It's nothing,' she said evasively.

'It would have been something had it not been attended to, I would say. Who did attend to it?'

'I did.'

'You did *later*, I think ... but I also think it was attended to fairly promptly, and by someone who knew their job.'

'Like a doctor,' she said flippantly.

'Like a—vet.' He waited. 'So you met Gair,' he said when Jane did not comment.

'I did not.' Well, actually there hadn't been a meeting.

'I happen to know Gair's particular manner of bandaging ... good lord, I should, I've seen it often enough. That ankle, for instance' ... his glance went down ... 'has been bound in a different way from how a layman would bind it.'

'I bound it myself this morning,' she insisted.

'Borrowing Gair's method?'

Jane was silent. She *had* borrowed it.

'All right, then,' Bower shrugged, 'it's not important, you're not stepping on anyone's corns, Maureen isn't interested any more. You have an All Clear.'

'I don't want it.'

'Why not? Dead sea fruit?'

Jane was silent, furiously so.

'He's a clever fellow,' said Bower.

'Yet you're getting rid of him?'

'Let me finish, please. But not my kind of clever fellow. He'll do much more and in a shorter time in a different sort of place from Bowers.'

'He told me you'd sacked him.'

'When you met him?' he said deliberately.

'When we encountered,' she corrected coolly.

'Where was that?'

'Oh—somewhere along a track.'

'You surely know *where*,' William Bower said angrily. 'Good lord, if you didn't know you could have got lost. Getting lost in our bush is very easy, but not easy on the searchers. It's sometimes proved fatal for both sides.'

'I'm here, aren't I?' Jane wondered how his reaction would have been had she confessed that she *had* been lost.

'So you can't indicate the spot?'

She could have told him the place where she had emerged, but she had promised Rodden to keep his retreat a secret, and she would not go back on that.

'Nor the track Gretel and I took,' she replied.

'What was Gair doing in the bush?'

'What I was, probably—exploring.'

'Not Rodden.' He looked at her sharply. 'Did you see anyone else?'

'No.' For a moment she forgot that first figure that Rod-

349

den had laughed over when she had told him, had said was his, of course. 'Why should I?' she asked.

'No reason at all,' he agreed, but he seemed somehow uncertain.

He began talking about the new contingent. Devil May Care was going to start training at once. William Bower said he had been studying his records and believed they could expect a lot from him. Dotsy they must leave for Tim's verdict, or for when Miss Sidney got a reply from the letter she *still* had not written to Rusty.

'How about Dandy?' Jane asked.

'I can't see much of a sire in him, nor can I see a racer.'

'Does there have to be?'

'A stud isn't run for fun, Miss Sidney.'

'I know that now,' Jane said coldly.

'Keep the fellow for your own mount, I think we can run to that.'

'You're very magnanimous, Mr. Bower.'

He looked as though he was searching for a retort, but, unbelievable in William Bower, evidently he found none.

'Write that letter,' he directed, and went away.

'Dear Rusty,' Jane recited to her pretty brown girl, 'is Dotsy, or isn't she, for she won't say, and if so, when, and from whom?'

She wrote just that, that night.

Dandy and Jane had fine rides together. The pony was more venturesome than Gretel, and would have explored anywhere that Jane asked, but that last experience had given Jane an extra sense of caution, and, apart from a few woodsy rides along the upper valleys, the pair kept to the top, sometimes towing Wendy's Pride behind them, for the filly was out of her box now and testing her slender legs on the soft grass flats.

On one of Jane's rides, William Bower joined her. He rode a very large bay, Major, and beside Major, Dandy looked small and insignificant. Jane knew she must look the same.

'You like this, don't you?' They had come to the breath-less end of an exhilarating gallop. Jane, not towing Wendy's Pride today, had given Dandy his head. The pair had come first in the unofficial race. Perhaps, and probably, William had held Major back, but it was a nice feeling to win.

'I love it,' said Jane.

'I wish the twins were more enthusiastic. I've provided them with suitable mounts, but the interest just isn't there, only down the valley. It's discouraging to say the least, the Bowers always have had racing in their blood.'

'But they're not,' Jane reminded him tactfully. 'You must look to your own for that.'

'I have thought of it,' he said coolly.

The practicality of it irked Jane. She could not have said why she was so irritated; after all, it was no concern of hers whether this man married, or not, had a family, or not.

'You're disapproving,' he said, taking out his pipe, 'yet a union on that basis would possibly, even probably, make a much better union than the usual maudlin reasons.' He said the maudlin deliberately, she knew, to bait her.

'I've read,' he went on, 'that in spite of what people think, arranged marriages are much more successful than the eyes-meeting variety. Each partner knows what to ex-pect, and doesn't ask for more than that. Do you agree?'

'I think,' said Jane, 'you have the right idea. For your-self.'

'Anyone else I should think of?' he asked.

'I also think,' she continued, 'that a grand tour of some of the studs might bring forth good material.'

'There's fair material here. I'm not the little boy who sees golden windows across the valley, I feel the talent is just as promising at home.'

'I thought stablehands were out?'

'A man can change.'

'Why not line up the candidates and see who wins the race?' Jane said, not far from open anger.

'It wouldn't be fair, unless I adopted a handicap.'

'Mr. Bower, this is all in bad taste.'

'I agree,' he said rather surprisingly, 'but you did carry it on, didn't you? I meant what I said about being regretful that the kids are not horse-minded. However, even if they were, it wouldn't matter, for they'll be leaving soon. I've had a letter from the parents. They've met up after their respective overseas assignments, and will be flying home within the fortnight.'

'The children will love that.'

'Yes, they will. Although lately I've thought...' But William Bower left it at that.

The next day invitations came up from the valley for the hop-picking celebrations, and immediately rosters were drawn up for attendance, since everyone wanted to go, and, on a stud, someone must always be on duty.

The girls consulted each other as to clothes. Because they were the fair sex, and the fair sex would be very much in demand at the celebrations, they were not rostered. Kate said that they must take an extra dress for the dance at night. Slacks, shorts or shifts would be all right for the day's entertainment, but long swinging skirts were called for after seven.

Jane, who had only her pink cotton bought from Ahmed ... and that negligée ... sent down to Sydney at once for some gay floral material. The girls did the same, and, their day's work finished, they met up in a bedroom for mutual sewing and advice. Maureen, as Jane had thought, was entirely out of her resentment by now, though still obviously a little embarrassed over herself and what she had said to Jane. One day they would shake hands and laugh over it all, Jane knew. Until then they both smiled a little shyly and a little uncertainly at each other, and the rift closed another inch.

Jane's dress featured large sunflowers, and, because she was slim and needed more bulk, she was advised by Maureen and Kate to gather the waist instead of adopting a more slenderizing line. She was also persuaded to send for tangerine sandals and to wear a matching band in her hair.

'I'll look like an orange festival, not a hop variety,' she complained mildly.

'So long as you look festive,' they advised. They had chosen pink and blue respectively; Maureen would wear splashy roses, Kate spiky cornflowers.

Jane spoke to William regarding the children.

'They've enough clothes surely already. It seems to me I'm settling an account every week.'

'Not after-six clothes.'

'After six that pair will be in bed.'

'Oh, no, not when the hop festival's on. Roberta has been practising her steps for weeks, and I did hear Robert say he may join the Greek group, seeing it's strictly male. You can't expect them to do things like that in shorts and T-shirts.'

'I don't expect them to, I expect them to be put to bed.'

'By whom?' Jane ventured to ask. 'As far as I can see no one will be left here except Sam.' Sam was a pensioner-rouseabout, and not interested in festivals; quite definitely also, believed Jane, not interested in putting juveniles to bed.

'There'll be others rostered.'

Jane said nothing.

'Then I,' proceeded William Bower, 'am not incapable of putting a child to bed.'

'Two children.'

'Two children,' he said coldly.

There was a silence. Jane could see she would get no-where like this, and she knew how terribly keen the twins were to stop for the night's festivities.

'I would look after them,' she offered humbly.

'Between the reels, the flings, the jigs, the cariocas, the tangos and the rhumbas,' he came back disbelievingly, 'and that's only half the list. Every nationality down there, and, believe me, there'll be few nations left out, will insist

353

on their dance, and with women-shortage as prevails every-where here, you won't be off the floor to watch anyone.'

She could not argue that, not having been to such a func-tion before. She stood uncertain a moment, then spontane-ously she appealed: 'Please let them, William.' The mo-ment she heard it, she could not believe it of herself. Not only the appeal to this man, but his *name*.

There was a silence. A long one.

'Very well then.' His voice was gruff. He did not look at her. 'Send down to David Jones for anything you need.' He walked away before she could thank him.

Robert wanted some mod gear. He made a list of it, and Jane, when ordering it, made the request that if it was not store-available, could someone get it for them from an In shop. Roberta simply wanted long skirts.

The clothes arrived, to both their satisfaction, and on Hop Day Jane packed their evening gear separate with her own, and sent them off ... they were going in a decorated haycart that one of the hands was entering in the procession ... in serviceable overalls.

She went in one of the jeeps, the rest of the unrostered staff in cars, bikes, vans, even horse-boxes. She noted that William Bower's car remained at his house, but then she had expected that, it would not be the sort of function, she, thought, that a Big Boss would attend.

The barbecue and sporting events were to be held in the reserve at the creek, the hop-picking competition at one of the larger fields, and the dance on a floor that had been laid down on perhaps the only level ground of all the lower district. As Jane passed the setting for the night festivities, she saw that coloured lights were being strung between the trees.

It was impossible to believe that this busy, bustling place was their sleepy valley. The quiet, almost dreaming little community had burst into cheerful laughing life. The sound of the river that punctuated the gully silences, the songs of the birds, could not be heard for human noise.

There were tents and caravans everywhere, cars turned into beds, stretchers on tabletop lorries, sleeping bags and simply folded blankets.

The Bowers crowd went straight to the hop-picking, which, Jane was assured, was worth seeing. The picking was being done by families, and it was fiercely competitive. Each family was supplied a large timber-framed receptacle, and that was all the equipment needed besides nimble fingers. Jane appreciated the size of the receptacle, for it was as big as a horse trough, after she had tried hop-picking herself. She admitted ruefully that it would take a lot of leafy cones to reach one pound. Also, she was told, no leaves or stems were allowed.

The signal was given, and the families began to pick. It was really something to watch, Dad's large yet nimble fingers, Mum's, the children's, sometimes cousins' and aunts', all darting and dancing through the vine's thick leaves and sending continuous streams of little hops into the bin.

Jane did not wait for the winner, it would go on for hours, but she did do a tour of a kiln, its upper level spread with a ten-inch layer of hops under covering mesh, the drying floor on the lower level. The hot air was being drawn through now, and John, who had offered to show her, said, 'That steam should make you hungry. Feel like coming to the house for a bite?'

She had been looking at all the good things laid out for the pickers—chunks of sausage, slabs of cheese, pyramids of boiled eggs and tomatoes—and gave an eager yes.

'No Johnny cakes?' she asked, and John gave her a rather curious look.

'No. No, Jane. I thought ... well, I thought you knew.'

'Knew what?'

'Come and have a bite,' he said.

But it was not a bite, it was a feast. An exciting foreign feast redolent of olives, capsicum and spice.

'It's wonderful, John!' she exclaimed.

355

'It's Estonian. The same' ... John smiled boyishly ... 'as my girl.'

'Your—— But John, I didn't know. I knew that you were—well——'

'Anxious? I was. What's the good of a house without its woman? a home without its heart? Jane' ... a little concerned ... you don't mind?'

'*I* mind,' Jane leaned over and touched John's hand. 'I think it's great. What's her name?'

'I'll have her tell you herself, it's rather a mouthful, for us, anyway. She'll be back soon ... her family are down for the picking ... that's how I met her, Jane. She's lovely. I'm sure you'll think so. I call her Ennie.'

'And you're terribly happy, I can see that.'

'Terribly happy. And don't think it was as it must sound to you, I mean you knew I wanted to settle and settle soon. Well, it was like that, I suppose, but it was also a——'

'Mutual look?'

'Exactly, Jane. The very words.' He beamed on her.

But Jane could not entirely beam back. Then where did Kate come in, she was wondering, Kate who had been so anxious to keep on her valley commitments, Kate who had grown so much more mature lately, so much more attractive. Everyone had commented on it. She started to ask John, but his Ennie arrived, just as lovely as he had said, and after they had talked there was a Polish wrestling match to attend, a Latvian boxing bout and an afternoon singsong.

Then it was time to change for the night. Jane, Maureen and the twins changed at John's. When Jane asked about Kate, everyone was so intent on themselves she received no answer, but Kate must have changed somewhere, for later, half dusk now, and the lights by the dancing floor being switched on, she saw Kate in her cornflower skirts, and beside her a man Jane vaguely felt she had seen before ... but where? There was no time to think about it, though, an Italian who had been strumming a serenade on a guitar

356

nodded to several companions with fiddles, then drums came in, saxes, every instrument that could be carried along, the children even wrapping combs in paper, and the music began.

Oh, what music! As William Bower had told Jane, it went on the whole gamut. Jane was claimed at once and not let go through any national dance, even though she protested she did not know it. Even in the Greek dances, those strict prerogatives of males, Jane danced, as did all the girls ... Maureen with Tim, John with his Ennie, Kate with that man whom Jane had felt she had seen before.

A party of Spaniards down for the picking did the saraband and the fandango, the bolero was performed, some very spirited Polish steps, then an English group were showing quadrilles and Lancers, some Americans the old Cakewalk and the less old Charleston, and after that the foxtrots and one-steps were getting the crowd to their feet ... then the fiddles were becoming more muted, the guitars were picking sweeter notes, and the waltz was beginning.

Jane was in the arms of a young South American who had previously been showing her the intricacies of the tango, when the man cut in. It was such a definite cut there could be no protest. The handsome Argentinian stepped back ruefully as—— It was William Bower who calmly took over.

'You!' Jane murmured.

'Why not?'

'No reason, except——'

'Except you couldn't see me one-stepping and foxtrotting, Miss Sidney? You're right. But I think I can manage this one. Please complain to me if I can't.'

'I will,' she promised. Then: 'I didn't know you were here.'

'You know now.'

Yes, she knew. His arms were iron-hard around her, his fingers held hers lightly yet she knew the grasp was inescapable.

'You've been impolite,' she said for something to say. 'It's not a cutting-in evening.'

'It *was* not,' he corrected.

'Do you always ride roughshod over people?'

'I breed horses, I don't go in for the intricacies of riding them.'

'And other intricacies, Mr. Bower?'

'You're never explicit, are you, Miss Sidney? You deal in subtleties and innuendoes, never a spade's a spade.'

'Shall I now?' she asked demurely.

'Just now, little girl, you will shut that very pretty but tiresome mouth of yours. Have you no ear for music?'

She had, and for that very reason she had been chattering frantically, trying to escape the sweet gipsy strains that the strolling players were coaxing from their strings. For the penetrating beauty of the soft throbbing waltz was taking possession of Jane. She felt herself drawn closer and knew that he was taking possession, too. She knew by her instinctive response that she was not withdrawing from him. She half-closed her eyes, gave herself over to the tender music, to his light yet firm guidance, to the heady rapture of the swelling rhythm.

'Don't look now,' he said in her ear. 'We're the spotlight, Jane.'

He had never called her Jane, and for a while in her surprise she did not look. Then she realized that all the other couples had left the floor and that they alone danced as one person.

'Embarrassed?' he asked.

'No,' she said truthfully.

'I'm not, either. I think we're a team, Jane. I think...' William stopped at an arm on his shoulder. He looked thunderous. But it was not a cut, it was one of the Bower men. Chad Addison's face was grave. Jane tried rather hazily to recall which mare was due, or whether one of the horses ailed.

William went to the side of the floor with the man. The

358

spell broken, the other couples resumed dancing again. Presently the stud boss came to Jane and said: 'Addison tells me I'm wanted up top at once. I feel for all his insistence that it can't be urgent, because I checked everything before I came down. So wait for me, Jane.' Again he said Jane. This time: 'Wait for me, Jane.'

And Jane knew she would wait.

She did wait. She waited all that evening. As though they knew she was waiting, no one came after William went to ask her to dance.

After a long while she sat down to wait. She grew cold ... and as an hour, two hours went past, she grew indignant as well as chilled. How dared he treat her like this?

When she saw the dancers forming more intimate pairs, she knew she could stand it no longer. A group of the Bowers people were leaving on one of the lorries, so she went with them.

In her indignation she felt like seeking out William Bower, telling him what she thought of his conduct, but that could emphasize everything, suggest an importance that she might have put on the night's events, and she didn't want any importance conveyed to that man. Besides ... furiously ... there had been no importance, not to her. She repeated that to herself as she got down from the table-top and ran across to the big house.

He was coming out of it as she went to enter, and at once he flung out an arm and guided her away.

'I thought you'd never come,' he said hoarsely.

'I—I waited. You said to.' Her voice shook with resentment and she hated its betrayal.

'I know, I know.' He shrugged his shoulders as though to shrug all that away.

She could not understand him, he had been so different down there. Was he going on like this now to tell her that down there was not here, that the gipsy music and what it could have meant had stopped?

'It's the kids,' he said shortly.

'They're all right. Maureen and Tim are bringing them up.'

'I should have said their parents, adopted parents, foster-parents, whatever you like to call Gareth and Dorothy.'

'They're home?'

'They're not coming home, Jane, not this home—any earthly home. There's been a major plane disaster. Only a few survived. They were on that plane and their names are not among the survivors.'

He turned away.

CHAPTER NINE

WILLIAM had drawn Jane away from the big house, but they had not got as far as his house. A cloud had temporarily obliterated the moon, but Jane could still see the droop to his big shoulders, the tug to his long sensitive mouth.

'There could be some mistake,' she whispered.

'No,' he said. 'They were on that flight and the list is official.'

'The children.' She said that tremblingly, and he answered just one word.

'Yes.'

A silence encompassed them. It seemed to encompass Plateau as well. No leaf stirred, no night jay called.

'Poor little mutts,' the man said troublously at last, 'they've had more than their share, Jane.'

'Yes, William.' It came as instinctively, she knew, as his 'Jane' had come.

'Children are resilient,' she said presently, and he nodded back soberly.

'I know that, I know they'll recover. Thank heaven Gareth and Dorothy possessed the wisdom to tell them the truth. The question is how much did they know of it themselves?'

'Your cousin and his wife?'

'Yes.'

Jane looked at him in inquiry, and he went on, 'Did they know the real parents and the situation?'

'It's not usual,' Jane said.

'But, I think, in Gareth's and Dorothy's position very probable. I believe the twins came from their own circle, Jane. In time, being the wise people they were, I believe they intended to tell Robert and Roberta. But meanwhile they never got round to telling me, and now I don't know. I just don't know.'

'Do you have to know?' she asked gently. 'Can't you just accept them with love?'

'Of course. What do you think I am? But it's not as easy as that. Those kids are not a studman's children, they're a different breed. How can I make them happy when I don't understand?'

'They're children, William. *Children.*'

'Whose?' he asked. 'And how can they ever know now?'

'I think you're creating something.'

'I don't want to. I want to go and say to that pair: You're home. *Home.*—But they're not. I know it. They know it.' He looked at Jane. 'You do.'

'I don't, William. They like here. They're fond of you.'

'Fond,' he repeated hoarsely.

'Children are adopted every day,' Jane said. 'It happens smoothly, it's not the rough passage you anticipate.'

He listened to her, but his face remained crumpled.

'The thing is—I don't believe Gareth and Dorothy ever did adopt them. Oh, I know to all appearances they did, but I think they were really "keeping" them for someone, someone who might not have known, though Gareth and Dorothy did. Now—well, no one knows.'

'I really meant when I said that,' Jane came in, '*your* adoption of them.' She looked up at him.

'The studman takes a child?' he interpreted. 'Heaven knows I wish it was as simple as that. But it isn't, Jane. No, I was right when I told you I had to grow my own.'

'Love——' Jane endeavoured.

'Doesn't come into this. The kids like me, yes, but I don't *belong*, Jane. I'm an outdoor man, a factual character, anything but a person of finer perceptions, but I still know that, that I don't belong.'

'Then,' said Jane practically, 'the second-best will have to do, won't it? And children being resilient, it will do.'

'I suppose you're right. I suppose it's just the impact making me see a distortion like this. They'll recover. They'll settle down. Incidentally, in the shock I opened a

362

letter that was your—my uncle's. I'm sorry.' He handed the letter over.

Jane read it absently, her mind not on Rusty and what he had to say.

'You were right about Dotsy,' she said tonelessly to William. 'She is. Your uncle says when but not by whom.'

He nodded, and her heart went out to him because of the wretchedness in his face. She pushed the letter into her pocket.

'I'll write again and remind him, for you would want to know the sire. It makes a difference even before foaling if you're aware what you are about to handle.' She knew she was talking in the hope of diverting him.

He nodded dumbly again, William Bower, the self-assured studman without words! Gently Jane said: 'Do you want me there when you tell them?'

'Would you?'

'Of course.'

'Not tonight.'

'No,' she agreed.

'The morning?'

'Yes.'

In the distance there was the sound of returning cars, bikes, vans. In one of those vehicles would be two exhausted children.

They stood in silence as the revellers completed the run, drew up and tumbled out.

'It was fab, Father William!' Robert called.

'Jane looked the second-best of the ladies. Kate looked the best,' Roberta announced quite as a matter of course.

Then the pair both saw something together and called together: 'Look, two stars fell!' And watched them.

'Goodnight, darlings,' Jane said, and went back to the big house.

She awoke earlier than usual the next day, and put it down to the troubled sleep she had had. Then she heard the noise in the house, saw the glow at the window. She ran across and looked out. The glow was to the east, but it was not the glow of sunrise but fire. Jane knew that glow now after the fire at the hotel.

She pulled on her dressing gown and went down to the canteen. It seemed everyone was there, and giving their theory. It came from the valley, one said, and had been caused by a short in the lights. Someone else said that the night had been just a bit too merry and some camper hadn't properly extinguished his fire.

One thing, it didn't appear much to date, and once the Urara volunteer brigade got on the scene . . .

Jane went back, dressed and returned to swallow a cup of tea. She could not eat anything, she kept on thinking what lay ahead.

She crossed to the house, but no one answered her soft knock. Probably William was letting the twins sleep as long as they could. Probably he was too wretched still to come to the door.

Around ten, the glow that had been only just that, nothing more serious, considerably deepened. The news of the tragedy must have reached the staff, for as well as apprehensive about that spreading red-black cloud coming from the valley, the men were visibly shocked and quiet.

Jane set her shoulders and walked across again to the house. This time her knock was answered by Teresa. Teresa's eyes were red and when she saw Jane she whimpered. William must have heard, for he came down the hall, and if he had looked wretched yesterday, now he looked positively distraught.

'William——'

'They're gone,' he said flatly.

'Gone? You mean the twins?'

'Yes.'

'Then you told them?'

'No. They must have heard.'

'No one here would say.'

'Not intentionally. I'm not blaming Anders.'

364

'He told them?'

'No, but he's come to me and said that when his attention was drawn to the fire ... you know about that, of course?'

'Yes.'

'That he cried out: "Not that on top of the other!"'

'Well?'

'The twins were in earshot. They're not the usual kids, you know that.'

'Yes.'

'They must have checked. I can just see Robert doing that. He has his own transistor.'

'They knew their parents were coming?'

'They knew they were on that flight. I'd told them.'

'Perhaps they didn't check. Perhaps Anders only thought they heard.'

'I don't know,' William said wearily, 'I only know I've looked everywhere, and they're not here. Jane, what am I to do?'

How had she ever thought him self-sufficient, not merely self-sufficient but repelling even the smallest gesture of help? He wasn't now, for all his maturity, and Jane knew she had never known a more mature person than William Bower, he was still a little boy crying for help.

'Help me, Jane,' he said.

'When did you discover they'd gone?'

'The entire night I'd been thrashing over the thing. I came at last to the conclusion that I must tell them, tell them alone, that it wasn't fair to call on you.'

'That's not so,' Jane said quietly.

'After I reached that decision I must have slept at last. Anyway' ... a resigned movement of his hands ... 'I didn't hear the twins get up, go out of the house.'

'They must have crossed to the stables.'

'They did. Several of the hands saw them. Then later Anders must have remembered saying what he did. Being the pair they are, they would be consumed with curiosity. Hearing Anders say: "Not that on top of the other!"

would determine them to know what he meant. They would have come back to the house, listened to the radio, and——' Again that gesture of the big strong hands.

'But why would they go away?'

'I don't know. I was hoping you could tell me that.'

'William' ... how instinctively William came now ... 'how could I know? Ever since Kate has taken over I've barely seen them. They liked Kate, so I didn't intrude.' As she said it Jane remembered Roberta calling: 'Jane looked the second-best. Kate looked the best.' She recalled experiencing a slight pang of resentment, just a very small tinge, but there was no resentment now, only a great hope.

'Kate,' Jane said to William.

'Oh, yes,' he replied, 'I thought of that, too. But she's not here.'

'Then the twins could be with her.'

'No, Jane, Kate never returned last night. It appears she wasn't expected, she's on vacation. I didn't know, but then I wouldn't be expected to know. I leave these things to the bookkeeper.'

'Maureen could know where she's gone.'

'She doesn't. I've asked her. Though——'

'Yes, William?'

'I feel she might know something ... just a feeling. However, all I want to know is what's concerning me. The kids.'

'Have they taken any ponies?'

'No. You know how they are in that section.'

'But if they wanted to get somewhere——'

'They're also very good on their own two feet.'

'But not too far,' Jane said. 'They're only young children.'

'And already they've been gone three hours. It could be more. Jane, can't you think?'

Jane said wretchedly, 'I'm trying ... trying, but nothing comes.'

She left William and came back to the canteen and had a meal. She knew it was no use trying to think, to do anything at all on an empty stomach, and she had not eaten at all this morning. She knew if something did occur to her, and she went off, at least she would go replenished. She could tell by the look on Harry's face that he was glad to have a customer.

'Terrible food wastage today,' he sighed, 'breakfast hardly touched.'

'That cloud is getting bigger and darker, Harry. What will happen?'

'If the volunteer brigade can't handle it, it'll be all hands to the job.'

'Plateau, too?'

'Of course.'

'Has fire happened before?'

'Oh yes.' Harry seemed surprised at Jane's question.

'The valley looks so green,' Jane explained her remark.

'Eucalypts thrive on fires, they look dead, then the next spring they branch out bigger and better than ever. The ground section of the fires clear the undergrowth and the sun gets in and stimulates the sap, I expect.'

'How will Plateau know if help is needed?'

'There's a siren system been fixed up,' Harry said. 'I'm getting ready anyway, just in case.' He pointed to piles of sandwiches he was preparing. 'Have to keep the fighters well stoked,' he said.

The rest of the morning went leadenly. Although time was what they all needed, it seemed to Jane that the hand of her watch never moved. She tended Wendy's Pride, looked in on Dotsy, then went and saddled Dandy.

No one called out a warning to her as she cantered from the stable, they were all wrapped up in their own concerns, everyone was depending on everyone else to use caution and common sense. Jane would have used these, too; when she left the stud she had no intention of doing what she eventually did. But after she saw Maureen in the distance and crossed the eastern paddock to talk to her, caution and common sense did not come into it any more. Only a sudden, desperate feeling that the twins could be——

The words that Maureen and Jane had had together were back in the past now. Maureen met Jane with the same anxious look that Jane wore.

'It's frightful, Jane!'

'Can you help in any way, Maureen?'

'You mean as regards Kate, and where she is, and if the twins could be with her? No. I told Mr. Bower so. Definitely Robert and Roberta would not be with Kate.'

'But you couldn't be absolutely definite, you couldn't know for certain, could you?'

'Yes. Definite. Certain. You see——'

'Yes, Maureen?'

Maureen looked upset. 'I can't tell you,' she confided. 'It's not for me to tell.'

'Tell what?'

'About Kate. Anyway, she's on vacation, and she doesn't have to say where.'

'Do you know where?'

'Not exactly.'

'But fairly exactly.' Jane knew that was absurd, but she knew that Maureen would know what she meant.

'Somewhere on the coast.' Maureen sighed. 'She ... Roger ... well, I think they're being married.'

'You mean John and Kate.'

'No, Jane, you must have seen John and Ennie. It's Roger.'

'Who is Roger?' asked Jane.

'I don't know. I should, and poor Kate has tried to confide in me, but—well, I've had my own things on my mind.'

'Of course,' Jane hurried to reassure her, 'Then you would say the children are definitely not with Kate.'

'No. Not at her marriage. Oh dear, I wonder if I've said too much. Kate did ask me to keep it to myself. That's why I didn't tell Mr. Bower.'

'You haven't said too much, Maureen. Anything ... anything at all in a situation like this could be a help. Though what help this can be . . .' Jane bit her lip.

As she rode away again, she decided to report it all to William. It had no connection, but at least it explained Kate.

When she got to the house, William was not there. Teresa was still crying, so Jane came away and mounted Dandy again. She rode across the flats, taking several detours to look down to the valley. The pall of smoke had blackened and thickened. A wind was blowing up, and she watched it tear at the solid dark smudge, eventually severing it into two masses. Between and beneath them she saw a charred wilderness, and it horrified her. She had never known that fire could move so cruelly and so quickly.

In the canteen this morning she had heard men talk of wallabies caught in fire corners, of birds dropping out of the sky from heat when the flames leapt up. Flames were leaping up now. The wind, Jane saw, was changing again. All at once the billows of smoke had turned their direction, and red streaks of fire were whipping through the black. Even up here you can hear the roar. Down there it would be like thunder.

She watched until her eyes, red even this far away from the smoke, could not focus any more. She thought of all the people who had been down there yesterday. Thank heaven for the creek. Also for past experience, for she had been told, too, that no human loss of life was anticipated, not in a place that had had all this before, that knew explicitly what steps to take.

She went back to Dandy, a Dandy as usual unconcerned and contentedly cropping. They resumed their way until something that Maureen had said hit Jane. That was the only way she could have described it. It was like a blow at her thoughts.

Maureen had said: 'No, Jane. You must have seen John with Ennie. It's Roger.'

Roger? Who was Roger? Then Jane was recalling that as well as seeing John with Ennie, she had seen Kate with a

369

man. A man ... and her grasp tightened on the rein ... whom somehow she had felt she had seen before. But how? Where?

They had come to the section where the small track left the flat to go down to that part of the valley that Jane had explored on Gretel. Just here, Jane saw, you would not have known there was a fire; the wind, and therefore any tattered flames, had missed this section.

She pulled on Dandy and looked down. You could not see Rodden's retreat from here, but that, of course, had been Rodden's purpose.

Jane remembered that day when she had discovered it, remembered seeing the humpy between the trees. At the time Rodden had been the last owner of a retreat she could have dreamed up, she half-smiled.

Then the smile was fading. She was recalling that *first* figure, that figure that had *not* been Rodden's. Rodden had laughed at her, had said it was, but it hadn't been. She knew it now. The shack might belong to Rodden, though she doubted that, too, and undoubtedly it had been Rodden who had faced her there, who had taken her up the cliff again, but it had not been Rodden on that first glance. It had been——

Yes, it had.

Jane thought of Kate, Kate looking older, maturer, looking a woman at last, as she had walked beside that man yesterday, a man Jane had felt mildly curious about. She had felt she had seen him before, and now she knew where. It had been down there, down in the humpy between the trees. He had been the figure before Rodden.

Kate had been so different lately, Jane's mind ran on, so—so lit up. Jane knew Kate had liked her role of looking after the children, but had there been another attraction? A glow like Kate had worn had indicated more than the twins, it had indicated—— Indicated a man?

She was still asking herself questions as Dandy, obeying her touch, left the flat and began to descend.

The way seemed quite clear now. Strange how on a second journey you wondered how you had lost yourself the first time. Even when the track petered out, Jane still found a minor but clear path between bent bushes, by the pushed-back branches of trees, things that had not helped her before.

There was no sign of fire. As she had marked carefully on top, the wind had ignored this section. When eventually Jane did glimpse the humpy between the trees it was just as she first had glimpsed it. A cool retreat.

She had had to leave Gretel, she recalled, but Dandy just proceeded as though it was any ordinary bridle track. He stepped over fallen logs. He stooped and scraped under impeding trees. He showed none of Gretel's disapproval. The last steep decline he took sidewise, and finally delivered Jane at the bottom of it just as though she had been doing a leisurely round of the stables. She patted him lovingly, noticing, as she had several times this morning, a rather clammy sweat on him. She said: 'Dandy, you're not in such good trim as I thought—you and I will have to look into that.' Then, leaving him untethered, as she always did, since Dandy was no Gretel and would never leave unless told, she went across to the humpy.

'Is anyone there?' she called. 'Are you there, Rodden? Roger?' As an afterthought, she added: 'Kate?'

There was movement in the shack. The door opened. The sight she had longed for, yet not dared expect, met her eager eyes—the twins, red-eyed themselves. Robert and Roberta.

'Oh, darlings!' Jane called, and ran to the pair.

They stayed in her arms for a long while. No one spoke. They did not cry, Jane could see by their stained cheeks that their tears had been exhausted. She looked round to check if Dandy was all right and saw he was, then pushed the children gently back into the little hut.

'Why are you here?' she asked.

They had no answer for that; it wasn't that they didn't

want to tell her, thought Jane, it was simply that they didn't quite know themselves. And yet they must have had something in mind when they had fled here.

'They're never coming home.' It was Robert in a low but controlled voice.

'No, darling,' Jane agreed.

'Everyone was kind to us,' said Roberta, 'sort of special kind, so then we wondered.'

'We'd heard about a crash on our transistor.' Robert took up the story. 'We knew Gareth and Dorothy had left, so when people kept on being kind, we checked, and——' His little face crumpled, but he still kept back the tears.

'You wanted to be away from everybody,' nodded Jane. 'But why hide yourself here?' she asked again. She did not expect an answer . . . or the answer, anyway, that she got.

'To tell Roger,' the twins said.

'Who's Roger?'

'This is his place. He sculps here.'

'It should be sculpts,' said the other twin.

'You remember, Jane,' tacked on Roberta, 'the first time we went to John's and he showed us the stillery.'

'The distillery. Yes.'

'We got tired of it and came up here instead.'

'That was to an old man whom John knew, an old man who came down each year.'

'I told you,' reminded Roberta, 'that this man wasn't so old.'

'That old one never came this time,' Robert added.

'But why did you come now? You've worried us, children. We wanted to comfort you.'

They said, together again: 'We had to tell Roger.'

'*Why*, darlings?'

But they didn't know.

Jane didn't persist; they had had enough already. 'More than their share,' William had sighed.

'There's a bad fire,' she told them, 'and that's why we were especially worried. Everyone is out looking for you.'

'Not Kate,' said Roberta, brightening a little.

'She's being married to Roger,' said Robert.

'We knew Roger wouldn't be here, but we thought he might bring Kate back after the wedding. They call it a honeymoon then.'

'And you wanted to tell Roger?'

'And Kate.'

Roberta said, 'We're a bite hungry, Jane. You haven't any chocolate or anything?'

'We'll go up at once. Dandy is here and can carry you two. I'll keep close behind.'

They went immediately, and Dandy, cropping outside, came across almost as though he had overheard the conversation and had only been waiting for them. He stood docile as Jane lifted first Roberta, then Robert, up. She patted Dandy and they started off.

Afterwards Jane was to wonder agonizingly whether, if she hadn't put the two of them on Dandy, if—— But then if she had kept them by her, with her, could any of them have made it?

They did not reach the path before it came rushing at them, the wall of fire. This time the wind must have done a complete turn around, for previously the flames had licked only at the other side of the valley.

Jane looked behind her, the fire was spreading there, too. The only escape was up, and she slapped Dandy smartly and called: 'Up, up, take them up, boy!'

Dandy, now streaming with sweat, his soft brown eyes growing red as he blinked from the acrid smoke, obeyed at once, but Jane could see it would be an effort, the twins were solid children, and the incline almost precipitous. She ran behind Dandy, urging him, encouraging him, pleading with him. The fire still came.

Only that the tree fell between them, she would still have run with Dandy, though how, her breath coming now in gasps, she did not know, but the great trunk divided them, and in the roar of its descent, its flurry of leaves, Dandy could not tell that no longer was he being impelled up, and that was good, Jane knew helplessly, for Dandy would never have left her. He would have come back.

As it was, she saw him joining the track, racing up the track, the children hanging on.

'Thank heaven!' Jane said, saw another wall of flame coming towards her, and raced back to the shack.

She did not know whether it was a wise move or not, but at least the shack stood in a clearing, it was mostly iron, and there was a tank. She searched around for cloths of any sort, and soaked them in water. She splashed water around with her hands, for there was no can, no hose, as far as she could reach. She soaked herself. She did it until smoke overcame her, then she lay down. She remembered reading once that air circulated more freely on the ground.

She must have passed out, for she did not remember anything else. The first she knew was someone lifting her up. The air was still smoky, but she could see no flames.

'William,' she said to the face above hers.

'Yes, Jane.'

'Did Dandy fetch you?'

'. . . In a way.'

'Did he get the children up safely?'

'Yes.'

'Then bring you down here?'

A pause. 'I reckoned he'd done enough, girl, so I did the rest myself.'

'But he made it all right?' There was pride in Jane's voice.

'He made it,' William said, and there was pride in his, too. 'Now be quiet a while, Jane. There's a gang on the way with a stretcher. We'll soon have you in bed.'

'I'm not hurt,' she insisted.

'No, just smoke-filled, wrenched, scratched, sprained and what-have-you.'

'Is there anyone really hurt?'

'No.'

374

'Any*thing*?'

'Just relax, Jane.'

'Any——' The gang and the stretcher were approaching them.

'Just to make it easier for the boys, Jane, Tim's going to—well, after all, it's a steep haul.' Apologetically William stepped aside and Tim stepped forward and inserted a needle expertly into Jane's upper arm.

She knew no more until she wakened in a bed she did not know.

'You're in my house.' William Bower was sitting beside her. 'I thought it would be quieter.'

'But there's nothing wrong with me.'

'No,' William Bower agreed, 'nothing that won't mend.'

'There's nothing wrong with anybody,' Jane recalled from him.

'True.'

'Nor anything.' But he hadn't said that, she remembered. Her brain, still fuzzy, still uncertain, at least registered that fact.

'William.' She struggled up to a sitting position.

'Lie back, Jane.'

'You said—you said relax.'

'Then do it.'

'You said "Relax" when I asked you before.'

'Then don't ask now, girl.'

She looked at him ... and read him. Read what he didn't want to say.

'It's Dandy, isn't it?'

'Yes.'

'He didn't get up. Then how are the twins all right?'

'He got up. They're all right. But then——'

'Then you found he was injured? You found he was burned?'

'No,' William said quietly, 'then he died, Jane.'

He reached out his big hands to hers.

375

CHAPTER TEN

IT was a severance. It was almost like an amputation. Right from his shaky beginnings Dandy had been Jane's fellow.

'Cry,' encouraged William, and Jane did.

'Why?' she asked at last.

'He had a weak heart, Jane, it's as answerable as that. Dandy climbed to the top, then that was it. Fortunately a party of us were scouting around there at the time and saw Dandy coming up with the kids.'

'You say Dandy had a weak heart,' echoed Jane. She was remembering Dandy's clamminess today, remembering telling Dandy she would look into it. Only she had never guessed . . .

'Yes. Tim had suspected it and tested him. He had reported it to me.'

'Then why didn't you . . . I wouldn't have ridden him.'

'*That* was why,' William said simply.

After a while he went on, 'He was going to go, anyhow, Jane, how much better then with turf under his hoof and wind through his mane.'

'I can't understand Rusty,' Jane cried next.

'Not telling you? Or for sending him? The first would have deprived you of each other, you would have kept him in his box, cosseted him, and that would have been an earlier putting down for Dandy, a putting down in a manner for you. As for sending him . . . what else would Rusty have done?'

'Yes,' Jane said slowly, for Rusty would never have abandoned Dandy to someone else, and he never would have had him destroyed.

'It seems so purposeless for Dandy,' she fretted uselessly.

'With two kids' lives on his honour roll? Oh, no, girl.'

Jane was silent as she thought of that.

'We've both a few things to say.' William began again.

'Why did you go there, Jane? To the valley? Had you been before?'

'Yes.'

'And not told me?'

'I suppose I could say you hadn't asked.'

'Yes, you could,' he nodded. 'We'd never reached the confiding stage.' He paused. 'Then.'

She looked up at him, but he left it at that.

'You better tell me,' he said. 'I intend to know.'

'I went exploring on Gretel . . . you might remember you commented that day on my several cuts and bruises.'

'I do remember. They'd been professionally attended to.'

'By a vet.'

'You received a shot a few hours ago also by a vet. Tim. But I don't think it was Tim then.'

'It was Rodden. I didn't lie to you, I told you we'd met.'

'By design?'

'I went down to see the hut, and Rodden came out.'

'What was he doing there?'

'It was his retreat.'

'Oh, come off it, Jane, does Rodden look like that? Like a pilgrim to a poetic retreat?'

'No,' she said slowly, 'and I know now that it wasn't his place, then how was he there?'

'It's my turn for a while. I'll try to be brief. Gair had gone down to claim his pickings.'

'What do you mean?'

'My ex-vet had met Roger Reynolds in some pub and the usual talk had evolved. Reynolds had put feelers out concerning friends he once had, a Mr. and Mrs. Courtney, cousins, he believed, of the Bower Gair worked for. In a carefully offhand way, but not carefully offhand enough for our shrewd Rodden, Reynolds mentioned children.'

'Whatever for?'

'You haven't guessed?'

'No.'

'I'll tell you now, then. It hasn't been substantiated personally, but when Roger and Kate return I believe it will.'

'The children said those two were being married.'

'Yes.'

'I never thought ... I never guessed ...'

William lit his pipe, and they both waited for the smoke to wreathe up.

'Rodden saw Reynolds' deep interest and reached a conclusion. He told Roger he knew somewhere he could stay if he wanted to delve further.'

'It wasn't Rodden's place, then?' asked Jane.

'No one's place particularly, though John Rivers did say some old man came now and then. Reynolds rushed it, made up some kind of art reason he knew Rodden would accept, a reward being Gair's real and only concern, and Roger undoubtedly guessing that.' A pause. 'I'm sorry, Jane.'

'It's all right,' Jane said.

'So Roger took up residence,' William shrugged.

'How did he meet up with the children?'

'Through you, actually, in the beginning.'

'Yes, they wandered away from the eucalyptus distillery.'

'Later,' said William, 'through Kate. She followed them, being a responsible young woman, and then——' He smiled.

'I didn't know,' Jane said again. 'I could see that Kate had changed, matured, that there was a look to her.'

'A mutual look,' William said.

'But I still don't understand about this man and the children,' Jane continued.

'Do you recall that I told you I believed Gareth and Dorothy knew the real parents? That I suspected they were from the same circle?'

'That man is a sculptor,' Jane said quietly, remembering the twins' chatter.

'He was a very young member of that art circle, and because of his youth we must forgive him.' William tapped at his pipe.

378

'Forgive?'

'Forgive him for not waiting to find if a natural conclusion had brought a natural yield.'

'You mean——' Jane asked.

'Yes,' said William.

'Roger didn't wait,' he went on presently, 'he didn't even think. Not then. He had won himself an American scholarship, and he just left Lilith.'

'She was the girl?'

William nodded.

'Where is she?' Jane asked.

'She died. She was delicate, evidently. According to Dorothy's letter ... oh yes, there was a letter left for me by my cousin and his wife *in case*, but I didn't know that when I spoke to you before, I believed it was only a monetary direction.'

'According to the letter——' prompted Jane.

'Lilith was a leaf in the wind. Gareth and Dorothy were both artistic; they spoke that way.' William half-sighed. 'A leaf that would fall, were the actual words, and the leaf that was Lilith did fall, but the twins were born fine and sturdy, and they were adopted by my cousins.'

'Then Roger Reynolds returned?'

'Years after, and to a new circle. There must have been something nagging in him, for he asked questions, but no one had the answers. Then he remembered that Gareth and Dorothy Courtney had been closest to Lilith, a Lilith he had learned had since died. Then hearing in the way one does hear things that there were two children now with the Courtneys and of a certain age, he tracked Gareth and Dorothy down here just in time to miss them to ask them outright. Then he met up with Gair.'

'How do you know all this?'

'I told you, I have the letter.'

'Not your cousins' part of it, William, Roger's.'

'I spoke to Roger Reynolds an hour ago. He was just leaving for the church.'

Jane said: 'He will not have our children!' She said it hotly, unaware of herself.

But William was aware.

'They are not, Jane, and never were.'

'I love them.'

'I'm not exactly antagonistic myself. But they were not for me. When they learned of the tragedy, was it to me they turned? No, they went instinctively to Roger, and you know why, don't you? It was the call of the same blood. They're Roger Reynolds' kids ... and Kate's, too, now. I don't know if you noticed, Jane, but' ... whimsically ... 'Kate wore the best dress.'

'I noticed,' Jane said.

'A lot of water has gone under the bridge that Roger stands on. He's a mature man now. He can't be penalized for youth, Jane. Also, he wants them, and they, though they don't realize or understand it, want him.'

'And what about Kate?'

'Kate wants them, too. It's all part of what happens when there's a mutual look.'

'How is the valley?' Jane broke in a little frantically; she found she wanted to hold something off until she caught her breath, as it were. She needed time.

'It will recover. Australian fires clean up, but rarely destroy.'

'And John's place?'

'Untouched. He and his Ennie defended it successfully, they'll be a great team.' As before, William said: 'I'm sorry, Jane,' and she knew he meant John.

'It's all right.' Jane repeated her reply.

'Then it appears I'm quite clear,' William said matter-of-factly. 'No use you bringing out Tim, he and Maureen practically have announced their engagement.'

'At no time had I any intention of bringing out Tim, as you put it, and I'm happy about them.' Jane stopped and looked at William. 'What do you mean you're clear?' she demanded.

'To put it to you.'

'Put what?' Jane stared incredulously at him.

'I want us to be married. Frankly I wanted that the first moment I saw you making a mess of your shipboard strapper chores.'

'I didn't!'

'You tethered them the wrong way, remember? But' ... a pause ... 'you knew how to tether my heart. I knew who you were, and I was determined to dislike you. You'd let Gair down.'

'I hadn't!'

'I know that now. In a way I knew it then. Rodden Gair was clever, but never an intrinsic character. However, in black and white it sounded as though you'd taken him up the garden path. I had to go on facts, Jane.'

'Where is Rodden now?'

'Oh, I haven't victimized him, in fact quite the opposite. I've secured him a very good city job, where he'll undoubtedly go right to the top by marrying the boss's daughter.'

'He only looked on the commercial side,' Jane murmured, 'naturally I thought it was his boss's way, too.'

'And you still don't know, do you? You know nothing about your boss's ways, nor' ... an oblique look ... 'your boss.'

'Co-director,' Jane corrected.

'Of four-fifths. You have only one-fifth. Jane, *Jane*, one-fifth of what?'

'Of Gretel, San Marco, Ruthven, of—Mr. Bower! William! William, what on earth——'

For William Bower had lifted her right out of the bed into his arms, she was in those arms tightly, so tightly that unless she struggled very effectively she would never break loose.

'One-fifth will do, Jane,' William Bower was saying. 'I would sooner you met me halfway, but I've enough for the whole way, and if you find you can't contribute——'

'Contribute what?'

'What it takes to make two. You see, girl, I love you. It

only took one look.'

'But a mutual look,' Jane said quietly, unprepared for the almost violent manner he now put her on her feet.

'Don't say that if you don't mean it, Jane.' William held her at arm's length.

'And if I do mean it, William?'

'Then say it. Say it.'

'What I have is five-fifths,' she told him. 'That makes the whole, doesn't it, William?'

'And the look?' he reminded her jealously.

'A mutual one. I said so. Oh, William' ... up in his big arms again ... 'everything is so perfect, so very perfect, yet Dandy...'

'Yes, Dandy. But it was to be, my sweet. Try to accept that.'

She did accept it, though sadly, her head against his shoulder, his fingers tight on the flimsy stuff of the night-gown in which Teresa must have encased her. In a bitter sweetness she heard him say, 'Oh, there was a cable from my uncle for you. Evidently he must have left out something in his answer regarding Dotsy.'

'Dotsy's condition, when, but not by whom,' Jane murmured.

'Yes, darling.' He handed her the envelope and she opened it up.

She was crying and smiling as she looked up again from the message, crying because something was over, smiling because something would soon begin. A little shaky foal would begin, a fragment of wet ears, soft eyes and bewildered expression. Dotsy's foal.

And ... handing William the cable ... *Dandy's* doing. For that was what was written.

MISS SIDNEY STOP BOWERS STUD STOP PLATEAU STOP IT WAS DANDY STOP

Then there was signed: RUSTY.

All this, knew Jane in William's arms, and *still* Dandy.

THERE WERE THREE PRINCES

There Were Three Princes

Verity's plans for joining forces with her brother evaporated when she reached Australia to find he'd married a woman she disliked.

Working for Mrs. Prince in the antique store made her feel more settled, however, especially when Mrs. Prince, the mother of three grown sons, talked about her family.

"Two of them," she told Verity, "are accounted for." But she didn't say which ones. Was it Dr. Matt, the gracious Prince; playboy Peter, the charmer; or Bart who... well, just like in the fairy tale, was just in-between?

CHAPTER I

... "ONCE upon a time there were three princes, a gracious prince, a charming prince, and a prince who was in-between."

Verity smiled nostalgically to herself as the old fairytale came back down the years to her. What favourite book of hers, or Robin's, had it been in? Not Hans Andersen, she knew. Certainly not Grimm.

She put the thought aside to listen attentively to Mrs. Prince who had prompted the childhood memory with her recounting of her trio of sons.

"Matthew is a wonderful person," she had told Verity, "Peter is a fascinating fellow, and Bart –"

"Yes, Mrs. Prince?"

"Is just Bart," his mother had related.

"Bart comes in the middle?"

"Matthew was our first, Bartley our second and Peter was our baby. Though none of them are babies now." Mrs. Prince had laughed ruefully. "In fact well into that stage of life when they should be providing me with grandbabies. If you can see your way to fall in love with any of them and marry him while I'm away, Miss Tyler, I'll be very pleased indeed."

"Do you say that to all your employees?" Verity had laughed.

"Only you and Priscilla. Oh, no, I'm a very discerning person." She had smiled warmly on Verity, and Verity who had liked her at once had smiled back.

"Priscilla is your secretary?"

"The firm's secretary for some years now. I don't know what holds up Bart."

"Then it's Bart and Priscilla?" As Mrs. Prince had broached the subject, Verity did not mind adding her bit to the cosy chat.

"Not officially, as I just said." Mrs. Prince had glanced down at the references that Verity had given her. "They do seem very promising," she praised ... then she had paused. "There is just one thing –"

"Yes, Mrs. Prince?"

"Do you think you'll stay on with us, or is this just a temporary fill-in for you? Oh, I'm sorry, my dear, and you don't have to answer, but so many of you English girls come to Australia just to look around. Not that I blame you, but –"

"You mightn't want me to stop after you've sampled me," Verity had laughed back. Then seriously she had promised: "I will stay." For she had to stay. *Now*.

It hadn't been the money, though certainly her fare out from England had depleted her savings, it had been her half-brother Robin. Robin was her junior, and the sole inheritor of her stepfather's very comfortable estate ... at least it had been that. A slight biting of Verity's bottom lip. For so long as he had been grown up, Robin had fallen in and out of affairs, from everywhere his restless feet had taken him he had written back to Verity that he was in love. He was reckless, scatterbrained, completely irresponsible, but endearingly vulnerable – anyway, Verity found him that. Possibly, she conceded, she felt like this since he had been so delicate as an infant. Her mother, seeing the adoration her young daughter of her first marriage had had for the baby of her second marriage, had declared him Verity's child.

There were only four years between them, but Robin had

used those years abominably, Verity often thought ruefully, with his calls and demands, his S.O.S.'s for help. Mature beside his immaturity, she had been at his beck and call.

But it had been when he had written to England that he would need her no longer, that Adele would take over the "child" now, that Verity had made the longest journey of all. She had come from England to Australia to see Adele, assess her, because if Adele was marrying Robin with that inheritance in view, that comfortable estate that was to eventuate in several years' time on his twenty-fifth birthday, she had to tell her that circumstances had suddenly altered, that the Ramsay assets had dwindled, that Robin no longer was the favourable proposition he had previously been. It was interference, she was aware of that, but she was painfully aware, too, of the type of girl Robin had previously selected.

Of course, she had known intrinsically, if she had looked at Adele and seen love there, she would not have spoken, because it would not have mattered, love needs no reward. And as it had happened she had not spoken. But not because of any love, that had been apparent, but because Robin was not going to live long enough for any words to be needed to be said.

"A few months," the doctor had told Verity sympathetically when she had gone to him after one of Robin's frightening attacks that had occurred soon after her arrival. "But you would have suspected that, of course."

"Well, he was a delicate child."

"You knew him even then?'

"I'm his sister . . . at least a half-sister."

"I'm sorry – I thought you were his wife."

No, Adele was his wife. By the time Verity had arrived in Sydney, the girl had seen to that. She had also seen to it that Verity knew what she now intended.

"I have been in touch with a solicitor," she had said quite

389

coolly, "and he has told me that even if Robin doesn't reach the prescribed age, which by the way he seems to be going could happen, the money still comes to me."

What money? Verity had thought.

She had not told the girl, though, for she had known that she must keep her by Robin's side. Either this last love was a true love or Robin was too tired to change, but this time his infatuation was persisting. Verity had not dared risk Adele leaving her brother because of what that shock could mean. Because her own money was gone and she must refurbish it, because if by some means Adele found out the truth and left Robin she had to be here to pick up the pieces, finally but tellingly because she simply loved him for the little vulnerable boy he had been, she had refused to listen to Adele's pointed suggestions that she return to England . . . Robin's suggestions, too, when Adele prompted him, because Robin was pitifully weak.

"If you're waiting for a hand-out –" Adele had said baldly.

"I have a wife now, Verity," Robin had hinted more kindly.

But she had still remained. And she would remain. She *must.*

"I'll be staying, Mrs. Prince," she repeated. Repeated it definitely.

The business was a superior antique and furnishing business in a very superior Sydney suburb. Verity had worked in such a business in Chelsea, but the moment she had crossed the threshold of "Woman's Castle", she had known that this was an even more encompassing concern. The displays were beautiful, everything was elegant, in perfect taste.

"The woman in this Woman's Castle," she had praised Mrs. Prince, for that was the establishment's name, "knows what goes to make a home." She had quoted: "A home is a woman's castle."

"Only," Mrs. Prince had smiled, "it's a man."

"One of the three sons?"

"Originally my husband, he had the unerring touch. I'm afraid" ... ruefully ... "all I know is not to match pink and yellow. Oh, I got by after Grant died, and the boys were still young, but only with the help of his books and sketches. Then Bart took over."

"Then he is the inspiration?" For, Verity thought, looking around again, inspiration was the only word.

"Well ... at present."

"Only at present?"

"Bart always considers it strictly that."

"He doesn't want the business?"

"Bart," said Mrs. Prince unhappily, "just wants his health."

"Oh, I'm sorry. I mean I didn't want to intrude."

"You're not intruding, and anyway, you'll see."

"See?" she queried.

"Bart suffered an accident. He was badly injured. He has undergone several superficial operations, and he faces the real thing now." A troubled sigh. "When he agrees."

"Will there be complete recovery?"

"We hope so, and Matthew is very confident." Before Verity could ask, Mrs. Prince had explained, "Matthew is my doctor son. He's the eldest."

The mother had sat silent for a while, and Verity had not liked to break in on her thoughts.

"Perhaps Bart would have been, too," she had shrugged at length, "if it hadn't happened. I mean, there was that time lapse in his medical studies, and a man loses his enthusiasm."

"And Peter? Your youngest? Medically inclined as well?"

"Oh, no, though doubtless he could have skated through.

391

Everything comes much too easy to our Peter. Just now he's a dabbler, in anything and everything, profitably dabbling, or he wouldn't do it. Well, there are my three sons."

"But only the in-between concerned with Woman's Castle."

... "Once upon a time there were three princes, a gracious prince, a charming prince, and a prince who was in-between."

"Until he finds himself," Mrs. Prince nodded.

"Can't Priscilla help? I mean" ... apologetically ... "you did tell me that she and Bart –"

"I don't know, my dear. Really, I don't know much about any of my sons. Does any mother these days?" Mrs. Prince had finished with a laughing note before she repeated the business information she had given Verity upon her arrival.

"If you're agreeable you can start as promptly as tomorrow. Priscilla looks after the secretarial side. The buying, selling and display will be entirely yours."

"And Mr. Bartley Prince's?"

A little cloud as Mrs. Prince warned, "He never actually attaches himself here. I told you."

"Yet he is attached?"

"Yes, though not at the moment. He has been having a series of exploratory examinations in St. Martin's. When he does come back . . ." a rueful little laugh.

"He won't like me?"

"It's hard to say. My last effort when Bart was away was a bathroom setting, and all he said was 'Oh, Mother!'"

Now Verity laughed, too.

"One thing," Mrs. Prince went on, "I won't be here to hear 'Oh, Mother!' when he sees you. I'm leaving at once."

"Canada, wasn't it?"

"Yes, my sister's daughter is being married. I don't know how these mothers marry off their children. Don't forget, Miss Tyler, what I told you about that."

"I won't," smiled Verity.

She left soon afterwards, left for the little flat in Balmain that Robin had rather unhappily suggested.

"We can't have you here with us, you understand that, as Adele said we're married now."

"Of course, Robin. I understand perfectly. But I'd like to remain in Sydney a little longer. I won't get in your hair."

"You're a good scout, Verity. You always were," Robin had said awkwardly. "It's just that Adele thinks —"

"Adele is perfectly right: You must always think of her as right," Verity had urged with an ache in her heart. At the very least, she thought, let Robin not *know* Adele, the real Adele.

She had opened the attic window of the small apartment in the old terrace; Balmain was full of these charming nineteenth-century remnants of sandstock and iron lace. She had looked down on the shining green waterway of Johnston's Bay. Once, a century ago, the agent who had leased her the flat had told her, the bay had been full of American sail, for they had been allotted this portion of the harbour. In their ballast had come American earth and in some of the earth sprinklings of American seed. Houses had sprung up later on exotic flowers, stifling them, but there were still occasional strangers among the freesias and marigolds. Strangers. And that was what she was now, knew Verity, looking down on the bay, now that Robin was accounted for by Adele. She belonged to no one here, she was a stranger.

She smiled slightly at Mrs. Prince's fervent hope for a daughter-in-law and in time a grandchild. With Bart reserved for Priscilla, and from the difficult sound of him Verity did not envy Priscilla, there remained Matthew and Peter. A gracious prince. A charming prince. Which, she said flippantly to the green water, to choose?

She turned back to the small but adequate room and cooked

a small but adequate meal. After which she went to bed early as befitted the night before a new job.

But after she had switched off, and before she climbed into bed, she stood again at the attic window, looking down at lights now, hundreds of city lights reflected in the darkling water, for Balmain was wedded both to the harbour and to Sydney, golden ladders from soaring buildings, rainbow streamers from their neon lights.

For some absurd reason she was thinking of that old fairy-tale again. "Once upon a time there were three princes, a gracious prince, a charming prince, and a prince who was in-between."

Matthew, the gracious, she tagged. Peter, the charming. She finished rather drowsily: "Bart, the in-between," as she pulled up the rugs.

Though there had been no nine-to-five rule laid down . . . "In a place like Woman's Castle customers never come at nine but frequently linger after five," Mrs. Prince had smiled . . . Verity saw to it the next morning that she was on time.

The shop was one of a leisurely row of tasteful salons and boutiques, set in a small courtyard with its own miniature fountain. The street in which it stood was leafy and quiet and there were glimpses between the ornamental trees of Sydney Harbour. Apart from a tasteful sign in the form of artistically in-beckoning arms reading "Woman's Castle", there was no announcement and no display. Verity knew now that one had to enter for these.

The business was not actually opened, but the door was un-locked, so Verity went in. She could hear the tap of a type-writer, so crossed to the room from where the sound came. Here, too, the door was unlocked, on this occasion also ajar.

At her quiet knock, a girl got up at once, but in those few

moments Verity had time to look at Priscilla ... for it would be Priscilla ... and she liked what she saw. A serene girl. Could anyone ask for more? Brown-haired, brown-eyed, rather self-effacing, Verity judged. But if you received a first impression of plainness, the sweet smile that slowly took over the gentle face soon altered that impression. Verity found herself thinking with Mrs. Prince that Bart was certainly wasting time.

"Miss Tyler?" Priscilla asked pleasantly.

"Verity."

"And I'm Priscilla Burnett – Priscilla or Cilla or Prissie, I get them all. There was no need for you to get here this early, Verity."

"You're here," Verity pointed out.

"Accounts are different, they require office hours. Also I leave at five, and I'm afraid if you've a customer ..." Priscilla looked apologetically at Verity.

"Oh, I understand that perfectly. I worked in England in a business like this. But I must be honest: it wasn't as beautiful or expansive as this."

"It is, isn't it? That's Bart for you." Priscilla's eyes were soft and loving, and once again Verity thought – what holds that man up?

Already Priscilla was busy with teapot and packet of biscuits. "We have lots of short breaks here," she smiled, "Mrs. Prince loves time off for a natter, and Bart ... well, Bart just has to have time off." Again the gentle look.

"I'm looking forward to going through the shop," Verity proffered. "It's much larger than you might think from the front. I see there's an annexe at the back."

"Bart's collection of colonial and antique oil lamps. You'll love them. The trouble is they're not profitable."

"But surely people are interested –"

"Bart makes excuses not to let them go. Milk, Verity?"

Over the companionable cup, Verity learned more of the Princes. Matthew, the eldest, was just starting out in his first G.P. Woman's Castle did not see him very often, Priscilla confided, for you know how called-upon doctors always are . . .

Bart would account for himself when he came in, Priscilla said next, but when Verity suggested that that might also be some time away since he was in hospital, she corrected, no, it was a brief exploratory stay only, and he could arrive at any moment.

"That leaves Peter," said Verity. The charming prince, she thought to herself.

"Yes. Peter." Now there was something in Priscilla's voice that Verity could not pigeonhole for herself. She looked at the girl, but her expression remained as calm and gentle, there was simply nothing there to read.

"Will Peter come in?" she asked.

"You ask Peter and he won't be able to tell you," laughed Priscilla. But as she laughed with her, Verity wondered why she heard somewhere a bleak note in that laughter.

She learned that Priscilla was always busy on mail orders.

"Yet we don't advertise. It's just that once you buy from Woman's Castle it seems you always buy there. Customers move to the country, they go interstate, but they don't buy elsewhere. Then, of course, friends see their treasures and become customers, too. And so it builds up and up."

"Yet it has no one to keep it on – I mean not personally." Verity explained how Mrs. Prince had said several times that Bart, who was its present manager, had no real heart for the business, that he always considered himself as only on loan to it.

"That's so, but it still might have to be Bart's thing," said Priscilla in the loving voice again, "if that first indicative operation that Bart keeps on delaying comes out contra. I think that that is why Bart hesitates. While he doesn't know the truth, there's still hope. But he must submit eventually." She sighed. "Peter, of course, could do it. Peter can do anything."

"Except settle down? Oh, do forgive me. I don't usually gossip like this."

"It's not gossip, it's fact. You have to know more than the things you sell in a job to make it a success."

"Thank you, Priscilla," appreciated Verity. "Thank you, too, for the tea. Now I really must get to work. What time do I open the doors?"

"We don't. We leave them unfastened and customers just browse in as though it was their own house."

"That's perfect," applauded Verity. She took her cup to a sink in the corner of the office, washed, dried and replaced it, then went out to look around.

The shop was formed like the rooms of a house. She went from room to room, becoming progressively enthralled. There was a bathroom done in black and aqua. A kitchen in cherry red and white. A grey and coral lounge. An apple green dining setting. A bedroom entirely in white. Apart from these offices there was a purely antique room that she longed to explore, and beyond it the annexe she had spoken with Priscilla about, and where the secretary had said that Bart Prince housed his collection of oil lamps.

She went there first.

It was pure delight, she found — superb ruby, opaque amber and cranberry-coloured majolica, brass lamps, venetian lamps, iron, marble and copper. There were hanging lamps, bracket lamps, barn lanterns, conductor's and policeman's lamps, piano sconce lamps. — She had no doubt there were all the lamps of China.

In the antique room there were the expected treasures, yet

in this instance *very* treasured, Verity sensed. That French walnut bureau, for instance. That embroidery frame. The Georgian dropside table. The rouge marble wash stand.

She came out of the antique room to find there was a browser in the pretty kitchen setting. The women wanted a biscuit barrel. As a child she had always reached up for biscuits from a barrel, she related nostalgically, and now she wanted her children to do the same. Verity found a variety of barrels, one in floral china that the customer chose at once. – "Because," she said, "I change my colours around."

Closely following the biscuit barrel, she sold a jardinière, and later in the morning a wall tapestry. The time raced and she loved every second of it, she told Priscilla at lunch.

After the secretary got back to her typing, Verity decided, business having drowsed away like the drowsy day, or so it appeared, to change a setting. At the Chelsea place at which she had worked they had changed the settings often, many customers laughingly complaining that barely had they time to get used to something than it was whisked away. However, the proprietor had believed in showing what he had, and every afternoon it had been Verity's job to re-set a room.

The sun porch in tawny golds seemed a likely change, and Verity decided to offer the customers a study in its place. A brown study, she thought, inspired.

She whisked away the gaily striped cushions and took down the sunflower curtains. The neutral furniture in the room, concealed before by gay covers and bright hangings, now lent itself to a more sober corner. Verity chose plain brown hopsack from a chest of drapes to hang at the mock windows, took the chintz off the table and left the table bare except for some books, a blotter sheet and a desk calendar, then she stepped back. Now was the time to add a touch of colour, she knew. One orange cushion, perhaps? Or a butter yellow? Or would she keep to a bookish fawn?

She opened a cushion box and went despairingly through it, despairing because not one cushion seemed to fit the bill. She tried several, only to discard them at once, and was just sampling a muted green when a male voice behind her called: "No."

She turned round.

Her first impression of the objector was not one of height, and yet she saw that he was a tall person. She supposed it was the slight stoop that took away the inches – that, and a perceptible droop to the shoulders. The man was flint-hard, she also saw, but she received the impression that he had *forced* himself into this near-whipcord condition, almost a kind of challenge to what fate had delivered him. For the rest, she had only a quick impression of dark unsmiling eyes, dark unruly hair, and from the forehead to the beginning of a brown throat, a scar. It was, she thought at once, not a disfigurement, rather it was one of those flaws that seemed to make up a man's character.

"Seen enough?" The voice was cool, and Verity reddened. She searched for an apology that was not the usual trite excuse and during that moment he moved a few steps. He had a faint hesitation when he did so, not a limp so much as a deliberation, a pause.

Undoubtedly, Verity decided, it was Bartley Prince.

"I'm sorry." She gave up looking for the right apology.

He shrugged. "Excused. It does come as a shock at first."

"It does not," she came back. "I would have looked at anyone. You're my first customer this afternoon ... or so I thought."

That halted his deliberate movement. "*Your* first customer? Who are you?"

"The new assistant." She remembered what Mrs. Prince

399

had related about the bathroom setting, and added before she could stop herself: "Now you say 'Oh, Mother!'"

"Oh, Mother!" he obliged.

There was an awkward moment, then, meeting each other's eyes, they both laughed.

"I'm sorry you weren't told about me," apologized Verity.

"Now I know why my parent kept changing the subject when I asked about filling her void at Woman's Castle while she was away. Sly puss, that mother of mine. She flew out last night and knows I can't put her in her place."

"Woman's place?" As she said it, Verity glanced around her. Surely of all places Woman's Castle was a woman's place, she appreciated.

"Yet not this particular room," Bart Prince said drily, evidently reading Verity's thoughts. "A study is intrinsically a man's place. Are you naming it Brown Study, by the way?"

"Yes," she said, a little surprised.

"Then why are you cluttering it up with another colour?"

"Because — well, there should be a contrast."

"Should there?" He walked across and took the green cushion she still had in her hand and threw it away. "A brown study should be brown," he said. Then he ordered: "Look."

She looked and saw he was correct. She might have been taught about the necessity for a contrast but undoubtedly in this instance he was right. The room was right.

Across the distance between them, the green cushion still where it had been flung, she met his dark unsmiling eyes. Bartley Prince's eyes. Not the prince who was gracious, not the prince who was charming, but the prince who was in-between.

"I'm Bart," he said. "No doubt" ... the merest flicker of anger ... "you've gathered that already. And you?"

"Miss Tyler." As he still waited, "Verity Tyler," Verity said.

CHAPTER II

"AND do you practise it?" Bart Prince said lazily, almost uninterestedly as he bent down to pick up the cushion.

She knew what he meant, it often had been said to her, but nonetheless Verity replied, "If you mean truth –"

"I meant that."

"Then the answer is yes. Unless, of course, it would hurt someone."

"In which instance you don't adopt it?"

"No."

"Then little use my coming to you for truth then, is there? Unless" . . . a brief laugh . . . "not knowing me, you would be indifferent to hurting."

"I don't know you, but I couldn't be indifferent."

"In short a tender-hearted lady."

"Mr. Prince," said Verity carefully, "do you always look for rebuffs like this?"

"No, but I look for truth. Can you in truth look at me and not look away?"

"Yes."

"Is that being kind?" he taunted.

"It's being truthful. I think" . . . daringly . . . "you vastly exaggerate yourself."

To her relief, for she knew she had overstepped somewhat, he grinned. It was a fascinating grin. The slight scar gave it an amusing, rather lopsided, puckish look. He appeared much less intimidating.

"I suppose I do. We're all over-important to ourselves. My personal trouble is that it was trouble for nothing. If I could only lose that . . ." There was a brief return of the anger, then he shook it off. "Seen over the place?" he asked.

"It's beautiful. I worked in a beautiful business in Chelsea, but this is more so," she said sincerely.

"My father did it."

"Yet you carried it on." In her enthusiasm she forgot what Mrs. Prince had said.

He did not let her forget long.

"Only until such time as I can do a man's work," he said, and again there was that harsh edge to his voice.

Quickly she diverted, "I like your lamp section," and was rewarded by his eager smile.

"In the dictionary," he proffered a little diffidently, "it says simply that a lamp gives light. I know that it gave that to me – the collecting, I mean."

"And that's why it's unprofitable," she asked. "You won't part with it?"

"It gave me light," he said stubbornly, "when I was needing it. When I find another light, I'll be as mercenary as the rest. – Ah, Cilla." They had reached the office and he stopped to smile across at the secretary.

But not to smile across a room for long. At once Cilla came over and put her hand in his. "Bart," she said quietly.

He held the hand, put his other hand over it to seal the grasp.

"How was it in hospital?" she asked.

"Easier, knowing your gentle concern."

"Apart from that?"

"No results yet. They'll be given to Matthew."

"Oh, Bart!" As Priscilla looked lovingly at him, quite oblivious of Verity he leaned down and kissed her brow.

But he must have become conscious of Verity's rather embarrassed audience, for he tossed, "Pay no attention, it's a business practice."

To the sound of Priscilla's amused but reproving, "Oh, Bart!" again, Verity and the man moved on once more.

"You're not put off by the business practice?" he taunted as he led her into one of the displays.

"It didn't concern me," she said stiffly.

"But a business practice should concern all employees."

"One of such a nature presumably only concerns old employees."

"You mean ones who saw me Before, not just After?"

Verity stopped short. "Mr. Prince, I don't know how you were Before, but I can see how you are After, and I see nothing even remotely remarkable about it. But I do find something remarkable in the chip you carry. Even watching you carry it makes me tired."

Again she had overstepped herself, but she didn't care, she had to work with this man, so she must have an understanding.

There was silence for a while, then he said, "I asked for that. Peace, Miss Truth, pax, please."

"I don't like Miss Truth."

"I don't like Miss Tyler."

"Verity," she agreed.

"Bart," he smiled.

They went on.

"Why did you change my display?" he asked.

"In my former place of employment it was Rule One."

"Then it wasn't my taste that prompted it?"

"Your taste is quite perfect," she awarded coolly.

"Are you speaking professionally?"

"How otherwise would I speak?" she asked, surprised.

"I don't know. I haven't learned about you yet."

"You're a very odd man," she said indignantly.

"In that way as well as physically. I'm sorry" ... at once ... "no harping on the subject, you said."

"Yes, I said." To really close the subject, she crossed to a small, very beautiful Jacobean bureau. "Do you, like my former boss used to, advise young people to go without until they can get the best?" she asked professionally.

"You mean the best is worth waiting for?"

"Yes."

"But is it, though?"

She looked around her, at all the beautiful things. "Can *you* say that?"

"I often think it. You can wait for the best." He stopped a long moment. "And you can wait and wait." Without another word he turned and left the room.

"Odd," Verity awarded him again.

She heard him later in the office. He was laughing now with Priscilla, and she was surprised at the annoyance she felt at her own failure with him.

Shrugging, she went back to the front room to find a customer trying to make up her mind over a set of kitchen jars, so she helped her decide. After that she sold a small curved stool and a slender long-stemmed vase. Which all made it, she tallied, Priscilla having left now, a rather satisfactory day. As there were no more customers, she decided she could leave as well, but not knowing the ropes of the place yet she went in search of Bart Prince to ask his permission.

She found him where she had anticipated she would, among his lamps.

"Oh, yes, go," he nodded. "No need ever to ask."

"If there was a customer I would wait, but the street is empty."

"That's all right," he nodded again.

She hesitated, she could not have said why.

"How long do you stay, Mr. – I mean Bart?"

"Like the young people waiting for good furniture, I just wait," he told her.

"But seriously."

"I was serious."

"I really meant . . . well, could I fix you something?"

"Would you?"

The answer surprised her, but she said at once, "Of course."

"That's extraordinarily good of you, but no, thank you. I live in city digs with a handy restaurant. None of the Princes live at home. Matthew is now doing his G.P., Peter is here, there and everywhere, and I found it necessary to snare an apartment either on the ground floor or supplied with a lift. But" . . . with a meaning look at her . . . "we won't talk about that."

"But you are, aren't you? You keep bringing it back by apparently not talking about it. I'm sorry, I wish I could help."

"With fixing me up something?"

"No, with –" She stopped herself in time. "Good evening," she proffered, and went out.

It was a pleasant hour to leave, the office rush over, the rush to the city for the night's entertainments not yet begun. Verity went down to Circular Quay and caught the number five ferry.

The airy, green and white, "showboat" type of large launch that Sydneysiders still insisted on for their harbour transport was just drawing in. She boarded, then climbed the stairs to the upper deck. With a fuss and a flurry the ferry bustled off again, ignoring the more glamorous eastern aspect with its fine waterside houses to pass instead under the bridge and take the river way that the American sail once did. At the first little wharf Verity got off and climbed the steep hill.

When she got to her stone terrace house, she saw a car there, and eagerly she quickened her pace. It would be Robin.

Her half-brother was waiting in the flat for her . . . she had given him a key . . . and at once they ran to each other. For a moment Verity thought uneasily that it was not usually like this, it was not like Robin to show his affection in such a way — not, anyway, to her — and she searched his face, hoping her anxiety did not show.

He looked ill. She wondered if he had noticed it himself, but then . . . and thank heaven . . . it was the one to whom it happened who never noticed. One looked at oneself each day in the mirror and saw no change, or if you saw it, it was such a small change that it meant nothing at all.

But it meant a lot to Verity. She noticed bone structure in Robin's face she had never known before, a pull to his boyish mouth.

"How are you, darling?" She was glad she had always petted him and that now the endearment, almost fiercely felt, would not sound strange.

"Oh, fine, fine. I'm still a little below par after that 'flu thing, but then it was quite a bout, lots of people have been complaining that they haven't picked up. How are you, V?"

"Thriving."

"You look it." He gave her another hug. He had never been demonstrative, and it tore at Verity.

"Adele?" she asked as casually as she could.

"Beautiful. She is, isn't she? She's visiting an aunt tonight. That's why I'm here."

Verity restrained herself from saying, "Couldn't you have gone, too?" because she knew that Adele would not have been visiting an aunt at all. She made herself busy with cups and plates.

"Not for me, Verity," Robin declined.

"Eaten?"

"I'm just not hungry lately. This 'flu thing –"

"Yes, I know. It reacts like that. But some tea, surely."

"Tea," he agreed.

As she brewed it, he said abruptly: "It's not fair."

"What isn't, Robbie?"

"This place . . . I mean . . . well, it's so poor."

"Actually it's elegant. It's early colonial. If you don't believe me ask the agent who leased it to me," Verity laughed.

"Oh, it has a charm, I'll agree, but after our luxury apartment . . . I tell you, Verity, it's just not fair. Father was not fair. He shouldn't have left the entirety to me."

. . . Left what entirety? Verity secretly grieved.

"Oh, I don't know," she said casually, "you were his son."

"Yet you were the daughter of the woman he married to get that son."

"Robbie darling, he was a wonderful husband to Mother, he gave her everything. After she died, he gave me everything . . . the best of schools, of opportunities –"

"He didn't include you in the will, though, you didn't benefit."

. . . Who has benefited? Verity thought achingly for Robin.

"You were his son," she repeated stubbornly.

"Well, if you think like that, though I know I couldn't have thought so generously, keep it up, please, V. You see, Sis, now that I'm married, now that I have Adele –"

"Darling, I understand perfectly, a man must always put his wife first. Never think, or do, any other way."

"No," agreed Robin, "but sometimes the unfairness creeps in. I do worry, Verity."

"But why?"

"I with so much, you finding your own way in the world."

"You've changed, Robin." – He had. Once he never would

407

have thought of such things. Again Verity felt uneasy.

"Perhaps. I suppose it could be Adele. All I know is I worry where I didn't before. Or at least" ... a laugh ... "I think of someone other than myself." He looked fondly across at Verity.

"Then perish that thought, unless it's for your wife. I" ... in a sudden inspiration ... "have never been so – forward-looking in all my life."

"What do you mean, Verity?" When she did not answer, not knowing *what* to answer, wondering why she had made the rash statement, he said, "Is there someone, then? I mean is that why you're so – well, confident?"

"Could be," she evaded with a deliberate show of coyness.

"Like to tell?"

"I couldn't."

"I suppose not." A pause. "Could it be what Adele said recently?"

"What was that?"

"I was telling her where you were working. Prince's, isn't it? She said, 'Which one of the three Princes is she after?' Then she added, 'Any one of them would do.' I gathered," Robin smiled, "that money is no object there."

"No object," Verity said faintly.

"Then which?" he laughed.

"That would be telling," she came back. "Just leave it at that. Leave it at 'Once upon a time there were three princes.' Remember, Robin?"

"I remember. You were always one for stories," he recalled boyishly. "You used to read them to me, you were a wonderful reader, Verity. Yes, I remember 'The Three Princes.' " He smiled. " 'Once upon a time there were three princes, a gracious prince, a charming prince –' "

Verity finished, "And a prince who was in-between."

"And which is it for you?" he persisted.

"Again, that would be telling." Better this, she thought, than to admit that there was no prince, nobody at all to keep her in Australia, except . . .

"Love – and the means, too," he commended, "what else can you ask? I'm always happy for Adele that as well as me she has expectations. I mean, it's a nice feeling for a girl, isn't it?"

"A nice feeling, darling," Verity assured him.

They drank tea together, but Robin ate nothing. She noticed the thinness of his fingers, the slight tremble as he held the cup.

When he left, he said, "You can't imagine how much easier I feel, Verity, I had no idea that you – I mean I thought you might just be staying on here for me."

She laughed at that . . . and hoped he did not hear a hollow note.

"But now that I know–" he went on.

"Robin, you don't know. I mean" . . . with concern, for after all a lie like this could have an unfortunate result . . . "I don't know myself."

"Verity, I'm not going to shout it out, I'm just going to re-peat to myself for my own peace of mind: 'There were three princes.' "

He was repeating it with amused satisfaction as he left her and went down to the car.

Well, it seemed a harmless fabrication, and if it appeased him, it satisfied her. She waved to the car as it left the kerb.

The next morning there was only Priscilla again in attendance at Woman's Castle, but Verity expected this would be the gen-eral rule, since as boss of the concern, for he was that even though he did not associate himself, Bart would need to be away frequently accruing more stock. She knew from the Chelsea shop how supplies must always be safeguarded a long way ahead.

She had a cup of tea with Priscilla, then got herself up to date with the goods in hand as she carefully dusted them. There were some beautiful pieces and the dusting was more pleasure than task.

Between the conning and the tidying, she sold a bed lamp and a tray, so felt she had earned her morning's salary.

After lunch she looked hard at the displays, not wanting to change them if they had been newly done. Priscilla, coming down the corridor, told her that the second bedroom setting had not been altered for some time, so she decided to change that.

But she voted against altering the purpose of the room, as she had altered the sun porch into a brown study. The study, she was pleased to see, was attracting much favourable attention. The only flaw was that it had not been entirely her inspiration. She would have added another colour and lost that brown impact.

She felt a challenge now to do something that was not added to or taken away from, and she stood regarding the minor bedroom a long time. It was a pretty setting in its present form, aimed at the gay teenager. Verity knew that she could not improve on it, so she decided to tackle a different age group.

She rummaged around the props, as it were, and inspiration came to her in the form of a very beautiful marcella quilt. From there on she unearthed more and more things that would be just right for the setting she had in mind – a Victorian bedroom for the older, more perceptive young woman, quiet, unassuming, in very good taste.

The plain narrow bed fortunately applied itself to the chaste scene. She removed every bit of bric-à-brac, but she allowed small white linen mats under a brush and mirror set she also found in the big box. To her delight she unearthed an antiquated washbasin and jug, remembering as she looked appreciatively at the flowered china that there was an appropriate stand in the back room storage. She had noticed it yesterday and admired the dark unpolished oak. She also recalled that it was on rollers, which would make it easy to wheel in.

Now she worked eagerly, with inspiration. She had always loved being urged on to an end she had in mind, but this time she found herself more anxious than she had ever been in Chelsea. For it had to be right. Just right. She pressed in a final thumb tack to secure something, then sat back on her heels to regard the finished scene, for as far as she was concerned it was finished. Yesterday she had felt somehow uncertain, and the feeling had been right, for the room had not been right, but now she looked and was confident. But would he ... would Bart Prince ...

"Perfect," the man in the doorway said so certainly that there was no disbelieving the sincerity. Aware of ridiculous tears of relief, for they were ridiculous – this person's opinion could not matter that much – Verity scrambled to her feet.

"It's right?" she repeated.

"I said so." Bart Prince was looking at her quizzically, and, flushing, she looked away.

She hoped desperately that he would not query the anxiety she had so obviously betrayed. Whether he felt her sensitiveness or simply was not interested, he did not.

Together they left the setting.

"Tomorrow, Verity," Bart said, "the Castle will be closed."

"A holiday?" As a newchum she had not yet sorted out Australian festivals.

"The very opposite – we'll be working very hard."

"Stocktaking?"

"Stock gathering. I've had an offer from Lilith Vale, a small valley town on the other side of the Blue Mountains. I'm hoping to pick up quite a few treasures. Early colonials settled there on land grants."

"Can it be done in a day?"

"The distance there and back, yes, but not the examination of what offers. No, I'll take the van, and we'll stay overnight."

She opened her mouth to say something, then shut it. What she wanted to know was whom he meant by "we".

Deliberately, or so she thought, he misconstrued her unasked question.

"It has to be the van and a camp, there are no hotels at the Vale."

Now she moistened her lips. "There's no need to close shop. I can handle the business."

"Up at Lilith Vale?"

"You mean I—"

"I mean you come, too. Don't tell me" . . . impatiently . . . "you never left that Chelsea concern."

"Oh, no, I used to go buying with—" She had gone buying with Mr. Felix, but Mr. Felix had been plump, fatherly, and — well, Mr. Felix. They had also stayed in hotels. Mrs. Felix, too, had been with them.

He was looking at her quizzically again, but not sparing her this time as he had before.

"I do believe," he drawled, "you're that rare thing, a conventional female. I do believe, too, you don't want to come on that account." Before she could blurt something, though what it would have been she did not know, he said, "Be of good heart, Miss Grundy, Priscilla comes, too, of course."

"That's unfair," she said of his Miss Grundy, and to her surprise he agreed with her. She had noticed before that for all

412

his positiveness, suddenly and completely he could capitulate.

"It was just your uncertain little face," he grinned. "By rights a wreck like I am should take a bow, I suppose. But then" . . . hard and clipped again . . . "that subject is taboo. I must try to remember."

She did not comment . . . but she did wonder who had gone along with Priscilla on previous occasions. To her horror she heard herself asking: "Did you have an attendant here before me, Mr. Bart?" and heard at once his amused laugh.

"No. But Priscilla is entirely different. For that's what you're *really* asking, isn't it?"

She felt her cheeks burning. She could think of nothing to say.

"The van will call for you promptly at eight. Priscilla has your address. Please be ready." He turned and left her. Presently she heard him in the office, laughing with Priscilla. She wondered whether he was repeating her clumsy question and if they were both amused by it. It sounded as though they were exchanging something funny. Not feeling funny herself, feeling priggish and rather schoolgirlish, Verity was glad to see a customer enter the Castle, and she went forward at once.

The afternoon proved quite busy, for which she was very grateful, yet for all her absorption between her discussing and wrapping something kept coming back to her. It was Bart Prince's confident: "Priscilla is entirely different." She had known it, of course. Mrs. Prince had said it. The man's eyes as he had looked at Priscilla had said it. And now he himself had said it. Priscilla is entirely different. Suddenly and bleakly it came to Verity that at the age of twenty-seven, absorbed with Robin as she had always been, she had never been "entirely different" to a man. Any man.

Promptly at eight the next morning, as Bart Prince had said,

413

the van pulled up at the Balmain terrace. It looked a roomy vehicle, and when Priscilla moved up closer to Bart and Verity got in, she found there was ample space.

As it was the peak hour for morning traffic, little was said as Bart ably threaded his way in and out of cars. Verity decided that if it had been in a motor accident the man had sustained his injuries, then certainly his driving skill and nerve had not been impaired.

Because of Sydney's sprawl it was some time before they were free of the city. It must have rained through the night, for the paddocks on either side of the Western Highway were still wet. After they had passed Penrith and climbed up, there was a tantalising smell of woodsmoke from the mountain cottages mixed up with the tang of drying mountain earth.

Now the air was apple crisp, and it kept it up even after they descended from Mount Victoria, then proceeded along an off-shoot ribbon of road. The minor track was narrow and bumpy but offering beauty at every turn, with the scallops of looming blue mountains between the leafy twigs of the bordering trees and the splashing streams.

A twist in the winding way and there was Lilith Vale: one old post-office hung with pink briar roses and no longer in use, one old courthouse, window-deep in encroaching sunflowers, and no longer in use, one old house, by the look of it barely in use, and that was it. "And after today, nothing in use," Bart said.

"What we don't take will be left to the possums," he told the girls. "Once Lilith Vale was on the main road to Lithgow, but many years ago, as you can see."

It had been a lovely old house, strictly in the early sprawling colonial style, plenty of space to stretch out, to breathe. Even now in its shabbiness there persisted that air of inbred pride.

Bart found a key in a prearranged place and they went in,

Priscilla at once busy on her notebook, the other two just gazing around them.

The rooms were rather low-ceilinged for their period, and the walls were panelled in dark rough wood. Because of the house's age the floor was buckled here and there and plaster had come down in several spots to lay on the planks like snow. The windows, as was usual in that era, were rather meagre, yet still extremely attractive, letting in sufficiently suffused primrose light to enhance the furniture that Bart had come about.

It was good furniture – simple, uncluttered and upon occasion quite lovely. There was a little cedar, a lot of mahogany and some warm old oak.

Bart called Priscilla and she made notes as he examined each piece.

Meanwhile Verity wandered round the house. There was no bric-à-brac; evidently only what could not be moved easily had been left. She wondered how Bart Prince would shift the stuff he decided to buy from the house, for like all old furniture it was heavy.

She browsed on . . . then all at once she stopped.

She had reached a fireplace, empty and cold, of course, but the width and depth and friendly accommodation of it somehow caught at her. She could see a family gathered here, a chair for the man of the house, a chair for the woman, a cradle for a child. She could see logs waiting that the man had cut, tea waiting that the woman had brewed. The child slept.

It was so real she could smell it, and hear it, and in her enchantment she half-turned as though to embrace it . . . and found herself breath-close to Bart Prince. He must have come in and in her absorption she had not heard him. What an idiot he must think her!

He did not speak for a long moment, then he put his hands out to the grate.

"Were you cold?" he asked, and she knew that he, too, was seeing the logs, the tea, the sleeping child.

Priscilla was calling out that a piece he had chosen appeared to have woodworm. Without another word, he went.

They had lunch from a hamper and a flask, then some men arrived in a utility to help Bart store the chosen pieces in the van. Verity was a little disturbed over this, for she had thought the inside of the van would be used as sleeping quarters. that the furniture would be consigned separately. Where then did they sleep?

She heard Bart arranging for the men to finish loading in the morning, and saw with surprise that this would be necessary, as already the sun was slipping away.

"Do we use the house tonight?" she asked Priscilla.

"No, it would be musty through being closed up – besides, Bart is a great one for stars." Priscilla gave that fond little laugh.

Bart drove the van to a small clearing he must have known about, and in an astonishingly short time had erected a tent for the girls and swung a hammock for himself.

"Now for tea," he said.

It was no hamper meal this time but steaks on green sticks, and damper. After they finished they just stopped where they were, talking idly, relapsing into comfortable silences, looking at the sky.

Then Priscilla, yawning widely, said that the mountain air always rocked her ... how often? Verity wondered, and with whom? ... and declared that she would go to bed.

Verity got up, too, but she did not cross as Priscilla did and lightly kiss Bart's brow, though Bart's bantering eyes challenged her to. It would amuse him, Verity thought, to be bid goodnight by *both* girls.

Inside the tent Bart had placed two inflated mattresses.

"They're wonderfully comfortable," Priscilla assured her, getting into sensible pyjamas.

Verity felt all varieties of a fool. Never having lived much of a social life, she had always expressed her instinctive femininity in pretty nightwear, fluffy concoctions like the scant apple green waltz-length gown she had brought now. She looked at Priscilla's cotton and then at her own gear with dismay.

"Oh, I'm sorry," regretted Priscilla genuinely, "I should have told you, Verity."

"I thought we'd be inside," Verity explained.

"I should have told you it would be canvas. Never mind, it's only tonight."

Priscilla was in bed by now, and grateful at least that Bart Prince could not see just how new was this newchum he now had in his employ, Verity stretched down on the pump-up and took up a magazine.

Priscilla had gone to sleep at once – she must have spoken genuinely when she said what the mountain air did to her – but Verity stayed awake for a long time.

At length she did feel a little drowsy, and decided to put out the lantern that Priscilla had left alight for her. Instead of getting right up, she leaned across, and in her inexperience she turned the wick up, not down, instantly flooding the tent with flaring light. Still uncertain which way to work it, not wanting to waken or alarm Priscilla, not at all happy over the ferocious leaping of the flame, she stepped carefully out of the tent with it . . . and into Bart Prince's arms.

"What in tarnation –" he began.

"I was frightened," she admitted.

"No need to be, the hurricane is foolproof, it won't start a fire." He took the lantern from her.

"I was frightened of waking Priscilla. She went to sleep at once."

"Presumably sleep is the idea." He was turning down the wick . . . and then he stopped. Without looking up at him to check, Verity still knew that now he was looking at *her*.

"You're a fool, Miss Tyler," he said at length.

"I'm sorry, I'm not used to lanterns."

"You're a fool to wear gear like that," he went on, ignoring the subject of the lamp. His eyes were taking in the soft revealing folds of the gown.

"You mean if fire did start . . ."

"Fire?" The way he said it she knew he had not been thinking that at all.

There was a long moment of complete silence. Not even the bush cracked. Not even a nightjar called.

"*Not* fire," he told her a little thickly, "man. A man can stand so much. Even my kind of a wreck of a man."

"Bart . . . Mr. Prince . . ." she stammered.

"Which I mustn't harp on. You've told me so."

Another silence, then:

"For heaven's sake, woman, get back to bed!"

CHAPTER III

IN THE week that followed, Verity often wondered if Bart Prince had really come to stand beside her at an empty grate to ask quietly: "Were you cold?"

Lilith Vale seemed a long way away now, much further than its seventy miles, as far away from Woman's Castle as the ends of the earth. The man was far away, too. She knew that a business background was totally different from a mountain one, but Bart Prince was more coolly remote than he had been when she had first started here, and, ruefully, he had not been exactly friendly then.

She wondered about it during her day's activities. Had he been so angry with her for not bringing a sensible sleeping suit, as Priscilla had, that he still rankled? But no, the following day after the lantern episode the subject had not been mentioned, and driving home had been pleasant enough.

But afterwards . . .

He was away a lot, and in his astringent mood Verity was glad of this. She had enough troubles. Robin had not been to see her, and though she disliked doing it in case she might be considered intrusive, she had gone to see him. Adele had been home.

It had been soon afterwards, she mused later, that Bart had come in and corrected very pointedly her new arrangement of wall panels. Before, his correction had piqued her, but she had seen how right he was, but on this occasion she had not seen it. He must have sensed her mortification, for he had reminded her blandly: "The boss is always right."

"I thought it was the customer."

"Which still makes me right, because this correction will ensure us a customer."

She had bitten her lip . . . and it had hurt . . . but much more hurting was the knowledgeable look he had given her, that knowledge that he was the boss and she could not answer back. Oh, why did she stay here?

Reading her in that uncanny way of his, he had agreed, "Yes, why? There are other jobs." Then, when she had not answered, "But you want *this* one, don't you?"

"I just want a job."

He had smiled thinly at that. It had been a disbelieving smile.

He had waited pointedly for a while, then he had inquired: "And for how long do you want 'just a job'?"

"I said I just want a job," she had answered flatly.

"For how long?" he had repeated. Mrs. Prince, his mother, had asked that, too, but very differently. "You came out to Australia to visit your brother, I hear," came next.

"I don't know how you heard that, but yes, I did. Only Robin is a half-brother."

"And a very comfortable one, I believe."

"Why should you believe it?"

"Isn't it true?"

It wasn't . . . but no one must know. "I meant how did you learn this?" she had corrected herself.

"The world," he had reminded her, "is a small place."

As she did not comment, he had said, "Among my acquaintance still on nodding and not wincing terms . . . sorry, I forgot, no self-pity . . . is Dellie."

As she looked at him in puzzlement, he said a little angrily, "Your half-brother's wife."

420

"Oh, Adele. Robin always calls her Adele."

"And you? What do you call her?"

"I haven't got to know her very well."

"So she remarked." His voice was dry, and he had said no more.

The next day they had classified his lantern collection, a fascinating business had he not been difficult again.

"A point, Miss Tyler." They had been pausing a few minutes; Verity had mused on the fact that he had been calling her Miss Tyler all the week.

"Yes, Mr. Prince?" she came back.

"I think it only fair to tell you that in a family of three apparently eligible males, there is actually only one eligible Prince."

She had gone a vivid pink. "And why are you telling me this?"

"Because of certain things –"

"What things?"

He had ignored that and continued, "Because of certain things I believe it would be wise. So often a girl wastes time, and if wastage can be avoided –"

"I don't care for your subject!" she said coldly.

"Nonetheless" . . . he had raised his voice . . . "*listen*. Matthew, though he won't admit it yet, is positively accounted for, even though the fool is not helping himself by adopting a wait-and-see attitude with Cassandra. Had I a raging beauty like Cassandra –"

"You would rush in where angels fear to tread? Is Matthew an angel? Your mother said he was a wonderful person."

"A wonderful idiot. But yes, Matthew is one of the best."

"Once upon a time there were three princes," said Verity absently, "a gracious prince, a charming prince, and a prince who was in-between."

"You go in for fairytales?"

"I did."

"It never dies out, I think – in which case, keeping a happy ending in view, forget Matthew, forget one of the other two, then keep strictly in mind that the field is reduced to only one."

Yes, Verity thought: Peter, the charmer. He is the sole one left if Matthew is written down for Cassandra, because you, Mr. Bart Prince, belong to Priscilla. She added to herself, rankling at his bald words: "Poor Priscilla!"

"I find all this in bad taste," she said aloud.

"It's in rotten taste, but it makes sense. If everybody was outspoken there'd be fewer broken hearts."

"I have no intention of breaking my heart," she told him.

"Or of breaking any other hearts?"

"You flatter me."

"I never flatter."

The next few days he was away. Verity, thinking it was business, never inquired from Priscilla, and was surprised one evening when the secretary asked her to visit Bart with her.

"Visit him?" she queried.

"He's in St. Martin's again. More tests."

"I didn't know." Verity had paused. "I hardly think he'd want to see me."

"Fresh faces," persuaded Priscilla. "Poor Bart gets terribly bored. Besides, even though he says he's not attached here, he's still very interested in how things are going. I can only tell him the clerical side. Will you come after we shut up, Verity?"

Verity, though not enthusiastically, agreed.

As the girls walked from Woman's Castle down the leafy street, Verity inquired from Priscilla as to what injury of Bart's was receiving the current attention.

"The leg. The doctors believe some of the drag can be eliminated – at least that's Matthew's report. Bart always persists that it's an examination to decide whether they'll take the leg altogether."

"Oh, no!" exclaimed Verity.

"No . . . but that's how Bart gets. If only . . ." But Priscilla left it at that.

If only he would let me share it all, Verity interpreted for herself. She asked if there was any other injury that was to be explored.

"No. Bart was in a very bad way, but everything else was patched up. Of course the scar will always be there."

"It's nothing," said Verity spontaneously. "I really mean if anything it lends something to him."

Priscilla turned quite radiantly to her. "I'm glad you said that. It's how I feel."

But not how Bart feels, thought Verity. "Can you in truth look at me and not look away?" he had said.

On an impulse, she took and pressed Priscilla's hand, and was surprised . . . yet why should she be surprised? . . . at the pressure the girl returned.

"I couldn't tell you what Bart means to me, has always meant," Priscilla proffered. "Without Bart . . ."

"Then why don't you –" But Verity stopped herself at that.

They turned into the hospital, and Priscilla led the way unerringly down a maze of corridors . . . "Yes, I come every day," she smiled, "so I should know" . . . to a verandah room.

Because it was the leg that was receiving attention, Bart was propped up in bed. He looked very fit, though, and Verity recalled that his whipcord virility had been her first sharp impression of him, an impact of determined vigour in spite of what fate had dealt him.

Priscilla went at once to him and kissed his forehead lightly. He took her fingers in his. When he turned his glance to Verity, raising his brows as he did, he said, "The other member of the staff! But not affording the same warm greeting."

"How do you do, Mr. Prince." Verity extended a cool hand.

"How do I do?" It seemed to amuse him. "I do well. The limb will remain with me a further week or so."

"Bart dear!" Priscilla's gentle voice reproached him, and he grinned and said, "Sorry, Cilla," and touched her fingers again.

"Sit down," he invited, his eyes now on Verity again, "and distribute the grapes."

"I'm afraid I didn't bring any," she said.

"No grapes?"

"I – well, as a matter of fact I didn't know you were in hospital until Priscilla told me. I mean" . . . for some reason becoming confused, and that fact annoying her . . . "you'd only just come out, and –" She knew that was the wrong thing to say, and he did not scruple to tell her.

"Didn't you know," he said harshly, "I have a permanent booking."

"Bart!" Again it was Priscilla.

"Sorry," he repeated. "I should remember, especially when I've been told how Miss Tyler doesn't like such conversation. What shall we talk about? Sealing wax?"

"There was a traveller called with a new furniture wax," related Priscilla equably. "Much less abrasive, I'd say. I thought on that last mahogany you bought –"

The talk veered to shop. When the hour was up, Priscilla again kissed Bart's brow . . . and Verity again extended her hand.

"I'll be back on deck again next week," he warned her, "so get your slacking over while you can."

"Bart, she never slacks," Priscilla objected.

"Only the boss."

"You most of all never do that."

"What's this now, then?" He looked down at the sheets. Then he glanced obliquely and ironically at Verity.

As they emerged from the hospital, Verity said, "Must he be so bitter?"

"It was very bitter for him."

"But lots of people are involved in bitter things."

Priscilla looked as though she was about to explain, then must have changed her mind. "It's Bart's story," she sighed, "not mine."

Yet your consequence, thought Verity, because of Bart's bitterness at what has happened to him, even though he loves you, the position is to remain at that. For now, anyway.

"Goodnight, Verity," Priscilla said, "thank you for coming, and that thanks is for Bart, too, for I don't believe he thanked you himself."

As she left the secretary, Verity thought that probably Priscilla had to perform a lot of social niceties for Bart Prince, but then Priscilla would not mind. What had she said? "I couldn't tell you what Bart means to me, has always meant." And then she had said: "Without Bart..."

A little bleakly, Verity boarded the ferry to Balmain.

She was pleased to see Robin's car drawn up at the terrace, but not so pleased, though she reproached herself over that, when, after opening up, it was Adele who greeted her.

"Hope you don't mind," smiled the girl ... a smile for a change? ... "but Robbie gave me the key. I suppose I could have sat in the car –" She shrugged.

"Of course you had to come in." Verity wondered unhappily if her voice sounded as false as she felt. No matter how hard she tried she could not warm to Adele ... Dellie, as Bart had called her.

As she brewed coffee, she wondered why she didn't like her.

425

She was certainly a very attractive girl, but then only an attractive girl would have appealed to her half-brother. Indulged always, he had had the time and the means to look around.

But the means were almost gone now, she sighed to herself, and as for the time . . .

Almost as if she read her thoughts, Adele said: "He had another turn."

Her abrupt announcement, not even Robin's name spoken, choked at Verity, but she knew she could only harm Robin by being aggressive.

"What did the doctor say?" she asked, controlling herself with some great effort.

"The same, no doubt, as he said to you."

"Did Robbie question the attack?"

"No. He simply doesn't know because he never asks." The dark eyes, remarkably dark and large, rested on Verity. "That's what I've come about. He mustn't know."

This at least was one thing on which they could be agreed, and Verity said at once that she felt the same.

"For different reasons, though," suggested Adele thinly. "You're thinking of his peace of mind . . . well, perhaps I am, too, I'm not that hard, also I can't stand heroics — I mean, it would be awful to live with a man if he knew that."

The callousness of her shocked Verity, but in the shock she wondered how Adele would react if she told her more of the truth, told her of her husband's changed financial conditions. She could see the rising colour, the incredulous look, finally the mental checking of where she stood showing plainly in those lovely eyes, and then the girl turning and walking out. Walking out from Robin as well. No, Adele must not know. If Robbie lasted longer than the money lasted, she must still not know. Somewhere I'll get money, Verity thought. I don't know how, but Robin . . . my Robin . . .

426

"I also don't wish Robin to know because lately he has become quite concerned over you," Adele said coldly. "I have no doubt," she went on, "that faced with that he could get quite maudlin, even wish to make a future settlement on you."

"That's absurd!" Absurd in more ways than you think, Verity could have added. Aloud, she reasoned, "It was his father's money. I wasn't his father's child."

"No, and evidently it hasn't worried him until now. There is an obvious solution, you know. Why don't you go back to England?"

"We had that out before," said Verity dully. "I can't go until – until Robbie goes. I've always loved Robin."

"Yes." Adele yawned. "He's told me countless times how you practically reared him. Quite touching ... so long as there's no other motive."

"You're an unrewarding person, Adele," Verity said with considerable restraint.

"I haven't enjoyed the most rewarding of experiences." The girl lit a cigarette, and Verity saw the line to her mouth and thought yes, that would be so, and she's let it harden her.

"Anyhow, we two are agreed," she shrugged. "If not about your return to England, perhaps, then about not letting Robin know. Of course" ... another shrug ... "we wouldn't actually see you stuck, at least I won't see you stuck. But you're doing quite well, aren't you? Anyone would – with the Princes."

"I believe you know them."

"Most Sydney people would, if only by repute. They're very rich. Riches seem to broadcast themselves." Adele laughed. "Which one are you setting your cap at? Financially they would all bring the same reward."

"Do you have to talk like this?" jerked Verity.

"You don't like truths?"

"It's not the truth."

"Time will tell," smiled Adele. She glanced at her watch. "Is that the time now? I must go."

She went without any more discussion, and as soon as the car moved away from the kerb, Verity came back into the house, left the door open, pushed wide the windows, let the wind come in. She felt stifled.

She did not visit Bart any more, and one morning, asking Priscilla a little offhandedly how he was, learned from the secretary that she was not visiting him either, since he had left St. Martin's and was undergoing some remedial treatment at an out-of-town clinic.

"That's the pattern for Bart," Priscilla said regretfully. "Perhaps one day he won't need these attendances. Matthew believes so, anyway."

"How long will he be away?" Verity asked.

"As long as they can prevail upon him to stop – but he can be very stubborn."

Yes, thought Verity, you of all people would know that.

"Matthew is a clever doctor, his mother said," she said instead.

"He graduated very highly. But like all the Princes, he's extremely obstinate. He has the means to set up a successful practice – all the sons have their own means."

Yes, thought Verity, remembering Adele, financially they would all bring the same reward.

"But Matthew wouldn't be content with that," Priscilla went on. "He must earn his own way, he thinks. He has taken this practice in an outer suburb, a suburb with a distinctly industrial slant, so you can guess how busy he'll be. While he works his way up he won't avail himself of any of his inheritance. He feels the manner he's doing his thing is putting him on his mettle."

428

"And does Cassandra ... oh, yes, I know about Cassandra ... think that, too?" They were having coffee, and coffee was a time for confidences. But perhaps this one was too close for comfort, for Verity noticed that Priscilla went a dull red, that she looked uneasy.

The girl did not speak for quite a while, then she asked Verity: "And what do you know about Cassandra?"

"Only that she's beautiful."

"Yes. Beautiful." Again the strained look.

Now Verity believed she knew what was worrying the secretary. Bart had spoken enthusiastically about Cassandra's loveliness, and seeing that he had said it to her, Verity, he must have also said it at some time to Priscilla. She looked sympathetically at the girl.

"Yes," sighed Priscilla again, "beautiful. She's all that Bart described."

"Bart also said," repeated Verity, hoping to cheer Priscilla, "that Matthew was a fool not to rush in."

"It wasn't Matthew I was thinking of," Priscilla said wretchedly. She pushed her cup aside and walked the length of the room.

"Have you ever guessed," she broke in abruptly, "the misery of being a plain girl?"

"All my life," answered Verity candidly.

"You?" There was no denying the surprise in Priscilla's voice. "Don't you ever look in a mirror?" At Verity's blank face, she went on, "No, perhaps you don't know that you're attractive – some girls are like that, and it is, I think, their main attraction. But look, please, at me, plain Priscilla, without any attraction."

"The eye of the beholder," refused Verity definitely. "You have a sweet serenity that wins through, and I'm sincere about that."

"Well, little good it's done me," sighed Priscilla.

"But your position is quite different, isn't it, your — well, your man is different."

"Yes," said Priscilla quietly, "my man is very different."

"Then why are you worrying? Why is Cassandra concerning you?"

"Because she's everything you heard. I . . . I'm not a jealous person, Verity. For instance, I can't be jealous of you. But Cassandra . . . well, I just don't know," she sighed.

Verity wished she could find the right words for her, but what were the right words? She waited a while, then went back to work.

It seemed odd after their talk that the subject of the talk should make herself known that afternoon. Cassandra called in.

Though she had been told the girl was lovely, Verity still experienced that sudden sharp impact that beauty does to you. For Cassandra was *very* lovely. She stood at the door smiling at Verity, and Verity knew at once that she must be Cassandra, knew it because beauty, beauty such as Bart Prince had described, was a rare thing, and this girl had it.

Cassandra's colouring was magnificent — bright copper hair, the white skin that sometimes goes with it, a naturally scarlet mouth. Verity looked at her in admiration, thinking how mousy her own acorn top and acorn eyes must seem in comparison.

However, there was a debit side to the beauty. Cassandra had none of Priscilla's quietude and composure, that trait that Verity had told the secretary in her opinion won through. Also, there was a certain discontent in the lovely eyes, a frustration, a restlessness. She seemed vaguely unhappy, and perhaps because of that unhappiness there was a slight challenge, a touch of recklessness there.

But the smile now was genuine; there was an obvious anxiety to be friendly. This girl, for all her beauty, is lonely, Verity thought. She smiled back.

"Cassandra, I think."

"Now why would you think that?"

"I was told you were a beautiful girl."

"Oh, please!" There was no coyness in Cassandra's appeal, she meant it. Verity could see that often her beauty set her back.

"I'm the new girl," Verity introduced herself, "name of Verity Tyler."

"I'm glad to meet you, Verity. Thank you for greeting me. Priscilla" . . . a little troublously . . . "does, but doesn't, if you understand."

Verity fully understood, but she doubted if Cassandra did, Cassandra would never remotely understand how Priscilla would feel about her man, or her man she one day hoped, saying, "She's beautiful."

She cleared a chair and invited Cassandra to sit down. For a few minutes they talked shop, though not very astutely. Cassandra, Verity could see, was pleased but by no means enchanted with rare things. Why should she be? she thought wryly. She was a rare thing herself.

"All very lovely," agreed the lovely girl, "but I must admit I'm a realist. I'm like that American I read about, who remarked of the vanishing wildlife in the American Everglades that he didn't think about alligators, he thought about people." She looked moodily out of the shop door at snippets of harbour dancing between the leaves of the trees. "I like people," she said. As Verity waited, she went on, "I'm a nurse, but not a brilliant one, I'm afraid. I didn't join out of dedication but because . . . again . . . I like people."

"Surely reason enough. Are you still nursing?"

"I graduated," said Cassandra but without pride, "and I

431

take on relief jobs. You see I did hope to . . ." Her voice trailed off.

Now another one, thought Verity, another girl emotionally tied to a Prince and Prince doing nothing about it. Bart and Priscilla. Matthew and Cassandra. In Bart's case, it was his health. In Matthew's case, it was his career. How much of a fool can a man be?

"I met Matthew nursing," said Cassandra. "Have you met Matthew?"

"I've only met Bart," Verity told her.

"Bart is sweet." Cassandra took out and lit a cigarette.

"Yet as stubborn as Matthew," Verity dared.

"Bart? No, I wouldn't think so."

He must be, decided Verity for herself, otherwise he would not be holding out from Priscilla as Matthew is holding out from you.

"It's Matthew who's the stubborn one," Cassandra told Verity. "He must be established before he . . . well, before . . ." She got up restlessly to pace the room, take things up, put them down again.

"I'm going away," she said abruptly. "I have had the offer of a temporary post in Melbourne. I have accepted it. I think it might do good."

Do good for you or Matthew? wondered Verity, but aloud she murmured that a change was always advisable.

"Well, we'll see." Cassandra did not sound very hopeful. She looked at Priscilla, now standing at the door and offering coffee. She smiled at her, and Verity could see the distinct effort it cost Priscilla to smile back. Bart was a fool, she thought angrily, to worry this sweet girl like he did. Why didn't he . . . Then why didn't Matthew . . .

It seemed that only Peter Prince stood outside the tangle.

"You can tell Bart I've gone," Cassandra said in the office.

432

"You can tell – Matthew if you see him."

"How long will you be away, Cassandra?" It was Priscilla.

"I don't know." Cassandra's voice seemed tired.

She went soon after that, and the rooms filled with beauty were less beautiful without her.

"Well?" asked Priscilla.

"Yes," agreed Verity, "she's the loveliest girl I've ever seen."

She was busy for the rest of the day. No time for display altering, even for dusting. Customers came and bought. She was there long after Priscilla had gone, having assured the secretary that she should leave, that there was nothing here for her to do, that this was what an attendant expected, and, when sales were being won, really enjoyed.

Verity had wrapped up an etching, her final transaction, and accompanied the buyer to the door with the intention of closing up at last, when one more customer, or customer she thought, came in. Well, it didn't matter, there was only the empty flat to go home to. She turned to the man . . . and gave a half step forward. Bart.

Then she saw it wasn't Bart, though a strong family resemblance was still there. Yet with a difference. This man was infinitely more sophisticated, more carefully tailored; there was none of Bart's whipcord strength, that strength that always seemed so carefully, so jealously guarded, as though it was all he had left. Peter. She supposed it must be Peter, for he was obviously younger, not older, than Bart. He was also better looking. There was no slight scar. As he moved forward, she noted no hesitancy. He was what Bart might have been and wasn't. – He was the charming prince.

Peter Prince for his part saw a girl in a pastel overall, pale brown hair, pastel colouring to match. A cool pretty girl.

"Cassandra," he claimed. "They told me you were a beauty, but they didn't tell me enough."

433

"They?" she queried.

"Matthew. Old Bart."

She did not say she did not believe that of Bart, she simply corrected: "Then they told you about someone else. I'm not Cassandra."

"Then –?"

"Verity Tyler," she introduced, "I work here."

"Verity." At once he discarded the Tyler. "Meet Peter, the third Prince." He bowed.

Once upon a time there were three princes ... Verity was thinking this as she put her hand into his. He enfolded it with his other hand, kept her hand there. She did not try to withdraw it. She stood smiling back at him. The fairytale was true, she thought a little headily, trying not to be carried away, but – being carried.

He was the most charming man she had ever met.

CHAPTER IV

NEVER had Verity been so late leaving Woman's Castle. She had sat talking with Peter Prince until the lengthening shadows had told her it was time ... and more than time ... to lock the doors. When she had done so, she had come back to Peter now in Priscilla's office, and brewing coffee with the air of someone who knew his way about.

"Oh, yes," he said breezily, "I always help myself here, Verity." His bright blue eyes flicked across at hers.

She found biscuits, and they sat and talked again. Talked and talked. He was the easiest man to talk to she had ever met.

When he said in a pause of the conversation that it was after eight, she looked at him in amazement.

When he said also, "You're having dinner with me," she did not protest.

Verity went into the washroom and took off her overall, wishing she had something smarter to wear than her utilitarian navy suit. She had a scarf, though, and tucked it at her throat. She loosened her straight acorn hair, let it hang free. She put on more lipstick than she usually wore. When she came out he was waiting for her, and he looked her up and down. He said in a voice that caught sharply and deliciously at her: "You're an English rose."

She flushed at the compliment, and in Priscilla's mirror saw that she *was* looking pretty — never a Cassandra, but appealing and nice to be with. He seemed to find her nice to be with, anyhow. He extended his hand and she went to him.

"Goodnight, old Prissie," he said to the office ... and it was the first discordant note.

"Why do you say that?" Verity asked, not caring for the feeling his carefree words had given her.

"Oh, I know Pris isn't old, no older, my rose, than you, but she is a solemn stick, isn't she, and bless her for it. We must have a sobering touch. Now, where shall we go?"

He chose an Italian restaurant, a very intimate place with red-checked tablecloths on secluded tables for two. He ordered heady wine, ravioli and a delicious salad. He also ordered a string of personal songs for the wandering musician. Verity, seeing the banknote he took from his pocket, protested, but he silenced her with a finger on his lips.

"Quiet, rose."

She was quiet.

It was a delightful evening. After he had left her at the flat, not spoiling anything by hurrying the magic moment, being content merely to touch her cheek with light lips. Verity knew she had never had such a night.

She stood at the window a long while, looking out on the glittering bay, for the first time in a long time not thinking of Robin, of Adele, of Woman's Castle and those who attended it, not even remembering the impact of the beautiful Cassandra ... Bart ... just thinking of Peter, the youngest Prince, the charming prince.

Well, she smiled, not far from enchantment, if nothing more ever happens to me, that's enough for dreams.

The next day she knew she had only just begun.

Peter was at Woman's Castle before she was. The first she saw of him was his swinging leg, swinging as he perched on Priscilla's desk and no doubt teased the secretary abominably. What had he said? "She's a solemn stick, and bless her for it." Verity wondered how Priscilla felt about that.

But when she entered, and Peter jumped off the desk and came across to greet her, bowing low in exaggerated chivalry as he kissed her hand but his upturned eyes telling her unmistakably that he was kissing her mouth, there was no question how Priscilla felt: she was not happy over the little scene.

Not understanding the secretary's cool attitude, for after all Peter was a free agent, Verity said weakly, "I didn't expect you here, Peter, or at least so early. Good morning, Priscilla. No need for you to introduce the third Prince. I met him last night."

"I see," said Priscilla drily.

Oddly uncomfortable, and why should she be, Verity hung up her coat and put on her smock. She was grateful that a customer entered, and, excusing herself, she went into the shop.

But Peter followed her. He not only followed her, he helped her with the sale. Verity was sure the customer bought more than she had intended. He was indeed the charming prince, she thought.

It was a busy morning. She had no time to talk to Peter. In the end their only interchange was over the midday snack, when Peter, still around, accepted one of the sandwiches that Priscilla had made, and said to Verity: "Tonight again? We'll try an Indonesian offering."

A little embarrassed, yet telling herself once more she had no need to be, that she was speaking to Bart's girl, even though Bart, according to his mother, and according to what she had seen, was doing very little about it, Verity said, "Perhaps Priscilla would like to come."

Priscilla's "No, thank you" and Peter's laugh came at the same time.

"I have an engagement," Priscilla said.

"Old sobersides," said Peter.

All the afternoon Peter stayed with Verity. They were busy, fortunately. Otherwise, Verity knew, Peter would have been doing more than help clinch a sale. There was no doubt about it that he had a talent for clinching sales. His mother had said that. Mrs. Prince had said that Peter, whatever he chose, would skate through.

Now he was skating through the afternoon hours, selling more with his easy charm than Verity knew she would with her knowledge and training. At half past five he called, "Down tools, Verity Tyler!"

"I never go till after six," she told him.

"Tonight you go now. I hope you're not tired, for we're dancing as well as dining, my girl."

"At an Indonesian restaurant?"

"Ever heard of the Tanka Bushi?" he laughed.

There was no one at the door. Verity peeped out and saw that there was no one in the street. A little self-conscious ... though heavens, why should she be? ... she went into the office and told Priscilla, who had evidently decided to work late, that she was leaving.

"Yes," was all Priscilla said.

Just as last night, the night was pure enchantment. In Peter's arms, as they tried the national dance, Verity felt a throb she had never felt before. But then she had never met a man like this man before.

"And I thought you were Cassandra," he said once.

"Cassandra is beautiful."

"You're a rose. You know" ... a confiding smile ... "I was always one for the glamour blooms – orchids, liliums, the rest. I never thought I'd lose my heart to a hedgerose."

"Oh, Peter!" she protested.

"It's true, darling." – Darling?

438

"You hardly know me."

"It's long enough," he assured her.

"Things don't happen so quickly ... I mean not lasting things."

"This will."

Yes, she thought in her heart, *this* will. It must be going to last, her heart ran on, because everything else is pushed out of my mind. I think of no one but Peter. Even Robbie has receded. Adele. Priscilla – Bart. Bart, the prince who was in-between.

"Darling, what are you thinking?" Peter asked.

"Actually of your brother."

"Matthew or Bart?"

"I haven't met Matthew."

"Then you were thinking of Bart." Peter made an absurd gesture of nervousness.

"Why do you do that?"

"Can't say really. All I know is he's the only one who ever scared daylights out of me. Did as a kid. I was a forthright youngster. I stood my ground – stood it with my mother, Matthew, all my teachers. But never with Bart. Even after the accident and Bart less ... well, less than what he had been ... that boyo still had the upper hand. I admire him to the ends of the earth, but let's not talk about him. He's safely out at the clinic, isn't he?"

"Yes, Peter," said Verity, a little puzzled.

The next night they tried a new restaurant. The music was soft, intimate. And soft and intimate was Peter's hand on Verity's hair.

"It's thistle silk," he said.

She did not pull away, she wanted his hand to stop there for ever. She wanted Peter to stop beside her for ever. She wanted to trap this moment and keep it for ever. She felt as frail as gossamer, as insubstantial as the thistle silk he had called her hair. Time counted for nothing. The world around her didn't matter, nor Robin, nor Adele, no one in the world, save Peter.

She was aware of an elation she had never known before. It was enchantment, it was magic, it was unreality . . . but after it she wanted no reality.

Across the table her acorn eyes met Peter's blue ones. For all the strong family resemblance Bart had brown eyes, not blue . . . but why had Bart occurred?

"It is true, isn't it?" Peter was smiling.

"What is?"

"That you feel like I do."

Verity tried to say, "And what is that?" but found she couldn't.

Instead she listened to Peter, Peter the charming prince, Peter saying: "So short a time . . . almost only hours . . . but darling, Verity my darling, already I believe we care."

I know *I* care, Verity said that night to the glittering bay, for she knew she had never felt like this before in her life. There had been men friends between her gentle guarding of Robin, and for some she had felt more than companionship, but never had she felt the excitement, the sweet madness that she did with Peter. If a feeling of gay rapture meant caring, then she knew she cared very much.

She gazed long out on Johnston's Bay, and the silky stillness was almost tender.

Then a little tug busies itself across the water, only visible by its winking light. It was quite an unimportant tug, but it left behind it a widening circle of shining ripples. And into Verity's new uncaring happiness, like a pebble flung into a pond, came the widening circles of an odd disquiet, a *Bart*

440

disquiet: unmistakably she knew it, for how could Bartley Prince keep out of this? How, she thought uneasily, would he react?

She stood on, telling herself it had nothing to do with Bart Prince, that love had nothing to do with anybody save the ones it concerned, but it was no use. There was something about Bart Prince . . .

She forgot all about it the next day, though, with Peter in attendance once more and Priscilla becoming more and more withdrawn.

They had dinner at an Indian restaurant this time, laughingly competing as to who could eat the hottest spices, then sobering suddenly and sweetly as their eyes met and held . . .

It continued, Priscilla still standing remote, all the week.

Then –

Unannounced, unadvised, just as he had before, Bart came back. Verity was hand-rubbing a piece of rosewood and she knew who owned that slightly, very slightly shuffling step without looking up. But she did look up. It was Bart.

Guiltily, and hating herself for it, for what had she to be guilty about, she said, "How are you, Mr. Prince?"

"That can wait," he said abruptly. "Where's my brother?"

"Peter?"

"You know it isn't Matthew."

"He – he's not here."

"When do you expect him?"

"I expect him?" she echoed.

"You heard aright. When?"

". . . Well, he's been coming in around eleven."

"Why didn't you say so at once?" Before she could answer, he went off.

Almost immediately Peter arrived, and with a wave, since a browser had entered with him, he crossed to the office before

441

Verity could warn him. At once voices were raised inside the office, and Verity discreetly closed the intervening door – but not before she heard the first fragments of a heated discussion. Mainly Bart's fragments, for Peter evidently found it hard to state his case.

... "Since when have you become so interested in Woman's Castle, Peter?"

... "If you really mean you want to try out this business you'll have to serve your cadetship like anyone else."

... "You'll go interstate, as I did, like it or not – good lord, man, who do you think you are?"

... "There's no short cut, no easy way, and if I accept you, *if*, you'll do what I tell you, work where I say."

"No, Peter, there's no alternative."

Yes, mainly Bart.

Then, breaking in at last, Peter's answers, undoubtedly protesting that he did not want to leave Sydney, that he wanted to work right here.

Bart still saying he must go.

And suddenly, surely, the fact coming to Verity that Peter *would* go, because Bart, for all his weakness, was strong. Stronger than Peter ever would be.

Later she heard Peter leave, no goodbye, just a quick appearance at her door ... she was serving the browser now ... and his finger on his lips to her in farewell.

"Did Peter ... did Mr. Prince .." she started to ask Priscilla later.

"Yes, Bart sent Peter interstate," finished Priscilla for her. "That is, if Peter is serious, and if he wants a future like this." Priscilla glanced indicatively around. "If he doesn't, then he can please himself, but otherwise he'll do what Bart says. Bart always wins, you know."

"I didn't know. I know now."

"Yes, you know now." It was Bart Prince at the door. "That last sale, Miss Tyler," he told her formally, "you very nearly lost. You can stay back after we close tonight and I'll suggest to you what you lack."

It sounded a suggestion, but Verity knew it was an order, an order she dared not disobey.

Priscilla had made no other comment. She had lost her withdrawn air and now she looked almost sorry for Verity. Well, Verity thought, not very happy for herself, even someone who loved Bart as Priscilla did would never take him lightly.

She spent more time over her last customer than the customer's two Japanese candles deserved. But at last she could eke out the moment no longer, and she was listening to Bart follow the customer to the doors to drive home the bolts.

He did the closing up slowly, deliberately, double checking. No thief, Verity thought abstractedly, would find it easy to break in here tonight.

Then he turned, slowly, deliberately again, to look at Verity.

"Well, Miss Tyler?" he said.

She pretended puzzlement, though she knew it would be no use, there would be no subterfuge with this man.

"I want an explanation," he said barely.

"I made the sale," she defended. "Sometimes it's like that, some customers aren't so easy as others, some – Mr. Prince!" For Bart had come across and taken her hand, and his grip was punitive.

He still did not release her, even though he must have seen her wince. "Stop misunderstanding me," he said. "You know what this is about."

She wanted still to pretend confusion. What right had this man to intrude like this? She wasn't hurting anyone, but one look at his angry face changed her mind.

443

"Yes, I know," she admitted instead.

"Then get any fancy ideas you may have right out of your head. You're not for my brother Peter."

"You could have put it that your brother Peter was not for me." She had gone a dull red.

"Put it whatever way you like, so long as you get the idea."

"I don't get the idea, as you put it, and I resent you speaking like this!" she snapped.

"You'll resent it a great deal more if you go any further."

This was too much! What did he think he was, his brother's keeper? Who was he to forbid love? She was not aware that she had said it aloud until he answered roughly, "Love! Don't give me that. You don't love Peter, and Peter —"

"Yes? Peter?"

"Peter is already accounted for," he said bluntly.

"Then that's something he doesn't know." But she was aware of a tension in her, a tension and *not* a confidence. It should be a confidence, she knew that, a confidence in what Peter had whispered to her. But now, when she wanted it, she could not gather any confidence to her. It simply wasn't there.

He was looking at her shrewdly, summing up her doubt. She wished she could wipe that small smile off his face, tell him he was wrong. — Yet was he wrong? Was Bart? And what about herself? How much had Peter meant ... that is, apart from that new enchantment, that new sweet madness? How much had he meant?

Peter is already accounted for.

For the first time she seemed *really* to hear Bart's words. Before, Bart had said that there was only one available Prince, and she had taken it to be Peter. If what Bart said now was true, then the only one must be — Bart. Matthew had already been discussed and dismissed. But Bart — why, Bart belonged ... His mother had said so ... Priscilla's soft eyes had ac-

444

claimed it ... Yet Bart, in Bart's own words, was the only Prince to remain.

"So the episode is now finished," Bart Prince was saying authoritatively. "It would have been, anyway, because I've sent Peter off."

"Yes, I heard you."

"And with my brother Peter it's out of sight out of mind. I'm really doing you a service, preparing you for a letdown in this way."

"Then thank you, Mr. Prince, for the service." She was looking round for her coat. She hoped he did not see that she was trembling.

But the keen eyes missed nothing. Abruptly, quite unexpectedly, he said: "Will you have dinner with me?"

"No."

"Yet you went ... frequently ... with my brother."

"That was different. You're my employer."

"Possibly Peter could be in the future. We'll discuss it over the meal."

"I still don't wish to come."

"If I make it an order?"

"When you make an order you don't make a question of it."

"Put on your coat," he said, and he went across, got the coat and handed it to her. For a moment she hesitated, saw there was no question in him now, and slowly, unwillingly complied. He barely touched her elbow and together they emerged into the street.

Peter's restaurants had been carefully chosen, Peter had studied the menu, conferred with the chef. But Bart simply led Verity to the end of the street to a small simple room with a red door beneath a red awning. At a window table he shrugged carelessly over the offerings, leaving it eventually to the waiter. When the waiter had gone, he pushed aside the

445

plate in front of him and put his elbows there instead.

"You've been a fool," he began.

"So it's to be that sort of dinner!"

"You didn't think I brought you here to feed you, did you?"

"You could have done your talking back at the Castle."

"Propriety," he reminded her coolly. "Behind closed doors. Though that hasn't worried you, has it?"

The first dish arrived, and in spite of everything it was delicious. It was a good restaurant. She said so, surprised, and he said, equally surprised, "Where else did you think I would have taken you?" After what he had just said about the type of dinner she was to receive, all Verity could think was: What a man!

They did not speak much until the waiter had removed the final plates, then Bart Prince said: "I want your promise."

"Yes?"

"To drop this fool affair now."

"You mean Peter?"

"I don't mean Woman's Castle."

"What business is it of yours?" she demanded.

"All my business."

"Your mother –" she began.

"My mother has three sons she loves but doesn't understand."

"She told me that she –"

"That she wanted you to nab one of the Princes, or something to that effect – oh, yes, that would be my mother. But the thing she did *not* say was to rule out the first and last."

"That leaves the in-between." Now Verity spoke out what she had thought . . . and incredulously . . . before.

"Precisely. Any objection?" His eyes were narrowed on her.

When she replied, it was not an answer for herself, but for Priscilla.

"There could well be, Mr. Prince."

"Namely?"

She stared at him in dislike. How could he use Priscilla as he did?

When she did not answer, for indeed she was so disgusted she was incapable of answering, he said sneeringly, "Why these evasions and innuendoes? Why that 'There could well be, Mr. Prince'? Why not come straight out and say, 'Yes, I would object.' Why, Miss Tyler?"

"Can we drop the subject?" she asked distastefully.

"And take up the subject of Peter?"

"Why not? Peter and I –"

"Have nothing," he said baldly.

"You could be wrong."

"Only I'm not."

"How could you know – I mean –"

Bart did not lean across the table, but all the same his eyes seemed to move forward to meet hers. "I know," he said quietly, and while hating him for that, she knew suddenly and with bitter chagrin that he did know. Why . . . oh, why had she had this change of heart? Or had it been only change of mind?

Angrily she cried, but secretly in challenge not conviction: "I care about Peter."

Bart smiled thinly and said nothing.

Needled now, she flung: "He cares about me."

This time he laughed scornfully. "*That* I do know about."

"And what is it you know?"

"That Peter has already near-forgotten you. I'm sorry, I mean I'm sorry if you're hurt, but that's our Peter."

"You're not a loyal brother," she said sarcastically.

"I am an aware brother, aware of Peter's –"

"Failings? And they would include me?"

"Your words, Miss Tyler, but since you put it that way,

447

yes. Peter is – what shall we say? – vulnerable. These things happen with monotonous frequency."

"What things?" Verity broke in, incensed.

"Boy meets girl," he said cruelly.

"You're impossible!"

"Yet knowledgeable. Peter meant every word he said ... but only for the length of time he said it. Already, and I have no doubt about this, he has forgotten."

"You don't understand –" she endeavoured.

"No," he came in quietly, "*you* don't. You don't understand that Peter must be understood – and that only one woman ever has understood him yet, and it's not our mother, nor" . . . gently, that is if this man could be gentle . . . "you."

One woman. Dully Verity remembered what Bart had said previously. He had said: "Peter is already accounted for."

But – but by whom?

He broke in on her thoughts, gentle no longer. "Look, Miss Tyler, you're not hurt, you're not even remotely affected. Drop that injured guise."

"I wasn't aware I looked injured," she muttered.

"You didn't look the way you looked when you first came to the Castle."

"And how was that?"

There was a pause. It went on so long she began to wonder if he had heard her. Then he said: "Beautiful."

But he did not add to it, he did not explain it, so perhaps she only imagined it.

Presently he said, "I'll take you home."

"Thank you, no."

"Is that what you said to Peter?"

"I don't need to be taken home."

For answer he rose, crossed and paid the bill, led the way out of the restaurant. Without asking her, he opened the

448

door of the car, and, not questioning his authority, she got in.

They drove in entire silence. Even when the bridge was open and they had to wait, they still did not speak. Verity looked down at the ship passing through the opened span up to Blackwattle Bay. She was thinking nothing at all; she seemed beyond thinking. She wondered what Bart Prince was thinking about, or whether he, too, was beyond thought.

As soon as the car stopped at her terrace, her hand went to the door. She must get out and inside the flat before he –

A hand covered hers, stopping any pressure on the catch.

"Why are you in such a hurry?"

"Please, Mr. Prince –"

"Please, Mr. Prince . . . is that what you gave Peter?"

"This is going too far," she said.

"On the contrary, it hasn't gone at all. Was it like that? Was it 'Please, Mr. Prince'?"

"No!" She fairly flung it at him.

"But it is to me?"

"You," she reminded him cruelly, not understanding her cruelty, not really believing she said it even after she had spoken it, "are not your brother."

It had immediate effect. She could see the old bitterness returning to him. His hand dropped away. He got out of his side of the car and came round and opened her door.

He said nothing but "Goodnight, Miss Tyler," then came back to his seat at the wheel. Before she reached her front door she heard the car draw away.

CHAPTER V

THE following day it seemed that Bart had spoken too quickly In the afternoon's mail there was a letter from Melbourne fo Verity.

Priscilla handed it to her without comment . . . Bart was ou . . . and Verity took it also without speaking.

She held it for quite a while before she opened it. Sh waited for the quickening of the pulses that such a letter Peter's letter, should bring. She wished desperately that sh could summon up something – what sort of woman was she t change her heart so quickly as this? Yet had her heart eve been involved? Even without Bart's raw words to start al this, wouldn't she still have been asking herself this?

Clutching the letter, she crossed to the antique room, try ing to stifle her feeling of guilt over Peter by anticipating wha he wrote before she read it. It would be as his brother hac said: Out of sight, out of mind. He might even have written ar apology over the pleasant but unimportant dalliance, for tha was all it had been, she knew it now, and she half-smiled. Though possibly if it was not an apology, it was an extrica- tion. She smiled all the way now, thinking that yes, an extri- cation would be Peter Prince.

She took out the letter.

"My darling."

My darling. Verity tested Peter's opening uneasily. It didn' sound an apology, or even a bowing out. She realized with shame, shamed at her shallowness, that she had hoped it would be.

"My darling, Were you let down when I allowed my big brother Bart to browbeat me so mercilessly, banish me to Melbourne? Then if so, my sweet, I did it for you. (For myself, too. After years of indecision I have decided after all that trade is for me, especially since it involves you. That it has to be in another state is saddening, but I don't think it will be for long. Anyway, let's hope.)

"Verity, the magic is still working, so it must be the real thing. I've thought of no one else since I left you. Everywhere I look I see only your little face. That might not surprise you, not after what we came to realize about each other, but I must admit it rather has surprised me. I've never been the stable Prince. I'm sorry, dearest, but that is a fact, that is Peter. But now it is another tale. Write and tell me the same story from you, and until then I'll still look round and see only one face. (That's quite good, isn't it?) P."

She realized she held the letter so tightly that she was crumpling it. It would not matter, she would remember the words, if not with thrall, then certainly with triumph. Triumph against Bart Prince. Bart had been so confident, so sure, and he had been wrong. She put the letter in her pocket.

She took out her writing things that night to answer Peter. Yet what to say? The same story, as he had asked her, as his to her? She looked at the paper a long time, finding no words, then put the pen down again. Although it was rather late she decided she would visit Robin.

As she caught the bus she felt remiss about the last week, Peter's week, that had passed without her seeing her half-brother. She had disciplined herself after meeting Adele not to go to see Robin as often as she wanted, but these last days she had not wanted, because she had not even thought of Robin.

One thing, her brother had always been a night subject; he

451

would see nothing amiss in her turning up now at this hour.

As it happened it was Adele who opened the door, and for the first time the girl greeted her with less than her usually thinly-veiled animosity.

"I was wondering when you would come."

About to remind Adele that she could have contacted her herself, Verity said anxiously, "How's Robin?"

"Oh, he's all right. Not picking up, of course, that's right out, but it wasn't Rob I was worrying about. We had no remittance this month."

Verity turned her head away so that Adele would not see the dismay in her face. Before she had left London she had had a long talk with Mr. Carstairs, Robin's solicitor, and he had warned her that the money from the Ramsay estate that was being allotted to Robin could not last indefinitely. But he had not said it would be depleted this soon. Verity remembered sitting down in the Balmain flat after Robin's attack and going through figures, trying to approach the subject keenly and practically, not with a numbness in her heart. She had estimated that the money should see her brother out.

She glanced around at the lavish apartment. Obviously the way it was being spent it was not going to last, but even then it should still be forthcoming for a period at least.

"I'll see to it," she promised. "I'll write at once."

"That will take time, and right now we're down to our last cent. Really, I've never seen such mismanagement! That solicitor must be a fool. Why, without you we'd be stuck." Adele looked irritated.

Without you ... The meaning of the words came abruptly to Verity. Adele was obviously expecting her to ... she was relying on her for ...

She thought dully that ordinarily she would have rushed the chance to help Robbie, she would have made a jealous privilege of it, but at this present moment all she possessed was in the handbag under her arm, and though quite sufficient for herself, in fact generous, by Robin's and Adele's standards it would not be worth the taking. But she was wrong, for Adele said, "Anything will do until the cheque comes through. And see you don't forget to jerk that lawyer." She waited as Verity opened up the purse, then coolly accepted the entire contents.

Hiding her dismay, for she had only been paid that day, Verity allowed Adele gather up the notes. She did a quick mental arithmetic as Robin's wife pocketed the money briskly, saying, "Rob's asleep . . . he has these sedation things . . . you can look in on him, though, if you like." Her arithmetic told her that it was fortunate that she had paid the rent ahead, also bought her ferry tokens, but as for food . . .

Yet when she looked down on Robin, she forgot her own living in Robbie's now apparent less-than-living. Couldn't Adele see that this was no sedation but progressive slackening on her husband's frail grip of life?

Kissing him gently, she went out again.

In the flat she analysed her position. She had not accrued even one cent yet in her job, she had not been able to build up any supplies. Well, not to worry. Priscilla, she knew, would forward her some of her wages in advance. She sat down at once and wrote to Mr. Carstairs. She knew he would tell her the position honestly, how far the money had gone down, how long it could hold out. Then ruefully telling herself she would not have minded some of that meal that Bart had pushed away so uncaringly last night, she went to bed.

The next morning she arrived before Priscilla. At ten o'clock the secretary was still not there.

At noon Bart came in, asking Verity if she was inconvenienced without Cilla – had the phone been worrying her when she had a customer?

"Fortunately business has been rather quiet, so I was able to cope. Where is Priscilla?"

"Laid low," he told her.

"She's sick?"

"Quite, according to report."

"Oh." It was a blow. Verity had intended to ask Priscilla today. Well, there was always the Castle's tea or coffee and biscuits to eke her out until tomorrow, and at least her rent and fares were prepaid.

"Looks like you'll be coping for a while," Bart said a little anxiously. "The doc has forbidden her work for ten days."

"Ten days!" exclaimed Verity.

"Look, I'll be around." He took her dismay as concern for her ability to manage the business.

"Yes, I know." She tried to hide a note in her voice she felt sure must be as obvious as a shout, the note of panic at living on a handful of coins and raidings from a tin of biscuits for ten days.

For she would never ask from Bart.

She had no groceries in the flat – very unhousewife-like, but she had not been employed long enough yet to collect a supply. She was thinking this as she went home that night. In her bag were some of Priscilla's office biscuits. They had to eke her out for tea and breakfast. She wondered if Bart Prince kept as seeing an eye on the domestic side of the Castle as he did on the business side ... and the emotional. If he did, she was going to have some awkward explaining to do, for it was a funny thing, she half smiled whimsically, how, like A. A. Milne's bear who had helped himself to ham, jam, plum and pear, that the more you ate the less was there. In this instance, biscuits. She knew she could tell Priscilla later, receive a smile in response, but if Bart Prince kept a petty cash record it was going to be hard.

The first few days the biscuits kept her going, not very satisfactorily, but she felt little the worse. Then, while she was busy on a rather demanding customer one afternoon, Bart made the coffee instead.

"The bix are going down," he remarked casually. It was an innocent statement, probably meaning nothing at all, but Verity shrivelled sensitively, finding something implied in it. She was being foolish, her common sense told her that, but that night she took home no biscuits. She went to bed without any sustenance, went to work again the next morning still fasting. She was so hungry at morning tea-time she knew that if she started she probably would finish up the tin's entire contents. So she did not eat at all.

It wasn't until late afternoon that she found herself feeling weak and giddy. Whenever Bart was not around, she sat down and closed her eyes.

She had not long to go now. Bart had said casually earlier that Priscilla had phoned to say that she had made a quicker recovery than her doctor had anticipated, and would be back tomorrow. Verity felt she could last till tomorrow. She *must*.

Like all fainting attacks, later she could not have said at what precise moment this one occurred. At one moment she was sitting conserving herself, relaxing to try to help herself, to dispel her giddiness, the next moment she was prone and unaware on the floor. She had no memory of anything occurring, no feeling of consciousness returning. All she knew when she fluttered her eyes open again was Bart Prince wavering before her, his face gradually becoming steadier, then at last keeping still.

"Do you feel better now?" he asked.

"Yes, thank you."

"Are you prone to spells like this?"

"No."

"Then what brought this one about?" he asked forcefully, probingly, and she remembered his mother saying that he had begun a medical career.

"I don't know."

"Oh, come, you can do better than that."

"A virus of some sort, I expect. I – probably caught it from Priscilla."

"*Her* complaint is an old ankle injury," he said drily. He waited. "Have you any other symptoms? A chill? A headache?"

"No."

"Then have you eaten?" He asked it so sharply, so pertinently, so unexpectedly that she knew for all her pallor that her cheeks were reddening.

"Ah," he said.

He lifted more than helped her up, then he went and closed the doors of the Castle.

"Mr. Prince –" she objected, for it was not yet closing time, but he made a dismissive gesture with his hands and left her.

He came back almost at once, at least in her depletion it seemed at once, but in that brief time he had made strong sweetened coffee. He also had put biscuits at the side of it, the biscuits that today she had not touched.

Verity tried not to eat eagerly. He must never know the position she had got herself into. But there was no deceiving this man, she thought ruefully. Watching her keenly, he said: "So that's why the biscuit supply has been going down."

"No . . . I mean . . . that is –"

"What is it? A slimming project?"

"No."

"Some health project, then?"

"You really are mistaken, Mr. Prince, there's nothing at all."

456

"Look, I may not be the doctor of the family, but I still got myself up to the stage of knowing when someone is suffering from depletion. In other words, when they're hungry," he said sharply.

There was no arguing with him – anyway, she did not have the strength. She did not have the strength either to sit and hear his tirade, but that, she heard thankfully, was not to be. He had got up and left her. She heard his steps in the next room, that slightly dragging gait that marked Bart.

After that there was silence for a while.

Then he returned, and there was a noise she could not recognize and was too listless to try to recognize. It came from the office. Then he came back to where she still sat, and, without any preliminary words picked her up bodily and carried her to the office, to a seat at a cleared desk. There he had set a table. When he had gone away it must have been to buy food. With it he had hired the necessary plates and cutlery. He had even brought two napkins.

"We cut short our meal the other night," he said. "Now let's make amends."

For a few moments she felt stiff and awkward, and then hunger took over. With cheeks red with embarrassment, Verity ate ravenously.

To spare her, she suspected, he ate, too. The main course over, he poured a hearty red wine and produced a cheese. Later he brewed more coffee.

Only then did he lean across to her, and she wondered what it was he would say.

He said: "Before you explain, which I fully intend you to, let me tell you that if you ever do this again, young woman, you'll answer to me. Is that understood?"

"Yes," accepted Verity.

He had lit himself a cigarette.

"All right," he said, "why?" When she did not answer, he prompted, "You're sitting there until you tell me, Miss Tyler."

"I overspent myself," she said with a rush.

His brows raised. "But weren't you paid recently?"

"It happened that day," she confessed with pretended shame.

"So you're a spendthrift," he nodded. It seemed to amuse him, and she was willing for him to be amused with her, until his smile suddenly stopped and he said, "Now start again, and don't lie."

"It's not a lie. I didn't have any money. I'd paid my rent and I'd pre-purchased my ferry tokens, but I had no money. I didn't worry, because I knew Priscilla would advance me some, but Priscilla wasn't here and – and –"

"And you wouldn't ask me?"

"No."

"How long did all this last?"

"Not long."

"Priscilla went off last Tuesday. Was it that long?"

"Well – yes."

"You damn little fool," he said.

There was silence. She could see from the whitened knuckle bones of his long thin hands that he was angry, that he was trying to keep the anger in check.

"What did you find that was so important that you had to buy it at once?" he demanded at last.

"I . . . well . . ." she stammered.

"Yes?"

"It wasn't like that."

"I'll believe that. Because you didn't buy anything, did you, you gave something away."

"No. No – I didn't. I –"

"Don't lie. You gave it to your brother."

"No."

"Then to Dellie."

She tried to fabricate, she didn't want this man in this, but she could not find the words.

"I know," he continued, "because Adele also spoke to me."

"Spoke to you?" she gasped.

"Why not? I told you we were old acquaintances."

"She spoke to you – regarding money?"

"Regarding it only. She didn't ask for it. She was very concerned, because nothing had come through. It's a pity" ... he said coldly ... "that that pair were not left to manage their own affairs without having to ask you to act for them."

"If you mean I'm doling out their money, you're very, very wrong. I wasn't aware that they were in the position they are until Adele told me. I – I wrote to the solicitor at once."

He shrugged meanly at that. "As I said, managing their affairs."

She decided to pass that. She said stiffly, "I'm sorry Adele bothered you. She should have come to me."

"She did." A thin reminding smile.

"But to you, too."

"I'm not blaming her, when a certain standard of living has been enjoyed it's hard to accept anything less. Besides" ... deliberately ... "you hadn't been to see them for some time to *know* their position." He left it at that, but Verity knew he was telling her silently what that time had comprised. It had been her Peter episode.

"Well, enough of that," he said presently. "You say you've written to England?"

"Yes."

"Good. But until the matter is fixed up, we must not, of

459

course, have a repetition of this." He made a gesture to the table.

"I'll clear up," she began childishly, pretending it was the office disarray he was decrying, but she was stopped by his angry frown.

"You know what I mean, Miss Tyler, you know I refer to this stupid starvation of yours. You must give me a promise now that you'll never do this again."

"And if I don't give it?"

"Then we spend the night here. After all, we have plenty of beds." Now he gave a maddening smile.

Verity looked down. "I know you mean well," she said at last, "but – well, none of this is your affair."

"Fainting on my floor is my affair, causing me to close early is my affair!" he snapped.

"Always business."

"Why not?" A small significant pause. "What else is there? But there, I do it again, that self-pity. Please consider it unsaid. And to ease your mind until this remittance detail is adjusted, you must accept this sum to give to your brother."

"No!"

"Have no fears, it will be deducted from your salary," he answered her.

"No."

"Then I'll have to offer it to Dellie myself."

"*No.*" This time Verity spoke with distress.

"Please yourself," he shrugged.

"You're sure you'll record this loan?" she insisted.

"Just you try to get out of it."

"Then – thank you," she said.

She watched him as he rose and went to a desk, unlocked it and took out some notes. When he came back he did not hand them to her at once. He sat down and flicked them through his

460

long fingers, not counting them, just flicking them. His eyes held hers. At length he pushed them over.

"There's a separate bundle," he said drily, "for yourself. Don't give that to the Ramsays as well and so repeat this performance, or I mightn't be as tolerant as I am today."

"Tolerant?" She said faintly.

"Tolerant. Then it would really be a case of 'Please, Mr. Prince.'"

He sat back and watched her go.

CHAPTER VI

IN the week that followed Verity had the embarrassment, if not the personal pang, of seeing everything that Bart had said of Peter eventuate.

As each letter arrived there was a progressive diminishing of Peter's warm interest in her. From the second letter, which still declared that he "saw her face wherever he looked" but no longer talked of any "magic", the correspondence went on, until, with the latest letter, "seeing her" went the same lost way as the "magic."

Relieved, yet still rankling because of Bart's unerring pre-knowledge, Verity accepted the episode as just one of those things, particularly when the correspondence stopped, only to renew itself with no mention at all of her but a thinly-concealed excitement in a brand-new interest – Cassandra.

"Talk of coincidences," wrote Peter, "in this bustling city where surely the only way to meet anyone is by rendezvous, I have (at last) encountered the illustrious Cassandra. I say at last because I had heard so much of her. Remember, Verity, I believed you were her.

"It was unplanned, as I said. I caught my thumb in a car door . . . no, no damage . . . and was taken to an outpatients department. Who should deal with me there but Cassandra? Oh, what a girl!"

Then came another letter.

"You have met Cassandra, haven't you? The Prince legend

is that she's for Matthew, but, as Cassandra has pointed out, not that you would notice. My eldest brother must be a damn fool. She's glorious.

"She's as pleased as I am for us to be getting around together. I think that lovely girl is a bit confused with her world, and I intend to spare her any more confusion."

Later that week there was a further letter.

"Verity, I really have fallen for Cassandra. I've never felt like this before in all my life, and I'm certain she's feeling the same about me. It's just too bad for old Matthew, but anyone who would hold up a girl like Cass doesn't need any sympathy. As for me, I'm a free agent." – Oh, Peter!

"Anyway, old girl, I wanted you to know." – Old girl!

"Old girl." It was Priscilla, and she was standing at the door; she was watching Verity reading the letter, and she was wearing an enigmatical smile.

Caught out, Verity folded the letter and said, "You seem to know the drill."

"It's always the same with Peter," Priscilla said, and her tone conveyed nothing at all. "One attack follows the other. It chronic. I'm sorry if you're hurt, Verity, but somehow I don't think you really are."

"Not hurt," Verity confirmed, and waited.

After a few moments, Priscilla said, "One day there'll be no more of this. Peter will be different. He'll settle." There was a note in the secretary's voice that Verity could not quite place. Several times Priscilla had puzzled her with her concern for Peter. It had seemed more than the usual sisterly concern, since sister to Peter was what Priscilla would be on that day when Bart overcame whatever it was that stopped him now and instead married his Cilla, for at no time had Verity credited Bart's statement that he alone of the Princes remained not yet accounted for.

463

"Was it –" Priscilla paused. "Was it just a falling out once more that Peter wrote about?" Now there was a slightly strained note in her voice, a frown on her serene brow.

"No. A new face for Peter – Cassandra's."

"Cassandra?" Priscilla, who had turned to leave, whipped round again. Now she looked really upset. "Of course ... they're both in Melbourne," she recalled, "but how –"

"Peter had an accident. No" ... as Priscilla stepped quickly forward ... "only a minor one. It was Cassandra who attended him."

A few moments went by, then Priscilla said flatly, "Yes, that's just what would happen. Peter draws pretty girls to him like a magnet. But Cassandra isn't just pretty, she's –"

"Glorious," said Verity for her. She added: "Peter's words."

Mr. Carstairs had not replied to Verity as promptly as she had thought he would. She knew the solicitor well, and had expected he would write at once, perhaps cable. However, no news was good news, and when an answer did come, it would probably be an assurance that some minor detail had held the money up.

But when Verity saw the bulky air letter the following evening after work, she knew that the solicitor's time in replying had been because he had been taking the trouble to account in detail to her. And, as she flicked through the sheets reporting the different expenditures to see the final figure, the sum total was anything but good.

She went out that night to Robin's flat. Robin was up and at first glance seemed a little better. But Verity, experienced now, looked to the dulled eyes, the lacklustre general tone.

"What's got into Carstairs, V?" Robin complained testily. "The cheque was right down this time."

"Oh, you got one, then?"

"You didn't think," cut in Adele, "that we were still living on what you handed out?"

Robin looked upset over that, but years of only bothering about himself made his concern transitory.

"Write to him again, will you, Sis, explain to him what a foul run I've had, how I can't be put around like this. I'd do it myself, only I just can't seem to concentrate lately. Another aftermath, I suppose."

"And until we get satisfaction," said Adele, "can you –"

"Yes," said Verity, and handed across the notes that Bart had given her.

She left soon after that. She felt very disturbed.

She was glad that the work at the Castle completely absorbed her. Without it, she would have had time to brood, to worry herself more than she had time to worry now. She was glad, too, when Bart announced the winning of a contract to decorate the whole of a new multi-storey government building, adding that not only would he be away for a week to assess the situation but that he would require Priscilla for note-taking.

"Can you cope?" he asked Verity.

"I did before."

"With rather dire results," he reminded her thinly.

"This time," she said boldly, "I'll see that the biscuit tin is full to the brim."

"This time," he amended, "if I return to find a situation like before I'll –"

"Yes?"

"Just practise your plea for mercy," he advised shortly "your 'Please, Mr. Prince.' "

"You never forget anything, do you, Mr. Prince?"

There was a silence. It grew to such a long silence that Verity looked at him uneasily. With an effort he seemed to bring

465

himself back from something that tortured him.

"I wish to heaven I could!" It was more a cry, Verity thought.

He had tight control of himself, though. At once he went briefly through some of the stock with her, telling her what he wanted pushing. "I need space," he explained, "I'm expecting a new consignment. We don't exactly run sales, but I leave it to you to find a price suitable to all to get rid of an article. You'll be pushed, what with the urgent correspondence, but anything else can wait for Cilla, and the phone as well as the shop. In which case . . ." He paused a moment, looking at her. Then he said, "I want you to have this."

She looked at notes he was handing her in surprise, then she shook her head. "You already pay me generously."

"For one job. I don't ask anyone to do two jobs for the price of one."

"Mr. Prince" . . . they never called each other by their names now . . . "there is also the money you've already advanced me."

"Loans, and don't fret, as such they're safely down in my little black book. This is entirely different. This is business. I'm paying you for a job I expect to be well done."

"It will be," she gratefully assured him.

She got into the practice of arriving earlier in the morning and going through the mail. In that way she was free to concentrate on her own domain for the other working hours. It proved a good idea, for though there was much that only Priscilla could handle, there were also quite a number of inquiries that needed to be dealt with at once. It also, or so, taken by surprise, she thought at first, put her into the position of apprehending a thief.

Except . . . and one glance assured her of this . . . he was *not*. When Mrs. Prince had had her three sons, if they were not identical there was still an unmistakably close resemblance between them. Peter, for instance, was a more suave Bart, yet Peter, looking across at her "thief", was not so outstanding as this Prince. Noting his added maturity, Verity knew he must be Matthew Prince. The first Prince. The eldest. The gracious prince of the old fairytale. The one, Bart had said, earmarked for Cassandra . . . though by recent developments –

She went forward to where Matthew Prince was letting himself into the store with a personal key and held out her hand.

"Mr. Prince," she greeted him.

"You haven't added 'of course'," he smiled at Verity, "people usually do."

"Of course," she obliged.

"Yes, I am Matthew Prince. I'm sorry if I alarmed you, but there was something I needed from here, and I thought if I called early –"

"I've also been calling early," Verity told him. "Your brother has won a big contract for the Castle and has taken Priscilla to help him with it for the week, leaving me, the newcomer, to hold the fort."

"Which I have no doubt you do admirably," he said sincerely, his eyes estimating and approving her at the same time.

"Thank you. I try." Verity paused. "Can I help you find what you came fo?"

He frowned slightly. "I hope so." He got into step beside Verity and they went down the corridor. "I want Cassie's address. I rang her flat, but there's no reply. I think" . . . deepening of the frown . . . "she may have gone away. Have you met Cassandra?"

"Yes."

"Then –?"

"You didn't know she had left Sydney temporarily?" Verity asked tactfully.

"I know nothing, except that she doesn't answer me when I phone."

"Cassandra . . . I met her briefly before she went . . . has gone to Melbourne. She has taken a relief position in a hospital there."

"Do you know which hospital?"

"No . . . but your brother would," Verity said unthinkingly.

"My brother," said Matthew Prince quickly. "You mean —"

"I mean both, actually, for Bart would have the name, but really I was referring to Peter."

"Peter," Matthew said after her. "Peter," he said again. There was a pause. "So Peter would know, would he?" He gave a slight shrug.

She told him briefly about Peter's mishap. He nodded as she related it, then when she had finished he said, "It doesn't help much, does it?"

"No. I'm sorry."

He turned and smiled warmly at Verity. "Why should you be sorry? You told me all you know."

Something made her say impulsively, ". . . Sorry for you."

"Meaning?"

"What you meant when you shrugged like you did just now."

"You mean — our one and only Peter?"

"The charming prince," she nodded. She told him quickly about the old fairytale. She found him very easy to talk to.

"Well, I don't know," he said after she had finished. "I don't know if I was ever the gracious prince. Conscientious, perhaps, which is after all often a word for dull, or so I'm told by Cassie."

"I don't find you dull," said Verity.

Now he looked at her thoughtfully. "Do you know what," he said presently, "I don't believe you do. Look, I'm due at the

468

hospital. After that I've surgery. I have my own practice now, you know. Then there's home calls. However, *you* won't get away early, either, will you?"

"No –"

"Then – dinner?"

"I don't know. You see, I've already dined with two of the three Princes, and it could seem like I'm making a habit of it."

"But one couldn't be left out," he pleaded. As she still hesitated he said, "Please," and she found she could not resist the quiet appeal.

"I could be closed up and ready by eight," she agreed.

"That will be wonderful."

The day dragged, though of late she seemed barely to have arrived before it was time to close up and go; Verity had supposed it was because she was busy that the hours had flown. But today she was just as busy, yet the hours passed slowly. She realized with a little rueful smile that it was because she was having dinner with Matthew Prince. She had not been out for a while now, and the diversion appealed to her. – Matthew appealed.

He was at the Castle on time, a little tired-looking, and she supposed he had had a heavy day. She suggested coffee before they left, and he agreed eagerly, sitting back in Priscilla's chair as she brewed it, closing his eyes.

"We needn't go," she proffered gently.

"Of course we must go."

"There's a place not far up the avenue. I could bring something back."

He looked at her eagerly, but wiped the look off at once. "What kind of escort would you think me?"

"A nice one." He really was tired, there was a fatigue line from his eyes to his mouth. "Please, Mr. Prince –" Please, Mr. Prince, that was Bart's gibe.

469

"Matthew, Verity."

"Please, Matthew, you're obviously not up to the social graces tonight. Frankly, after a day coping by myself in this store, I don't think I am, either. Why don't we just relax and talk here? I mean, after we've had something to eat."

"It sounds attractive," he admitted wistfully, "I do feel I've met as many people as I want today, present company excluded. On the other hand it also sounds terribly mean."

"I don't know why," she laughed, "you'll be paying. Look, why not come with me and choose? It's only a few doors up."

He jumped up eagerly, enthusiasm making him seem much younger. "I haven't done anything like this for ages. Lead on, Verity."

The shop from which Bart had bought the supplies that night of Verity's hunger faint was a very attractive one. Paper carrier bags were produced by the obliging shopkeeper, and Matthew and Verity had a lot of fun choosing their take-away meal. Matthew insisted that although they were not dining out they must still go through the courses, and he not only ordered appetisers, soup, entrée and an elaborate sweet, but white wine as well.

"This is fun," he said, adding little white onions and red peppers to his purchases, "this is as much fun as I've had in a long time."

"Your fault?" Verity asked carefully.

"Why do you say that?"

"Having fun is usually your own thing," she said. "At the very least you have to make the effort."

"I've never been what you might call a funny fellow," he admitted. "I'm afraid I'm a bit of a sobersides."

"The fairytale said gracious," she smiled.

"Oh, that fairytale!"

They were walking back to the Castle now, both carrying

bags, occasionally their hands brushing. When they got to the office, Verity set the desk as Bart had set it that night – except that she had forgotten to pick up the paper plates.

"Oh, dear!" She looked rueful and nodded to her omission. "I'll go back."

"I'll go. No, neither of us will. You've brought the implements. What else do two people need when they like each other?" He smiled warmly as he said that "When they like each other."

Eating from one dish necessitated sitting close. They sat close. When they had finished, when the wine was finished, there seemed no reason to sit apart again. A comfortable silence encompassed them, for quite a while neither spoke.

When Matthew broke the silence at last it was tentatively, a little hesitantly, but only because of what he spoke about, not because he was saying it to Verity. Verity had the feeling that he was completely relaxed with her, as she was with him.

"So Cassie and Pete have met up at last?"

"Yes, according to Peter. But why did you say that?"

"At last?"

"Yes."

"Because I suppose in a way I've always tried to work it that they didn't meet."

"They had to, some time."

"I expect so, but Peter . . . well, if you know Peter . . ."

"I do know Peter." Her eyes met his a moment, then she smiled back ruefully to his own rueful smile. "The charming prince," she said. "Only" . . . a pause . . . "it doesn't last."

"But one day it could." Now it was Matthew who paused. "This time it could."

"Then why, Matthew, why? Oh, do please forgive the intrusion, but why?"

"Why haven't I done something about it?"

"Yes."

"You mean – like tie Cassandra down?"

Verity nodded.

"Because I wasn't ready, or rather my prospects weren't. I've always had this thing about a man building up something for his wife, not just – just –"

"Cassandra didn't want you a raving success, no woman would."

"I know, I know. But –" He fell silent again.

They left the subject at that point, and talked about generalities, coming to the general practice he now had, and how he hoped to extend it.

"It's a new district and I'm the first doctor. It's a challenge." Presently he said, "I can't tell you how good I feel having talked to you like this. You've unloosened me. I think I must have needed you."

"And the picnic meal?"

"That, too. It was much better than going out. But I still owe you a proper meal, Verity. When?"

"That's entirely up to a G.P. An assistant to Woman's Castle hasn't the same demands made on her. A dropside table is never a matter of life or death."

"Surgery is at the same hours throughout the week. I have no imminent cases. Of course if an emergency arose –"

"I'd understand," she assured him.

"Then when?"

"Tomorrow night?" She flushed, thinking she might be hurrying things, but for obvious reasons, Bart reasons, she wanted to meet Matthew while his brother was away from the Castle, and already the week was halfway through.

She became aware that he was laughing at her. "Do you know when tomorrow is?"

"Why – tomorrow."

"Right, but I really think you mean tonight."

"Tonight?" She looked at him in disbelief, then checked her watch. He was right. Tomorrow was now tonight, it was after midnight. She had never known time to go so quickly.

"I must go," she said hastily.

"Or the carriage will turn into a pumpkin and you'll be back sitting among the cinders?"

She laughed at him. "I'm a working woman. I can't keep these late hours and give the Castle what I want to give it."

"I must go, too. I suppose I shouldn't have stopped so long, but I just couldn't call a halt."

"Then you knew the time?"

"Yes."

"And you didn't tell me?"

"No." A pause. "Verity – I was lonely."

I was lonely. Matthew's quiet admission rang in Verity's ears long after she had gone to bed. I was lonely. Well, he hadn't been tonight. She hadn't been. She thought how the time had flown and what a pleasant evening it had been with the eldest Prince. She knew he had enjoyed it as she had. She did not try to sleep, she just lay relaxed.

When morning came she had snatched only a few naps, and as she joined the rush into town she knew she would not look her best for her formal night out.

At six the phone went and it was Matthew.

"Verity?"

"Yes."

"All beautifully dressed and desirable?"

"Most unbeautiful and undesirable."

"I know you could be neither, but you sound as drained-out as I am, as – well, an unforward-looking."

"You're quite right, Matthew," she said.

"Then I wonder could we . . . I mean it's not fair of me to

ask, but I did appreciate it. Somehow it was like being home –"

"You mean do what we did last night?"

"Yes." Diffidently.

"Matthew, I'd love that." Eagerly.

"Then you enjoyed it, too?"

"Very much."

"Then you stay on at the Castle. I'll bring the food."

"And the plates?" she laughed.

There was a short silence at the other end.

"We got along all right last night without them."

Now it was Verity's turn to hesitate. But she didn't. She said at once, and warmly: "Oh, yes."

After two nights it had become a pattern. Verity would finish the day's work, close the shop, then while the percolator bubbled she would wash, take off her smock and comb her hair. By then Matthew would have arrived, smiling like a delighted small boy over the goodies he had in the carrier bag, pleased when he could show her something they had not sampled before.

That he found pleasure in their relaxed meals was very apparent. "After our father died and my mother had to carry on the business, we three boys were put into boarding school. I liked it all right, I've always been fairly adaptable ... rather dull, as I said before ..."

"I would say adaptable."

"You're kind, Verity. Yes, I suffered no setbacks, but I do remember longing to sit at an unshared table."

"You're sitting at a shared one now."

"Not shared by thirty boys. Anyway, this is a desk, and yet –"

"And yet, Matthew?"

"It could be a family table in a home."

"It's a home," she reminded him, "and home's what a woman's castle is."

"Yes," he said quietly, and his eyes smiled into hers.

It was Verity who forced her glance away in the end. This won't do, she thought. Matthew and I are seeing far too much of each other: it means nothing, it *is* nothing, we're just two rather confused, rather lonely people who have turned to each other for company, for companionship . . . but it still won't do.

Yet when they parted that night and Matthew asked eagerly "Tomorrow?" she could not say no.

Occasionally during the day Bart called in to see how she was coping. He reported that he and Priscilla were progressing favourably with the assessment.

"It's going to be a bigger job than we thought. We may take longer. Is that all right with you?"

"Perfectly."

"You're sure?"

"Why the doubt? Isn't my work satisfactory?"

He frowned. "I didn't ask you that. Your work is quite satisfactory, so satisfactory I'm wondering if you are over-exerting yourself," he said probingly.

She *was* over-exerting herself. Though she would not have admitted it, there was always present an uneasy doubt, a reluctant knowledge that if Bart had frowned on her episode with Peter, he would more than frown on this. Though not fully aware of it, she had salved her conscience by putting more into Woman's Castle than she could have credited from herself. Bart had evidently noticed something. He was still looking at her searchingly.

"There's no prize at the end," he said briefly. "I require you only to cope, not create an all-time record."

"I'm only working normally," she assured him.

"I hope so. I also hope among other things that you are

keeping the regulation hours. Are you, Miss Tyler?"

A little nettled, she said, "What are the hours? Oh, I know Priscilla's are nine to five, but mine depend on other issues, don't they?"

There was a silence. Then Bart said, "Yes – other issues." He was still looking estimatingly at her.

Presently he said, "You look different."

"I assure you I'm the same."

"But what is the same?"

"What do you mean, Mr. Prince?"

There was another pause. He seemed about to say something, but he must have changed his mind.

"Everything seems as it should be, Miss Tyler," he said briskly. "We could wind up the assessment next week. Any queries before I go?"

"No."

"Any troubles?"

"No."

"In fact all plain sailing?"

"Yes, Mr. Prince. Thank you."

"On these records" . . . he tapped the ledger . . . "I should say gratefully to you to keep it up. – Whatever you're doing."

She waited . . . but he did not say it. He gave her another long steady look, then left the shop.

She did not see him again until the end of the week. *But she saw Matthew.*

Verity and Doctor Prince were on much closer terms now. He had listened sympathetically to her account of Robin, nodding now and then, inserting pertinent questions. When she had answered them, and when she had finished her report, he had said gently: "There's nothing I can add, Verity, you must know that."

"Yes. I know that nothing can be done, nothing except to

keep him as contented and happy as possible." She was silent a while; she was wondering how long the money that went a long way if not the entire way to Robin's contentment and happiness could last. "Matthew . . ."

"Yes, my dear?" The dear was said kindly, with understanding.

"How – how long?"

"Can a doctor ever say that? He can estimate, but finally it's another authority. Also, the man's will enters into it, his capacity to hold on."

"Then – an estimate?"

A pause. "Not long," Matthew said.

Matthew also talked about himself.

"The moment I saw Cassandra, Verity, I knew . . . at least I *think* now I knew."

She looked quickly at him at that "think."

"What are you saying, Matthew?"

"I don't know. For the life of me I don't know. Except" . . . he hesitated . . . "except why, oh, why can't she understand? Understand how important my work is to me, how I must find my roots in my work first." He looked at Verity. "*You* understand."

"Yes, but I may be differently constructed from Cassandra. I may not have another capacity that she has."

"Capacity for what?" he asked a little harshly, and in his harshness he reminded her more of Bart Prince than Peter, whom she had judged he most resembled before.

"Capacity for love?" she suggested . . . then she found herself meeting Matthew's eyes, and flushing vividly.

For a long time he said nothing, he just sat looking back at her, looking deeply. Then he rose and sighed. "Tomorrow is another day, little one." There was an infinite gentleness in that "little one."

There had been no more letters from Peter, and Verity had expected none. Unlike Priscilla, who had said of the third Prince's talent for collecting, and discarding, lovely girls a bleak "But *Cassandra* –" Verity had at no time anticipated anything else than the same as had been meted out to her.

She was wrong.

"Verity, be the first to know –" said the letter from Peter that came the following morning. Verity read it to the end, then put it down. Poor Matthew, she thought.

She would never have told the doctor had he not probed it out of her.

"Matthew, do you delve professionally as you're delving now?" she complained at length.

"Of course. I must." He paused. "You *have* had something from Peter, haven't you?"

"Yes."

"What does he say?"

"Oh, Matthew!" she sighed.

"All right then, just tell me one thing: Is it going the same way as it went with you, with the rest? Here today, gone to-morrow?"

She sat silent.

"Answer me, Verity."

"No, it's not going the same way."

"Then Peter and Cassandra –"

"Yes. I'm sorry, Matthew."

There was a dead silence. For quite a long time Verity could not bring herself to look up at Matthew. But when she did his first words to her completely surprised her. For Matthew said quite calmly, without any heroics, without any anger against anyone . . . with only emotion for her:

"Come away with me, Verity."

478

CHAPTER VII

"You're not serious, Matthew!" Verity looked back at him in disbelief. This could not be Doctor Prince, the first Prince. The "gracious prince."

"I think," Matthew said slowly, deliberately, "I've never been more serious in all my life."

"It's rebound. It has to be. You're hurt. You're lost. You're turning to someone, anyone at all, and it just happens to be me."

"Perhaps it could be rebound, Verity, but I can truthfully tell you that in this moment it doesn't seem like that at all. Instead . . . well, instead it seems the most wonderful moment in my life. It seems –" He took her hand in his strong surgeon hand. "It seems –" He paused. "Also," he went on presently, unable to finish what he had begun, "I don't feel hurt at all – indeed, I don't think I *feel* anything at all, except –"

"Except a numbness," she hazarded.

"Except a gratefulness to you," he corrected stubbornly.

"Gratefulness isn't enough."

"It's a start, everything has to have a start."

"And with anyone?"

"With you." Now he said it intentionally.

"Matthew –" she began.

"Oh, I know how this sounds to you, Verity, and I know it should sound like that, too, to me. But it still doesn't. This last week has been the happiest week of my life."

"Happiness," said Verity with a wisdom she did not know she possessed, "has to include more than we happen to have. Real happiness, the kind I believe you're talking about" ... she flushed ... "can't be built on just companionable happiness as we have known it, it has to go much deeper than that, it has to — well, it has to —" But her wisdom left her, and, as they had with him, the words ran out.

"I don't know about all that," said Matthew a little wearily. "I only know I've been able to talk with you as I've never talked to Cassie."

"Has Cassandra been able to talk to *you*?" probed Verity fairly.

"Two people should meet halfway," he said doggedly. "I talked to you, you listened to me, you talked to me, I listened to you."

"Did you ever listen to Cassandra?"

He grew silent.

"*Did* you, Matthew?" Verity persisted.

He answered, "Cassie never listened to me."

They were getting nowhere, nowhere on the subject of Cassandra, too deep on the subject of Matthew Prince and Verity Tyler.

"Matthew, go home now," Verity said. For a moment she thought he was going to refuse, then he smiled ruefully at her, kissed her cheek, then left.

Verity tidied up, then left, too. As she went down the street she wondered ... but was afraid to wonder too deeply ... what tomorrow would bring.

It brought Bart.

He was dragging his leg a little as he did when he was tired, but he wore that satisfied look of a job going well.

"Everything's falling into place," he told Verity, "a few hit-

480

ches here and there, but nothing really for an assignment of this size."

"I'm glad."

"You mightn't be," he shrugged. "Although we're progressing favourably Cilla now believes it will take even longer than the extra time I warned you. In other words, Miss Tyler, you'll be asked to cope another week."

"That's all right," she said.

He looked at her shrewdly. "Very confident, aren't you?"

"What do you want?" she came back, irritated. "A defeated attitude? A doubt if I can keep on?"

"No, I like assurance as much as the rest. Only . . ." He was looking at her curiously now.

"Yes, Mr. Prince?"

"You seem different somehow."

"You said that last time."

"I say it again. You *are* different."

"Then that should please you."

"Also," he said, ignoring her comment, "you seem *very* eager to continue here by yourself." As she did not speak, he asked sharply, "Which you are, Miss Tyler?"

He was silent for a while. Then: "Has my brother been around?"

She caught her breath, but in that breath he continued, "Because if Peter has chucked this Melbourne tour he'll have to answer for it."

"No," she came in smoothly, "he hasn't been around."

As he went through the records of her sales, the copies of any correspondence she had thought should be answered, he said casually, "If Matthew comes in, see to it that he gets Cassandra's address. I'll leave it with you. He doesn't deserve it, playing hard to get with a girl like that, but I like to be Cupid. Besides, with Peter in the same city, one never knows." – So he hadn't learned yet, Verity thought. The thought was pushed aside as Bart, glancing up at her, asked: "Has Matthew been in by any chance?"

"Yes. He's very like you. I mean you're like him, except–"

"All the Princes are alike," Bart drawled. "*Except.*" He gave that old bitter derogatory laugh, but he did not add the usual bitter comment. As Verity did not speak, he went on: "My dear mamma evidently knew only the one pattern. To give her her due, she had variations, or should it be a standard? Mediocre, better, best. You can allot the grades." As she still did not speak, he got up and moved towards the door. "Don't forget about Matthew."

"I won't."

How could she? Verity thought.

Sitting in her favourite position at the flat window last night, she had analysed, or tried to analyse, herself. It hadn't been easy. She had never been the sort of person that she was uncomfortably aware she must seem now. For instance one week Peter. Then soon after, *much too soon*: Matthew. She had wondered at the difference in herself, for she always had been a very stable girl. As a child, her mother had said that once Verity had a friend she had her for ever.

She could not understand it ... nor could she understand the undercurrents and the crosscurrents and the too swift currents that seemed to be upsetting the previously quiet flow of her life. Almost, she thought, as if a major change had taken place in her.

Matthew did not contact her for several days, and in her uncertainty she was glad of that.

Then he rang ... and she felt her concern going out to him as he said sensitively: "Verity? Verity, my dear, I'm sorry."

"That's all right, Matthew." She did not ask "Sorry for

what?" because she felt she knew already, she knew that he never really had meant that "Verity, come away with me." Never Matthew. She said so now, hoping it would help him.

"But I did mean it," he said at once, "that is I meant –"

"Matthew" . . . gently . . . "what did you mean?"

A silence at the other end, then, wretchedly: "I just don't know."

He told her he was working hard. He would not see her for several more days.

"I think that would be a good thing," she agreed. She related his brother's instruction to pass Cassandra's address on to him. When this was met with silence, and the silence grew, she called, "Did you hear me, Matthew?"

"Yes, I heard. But don't bother about the address."

"What do you mean, Matthew?"

"I'll ring on Thursday, V."

There was still no letter from Mr. Carstairs telling Verity how Robin now stood, and it was with trepidation that Verity visited Robin and Adele again; she would not know what to answer to Adele if she questioned her as to what held up the cheque.

As it happened Adele was in such a good mood that Verity knew some moments of doubt. Robin was a spender; she knew Adele would be the same; and the amount she had given Adele, though large by her own standards, would not have satisfied that pair for this long. Instantly her mind jumped to Bart, and she felt herself withdrawing in distaste at the thought of what Adele could have tried, and, from the look of her, could have succeeded in.

She could not ask, but she learned, anyway, without asking.

As she was leaving she made a complimentary remark on Adele's new dress. She had left Robin in the lounge. The two girls stood at the flat door.

"Not bad," acknowledged Adele.

"A Sydney make?"

"You could say" . . . a little laugh . . . "that it was locally inspired in every way." There was no mistaking Adele's emphasis, but in case Verity did mistake it, Adele said, "Bart is a dear."

"Bart!" It was out before Verity could stop it, dismay with it.

Adele pounced triumphantly on the dismay. "Why not? I knew Bart Prince a long time before you did. Yes" . . . another little laugh . . . "we knew each other *very well*."

Sickened, Verity turned and went down the apartment stairs.

But the next day what Adele had said was lost in a worry she had known she must face soon, but had not anticipated as soon as this. The answer came from Mr. Carstairs, and the news could not have been worse. There was nothing remaining, nothing at all, of the Ramsay estate.

"I have delayed my reply to you, Verity" . . . Mr. Carstairs was an old family friend . . . "for the reason that I have been exhausting every possible channel. I know how important it is" . . . Verity had told him of Robin's prognosis . . . "and I only wish my news could be more favourable."

There followed a detailed account, of which Verity took small notice. She had implicit trust in the solicitor . . . she even suspected that final debt written down did not include the fee that his services should entail.

She was shocked. She had not expected anything as bad as this. She did not know what she would do. It had been all right to make a vow that Robin would never be told, but when she had made it there had been something, very little admittedly, but something. Now there was only a debt. Debts had to be paid. But how? How?

She yearned to talk to someone, to confide in them, to be advised. If only Adele had been the right kind of wife, a wife she could have gone to and told the whole unfortunate story. But the right kind of wife would not have been interested in the story, only concerned with Robin, and Robin's health.

There must be someone, Verity despaired.

Almost as if in answer, the telephone pealed. As she picked it up mechanically, still wrapped in her abject thoughts, Matthew's voice came over the wire . . . and at once she felt cut loose from her forebodings. They were still there, of course, but Matthew's contact seemed to help her. She remembered reading once where a change of pain is almost as miraculous as a cessation of pain. Now Matthew with his own troubles seemed to help her with hers.

"Verity."

"Matthew."

"I said I'd ring."

"Yes."

"To say" . . . but a little smile somewhere now . . . "will you come away with me?"

"Matthew, not that again?"

"No, my dear, not that again. V, I'm sorry to the ends of the world. Of course I didn't mean it. You knew, didn't you, you sensed all the time that it was still Cassie with me, always was, always has been, is, always will be."

"Yes, Matthew, I sensed that."

"And for that reason I want you to come away with me."

"Matthew, are you mad?" she gasped.

"Hear me out, V. I'm not playing tit for tat, anything like that. I'm just flying down to Melbourne to put my cards on the table, to tell Cassie that she was right, that I was wrong, that building a career is very good, but that love comes first."

"Oh, Matthew, that's wonderful!"

"But only if you come, too. To lend me courage, to prod me. I'm a dull stick, I told you that. Most of all, if it is called for, I need you to take Peter out of the picture."

"Oh, Matthew, none of that is necessary. You should be able to handle it all yourself."

"Should, yes, but don't forget what I am."

"A good doctor."

"And a rotten executive. Verity, please come. I need your help."

"But, Matthew, it wouldn't be ... well, right." She had been thinking of Bart as she answered this, Bart who had said something of the sort, tongue in cheek probably, but still he had said it.

"Melbourne is all of an hour's flying time," said Matthew drily. "We would be back the same day." For a few moments Verity was silent.

"It's still impossible," she reminded him. "The store has to open."

"But it will be closed all of next week-end — it's a public holiday, even women's castles close up. Only hardworked doctors remain on deck, but I've snared myself the services of a good locum."

Again she was silent. It would be a break, she thought eagerly, and with Robin's troubles heavy on her shoulders she felt she needed a break. Besides, in her backing of Matthew, or so he had said, she certainly would be talking to him, he would be talking back to her. Talk, she yearned. Someone to spill things to.

"Verity?" came Matthew's voice, anxious, pleading. Poor Matthew, he really did need someone to nudge him on, she half-smiled.

But still something stopped her from answering ... yet not

486

something, she knew intrinsically, but some*one*. Bart. How would Bart take to this?

But need Bart know? Matthew saw very little of his brother. They were on excellent terms, but not the terms that would entail Matthew ringing Bart to say: "I took your assistant down with me to Melbourne."

It came down finally to a matter of conscience, everything came down eventually to that, and her conscience, Verity told herself, was clear. — It also came down to human contact, which in her present state she knew she must have ... and to the contributing fact that when it came to human contact, Matthew offered all the sympathy and comfort she could need. He was a sympathetic and comforting person, not like –

"Verity?"

"Yes, Matthew," she said, "I'll come."

The doctor called round just after closing time. He did not bring the carrier bags of goodies, that phase was over. But it had benefited both of them, Verity thought.

He waited long enough, though, for a coffee, telling her his arrangements as they drank together.

"I'm hurrying back now, V. Bryan, my locum, is calling round, and I want to go through some things with him. I've decided against flying after all, the times of departure don't suit me. I thought we'd drive instead. Would that be all right with you?"

"Yes, Matthew, but it is a long way." She was thinking it could entail an overnight stop.

He smiled, reading her thoughts. "I love driving; this restricted house-to-house process has been stifling me, I've been yearning to put my foot down on the accelerator for a long time. Besides, I believe you could take over now and then." He made a question of it, and she nodded. It would be easier, too, she thought, just to step into a car.

"It will be cosier coming home," he went on almost boyishly, "that is if Cassie – if she'll –"

"She will, and I'll fly back. No, Matthew, two's company."

"It could be for you as well. Peter might come."

"That," smiled Verity, "is finished."

The telephone rang and she picked it up. It was Bart.

"Still there?" he asked.

"Yes, Mr. Prince."

"Still coping?"

"Yes, Mr. Prince."

"Anything to tell me?"

"No – no, nothing out of the usual."

"It's a holiday week-end. I suppose you knew that?"

"I didn't, but I do know now."

A hesitancy at the other end, which, if it had not been Bart Prince, Verity would have put down to a wish to prolong the conversation.

"Well, if there's nothing –" Bart said.

"Nothing."

"Then goodnight, Miss Tyler."

"Goodnight, Mr. Prince." The receiver went down.

"Goodnight from me, too, V ... and V, thank you, my dear." Matthew kissed her lightly and left.

Verity went soon after, went home to the worry of Robin again. She had thought that the prospect of telling Matthew about it in the near future, of asking his advice, might have helped her, but she found it hadn't. She sat at the window again, trying to find a way out, finding nothing but the same despair. She knew she could go to Adele, state the case, tell her it was up to her now to raise enough out of the jewellery that Robin had bought her to see Robin through. But Adele was not that kind, Adele would not part with any possession ...

cept Robin. So the worry still had to belong solely to Verity.

The several days left to the long week-end went too quickly
r Verity. If she had been honest with herself, she would have
dmitted that she would have liked to have slowed up the
ours, delayed the minutes. For though she was looking for-
ard to talking to Matthew, and in those long hours on the
ad there would be plenty of opportunity, she found herself
inking instead of Bart ... seeing Bart's hard face, for hard
d bitter it would be if he ever knew.

On the morning of the day prior to the brief vacation, she
t a few things in an overnight bag. Though they would be
avelling all night, and she intended, after she saw Cassandra
d Matthew settled together ... or so she prayed ... to fly
ck at once, sometimes there could be delays.

Where the other days had flown, today seemed to drag. Now
at it had come to the end, Verity wanted to get it over.

She was not busy ... invariably the day before a holiday,
e remembered from Chelsea, is like that ... but at the last
oment there was a customer who took her time.

Always patient, tonight Verity felt impatient. She could see
car drawn up at the kerb, and knew that Matthew was wait-
g.

But at last the woman went, and calling out to the car,
Don't come in, I won't be long," Verity pulled off her overall,
ok up her overnight bag, snapped off the lights, closed up,
en ran out.

The car door was open for her, she got promptly in, and at
ace they started off. "You are in a hurry, Matthew!" she
ughed.

"Why not?" came the answer ... only not in Matthew's
ice.

Calmly, but not reducing his speed, Bart took the first cor-
r, then with an open stretch in front of him, and no traffic to

impede him, he put his foot down.

Bart . . . not Matthew.

"Surprise, surprise," he said laconically as they caught t
first green light and did not need to stop or reduce their speed.

"Yes," agreed Verity with a composure that she secre
marvelled at, though possibly she was beyond emotion, pro
ably she was numbed. "I didn't expect you."

"That," he said, "must be the understatement of the year."

They both were silent after that, they had encountered
outer city traffic snarl, and it was no time, Verity accepted,
start a heated discussion. A thought struck her when, for t
third time, the car was obliged to stop. She made no mov
ment, unless her glance had gone to the door, but at once
said, "Oh, no, you don't, but just to make certain . . ." I
leaned over and locked the door.

This was going too far, but Verity decided to restrain he
self until they reached the suburbs with their greater possib
ities. For after the suburbs they would be in the rural regio
long stretches of empty road only punctuated by towns mu
too far, as far as Verity was concerned, from the refuge of t
city.

"Where are you going?" she asked at length.

"Where were you?"

"That was not my question."

"It was mine."

"Melbourne," she said uncaringly . . . what was there left
care about now? She knew it must sound ridiculous . . . s
knew it must seem the end of the world at this moment. Mu
too far for a contemplated non-stop journey. She heard his l
laugh, and was aware that he was thinking so, too. She knew
disbelieved her.

"We were driving right through," she defended herself.
was going to relieve Matthew."

490

"Not very cosy," he commented slyly, and she rankled.

"Well, that was our plan." She barely contained herself.

"And the ultimate goal?"

"You know already."

As he still waited, she said, "I told you – Melbourne."

"I asked the *ultimate goal*. Matthew, who recently proved imself to be a very clever fellow when it comes to degrees, so proved himself years ago to be a very simple one. In short, a boy he would always blab his intentions. He did again this me, but only the fact that you and he were using the long eek-end to hit south. Not the ultimate goal." Again he waited.

"The goal," Verity said stiffly, "was Cassandra. I've seen mething of Matthew this week, and I've convinced him that e's been going the wrong way with her."

"They must have been very interesting lessons." A pause as light came up. "Practical, of course."

"Mr. Prince, what is this?" she demanded.

"Not what it looks. It looks like a kidnap, doesn't it? But 's not."

"I want to get out!" she snapped.

"You would have a long hike, we're halfway between . . ." e was silent while he estimated, then he told her. The towns ade no sense to Verity, so far her Australian geography only nbraced the eastern capitals.

"You're no wiser," he nodded, "then accept the fact that u'd find yourself bushed. You could hitch a lift perhaps, but t here that could be risky. A much more prudent move ould be to stay where you are."

"With you?"

"Is it that awful? After all, you were going with Matthew."

"I wasn't. I mean –" She lapsed into silence. What could e say to this man?

"Not to worry," he tossed carelessly. "I believe you . . . or

should I say I don't believe Matthew would ever think of a~~
one but Cassie." A pause that was more a probe, but Ver~~
did not speak.

"But of all the fool schemes," Bart went on presently,
take you along with him to state his case. No woman wo~~
ever respond to that. As a woman yourself you must h~~
known it. But perhaps" ... thinly ... "you weren't think~~
of Matthew and Cassandra but –"

"Or Peter," she came in quickly. "Also, you have the wr~~
idea. I was going with Matthew just to –" Her voice trai~~
off. It did seem ridiculous now.

She wondered what he would say if she added her ot~~
reason, that reason of talking with Matthew about Robin. ~~
she could never talk to the man beside her, the man wh~~
Adele, Robin's wife, had known ... to use her words
"*very well*."

"All right," Bart was saying, "the subject is closed. M~~
thew is on his way to Melbourne ... unaccompanied. I c~~
say how it will be on his way back, but I can hope. I suppos~~
should thank you, Miss Tyler, for giving my brother the g~~
eral idea, though I cannot commend the manner in which ~~
meant him to carry it out."

"It was not my thought."

"I well believe that, it's typical of the silly thing Matth~~
would do. All those years in university make a man so ~~
worldly it's a laughing matter to someone on the outside." ~~
all his scorn there was a note of envy in Bart's voice. It was ~~
there, however, when he spoke again. "We've dealt with M~~
thew, with Peter. Only one Prince left. Aren't there any qu~~
tions, Miss Tyler?"

"Yes. Where are you going?"

"Where are *we* going," he corrected.

"Where are we going?" she conceded thinly.

"To the first restaurant that's open so I can eat. I don't now what Matthew's arrangements were, but picking you up onight made me miss my dinner." He half-glanced at her. You would have been pushed, too. Have you dined?"

"I'm not hungry."

"All the same I want you to eat first."

"First?"

"Before I say what I have to say."

Angrily she asked him, "Hasn't it all been said?"

"No. As far as I'm concerned nothing has been said, I mean othing of real importance. For marriage is important, isn't ?"

"Matthew's?"

"I said that Matthew had been dealt with. Ah, lights at st." He swept the car from the road round a semi-circular rive leading to a small diner. As he pulled up he said quite nemotionally, "No, *your* marriage, Miss Tyler."

Then: "With me."

CHAPTER VIII

IT WAS an hour afterwards, and coffee had been brought. B
Prince had eaten a good meal, and during it he had spoken
everything, it seemed, but the subject he had exploded, for
explosion it had been, as he had stopped the car. Her m
riage. To him.

Several times during the meal she had tried to br
through, but he had stopped her.

"First things first."

"My marriage would be my first thing."

"Good. I'm glad to hear that. I trust, too, it will be a last
thing."

"Mr. Prince, this is a very poor joke," she snapped.

"It is not a joke, Miss Tyler; believe me, I've never be
more serious in my life."

"I would never marry you!" Verity declared.

"But you would have married Matthew . . . Peter?"

"No. I mean . . . Oh, I don't know."

"Then know this." He had leaned across the table. "Y
will be marrying me," he said.

"What makes you think that?" She tried to be coolly, c
temptuously amused, but she knew she sounded heated a
agitated.

"I know. Or at least I'm so sure of it you could call it kno
ledge. All the odds are stacked on my side."

"If you mean I'm with you in a place that I don't know
an hour that is getting rather late, that went out years ago. C

know you're a believer in propriety . . . behind closed doors,
think it was you once said . . . but these days I hardly think
" She stopped. He was laughing at her.

He finished his laugh, then he shook his head. "No, I was
ot meaning that at all. Brandy?"

As she declined, he suggested, "It might help you. I have
ome things to say."

She decided to accept the drink after all, and when he had
oured it, she drank it so quickly that she had to follow it up at
nce by the coffee. She still felt the brandy burning in her . . .
ut it lent her no courage. To make it worse he kept gazing
teadily at her, and with that cool amusement that she had
een unable to summon up for herself.

"Ready?" he asked presently.

"Yes."

"Then this is it. You will marry me because there is nothing
lse. No" . . . as she went to object . . . "note that I said 'noth-
g', not 'no one'. I know you would never lack a number of
andidates. But money . . . ah, that's a different thing."

"Money?" she queried.

"Which you must have. And in a sufficient degree."

"I have it now."

"For yourself . . . But for your brother?"

Verity put down the coffee spoon she had taken up and ner-
ously played with. "I believe I begin to understand," she said.
My brother's wife Adele has asked and received money from
ou. No doubt in the transaction, if transaction it's called,
he's told you that Robin's remittances have not been so satis-
actory of late."

"Yes," he nodded coolly, "I did give Dellie a cheque."

"For old times' sake." Verity's voice was pinched.

He was looking at her closely. He seemed amused again.
Jealous?" he asked.

"Jealous? Of you?"

"Why not? But then I forgot. I forgot you've only know me After. Adele knew me Before."

"Yes, she knew you very well."

"Perhaps." He shrugged. He was silent a moment. "But was not Dellie who told me. Perhaps she gave the indicatio when she asked for a tide-over, but I never thought then tha it could come to this."

"To what?"

"Our marriage."

"How could it come to it?"

He looked at her deliberately. Then he spoke deliberately "By your inability, at least your solicitor's inability, to squeez one cent from the Ramsay estate."

"But how can you know that?" she gasped. "Adel wouldn't know it."

"No, all she knows is that she'd like more money. But th male mind delves deeper. It wants to know *why* there is no the same money."

"When it doesn't concern him?"

"It concerned me."

"But – but why?"

"We will come to that later. I was up to the male mind. Re member?"

"Yes," she said in a low voice.

"After the thing that happened to me," he said a litt roughly, "and I got out of Med school, I tried my hand in sev eral avenues – advertising, law. I quite liked law, only I sti had that feeling for –" He paused; it was evidently, from h expression, a bitter pause.

"However," he went on, "if it was not to be that, then I de cided it didn't matter what. My mother needed me, so th

496

other avenues went by. I wept no tears over them." He gave a short laugh.

"But I got sufficiently through law before I tossed it to enable me to get what I wanted from my brother professionals, even though I myself was only a near-professional, in other words had I been a rank outsider I might still be outside my present knowledge. The knowledge that not only is Robin Ramsay dead broke, he's in debt as well."

"Mr. Carstairs told you that?"

"No." A smile. "But I wouldn't say that I didn't get it out of him."

"I didn't think Mr. Carstairs –"

"To be fair to him I must admit I used certain methods. Like claiming you for a fiancée, for instance."

". . . You didn't!"

"He was quite delighted," reported Bart Prince, "seemed to think it was time you had a restraining hand."

"You lied to him," she exclaimed.

"Call it white-lied. The ultimate purpose deserved that adjective, anyway."

"I still don't think Mr. Carstairs should have –"

"Look, you have more serious things to consider just now than your solicitor's scruples. You have your brother. Where are you finding next week's cheque?"

"I can't. But" . . . proudly . . . "that doesn't mean that I'd –"

"Marry to assure it? I'm not so sure about that. You think the world of him, don't you?"

"Yes. But if I told him, Robin would understand."

"But would you tell him?"

"Yes. I mean –" Suddenly unable to cope, Verity put her face in her hands.

She was aware of his getting her to her feet, leading her out of the restaurant, sheltering her all the way from curious eyes, to the car. His grasp was gentle, considerate, and the gentle consideration, so unexpected, was her undoing. The moment she gained the seclusion and privacy of the parked vehicle, she burst into tears.

"Robin is dying," she said desperately.

"I know, Verity." He said her name again, something he had not said for some time.

"If I tell him, then Adele will find out, possibly leave him."

"Yes, quite possibly."

"*You* can say that?" For a moment the grief left her; it seemed an odd agreement from a man who had known a woman "very well."

"Skip it," he said of her surprise. "Get on to facts. Adele would leave him, as you said, and would it matter?"

"Very much. Whether it's his present condition or whether this time he really cares, I don't know, all I do know is that for the little time left –"

"He must not know, he must live as he always has lived?"

"Yes."

"Then," he said deliberately, "you have no other choice than marriage with me. Oh" . . . as she went to object . . . "you could have, I suppose. You're certainly attractive enough to marry well. But rich men don't grow on trees, and even if they did, the actual clinching takes time, doesn't it? And time is something you don't have, Verity, but" . . . a significant pause . . . "you have me.

"I'm rich, and though compared to my brothers I'm no catch physically, I've still seen to it that I'm not . . . physically speaking again . . . a total loss."

. . . No, not with that deliberate whipcord strength, she thought.

"In other words, I'm bad, but I could be worse. Ordinarily

you'd be a fool even to consider me, but it's *extra*ordinary now, isn't it? Also there's that old enemy time."

"Mr. Prince" . . . she could not say Bart . . . "I can't believe all this."

"Then believe it," he advised her.

"But — but even if I do, what do you — what do you —" Her voice stammered to a silence.

"What do I get out of it? I think that's what you're trying to say."

"Yes."

"I can only tell you part, and this is the part: I get a satisfaction. A satisfaction that I'm acquiring something that my two brothers undoubtedly thought about . . . oh, yes, I know Peter, and even though I said what I did of Matthew and Cassandra, I know that Matthew is not that unworldly that he doesn't recognize beauty other than Cassie's. A satisfaction that an ugly wreck like I am can still show them something. A satisfaction —"

"Stop!" Verity interrupted at last.

But when he did all she could say was, "I'm not beautiful." She could not find the words for the disgust she felt.

"I think you are," he stated. But there was no feeling at all when he said it. "I think you're very beautiful, and I consider I would be very well recompensed."

"Recompensed?"

"By what you would give me in return. I would be the cripple with the lovely wife. And for that little thing, that triumph, your brother need never know the truth."

"It's horrible! I'm not listening."

"It's not a charming story, I'll give in, but you are listening, and you'll agree."

"What about — Priscilla?" she barely whispered.

"Well what about her?" he asked back.

Verity looked at him incredulously. Did anything matter to this man, anything at all? Because he would score more of a triumph by marrying someone his brother might have thought of . . . his own words . . . he would pass over Priscilla as though she never existed. And Cilla, she thought, quiet, unassuming Cilla, would never utter a word.

"It's impossible!" she said sharply.

"You're not answering yet, you're sleeping on it. Oh, no, my dear" . . . at her quick look . . . "in your own bed. As so you so triumphantly told me *that* doesn't matter any more. For which reason I'm taking you home now to do some serious thinking. Think all tonight . . . tomorrow . . . the next day. You have the entire week-end. It's happened quite opportunely, actually." He started the engine, and the car completed the half-circle of the drive.

They spoke little on the return trip. Once he glanced at his watch and remarked on the wonder of flying, how already Matthew and Cassandra would be reunited, how —

Verity turned away.

But she could not keep turning away. That fact came home to her, as, having left her at the flat, she ran upstairs and opened up to find a note pushed under the door. It was in Adele's writing, and for Adele to have called personally Verity knew the matter would be urgent. She tore away the envelope.

Adele had gone straight to the point. She had written:

"What's happened to our money? Robin had a bad attack today and our doctor called in some specialists in Robin's trouble. These men are coming again tomorrow, and, as you can guess, these private calls cost the world. There is also special medicine, and a nurse will be required. For heaven's sake, Verity, do something."

Verity read it again. Then she put the letter down. She had never felt so heavy, so burdened in all her life.

There seemed no way out. Except . . .

There was no awakening in the morning, for though at last she had left her seat by the window and gone to bed, she had not slept.

She wished the week-end was an ordinary working one, for then she could have occupied herself in the Castle, escaped, even briefly, from her crowding thoughts. But also she would have had the likelihood of Bart calling in upon her, waiting for her decision, even though he had assured her that she was not to answer him yet.

She did not know which would have been the most racking: the unnerving possibility of Bart – or her aching thoughts of Robin. For those thoughts . . . those memories . . . kept flashing through her tortured mind like the facets in a kaleidoscope. Robin, as the baby brother she had carried everywhere, Robin, as the toddler to whom she had taught his first steps, Robin, the schoolboy, getting help with his homework, Robin, the adolescent, getting help with his pocket money, Robin, the man, getting help with his love affairs. Robin . . . since he was Robin.

She supposed she had adored him so much because there had been no one else. There had been the warmest of feelings between her mother and herself, but her mother's real love had gone to the kindly man who had come later into her life to make a rich happiness out of her poor remnants. Louis had been sweet, and Verity had been glad Mother had returned his feelings for her. Most of all she had been glad that between them they had made Robin for her. "He's your baby," they had said.

And now the baby was a man, and the man was dying. Robin was dying. She felt she could not bear it, her grief seemed large enough to fill an eternity. But whatever she felt, the sit-

uation still existed. All she could do was keep it from Robin
... from Adele. Just as she had spared the little boy, she must
spare the man. And she was going to spare him.

So on the evening before her return to work, she picked up
the phone and dialled Bart's own number.

His voice came back immediately, he must have been waiting there. "Verity?"

"How did – how did you know?"

"I think I know everything about you. You haven't slept,
you haven't eaten, you've gone through every possible means
of escape." A dry laugh at that choice of words. "You've
turned over pictures in your mind of what-once-was until the
torture was unbearable. And now you're ringing to tell me –"

"Go on, please, Bart."

"No, *you* must say it." There was a final note in his voice
and she knew there would be no compromise.

"Then – it's yes," she said.

Now there was a silence at the other end, and for a hideous
moment she wondered if he had been joking with her, if it had
all been a kind of game. If he had, she thought ...

"Thank you." His voice came at last. It came as though he
was speaking from a long way off.

"Will you call at the Castle tomorrow to tell me?" She was
actually trembling and she hoped he didn't hear it in her
voice. "I mean – tell me – when? – That is – I mean –"

"No," he said, and the tone came stronger this time. "No,
we'll be married by then."

"We couldn't!" she gasped.

"But we shall. You can do your shopping in the morning
while I see to the necessary details. Then in the afternoon –"

She was holding on to the receiver so tightly that her fingers
hurt. She couldn't go into it that fast, she was thinking, she
had to have more time.

As if he read her over the wires as well as face-to-face, he drawled, "On second thoughts we'll start life as we intend to go on, doing all things together. You can come with me while we fill in the necessary papers – probably you'll be needed there, anyway – and I'll help you shop."

"I don't need anything." She said it blankly, just for something to say while she still withdrew from what he had just told her, and she was unprepared for his quick reply.

"Certainly you'll need things. How often do you think I've been married? At least my bride will wear a new gown."

"But I have dresses."

"*The* dress?"

"Well, I –"

"Or something suitable in navy?"

"It is, as it happens."

"It won't happen."

"Then – what about –?"

"I'll tell you when I see it."

She was quiet a moment. Then: "What about the Castle?" she asked.

"As we've concluded our assessing, Cilla can open up, keep an eye on the sales . . . for that matter she can close the shop section altogether, just attend to the accounts."

"Poor Cilla!" It was out before she knew it. Now the man must say something, she thought.

"Yes, poor Cilla," he agreed. Then, at once: "Tomorrow at nine, Verity."

She held on to the phone for minutes after he had rung off.

During the evening the phone pealed again. She looked at it warily. What did Bart Prince want now?

It was not Bart, it was Adele.

"The specialists have just left. Robin seems to be reacting favourably . . . well, anyway, he does seem as good as can be expected, to use the old hospital phrase."

"That's grand news."

"So was the cheque. You've certainly achieved something at last."

"You – you got it?"

"Yes. – Well, I thought I'd let you know about Rob."

Again the other end of the phone went down before Verity could cradle her own end.

Bart, she was thinking, had wasted no time. That was good for Robbie, so therefore it must be good, too, for her. Only Robin mattered, and she was grateful that Bart had acted at once. But the signed, sealed and delivered feeling that was encompassing her frightened her. It's too late, she thought, to go back now. Perhaps I could cheat, now that Adele has received the money, but other cheques will be needed. I'm closed in. I can't get out. Bart said nothing in navy blue, but I feel it should be black . . .

It was gold. Not the warm gold of the sun but the faintly green-gold of a young acorn. From the dress départment they went to the jewellery for a circle of yellow sapphires for Verity's engagement ring, a plain band to be tried for size for her wedding ring. For a string of amber to lighten up the dress.

"Now you're an acorn," Bart said.

"Usually it's a flower," she said for something to say.

"Flowers fade. You can keep an acorn in your pocket for years."

"I know," she nodded, still using words to hide behind. "You don't get rheumatism and you won't grow old."

He shrugged. "I only know the years," he told her. "If I leave you now will you promise not to disappear by two o' clock?"

"Is that – when –?" She had been beside him when the ar-

504

rangements had been made, but she realized now she barely had heard a word.

"Near enough," he said. "Will you promise?"

"But I couldn't not promise, could I? I mean it's too late. You see Adele rang and –" She stopped at a look on his face.

It was there so briefly she could not have said that it was what she first had felt ... pain. At once the look was impersonal again, nothing at all conveyed.

"Yes, a little late," he agreed coolly. "Two, then?"

"Two." She got off at the beauty shop and went through the usual ritual. – Afterwards Adele told her that she had rung and rung ... rung the Castle ... rung the flat. Rung to tell her that –

At two Bart came to the beauticians and took her to a small hotel where everything was laid out in readiness – dress, shoes, all she needed. She did not ask who had done it, there could be no one else but Bart.

She dressed, went downstairs, they drove round to the church that Bart had arranged, and were married within the hour.

An hour *after* Robin had died.

Only a witness supplied by the minister stood at the ceremony, and there was no one but themselves at the dinner in the same little hotel where Verity had changed.

They sat at the candled table opposite to each other, and Bart, lifting his wine glass, said: "There, it wasn't so bad, was it?"

"No," she answered him indistinctly, for she was all choked up.

She seemed to be thinking in too many channels at the same time, yet she still did not want to direct her tumbled thoughts into one channel, because she knew now what that

505

channel would be. For ever since the simple service her awareness had kept returning to that *incredulous but unmistakable
serenity that she had experienced as she had stood beside Bart
Prince and made her vows*. It had been so totally unexpected
she still could not believe it, and yet it had existed, it had been
there, a peace of mind she had never known before. And a happiness. – Happiness?

But she could never tell him. Not this man who had gone
into marriage with her for as well as an undisclosed reason ..
what reason? she wondered briefly ... for the blatantly
admitted reason of establishing himself in the eyes of the outsider. To use Bart's own unadorned words: "To get something that my two brothers undoubtedly thought about. – A
satisfaction than an ugly wreck can still show them something."

No, she could never tell him how she felt after that.

"When we're done," Bart said, "we're going up to the
Mountains." At a look on Verity's face, as, as always, she
thought of Robin, he reassured her: "I'll leave Cilla a number." He paused a little diffidently. "It won't be much of a
break, Verity, but we can catch up later."

She said something trite about the mountains being new to
her, anyway, avoiding his eyes as she said it, suddenly almost
girlishly shy because of those unfolding minutes standing beside him and knowing something so intrinsic she was afraid
now to try to recapture it. And so they finished the dinner.

She went upstairs and packed her few things, very conscious
of Bart standing behind her in the room ... and why not,
was their room? ... as he said: "It's only the night, Verity, so
just take a few articles. One day" ... a pause ... "we'll do
all properly."

She did not know quite what he meant by that until two
hours later when they had reached the mountain town with

506

the Swiss-inspired hotel where they were to lodge.

The air smelled of wet violets and fir trees, and there was a fire crackling in the suite to which they had been led ... a large bedroom, a smaller annexe with a bed, bathroom and dining alcove.

"It's an apartment," Verity cried.

He was putting her bag on the big bed, and he did not look at her as he said: "Yes." Then he paused. "You see, Verity, tonight this room is yours."

"What, Bart?" She looked round at him, but his glance was still averted.

Then he turned suddenly, and held her eyes until she lowered her gaze.

"We've a long way to go and all our lives to complete the journey. You're tired ... you're strung-up. So, little one, good night." He stepped towards her and lightly kissed her brow. It was the first time he had kissed her since the minister had smiled at them in the church and intoned: "The groom will now kiss the bride."

"But Bart —" She spoke impulsively, and he turned instantly, a world of eager inquiry, had Verity looked up into his dark eyes. But Verity's glance stayed down.

"Yes?" he asked.

"Bart, I'm not a child ... far from it. I mean I've mothered Robin all these years. What I really mean is — I'm adult. I understand that a man and a woman —"

"I'm glad you understand that." There was no eagerness in him now, rather a cool acceptance of basic facts. "Because I do intend us to live a full life."

"You may reassure yourself." In her shyness, she said it a little stiffly, she still did not look up, and when he did not respond, she burst out: "I'll keep my side of the bargain, never fear."

"Bargain!" He said it so faintly she was not sure she really heard it. When she did bring herself to turn round, he had left the room.

She could hear him in the annexe next door, moving around, probably taking out his things. Then she heard the door close between them . . . then his light snap out.

She put her own light out and undressed in the dark. Then, tremblingly, she got into bed. She felt sure she would not sleep, but when the telephone rang some hours later she woke up with a start.

Before she could grope for the receiver, Bart was there, already in his dressing gown although it had barely begun to peal. He took it up and asked: "Yes?" Then he said: "Yes. – Yes, I do understand. – Yes, I'll do that. – Yes." He put the phone down.

Already she was going off to sleep again, and for a long moment he stood looking down on her, she could see him faintly through her almost closed eyes, and for a second –

"Yes, Bart?"

"It's nothing. Go to sleep." He went out.

She did sleep. She slept until the next morning, and Bart standing beside her with coffee. He was dressed ready to leave. He had been right when he had said it would only be a brief break.

"Drink it, Verity." Something in his voice made her look quickly up at him.

"What is it?" she asked.

"Coffee."

"I didn't mean that, I meant –"

"Drink it first." He said it authoritatively, and after a moment she did so. He waited until she drained the final drop, then he said quietly: "That ring last night."

"Oh, yes?" Only now did she remember it.

508

"It was a message for you."

"For me?" She sat up straighter.

"From Cilla."

"Oh." She relaxed back again.

"You see" ... gently ... "Adele had been trying to get you, and when she failed she finally got Priscilla's home."

"Adele trying to get me? Bart – Bart – not Robin?"

"Yes, little one." He sat down on the bed beside her.

"He's – worse?"

"No, Verity. No. It's all over."

"All over?" She looked at him stupidly. For a moment she thought: Robin's better. The nightmare is finished. Robin is all right again.

And then the meaning of Bart's words became clear.

"No!" she cried.

"I'm sorry, but yes, Verity."

"And that was the phone call last night?"

"Yes."

"You should have told me."

"There was nothing to be done. I wanted you to have a night's rest at least. Besides, it had already been over for some hours."

For a while what he said did not sink in. Then Verity said in a muffled voice: "How many hours?"

"Does it matter?" he answered harshly, and but for the harshness she would have left it at that.

"Yes," she said, her pain because of Robin making her unreasonable, for what she said then she did not really mean. "Yes. Because I think you knew before you married me. Because if I'd known, I needn't have gone through this thing. I mean –"

She stopped at his hand on her, hard, relentless.

509

"I didn't know, but had I known I would have done jus what you said."

"To even up with your brothers." She shivered. "To show them something?"

"Verity . . ." he began.

"Isn't it true? Didn't you give me that reason? That rea son for this – this farce?" She was looking down at her ring.

"Verity . . ."

"To establish yourself, you said. To show them. And be cause of Robbie, I agreed. And now Robbie has died too early. She stopped to put a shaking hand to her quivering mouth "And I've found out – too late."

CHAPTER IX

THEY drove down to Sydney with the separation between two seats . . . and a world . . . dividing them. Neither of them spoke for the two hours that it took.

Only when they joined the snarl of the city traffic did Bart address Verity.

"I'll take you straight to your brother's apartment. Have you any money for the taxi fare home?"

Home? But where was home? When two people married it was presumed that they lived together. But she – But Bart –

Reading her thoughts, he said sharply, "Our home, of course." For a moment he took his eyes away from the stream of cars to give her a quick searching look.

"I may be late." She did not look back at him. "I'll have to go to my own flat to pick up some things."

"That can be attended to tomorrow."

She said stiffly, "Very well . . . but I still can't say what time it will be."

"That's all right, I'll be waiting. I'll be as near as the phone."

"Thank you . . . but I don't think Adele will be requiring anything." Her voice was brittle.

His mouth tightened. "I didn't say Adele."

"No, you didn't. I'm sorry. – Yet it does come down to the same thing, doesn't it? It was only because of Adele that we –"

His face had paled with suppressed anger. "You're under

strain. I'm not arguing with you. Later –" He hunched on
shoulder, the shoulder near hers. Briefly the pair of the
touched, and she withdrew slightly. She knew he felt her with
drawal, for his tightened mouth grew even tighter. In spite o
herself Verity shivered.

A few minutes afterwards he turned into a quiet avenue
went a short distance, then pulled up at the lavish block o
flats where Robin and Adele . . . where *Adele* . . . lived.

"Want me to come in with you?" he asked offhandedly, an
Verity knew that if he had not asked like that, she would hav
answered an eager Yes.

"Yes," she would have appealed, "yes, Bart." For, lookin
up at the window at which Robbie often had sat, she longe
for someone's hand now in hers. – But it could not be Bart
hand. Not with a carelessly tossed offer like that.

"No, thank you." She got out of the car.

"I'll be waiting," he said again.

"It will be late." It was her turn to repeat herself.

"It doesn't matter what time it is." He did not move the c
until she entered the building.

When she heard him leave . . . she did not look around
see . . . she knew a sudden devastating emptiness. She ha
never enjoyed coming to this apartment, Adele had not we
comed her, Robin had looked more ill each time she saw hir
And now . . . and now . . .

She went into the lift and pressed the button to Robin's .
Adele's floor.

Adele opened the door to her. She looked pale and shocke
at least Verity had to credit her with that. She led the way in
the lounge.

"I knew it was going to come," the girl said as she lit a ci
arette, "but I didn't expect it this soon. Also, when it happer
you're still not prepared, are you?"

512

"Was he in pain?" Robin always had been a bad sufferer, Verity thought tenderly; as a little boy he had cried over a cut knee, created over a stubbed toe. There had to be heaps of love administered as well as salve and bandages.

"No, he was sedated. Poor Rob!" Adele exhaled.

"I suppose," she said presently, "I come out of this as the archdemoness of all times, or whatever a female demon is. I know I'm an unrewarding character ... your word, Verity ... but I haven't had the most rewarding of experiences." – She had said this before, recalled Verity.

For a few moments the girl brooded, presumably over her unrewarded past, and, suddenly, unbidden, Bart came flashing into Verity's mind, Bart who had known "Dellie" *very well*. Yet still never married her. Had that been the less-than-reward she spoke of now?

"But with favourable circumstances I would have stuck with Rob," went on Adele. "He was the same type as I am, really. You mightn't like that, but we suited. Anyway" ... a shrug ... "it's all over now." She looked at Verity. "Anything you want? Sentimental section, naturally, working with the Princes you would never lack anything monetarily." She gave a short laugh.

Working with the Princes ... So Adele did not know about them. Priscilla did not know either. No one knew. We could be – not married, Verity thought.

"I want nothing, thank you, Adele." All she needed of Robin, Verity knew, was imprinted on her heart.

She wondered when she should break it to Adele that Robbie had not died the rich man his wife had thought. Not yet ... though already Adele looked much more composed than she had been when she had opened the door.

"When is the –" Verity began quietly.

Adele understood. "Tomorrow. Early." She gave a little shiver. "I hate these things."

Impulsively Verity said: "Would you like me to stop to-night?"

"Would you?" rushed Adele. "Bart brought you, didn't he? I saw his car pull up. I'll ring and tell him what's what. No" ... as Verity moved forward ... "I know the number I should." She crossed to the phone.

I know the number. I should. As she listened to Adele dialling Bart's apartment, Verity could not help herself wondering how many times Adele had done this before. Bart had never denied he had known Adele "very well". What had been between them?

She moved sensitively away again ... but she could not move away from her own nagging thoughts.

Had Adele's failure to tie Bart up been the incentive for Adele to marry Robin so promptly, for it had been all over by the time she had arrived from England. This was the painful trend of the thoughts.

Then ... following fast, following compulsively: Had that marriage been the "other" reason to Bart's frankly admitted one of "status", the one that had *really* urged him to force along his own marriage, to her, that reason as old as society itself; that retaliatory what you did, I can do, too, Adele.

He could have called on Priscilla, Verity thought abstractedly, sweet, loving Cilla, but his Cilla would be such an accustomed figure she would probably never occur to him for that. Possibly only his mother ... and Priscilla herself ... had dreamed in such a strain. But Verity Tyler was unaccustomed, so she did occur. She was also immediately available, because she was at her wits' end. Bart had known it. He had known he could make that tit-for-tat move at once. So he had married her. She was Mrs. Bartley Prince. She was Bart's wife for two reasons. Achievement. Repayment. But not for ... never for ...

She felt a throbbing in her head as she tried to work it all out, but in spite of her vagueness, and the distance she had put between herself and the phone, she still heard Adele:

"It's Dellie, Bart ... Thank you, my dear ... No, so far I'm holding up well. Verity will stay with me tonight, you know me of old, how I go to pieces. Yes ... Yes, Bart, I'll be here ... I'll be waiting."

The phone went down.

Thank you, my dear ... You know me of old.

Verity was still mulling over Adele's conversation long after she had put Adele to bed, then gone herself. She had finished her tears for Robin, she had accepted with final resignation the futility of grief. But she could not accept Adele's soft words, she found. Even when she pulled the pillow over her ears she still listened in retrospect. My dear. You know me of old. There had been something else, she recalled dully. It had been: "I'll be here." Then: "I'll be waiting."

Why had Adele said that?

The funeral service was short. Only Robin's wife and sister attended. When it was over, Adele said, "Thank you, Verity," and got in her car and left at once. A little confused, for she had believed Adele would need her longer, Verity called a taxi and went out to Balmain.

Once there she moved around the rooms, picking up things, putting them down again, oddly restless. She remembered to ring the agent to cancel the flat, she remembered to stop the milk, the bread — then that was that, she thought. Now she could leave. Go — home, as Bart had said. But all at once she knew she could not go without a previous word from Bart. Kind, or otherwise, but he had to tell her first. She dialled the number that Adele had dialled so much more expertly last night. She listened to the bell ring at Bart's end. There was no answer. She tried again, but still no answer. She put the phone down, feeling inexplicably hollow and very alone.

She knew she needed somebody, some human contact. She rang Woman's Castle, but either Priscilla had not come in, or was busy, but again there was no response.

She decided to ring Adele, ask her how she was feeling. The girl had made it obvious that she was finished with her, that she needed her no longer, but all at once all Verity cared about was to hold the phone to her ear *and hear a voice*.

It rang several times, and she had just begun to wonder whether anyone was answering telephones today, when the other end was taken up.

"Hullo." It was a male voice ... and she recognized it at once as Bart's.

"Hullo," he called impatiently again.

... "Yes," Verity was remembering from Adele last night, "I'll be here. I'll be waiting."

Bart's voice called a final Hullo, then the phone went down.

But – "I'll be here. I'll be waiting." Verity still heard those words.

An hour afterwards she was still sitting there at the phone staring blankly into space. She had not thought she was so prone to pain, that is pain apart from Robbie. She had not thought, anyway, that she could feel pain because of Bart. Bart, whom, whether she had liked him or not, she had instinctively trusted, for at no time since she had entered the Prince world had she not trusted and believed Bart Prince, but now –

Clumsily, probably ineptly, since her hurt made her inept, she pieced her story together.

Adele and Bart had been close friends ... hadn't they

516

known each other "very well"? . . . but Adele like all women had presumably wanted marriage. Reward, she had expressed it. Bart, like all men, had wanted freedom; either that or his accident had left him with an uncertainty that had delayed any matrimonial move.

So Adele, probably in frustration, for there had certainly not been love, had married Robin, and that had prompted Bart to retaliate later in the same way. With her. He had explained it as a status gesture, and she had believed that that embittered man could be capable of such an action. She had not cared for the idea . . . what woman would care to be only an achievement symbol? . . . but now she knew she liked her present position much less. For as well as being a feather in Bart's cap as he would have her believe, she was a substitute for the girl he really had wanted, but not got around to. Not until it was too late. If he had waited another day, waited another hour, he could have rectified that hideous mistake. – And I, Verity knew hollowly, would not have made mine.

This comedy of errors that was no comedy at all she knew she could have put aside, or at least passed over, *but never, never, could she forgive Bart seeking out Adele so soon . . . going to her at once.*

What was he saying to her now in her apartment? Were there recriminations? Regrets? Plans? Hopes? Schemes like: "Wait a while." Agreements like: "Very soon." Arrangements like: "Give it time." Anticipations like: "After that . . ."

"Oh, no!" Verity said aloud. I'm not really married to Bartley Prince, she was thinking wildly, *not really*. There's a signature on a form, but we're not man and wife. When I go round to Bart's apartment tonight . . . home, he had said, she recalled with a thin little smile . . . it will be to hear him tell me all this, tell me that as well as my misfortune, he has a misfortune on his own hands.

517

The indignity of it all gripped fiercely at her. I can't go on, she knew, not now, nor tomorrow. Not ever.

But what do women do in a situation like this? They go away, I would know that, but where can they go? What do they live on? How do they exist? I can work like anyone else works, but if I work as I'm working now, on what I've been trained for, Bart will be sure to find me, there is a closeness in businesses like his . . . and we would have that reckoning. It has to come, my common sense tells me that, but not now, not yet, not — not with Bart answering this soon from Adele's phone.

She tried desperately to think, to reason . . . to plan, but she found she could get no further than that . . . than Bart's voice on Adele's wire.

She had been nervously pleating a sheet of old newspaper, and, looking down, she read absently . . . then not so absently . . . the few lines of the advertisement in the middle column that somehow had caught her attention.

"Young Australian woman for conversation in English with two boys of eleven and thirteen years. Remote country home but every amenity and consideration. Telephone . . ."

The edition, she saw, was a week old. She was not Australian. But that "remote country home", remote from the turmoil in which she now found herself, the further turmoil in which she knew she would be placed, suddenly prompted her to take up the phone. She checked the given number.

She was aware she could not indefinitely run away from Bart, but just to remove herself from the scene for days, weeks . . . perhaps a month . . . Just to get away . . .

Verity put her finger on the first digit. The advertiser would have left by now, left with the young Australian, not English, woman; no one waited for an answer to an ad a week after. She turned round the final figure and heard a bell, and for the first

518

...me today there was a prompt reply. A young boy's voice, she
...dged. A pleasantly foreign voice.

"Yes?" he asked.

"I'm Verity Tyler." No, she was Verity Prince, she thought
...lly. "I've just read an advertisement in a week-old news-
...aper."

"Oh, yes," said the boy. "Will you come?"

Will you come? It seemed incredible . . . it was incredible.
She listened again.

"It's a long way away," the boy went on. "All the others
...id too far away. It's called Tetaparilly, and that means – Oh,
...[M]other, why can't I try this time? You did no good, and she
...ounds nice."

"Gunnar!" A woman's voice now came across the wire.
...[M]y sons!" she apologized to Verity with a laugh.

"This one sounded in little need of English conversation,"
...[p]raised Verity sincerely.

"He is the better," admitted his mother. "Ulf, the younger
...[b]oy, is quite bad, I fear. It would be wonderful if you could
...[c]ome."

"I'm English," Verity told her.

"Better still for English conversation. We have been delayed
...[fr]om leaving Sydney earlier because of a throat condition in
...[U]lf, but all is well now and the doctor says we can go at once.
...[Y]ou could come at your convenience, of course, if you will
...[on]ly agree. We are a Swedish family, and have settled in the
...[n]orth-west. My husband and I went some years ago, then,
...[w]hen we could bring them over, our two young sons. It is an
...[is]olated farm, so the boys must have school by correspond-
...[en]ce. Ordinarily they would have picked up English quite eas-
...[il]y if they had been able to mix, but with only parents to con-
...[ve]rse with –"

"You, anyway, are very fluent," said Verity.

"Yes, we both, Big Gunnar and I, can speak English. But I assist my husband a great deal on the farm, we are little more than beginners so can afford only a minimum of help, thus I have not the time for encouraging my sons as I would like. But our place is comfortable, as the advertisement says, yet" . . . ruefully . . . "also, I must admit, remote."

"The important thing to me," Verity broke in, "is – is it still available?"

"Is it – Why, yes. *Why, yes!*" There were delighted noises at the other end. "Does this mean –"

"I want to come," Verity said.

"Then – how soon? We could forward you the plane ticket to the nearest field, and we would pick you up."

"When are you leaving?"

"As early as an hour from now," said the voice. "I am driving the car, and my husband, who has been concluding a deal at Bathurst, will meet us there. But if you could tell me when –"

There was a moment's pause from Verity, during which time she could hear the Swedish woman breathing more quickly, probably fearing she had not gained her prize after all.

Then Verity said: "Could I come with you?"

"Come with us?"

"I'm sorry, perhaps your car is not big enough –"

"Our car is very big, as well as very clumsy, the boys call it the Tank. But this is wonderful."

"You may not think so," Verity laughed.

"I do think so. I think, like Gunnar did, that you sound nice. You *are* serious?"

"Very serious. When and where?"

"Within the hour that I told you." After some consideration the woman gave Verity a meeting place that even a newcomer would have no trouble in finding. Excited, she rang off.

More slowly, Verity put down her end of the phone. She knew that what she was about to do was immature, unreasonable, quite abominable ... but also that it was essential, essential to her own peace of mind. She could not face Bart yet. In time she could, and must, face him, but she had to have this breathing space.

She had already placed her things in her bag, so she had no packing now. She knew, though, she must leave some kind of note, otherwise Bart could think all sorts of fates for her, possibly raise an alarm.

She took out pen and paper, cursing her dullness as the clock hand went half way round the face before she could find any words to write. Then they could not have been sparser, less illuminating, though illumination was the last thing she wanted, she thought.

She wrote barely: "I have gone away. V." Then left it at that.

As she ran down the stairs, she heard her telephone ring ... but she did not turn back.

CHAPTER X

TETAPARILLY was far north-west, and, in spite of what Grete Dahlquist had said, a well-established little station. The reason that Grete was needed to help her husband so much was a new crop they had gone in for, one that reacted favourably in most instances to a woman's hands. It was herbs.

"Our parents went in for herbs in Europe," the Swedish couple explained, "and now the demand is growing out here."

They had come originally to Australia because of an inheritance. An uncle had left Gunnar the property.

"Yes, a Swede, of course," Grete had laughed. "Just look at that furniture!"

It was very old and very beautiful, Verity saw at once. The Chelsea house had handled such stuff. It was not seen much in Australia.

"No, Uncle Bent had it shipped out," Grete said when Verity remarked on this. "You find it good; we find it cumbersome. We both, my husband and I, incline to the modern pieces that our Nordic countries are now doing so beautifully. In fact we incline so much that we have already been doing some shipping out ourselves." She showed Verity the slim functional pieces that had arrived with much pride. "You do not like them?" she laughed.

"I do. Yet not so much in comparison. But perhaps I'm the old-fashioned type. What I definitely do not like is seeing them mixed up together."

"Neither do we, but slowly ... slowly ..." Grete Dahlquist spread her capable hands.

"You will sell the old stuff?"

"We have been selling ever since Big Gunnar and I started here." Grete often called her husband Big Gunnar. "As we gain a new piece, we sell Uncle Bent's old things. I'm sorry we disappoint you" ... another laugh ... "but it is balanced because you never disappoint us. We still can't believe our good fortune."

"You don't really disappoint me," refused Verity. "Your selections are in excellent taste, it's just that I like old things."

"In a new country?"

"It is old, too."

"Oh, yes, we have learned about that, also, but not old furniture old, at least not for us." Grete put her arm round Verity and they walked down to the herb section that was the Swedish woman's dream.

"I love it," she had confessed. "Do you think badly of me for preferring to raise a bed of rue to teaching my boys to enunciate more properly?"

"I think it shows your love of them to pay for me to do so."

"Not much, I'm afraid." Grete had looked worried. The salary was not large, but out here Verity did not need a large salary. She had everything she wanted. Most of all, a less troubled heart.

She liked the young couple very much, for they were still that in spite of their tall sons. "We were married early," Grete had said.

They had left the boys with her parents at the ages of seven and nine, Grete returning several times in the intervening years to see them, then at the end of that period bringing them out with her.

"They love it, as we do. They like new things, as we do.

Hence poor Uncle Bent's furniture." Another laugh. She was a happy person and laughed a lot.

From the moment the Tank had pulled up at the rendezvous that had been chosen, Verity had known she would be as happy as she could be anywhere with this nice family. When Big Gunnar had joined them in Bathurst and taken over the wheel, she had felt more confident still.

The homestead had proved a delight. Instead of the accepted spreading, leisurely one-storey edifice favoured in most instances, it had borrowed from native Sweden. It was a surprise to come across its three levels and its tucked-in attics and dormer windows, but it was a pleasant surprise.

The boys were likeable, and she felt they liked her. Big Gunnar had built a swimming pool, she had a mount to go riding with Gunnar and Ulf, in fact she could think of nothing that she needed.

Grete chatted about everything, but she never intruded into Verity's life. If Verity told her anything, she listened very eagerly, so Verity guessed she must be curious about her. But she never asked, and Verity never confided. Anyway, she thought, what would I have to say? You can't talk about emptiness.

There was a mixed plate at Tetaparilly, as Gunnar Dahlquist put it. A little sheep. A few cattle. A lot of crops. Their new herbs. Then they had leased the western and southern sections to a cotton starter. It was two weeks before Verity met Chris Boliver.

Grete had made only a superficial endeavour to hide her eagerness for Verity and Chris to like each other. "It is not good Chris living as he lives," she said. Then carefully, but still saying it: "It is not good for you, Verity."

"I'm contented, thank you, Grete." Verity was. – Well, she was as contented, anyway, as she could hope to be. At times the enormity of the things she had done, that outrageous walk-

ing out from her marriage without an explanation, with only:
"I have gone away. V," did appal her, as in all fairness she
knew it should, but in between she knew a degree of serenity
out in this serene western refuge, with its wide unclouded skies,
its distant horizons, and its nice people, for already she liked
them, parents and children, very much. She was aware that
Grete wanted her to like their neighbour, too.

Well, she was prepared ... a little ... for that. She was
young, and at times she thought wistfully of younger company
than Grete's and Big Gunnar's, yet older than the boys'. But
it must stop at that. She knew it, but Grete didn't, and she
listened rather uneasily as Grete explained how Chris was
American, but had left his native cotton fields to start again
in Australia after his young wife had died.

"I know what you will be thinking now," Grete had babbled eagerly. "You will ask yourself what does this Grete want
me to do, live with a ghost? And I would say yes, for I believe
from what Chris has told me it is a happy ghost, and I believe
from my own knowledge that it should be so. Male and female,
Verity. Why do you think I left my children all those years for
my mother to bring up? I missed them terribly, but I knew,
anyway, they were only on loan to me, but that my husband
was for ever. Two people together is as it should be. Don't
you think?"

"But, Grete, you don't understand ... and I'm afraid I can't
tell you."

"Then you, too, have thoughts behind you. Then I think it
could be very good for you and Chris to –"

"*Grete!*"

"I'm sorry. Big Gunnar always says I rush in. It is just that
I'd like you for a neighbour one day, Verity."

"I'd like you, Grete, but –"

"Then do not say any more. Wait till you meet our Chris."

With a sigh Verity had decided to leave it at that.

Chris Boliver came riding up one morning just before Verity's hour of conversation with Gunnar and Ulf.

"Look at him," said Grete as the fair American on the grey horse approached, "he has a large car and a landrover, but he rides." An inspiration came to her. "Why don't you ride with him, Verity?"

Verity burst out laughing.

"You are supposed to be asked," she pointed out. "I could hardly go up to Mr. Boliver and say 'Come riding with me.' "

"No," agreed a soft American drawl, and Verity realized her voice had carried in the clear air, "but you could say to *Chris* Boliver, 'Come riding with me.' "

"And your answer, Chris?" Grete came in eagerly.

"Yes, please," said Chris at once, his hazel eyes appreciatively on Verity.

He said he could do with English conversation, too, after all he also was a foreigner, and he followed Gunnar and Ulf into the schoolroom. Embarrassed at first, Verity found herself enjoying the hour. They compared their brands of English, the American way, the English way, the Swedish–Australian variety, for Gunnar and Ulf talked a mixture of what they had picked up from the farm hands and their parents' native tongue.

It became an established thing in the week that followed for Chris to "happen" along. That was what he always said. "I happened along."

When she laughed at him, he asked, "What would you say?"

"I came."

"I came, I saw . . . I conquered?"

Flushing, Verity started on other varieties of differences . . . paraffin where the Australian said kerosene, supper that meant a snack before bed in Australia but in England and America meant what the Australians called tea. She was aware that Chris was looking at her and not listening as attentively as she liked Gunnar and Ulf to listen. – She was aware, too, of her awareness of him. I must stop it, she knew.

A few days afterwards he said diffidently, "Knowing Grete, I have no doubt she has spoken about me, Verity."

"Well – yes."

"I was married. When Elvie died I knew I must get away. There will never be anyone like Elvie, yet would I want that? – Yet more important, would the one I now want want that?"

"I wouldn't know, Chris," she said honestly.

"Then I'm asking you to think about it, Verity. I can't offer you what I had for Elvie, but I can offer you what Elvie never had of me. She was my morning time, something that happens only once in a man's life. But a day can grow as lovely in a different way. The thing is whichever view you take, the day *will* grow, will reach night. So all the trying in the world to hold time back still will never hold it. Life must go on. Do you follow me, Verity?

"Yes. – Grete has been talking to you."

"She has," he admitted, "but I think I would still have reached this knowledge of my own accord, this acceptance that I can't live the rest of my days on only a dream. I've a lot of days yet, you see."

"I hope so, Chris. But Chris –"

"Yes, I know. There is something, too, with you. I could tell it at once when I first met you. Perhaps you're only at the stage that I was when I came out here. Still withdrawing from it all. But it will pass, Verity. And then –"

It will pass. Verity gave a bleak little smile. Oh, Chris dear, if you only knew!

He took her silence for thoughtfulness, and touched her shoulder gently.

"Think about it, anyway, Verity."

She could not reply to that.

The Dahlquists had taken delivery of some more of their chosen furniture. Plain, unpolished, simple to sparse in line though it was, Verity had to admit that the almost Biblical quality of this remote western terrain set off the uncluttered designs in cool perfecion.

"I knew you would see it in time," Grete nodded eagerly. "To put scrolls and curlicues in this basic land would be very wrong."

"Your uncle did it."

"Big Gunnar's dear old Uncle Bent. But that was years ago. Now his nephew is selling it."

"Surely not to anywhere at all?" asked Verity, shocked.

"Oh, no, we have our own dear man, our very dear man, and he has made us promise that we sell only to him. Each time we have a few pieces to let go to make room for the new, he comes and buys it."

"That is good." Verity felt relieved. She was still sufficiently the connoisseur to shudder at any indiscriminate disposal of such lovely stuff.

It was a month now since Robin had died ... so a month since she had married Bart Prince. Common sense told her that she must make a move soon, she had had her respite, had her time for constructive thought ... even though she had done very little of that ... and she could not go on like this. She must contact Bart, tell him he could start procedures, or whatever one did to begin a release. A release so he could go to Adele.

As it always did when she thought of Bart and Adele, the picture of Priscilla came to Verity's mind. Dear background Priscilla, whom once she had coupled with Bart, when all the time it had been her brother's wife. But even Mrs. Prince had assumed it was Bart and Priscilla, Verity recalled.

Priscilla was too worthwhile not to belong to someone, Verity's thoughts ran on. Then she smiled reprovingly at herself. I'm becoming a Grete, she accused.

Yet with little else to think about out here, it was a diversion, and she even got to the extent of bringing Priscilla and Chris together in her mind. — But at that she stopped, stopped at the thought of Chris's fair good looks, his serious gold-green eyes.

I am beginning to like him, she thought, appalled, and I can't, I mustn't.

She knew she could not go on much longer like this. But before she could do anything, admit what she should have told Gunnar and Grete . . . and Chris . . . right from the beginning something else happened to put any telling back for yet another day.

And a night. . . .

As Chris smilingly put it as he extended one arm of his jacket to include Verity, in olden days . . . as younger Gunnar and Ulf always expressed anything further back than their own years . . . this episode certainly would have "fixed things."

— "Even still does in some straitlaced New England towns," he admitted.

"How do you mean fixed?" Verity had been fastening herself in from the breeze biting at the other side from Chris.

"You shock me, Verity," he had teased. "Us, of course. This is unconventional, to say the least."

"Your coat? I find it warm and necessary."

"Can you find me necessary, too?" Chris had said then.

Before their predicament he had taken her out to see, and understand, he hoped, the cotton. "Elvie understood the process perfectly." He had pulled himself up sharply. "I'm sorry,

Verity," he had apologized at once.

"For what?"

"For bringing in Elvie."

"Oh, Chris, don't feel like that, keep keeping her in your mind."

"You don't mind?"

"I want you to."

"But if we –"

"Not now, Chris," she had evaded, reading his thoughts. But it had to be some time, her own thoughts had warned. She must not keep on like this.

They had gone through the different processes of the cotton. Chris even had shown Verity where he planned a future ginnery. He had said deprecatingly, "And I can have it, Verity. I really mean I have the means . . . I think you have the right to know that. You wouldn't be . . . well, I'm not a poor man."

And you, knew Verity wretchedly, have the right to know that I have a husband with more than just means, a rich husband, only he isn't really, because we – because I –

"Verity, didn't you like me telling you that?" Chris had asked with concern at her preoccupied silence.

"Telling me what?" She realized she had not been listening with attention, she had been thinking of something else.

"Money."

"Of course I didn't mind. And Chris, I love the source of your money. I love the cotton. I love those fluffy balls."

"Bridal," he had agreed, and as it often . . . unbidden . . . seemed to happen, he seemed to withdraw from her into another world. Poor Chris!

They had had a happy meal at his house before they had set out on the ride to the distant rocks that Verity always had wanted to see.

"I'm going to give you some good American fare," Chris had

told her. "I thought it would make a change from Swedish."

"And Australian – don't forget we have Australian hands, and to them all the choice Swedish offering in the world would not come up to steak and damper. But this looks wonderful, Chris. Is it –" She had examined the perfectly baked pie.

"Blueberry. From a can. But the pastry is my own doing. If it adds a few points to my score, it will be worth my having thrown out four pies before this one."

"Did you, Chris?"

"Yes. I remember once we were having a blueberry contest, Elvie and I, and –" As before, he stopped abruptly.

"It's a beautiful pie," Verity had come in quickly. Then she had said spontaneously: "You're wonderful husband material, Chris." As abruptly as he had, she had stopped, too.

They had both looked at each other, then smiled ruefully. He is completely nice, Verity had thought with a little catch at her heart.

The Outcrop was the only higher point in a vast world of plain. Once, Verity had been told, it would have been a mountain, but centuries of centuries had worn the mountain down to the small but in this flat country salient rise that it was now.

Because of its position it seemed to entrap every colour that the day chose to wear. Crimson in the morning. Pure amber at noon. Purples and deep burgundies at night. Verity had never got over turning to gaze at it and wondering what it would be like to gaze back from.

"Probably," Grete had warned, "it will be the same as the house with the golden windows, and we will have the colours."

"It must still be fine to stand there and look around."

Chris must have heard her say that, for as soon as the meal was over after the cotton inspection, he had said they would go across.

At first he had suggested taking his Rover to the closest

point, then they could climb up, but Verity had wanted to ride. If she had listened to him, she told him ruefully as later he had apportioned out his jacket, they would not be up here like this.

"I'm not complaining."

"But you did say about this 'fixing' it," she reminded him with a giggle.

"Perhaps wishfully," he suggested.

They had ridden as far as they could, then left their horses cropping. That, Chris had said, was where he had to take the blame, but Nomad had never needed before to be tethered. However, something must have scared the horse, he was a highly sensitive animal, and suddenly he had galloped down the hill. Before Verity could reach her mare, Sally had followed Nomad.

The sun had been well to the western rim. Even as they had stood looking at the retreating horses, it had started to sink. Verity knew, even though she had only been here some weeks, that dusk would only be a matter of minutes. It was instant night out here in the west.

Also, although the days were warm, it would be cold with the plain all around them. She had only a thin blouse on, and she shivered at the thought of what lay ahead. – That was when Chris had apportioned out his jacket ... one arm each, which meant they had to sit very close together, as close as one, not two.

The darkest moment had been just after the sun had slipped away and after elf light had deepened into night. For this was the time of no stars, once the stars pricked out it would be almost like putting on a lamp, for out here the heavens fairly blazed.

"Verity."

She had known it was coming, but the knowledge didn't

help her now. But before Chris said anything, Verity knew what *she* had to say.

She took a deep breath.

But finally it had been hours before she could tell him. All that time he had waited sympathetically, sensing her desperate need to spill out the words, appreciating the difficulty she found in doing so. When at length she had blurted the story, he had tightened his grasp on her hand.

"I felt there was something important."

"Not really important, Chris, although we were married we're not married. I mean —"

"I know, I know." He spared her. Then, after a pause: "But does it really finish at that, Verity?"

"Chris?"

"It doesn't, does it, girl?"

"Chris, I don't understand you."

"I believe deep down you do, but you just won't let yourself believe it. But it's still there, Verity, and even if you don't, or won't, know it, then I still do. If I didn't, then . . ." He gave a little smile.

"If you didn't know what, Chris?" she asked directly.

"Your love."

"What love?"

"For this man."

"You're wrong."

"I'm not wrong, girl, and if I didn't know it, I would wait and marry you. But what would be the use of marrying half a heart."

Now she *did* understand him. She understood that he was telling her that only that he sensed the impossibility of what Grete in her goodness had tried to bring about, that he would not be saying all this now, that instead he would be —

But . . . and Verity knew it with a sudden sure perception

533

. . . Chris Boliver would *not*.

Calmly, she told him so.

He listened to her silently. He heard her say, "You still would not have married me, dear Chris, because in your heart you're still married to Elvie. Some marriages are like that." He listened to her say it in different words once again.

There was a silence. It was such a long one it seemed hours before he spoke.

Then: "Thank you, Verity," Chris said.

After a while he blurted, "I just didn't know . . . I was confused . . . I just accepted what Grete advised, and she said —"

"There should be someone again?"

"Yes."

"Yet in your heart you didn't feel it?" Now it was Verity's turn to probe.

"No."

"Then —?"

"Then it doesn't have to be." He nodded at her in the dark. "You are right. Grete was wrong. Oh, she's kind, and she means well, but . . ." Another pause. "Thank you, Verity."

After that they just sat close together, each intent on their own thoughts. At times they spoke companionably, but that was all it was. Yet Verity saw that Chris had reached a new peace of mind. Probably what Grete in her kindness had urged would do for a lot of men, most men, but not Chris. He had been uncertain, but now he had found himself. There was a tug of sadness to his mouth, that would always be there, but there was a serenity and an acceptance he had not had before.

As for herself, the relief of spilling out everything had lightened her so considerably that with the first buttering of dawn she felt almost like the new day.

Taking Chris's hand in hers, she smiled up at him, and they descended from the Outcrop to start the long trek home.

"Possibly we'll be met halfway," Chris said. "Someone will see the horses, guess what took place, and come out for us."

They had gone only a short distance when this happened. Turning a bend with a concealing mulga blotting out the track beyond it, they came almost on the car.

"Hi," called out Big Gunnar from behind the wheel, "all well and accounted for?"

"All well, all accounted for," called back Verity cheerfully, Chris's hand still in hers, her eyes still smiling because of that smile now in his. Then she froze.

Sitting beside her employer was someone she had not expected, or wanted, out here.

It was Bart.

CHAPTER XI

BART made no attempt to claim Verity, but on the other han
he prevented any move on her part to claim him by insertin
blandly: "Very well, very accounted for, from the look of th
victims, so your worries were unnecessary, Gunnar. Being ac
quainted with the lady ... yes, I am ... and knowing her re
sourcefulness" ... the slightest of pauses ... "I should hav
reassured you previously. Careless of me, my friend. I mus
have been concentrating on the male side of the episode. You
neighbour, Chris Boliver, I should say?"

"Yes, you can say that." Chris had stepped forward an
extended a firm hand.

Verity was glad that when she had told the American he
story, she had used no names. Chris had an open way with hin
and certainly would have registered immediate pre-know
ledge of Bart. As it was, all that his likeable face expressed
was a continuance of that acceptance and serenity that he ha
thanked Verity for up on the Outcrop.

That Bart could interpret the look as something intrinsic
between the man and herself did not occur to Verity. She sim
ply was relieved that Chris did not know, that Gunnar did
not know, that Bart had the control to wait for a private mo
ment.

Gunnar was saying, "Well, it's a small world" of Bart's cas
ual acknowledgment of Verity. "But," he went on, "I should
have known, she's so keen on furniture, and it seems you an-

tique people are a race apart." There was a general laugh at that "antique people" which considerably lightened the strain for Verity. She was glad when Gunnar continued, "As Grete remarked last night: 'Fancy coming out all this way for Uncle Bent's old stuff.' Yes, a race apart, as I said." Gunnar spread his hands. "Not that we would have it any other way, thank you, Bart," he hastened to add.

He turned now to his American neighbour. "Was it as we guessed, Chris? Something startled Nomad, Sally took up the scare, and the two of them left you stranded?"

"Exactly," nodded Chris Boliver. "Still, it could have been worse, we could have had to walk right back." They were now getting into the car.

"And we could have frozen had Chris not had a jacket," came in Verity unthinkingly.

Chris finished, "And that jacket not been large enough to lend Verity one of the sleeves. I tell you my outsize tent saved our lives, or at least our comfort, last night."

"Closer settlement, no doubt," Bart said quite pleasantly, no undertone at all.

"Very close," laughed Chris. "Ever shared a jacket?"

"No. I must do it some time." Bart still kept up the mild amiability, he still did not look at Verity.

Gunnar backed the car, and they set off for the farm.

Chris was persuaded to continue on to the homestead for lunch. "And to tell Grete all about your adventure," added Gunnar with a laugh. "You know our Grete and her enthusiasms."

Verity, who had left some of her things at Chris's bungalow and would have been better pleased for them to remain there until later than have attracted more attention, heard Chris say, "But we must call first at the villa, Verity has belongings to pick up from yesterday."

She need not have concerned herself, Bart remained as supremely untouched, even uninterested. He did show interest in the cotton as they passed it, though, and the conversation ... thankfully for Verity ... changed focus.

The boys took over at the meal, proudly showing "Uncle Bart" how well they could speak now. Not just howareyoumate as learned from the hands as before, pointed out Ulf, but Big Words. He demonstrated, losing much of the effect by putting his Big Words in the wrong place. However, like his mother, Ulf was a cheerful person and did not mind the resultant laughter.

Much as she would have liked to have slipped away, Verity was included in Grete's furniture showing to Bart during the afternoon. Chris had gone, but not before he had arranged with Bart to view the cotton the following morning.

"Yes, I would like to see it," Bart had accepted at once, "I would like to find out the prospects of it. That's very important, I think." For the first time a look was flicked at Verity.

"The prospects are excellent," Chris assured him enthusiastically.

"Then excellent," said Bart. Although he did not look at her a second time, Verity still had a sense of being in his deliberate line of vision. It was not a comfortable feeling.

In the lumber room afterwards he accepted every piece that Grete offered. His price must have been very satisfactory, for Grete protested once: "You are too generous."

"My dear Grete, the last thing in the world I am is a benefactor, but I would never rest another moment if I was not fair." – Once again Verity had the impression of his estimating eyes on her, and yet his back was turned.

Grete went out to bring in a small piece she had forgotten, and Verity stiffened herself for the words she knew he would now say to her. A few minutes went by in silence, they seemed an eternity, then he remarked: "Quite an interesting line to that chiffonier, don't you think?"

"Bart —" If he wouldn't begin it, she must; she could not go on any longer like this.

"Also, the divan head is rather unique." Then, without drawing a breath: "Not until I see the cotton, please, see how you'll be placed."

"Placed?"

"That's what I said. You must have heard me tell Grete that I would never rest if I wasn't fair."

"What do you mean, Bart?"

"Oh, come!" he said impatiently, his head inclined to the corridor along which Grete should return at any moment. "I am well-placed ... extremely well-placed. Do you think I would let my" ... a deliberate pause ... "wife suffer with less than she could have snared?"

She realized what he was thinking. He had gathered the impression that she and Chris, that they —

"You're making a mistake, Bart," she said it urgently.

"I made it," he corrected coolly.

"Bart —"

"I made it ... but I am prepared to pay for it. Hence the cotton inspection to assess the position. No" ... as she went to speak again ... "there's nothing to be said that wasn't said in your two faces as you came along the track. But not to worry, I'll see you don't lose."

Indignation rose in Verity. "I would think you were being very magnaminous assuring that," she flung, "if I didn't know how important it all is to you." How important to get your release, she was thinking, a release without tears if possible, as it should be possible with your added money, if it's needed, to help it along. A release to go to Adele.

"Yes, it is important to me." He turned and looked at her

539

fully for the first time. "It's the most important thing in my life."

"Then why –" Why, she had been going to ask, didn't you wait for Robbie to die, for Adele to be free, why did you put us through all this?

"Grete is coming," he said, and his voice was cold.

The next day he spent over with Chris, then when he returned in the late afternoon she saw that his bag was in the hall and that Gunnar had the car out to take him to the airfield.

"Priscilla will be arriving," he said as he stood waiting for Grete and the boys to come and say goodbye.

"Priscilla." Verity said the name blankly, her attention elsewhere.

"She always does the after stuff." It was not a reminder of what she should know but a statement as to a stranger.

"Yes, of course," she murmured.

A short silence.

"I think you need have no fears," he said. "You know what I mean."

"I don't, Bart."

She might just as well not have spoken. "If you do have," he went on, "you know the address. However, I found that cotton very safe."

"Bart –" she began.

"Though if you believe you're not doing as well as you might have –"

"Bart. Bart, please."

He did not turn to her, but he did ask tersely, "Yes?"

"I'm sorry. It was abominable of me."

Now he must speak at last, she thought. He would agree, and she would tell him *why* she had left with only a few written words, tell him half of the fault had been his, that his voice

540

when it had answered . . . so soon . . . from Adele's apartment that evening had been the real reason she had gone away. Tell him of moments when she had stood beside him in the church. Tell him . . .

But what was she thinking of? This man was only interested in assuring himself that he was strictly fair and just. And only concerned for Adele.

"I'm sorry," she mumbled again.

"Not to worry." He had advised that before. He said again as he had said yesterday: "Grete is coming."

Within minutes he had left.

The week that followed prior to Priscilla's arrival to do the after-sale things was a very long one for Verity.

Chris, in his new acceptance, did not notice any difference in the girl, but sharp Grete did.

"You are not happy, Verity. It did not work out as I hoped. And yet in the beginning you two seemed to get on so well."

"What two?" For a moment Verity forgot what Grete had planned, what Chris himself almost believed he had wanted.

"You and Chris," said Grete, sharper than ever. "Who else?"

"Oh, Grete dear, it was never like that at all, and it never could have been."

"Yet Chris seems more contented," went on Grete, puzzled.

"He is, because he was one of the few who did not need your help, any of our help," said Verity gently. "For a while he believed what you urged, Grete, but it was only a phase. He is still married to that girl who died, you know."

Grete thought that over for a few minutes, then gave a little defeated smile. "Well, perhaps you are right, perhaps Chris is right."

"We are. We are sure of it."

Now Grete nodded soberly. "Yes, and I must believe it, seeing his serene face. But you, Verity, you look –" But at a look now in Verity's eyes, Grete simply touched her hand, then changed the subject.

Several days afterwards Priscilla flew in.

It seemed a lifetime since Verity had watched Priscilla go through her "after-ing" processes, the cataloguing, the recording, the describing for identification, all the necessary details that the girl did so efficiently, a lifetime away, and yet it was only a few weeks. So much had happened in those weeks. Robbie had died. She had been married. She had run away from the marriage and come here. She had met Chris, and her husband . . . for a moment Verity stopped, surprised at herself, it was the first time she had said that . . . and Bart had thought that she and Chris . . .

"There, I think that's all for that section." Priscilla turned a page of her book.

There was something different about the girl, Verity thought, coming out of her introspection. Priscilla, as Grete had remarked of Chris, looked more at peace with herself. In fact, she looked almost –

"I suppose," Priscilla smiled, "Bart supplied you with all the Prince news."

It was Verity's turn to smile back, but it was a thin little smile, for she was thinking how meagrely Bart had spoken about anything. She heard herself murmuring, "Not expansively. You know men."

"I don't," admitted Priscilla, but she did not look wistful about it as she used to look.

"As you would know, Matthew and Cassandra are married," she told Verity, "they have a flat above Matthew's surgery. They're both rapturous – that's the only way I could put it." Priscilla looked very pleased herself, and Verity recalled her saying once that Cassandra's beauty was something she felt she could never handle.

"So," Priscilla finished, "the first of the Princes is accounted for."

Now Verity darted a quick look at the secretary. So Priscilla still did not know. Well ... bitterly ... that made for belief, Bart had not had time to let anyone know *before*, then *after*, with Robbie not standing between anyone any more, it had been the last thing he would have wanted to be known.

She watched Priscilla now recording the chiffonier. Was the girl's new assurance based on the welcome fact that Cassandra had been removed from the scene ... as regarded Bart? Poor Cilla, if that was the case ...

"How about Peter?" she inquired automatically, concluding that it was expected of her ... then was shaken out of her polite interest by the almost dramatic change on Priscilla's face. There was no mistaking that change ... that very lovely change.

"Why, Cilla!" she said, caught up by the girl's cheeks that had flushed to a warm pink.

As she did not answer, Verity crossed to her and tilted her chin. "Cilla, I don't understand," she begged.

"You mean," said Priscilla incredulously, "that you don't understand that I ... that Peter ... that we ..." She paused to take a deep breath. "That I always –"

"No. No. I believed it was – Bart."

"Bart?" Now it was Priscilla's turn to look surprised.

"You were always so gentle with him."

"Could anyone be anything else with Bart?"

... Yes, thought Verity, *I* was. I was abominable with him. Even though he had been using me, how could I have done such an embarrasing, cruel thing?

"But you loved him," she said to Priscilla. "You always

543

loved Bart."

"Yes."

"He loved you."

"Yes ... but oh, Verity, never in the way you're thinking. How did you ever reach that conclusion?"

"He would look across at you. You would look back at him."

"Because there's something terribly close between us. If I could tell you –"

"You must tell me."

"It's Bart's story." – Priscilla had said this, Verity recalled, once before.

"You must tell me," she appealed with sudden urgency, "Prissie, you must."

For a few moments the girl hesitated, then with a little resigned gesture she sat down.

"If Bart hadn't done what he did, I wouldn't be here," she related soberly. "Bart saved my life. A thing like that leaves something, Verity, just as it should. I can never look at Bart now without remembering ... and thanking him for ever."

"Has this anything to do with his injuries?"

"Everything," Cilla replied.

"Then why is he still so bitter? What he has sustained can be surmounted, it has already been surmounted to a large degree, and at least he has the satisfaction that he achieved what he did with you." She waited ... then when Priscilla did not speak, she asked: "You did tell me he saved you, Priscilla?"

"But not the child," Cilla said quietly. "The little girl died."

There was silence in the room. Somewhere a clock chimed and the notes fell cool and clear. Then somewhere further away ... in the garden? ... small Ulf called. Ulf. Rising twelve robust years.

And a child had died.

Verity looked across to the secretary, and waited.

"We had this business call to this old suburban home that had been donated to a charity. Already a number of girl wards had been accepted, so more suitable furniture, child-suitable, I mean, was replacing the antique stuff. Bart, of course, was interested."

"But Bart," interrupted Verity, "wouldn't be in the business then, he only came after the accident." The accident, she thought, that had stopped his medical career.

"It should have been Peter," nodded Priscilla, "but Peter was suddenly somewhere else . . . that's Peter . . . so Bart, as he always did, stepped in to help.

"We were in the garden at the time, the little girl and I. Bart had gone into the house to talk to the matron.

"We shall never know how the hideous thing started, perhaps one of the children, even the little girl herself, had decided to burn up the dead leaves that the gardener had raked. Perhaps there was a spark from somewhere. An incinerator, or so." Priscilla sighed.

"Anyway, all I can recall is that all at once a child was aflame. I ran to her. Then" . . . a little shiver . . . "we were both alight."

"After that, I can't recall anything . . . but I've been told. I've been told that Bart leapt from the balcony from such a height and in such a way that he did much more than the usual damage a fall can do, yet in spite of the awful impact it must have been he still ran across and pulled me out and threw me to the ground, rolled me over to extinguish the flame . . . then he turned to the child and did the same."

"I didn't see it," Priscilla repeated. "I'd passed out, and anyway, people had run down and carried me off. I didn't see Bart's shocking injuries as he tried to save that child. The awful thing was he did save her, as he saved me, but what he did not know was the previous state of her heart, poor mite. As Matthew has tried to tell him a thousand times since, the child would never have grown to maturity, anyway. But Bart would never accept it. To him it was a failure on his part – a failure to save a child's life."

There was a long pause now.

"He was months . . . a year . . . in hospital. In that time he became very embittered. He gave away all thoughts of continuing his career. I think" . . . looking at Verity . . . "that that's why you coupled us. I visited Bart all the time, I understood what he was going through, because of what had happened. When two people are involved like that, there is, there has to be, an intrinsic understanding."

"Mrs. Prince also coupled you," said Verity absently. Her mind was on Bart and the horror he had known.

"I suppose so. There are things between us and I expect they must show." She looked directly at Verity. "Will you mind?"

"Mind? *I* mind?"

"Because," went on Priscilla, not heeding her, "it will always be that way . . . a look and a memory. You mustn't think that –"

"*Priscilla!*" Verity waited for Priscilla to come out of herself, then she demanded : "If it was not Bart with you, then –"

"Then who?" broke in Priscilla. "But I've just told you. The other Prince, of course."

"But that leaves –"

"Peter? Yes. Then – Peter. Are you astonished? Yes, I suppose you must be. Peter has everything, I am a dull mouse."

"You're not. You never have been."

"So," said Priscilla softly, "Peter told me . . . just before I

546

flew down. Verity ... oh, Verity, we're being married. I've always known for myself, and I've always sensed ... I suppose I'm being boastful ... that Peter would know, too, one day. He had to go through the gamut, he had to grow up. But he knew he was the type who needed tying ... there are people like that, you know ... and that I was the one to do it."

"A kind of mooring, Priscilla?"

"You understand it perfectly. So long as I have known the Princes, Verity, Peter has always been the 'scrape' one. As I said, he never grew up. Too much charm, too much of what it takes.

"But I knew one day he would need *me*, and when he came up from Melbourne to Sydney for Matthew's and Cassandra's wedding, it was That Day. He didn't need you, he didn't need any of the many women he had 'fallen in love with'" ... a little loving laugh ... "but old Prissie he did need. And," finished Priscilla, "I was there waiting for him."

She leaned forward to Verity. "I've sometimes wondered whether it would happen, whether it could happen, but always there persisted that feeling that it was going to happen, that it was going to be all right. Bart was aware of my feeling. He supported me. Each time he smiled at me he was telling me so ... and you thought –"

"Yes," said Verity, "I thought that."

"I'll be a restraint on Peter," admitted Priscilla, "but I think the youngest Prince has come to the stage when he's ready for that. Perhaps Peter is weak ... in fact I know he's weak ... but the weakness will pass, and even if it doesn't, I have the strength and capacity for both of us. And I feel that in time he won't resent that strength ... that he'll come to like me for it."

"He'll love you for it," said Verity, touched.

Now Priscilla's warm pink had deepened to a glowing rose.

"I know," she said softly. Then she smiled. "Because he's told me already."

A few minutes went by in happy silence.

"Another Prince accounted for," Verity said presently in a light tone.

"Yes. Only Bart to go."

Only Bart to go. If Priscilla knew the truth! Yet what was the truth? It was this: *Bart was less than married because he had a marriage that was not a marriage at all.*

"Priscilla," she broke in abruptly, "were you surprised when I went away?"

"No," answered Priscilla, surprised herself, "your brother had died, and after that you came down here for Bart. It was part of the job."

"Yes," said Verity dully, "part of the job." Then she said, finding every syllable hard but making herself say it: "Do you know that soon there'll be three Princes accounted for?"

"What do you mean, Verity?" There was a smile in Priscilla's voice, but Verity quickly stopped it.

"Bart – and my brother's wife," she said in a tight voice.

"Adele?"

"Yes. Adele."

"But you're so wrong." Priscilla was looking at her in amazement. "Never Adele," she refused.

"Always Adele ... In fact it would have happened before had Adele not lost her head when Robbie came out here."

"It would never have happened, not in a lifetime. I should know, Verity, I've been around the Princes for years. I don't say if Adele had had her way it wouldn't have come about, but never, never Bart."

"You know very little, then. You wouldn't know that Bart – that he –" But Verity's voice trailed off. How could she say to Priscilla: "You wouldn't know that my husband of only two days rang Adele as soon as he knew she was free, and that he . . . that she . . . that they . . ."

"I know a lot," Priscilla was saying confidently. "I know, and I'm going to tell it to you, Verity, whether you are ready for it, or not. And this is it: It's you whom Bart wants, and has wanted right from the start. No, don't try to stop me. I've gone through too much with Bart not to know that."

"But he never said anything."

"Bart couldn't. He was still too choked up with what had happened to his life. He was still uncertain of himself. He would have told you all this . . . had you helped."

Had she helped? Verity knew she had done everything – save help.

"But Adele –" she persisted wretchedly.

"Was never anything . . . except that perhaps he was sorry for the girl. She brought a lot of trouble on herself one way and another, and because Bart understood trouble . . . who would more? . . . he was always there to help a lame dog."

"He kept on helping," said Verity bitterly.

"He's a rich man."

"Not just that way." No, Verity was thinking, not just with money but with his presence that afternoon of Robbie's funeral. An afternoon that had run into a night? Into days? Weeks?

But it was the day of Robin . . . two days after a marriage . . . that comprised the sharp hurt.

"But mostly that way, mostly money," Priscilla was saying in her practical secretary way. "For instance on the occasion of your brother's death he went over to her apartment to hand Adele a cheque for –" She named an amount that fairly shocked Verity into a long, long silence.

"That much," she said at last.

"That much," Priscilla nodded.

"Are you sure?"

"I went with him. I made it out for him. Knowing Bart as I do, I suppose I must have looked astounded at it, for he said, 'It's to be for a long time, Cilla.' He might have meant a long time for Adele . . . or he might have meant a long time for him to make out any more. For, of course, he'll be out of it all for some months."

At first her words did not sink into Verity, then slowly, starkly, they did.

"How do you mean, Priscilla?" she asked.

"Bart is going into hospital. Didn't he say? It won't be like the other clinic stays, just brief ones, it will be much more than exploratory this time. It will be the real thing. Matthew has finally persuaded Bart to go through with it, and it will mean being totally invalided for a very long time."

"When?" Verity knew it must be she who asked it, but she was not aware of opening her mouth, of making any sound.

"The first of the operations, and the indicative one, for if it is not a success, then . . ." Priscilla paused to make a little movement with her shoulders.

"Yes? *Yes*, Cilla?"

"Should be very soon. It might even be now. – Why, Verity . . . Verity, what are you doing?"

For Verity was running through the house like a whirlwind, she was calling, "Grete . . . Grete dear, I'm so sorry!

"Grete, I'm going down to Sydney with Priscilla. One day I'll come back and finish off the boys with their howareyou-mate." She gave a breathless little laugh that ended in a half sob. "At least, Grete," she promised, "I'll come back to explain."

"Do you know what," said Grete who had appeared from the kitchen, "I might have been wrong about Chris, but I don't feel I'm wrong about something else. And it is this: You won't be back, Verity."

"I will, Grete. I promise."

"No, Verity, you – and Bart will be back," smiled Grete.

"Oh, Grete," Verity said, not pausing to wonder how the Swedish woman had guessed that, "please hope it. Please hope it." She added: 'Hope for us."

She was still crying "Please hope it for us", but to herself, as she threw her things into her bag.

CHAPTER XII

PRISCILLA asked no questions. She must have been curious about that mad whirlwind race through the house, the announcement that there would be two of them returning to Sydney, but when Verity came out carrying her bags, telling her that if she was finished they could leave today, that Gunnar was on the telephone now confirming their tickets, she simply, and typically, welcomed a travelling companion home.

The secretary must actually have said "home", for at once Verity was thinking: Home? But where is home? – Her Balmain flat was relinquished now, and even if Bart had not closed his own apartment to enter the hospital, could she – could she –

Oh, no, she knew, I'm not entitled.

"And I really mean home. My home." Verity's doubts must have conveyed themselves to Priscilla. "You would have cancelled your own place when you went to the Dahlquists, so now you must come with me until you start your own flatting again. That is . . . if you do." A careful smile.

Verity let that pass in her relief to have somewhere to go – and yet in an equal anxiety not to intrude now on Priscilla and Peter.

"I would appreciate it for several days, Priscilla," she admitted.

"For as long as you like?"

"And – Peter likes?" Verity smiled.

"Don't worry about that." Priscilla's rejoinder was shy but assured. "After waiting so long for Peter, it will do him good to wait for me."

"Then if you're certain –"

"Verity, I've never been more certain in my life." A pause. "Of everything. Otherwise would I be talking so confidently like this?"

"No, Pris, you wouldn't," Verity smiled back.

They had relapsed into silence, Priscilla to her dreams, Verity to her less than dreams.

The Dahlquists, Big Gunnar, Grete, Gunnar and Ulf, had come to wave them off. Just as the country plane had started along the narrow strip between the bleached grass and last year's dandelion, Chris had raced up in his Rover. Verity's final wave had been for Chris.

She looked down now at the country over which they were flying. The western plains had given way to tablelands, soon they would cross the mountains, cross the lodge on those mountains where she and Bart had spent the first night of their honeymoon . . . honeymoon? . . . one month and an eternity ago.

Then they would cover Sydney's suburban sprawl.

She dared not mull over the mess she had made of everything, and even if she had tried to do so her concern for Bart would have pushed it aside. Let him be all right, that was all she could think. Let this big, initial, indicative operation show what other operations can avail. Most of all, let Bart realize this, and persist. For, although she knew nothing of medicine, Verity was sharply conscious that half of the battle was to be Bart's, and that if he didn't offer his bit, then it would be of little use.

"Fasten up," prompted Priscilla at her side. "We're nearly there, Verity."

Verity snapped her seat belt catch, and their plane touched down.

On Priscilla's decision they went first to her flat.

"You can settle yourself in, Verity," she said. "The hospital may not want visitors around for some time yet. It will be better, anyway, to ring first."

"Yes, Pris." Verity felt she had to agree.

As they took a taxi to Priscilla's suburb, Verity repeated, "Pris, you are sure?"

"About staying with me? Very sure."

But Peter, in the flat waiting for his Priscilla, was not sure, and it was the most welcome thing, Verity told him frankly, that she had heard.

"You'll be hearing much more welcome things," Peter grinned, "but not from me. No, I'm not sure I want you here, Verity, in fact I'll be honest and assure you I don't. How long do you intend to interrupt my new love life? I don't mind a day or so, but –"

"Peter!" reproved Priscilla.

"Sorry, sweet." Peter flashed a smile at her.

As she went out to make coffee, he looked boyishly at Verity.

"When I said my new love life, I was wrong, you know, for, Verity, I think I've loved Prissie ever since I first saw her, which is a long time ago now. But I was completely self-absorbed, I wouldn't read any other signs but ones to do with me. Thank heaven Pris had the maturity to wait for me to come to my senses. I really have come to them, and all I regret now is that I never came earlier. Mad, isn't it?"

"It was mad of you, Pete," Verity replied.

He nodded whimsically. "Yet sweet, too, in a way," he went on. "There's something to be said for a late start. I know all that I'm saying now must sound pretty impossible to you, I mean after you and I . . . after we . . ."

"Go on, Peter," Verity encouraged with a smile.

"Then Cassie so soon afterwards. Girls before that. Girls before that again. But –"

"But?"

"But they were nothing. You" . . . apologetically . . . "were nothing. Cass was nothing – the rest. Only one ever stood out. I think I must have known it, but wouldn't accept it. I wanted life first, or what I thought was life." He gave a comical shrug.

"But Prissie *is* my life. She's my heart, Verity, and a man can't live without his heart. – I say now, there's a pretty speech if you like," he grinned.

After a pause, he went on again. "Don't think, either, that this is another Peter-phase. It's true. It's lasting. I've had my fling, and in more ways than one. For instance, I'll definitely take over the Castle. And don't think I'm being heroic about that, I'll be taking it over because I want to. I mean that, Verity."

"Then good for you . . . but what about Bart? What about his role in the business?"

Peter smiled across at her. "Bart will never come back to it, of course."

"You mean . . ." Peter could mean several things. For instance he could mean –

"No, nothing dramatic, Verity. It's simply that Bart never did attach himself to it. Sawbones were always in his veins. – I say, that isn't so good, is it? If I'm to handle the Castle's publicity I'll have to read up on metaphors."

"Oh, Peter!" she laughed.

"No, Bart never wanted business, not really, and after he's better –"

"But will he be better, Peter? I mean – properly better? Career better?"

"It's more likely than unlikely," cheered Peter. "If this first go is a success, then I think there'll be nothing to stop old Bart from finishing those years he began. That is, nothing except the lack of incentive."

"Yes," murmured Verity, "incentive." She looked directly at Peter. "Why did you think he might lack that?"

"Matthew wasn't sure at any time," admitted Peter. "There's a purposelessness about Bart, Matt says. — I say that's quite a word. Purposelessness."

"Peter" . . . Verity said jerkily . . . "I don't think I want to hear your words. I just want —"

"Coffee? Here it is now." Peter got up to take a tray from Priscilla.

But Verity knew she could drink no coffee, not until —

"No," she said, "I just want to see Bart."

Once she had spoken she felt much better.

She was aware that Peter and Priscilla were exchanging glances, that they were glancing back at her.

Then, at a nod from Priscilla, Peter said: "I don't know if you can, but, anyway, we'll try. Come on, old girl."

By the time they reached the hospital it was to learn that Bart's first operation had been successfully concluded. — Though Matthew's face as he told them this was not as pleased as it should have been.

"What is it?" Peter asked bluntly at once.

"He's not co-operating. Even this early that is quite apparent. He's not pulling out as he should. Surgically speaking, everything has gone off perfectly. According to text, he has come through A.1. But the fact remains —"

"That he still hasn't." It was Peter again.

"No," said Matthew gravely. "He's simply lying there. And don't think that because physically he's been passed as all right he can *not* be all right. Things can still happen. Even in successful cases like this, things sometimes do. In fact unless something turns the tide, he could –"

Matthew grew silent.

"All this is strictly unprofessional," he went on presently, "it is also between this family." – Family? wondered Verity, what family? But she did not wonder long in the impact of what Matthew said next.

"If Bart," he told them all, "doesn't exert himself . . . if he doesn't hold on, then –"

"Matthew." Verity's voice broke in quietly but definitely. "Can I see him, please?"

The eldest Prince looked gently at her, he even leaned over and touched her hand.

"Sorry, my dear."

"I must see him."

"He's not being seen by anyone – by that I mean anyone outside, Verity, he's not up to that stage. Why, even our mother –"

"And even his – wife?"

There was a silence. The two men looked at her, looked at each other. Priscilla looked at her. Then, without asking any questions, Matthew stood up and put out his hand to Verity.

"Come on, Mrs. Prince," he said.

Bart lay in the darkened post-op room, and one look at him told Verity *why* Matthew had spoken as he had. Bart looked frail.

"He's conscious," Matthew reported in a low voice, "but I would say barely so. He should be fully out of it by now, but it almost seems he doesn't want to be, that he's holding back on us. The thing is he *must* be out of it. Do you understand me, Verity?" He looked briefly at her. "I don't know what happened between you two, but something must have, but if you can forget it, if it should be forgotten, or remember it, if it can

557

help, then – try."

"There was nothing, Matthew" . . . well, that was the truth . . . "but I'll be trying." Verity sat down beside the still form.

She heard Matthew go out again, but she knew he would not go far. She knew the other doctors were waiting as well.

"Bart," she said softly, "Bart."

The man did not respond.

She sat on for a while, sat desperately. At times she repeated, "Bart –" but still he did not move. Then, unable to bear it any longer, Verity leaned over and called, "Bart, I'm here. Verity is here. Bart, your wife is here. I'm your wife," she repeated.

She said it several times more before he showed any response. Then, his eyes opening slowly, Bart Prince looked up at Verity and said : "My wife." He closed his eyes again.

Soon after, Matthew came back. Several of the doctors came with him. Verity was led outside.

It seemed an eternity before Matthew joined her, but when he came he was smiling.

"I'm not asking any questions, I'm not even asking if you went into there with a genuine reason, Mrs. Prince. No, all that can wait. Right now I'm only concerned with results."

"And they are?"

"Good. Almost miraculously so. It's remarkable how the tide has changed. He's fighting back now. Probably he'll have some tricky moments, and I have no doubt he will be a bad patient, but the thing is *he will be a patient, Verity*. He will be, my dear."

They walked along the corridor together. She asked Matthew about Cassandra, and listened, though abstractedly, to him telling her, enthusing over the newly decorated flat above the surgery, charming if not at all the grand first home he had wanted for his wife, but how Cassie adored it, how she insisted on being his receptionist-nurse, how he saw now he had been wasting his days before he married Cassandra.

"All the Princes waste their lives."

"What, Verity?"

"I'm sorry, Matthew, I was thinking of something else."

– Thinking of everything else, she could have added, than what I want to think about. "The tide has changed," Matthew had just said. "He'll be a bad patient, but the thing is he'll be a patient."

Without exactly awarding it, she was aware that he had been giving her the credit. But what did I do? she wondered dazedly. What did I say?

I want to remember ... I must remember ... but I still can't remember what I said to Bart.

Verity, at Priscilla's and Peter's urging, went back to Woman's Castle. She found she was glad to do so; at least the work helped fill in some of the dragging time.

She did not let herself think of the future, and she could not think of the past. It was too unhappy a past.

Bart was still in intensive care, Matthew had told Peter, and Peter had passed on to her. No visitors. No communications. Just day-by-day watchfulness. After the first tricky weeks, things should pick up.

Those weeks seemed years to Verity. When they were up, she thought, and I know, know for sure he's going to be all right, I'll step quietly out of the scene. But I'll leave an address this time, not mark it by anonymity. At least an address will be playing fair. Playing fair? She gave a little wry laugh. All's fair, she recalled, in love and war. Only as far as she and Bart had been concerned, it had been all war.

Yes, she would have to go, she continually told herself. What Priscilla said that day about Bart ... and about me, could

559

have been only Priscilla's imagination. It must have been her imagination, for certainly Bart had never given any sign. A girl in love, as Priscilla is, Verity shrugged, naturally would imagine love in everyone. She gave a resigned little smile.

Thinking of Priscilla brought up the subject of Adele. Had the girl also imagined something there as well? It wasn't like the efficient Prince secretary to make a mistake, but in her pink cloud nine that she lived these days. It could happen.

As though in answer to this, Adele turned up one afternoon. She was perfectly chic and very lovely, and no doubt well aware of this.

But she was a different Adele, though it took some time for Verity to believe it. Adele waited while Verity attended a customer, then she came straight to the point.

"I know you adored Robbie, Verity, and I was quite fond of him, too, in a way, so I feel I must tell you this myself, not let you hear it from someone else, and . . . well, be hurt."

For a moment Verity's heart pained her so much she felt she could not bear it. Could it be – No, Priscilla had said . . . Then Peter and Matthew had not reported . . . Besides, Bart was still not to be communicated with, so he could not have sent for Adele, have agreed with her that they –

She was not aware that in her agitation she had said Bart's name until Adele came in with a low laugh: "Oh, you're wrong to the ends of the earth there, my dear."

"But you – well, you –"

"Oh, yes, I know I let you gather that impression, it's this streak in me, I guess. I didn't have a very good time. I told you once."

"Unrewarding was your word."

"Yes, Karl was anything but rewarding." Another laugh, rueful this time.

"Karl?"

"The man I always loved but didn't get around to marry ... at least *he* didn't get around to marrying me. I wasted my best years on that fraud." A fond pout.

"I always thought you meant –"

"Yes, and I intended you to. I'm one of those mean people who have to distribute pain in the idea that it helps them with their own pain. I could never bear anyone else's happiness."

"Then Bart was never in it?"

"Only to the extent of a helping hand. That's always been Bart Prince. Incidentally, you can tell him from me that I now know the truth ... it doesn't matter how ... the truth that there's no Ramsay money, and that he came forward instead." A pause. "That's love if you like."

"For you?"

Adele stared incredulously at Verity for a long moment. "Oh, you little fool," she said at last. She waited a while, then went on. "You can tell him, too, I won't need any more handouts on your behalf. You see, Karl ..." She glanced significantly down at her hand, and Verity saw that Robbie's wedding ring had been removed ... poor Robbie ... and that another ring, a very showy diamond, now glittered there instead.

"Karl," affirmed Adele proudly. "Sometimes it's like that. Some people take a long time to come good. Karl did. And because he has, I have, too, Verity."

She was quiet for a while.

"I know what you're feeling about me, and I don't blame you, but believe me, if Robbie had to die, as he did, I made him happier than he would have been had I not come into his life. Can you at least think of it like that?"

"I'll try, Adele."

"Also, if I had been Robbie and if Robbie stood where I stand now, he would be doing what I'll be doing ... marrying again. You see" ... a reminding little smile ... "we were one of a kind."

"But something else has come into my way of looking at things. It's being really happy for the very first time, I expect ... for I want to clear things up before I go off."

"With Karl?"

"Yes." A shrug. "He has a bit of clearing up to do himself. But I want you to know, and to tell Bart, that I won't ever be asking for another handout. Anyway" ... proudly ... "Karl has more than enough for both of us. He's certainly got himself up in the world in those years between." A smile now for Karl's success.

"Also, I want you to understand that there was nothing ever between us, between Bart and me. I looked all the Princes over years ago, having heard of their possibilities, and having managed a contact, but saw that as far as they were concerned that that was all they would ever do to me, look me over, then let it stop at that, so I concentrated instead on the soft touch of the family. Bart, of course. You'll have to watch your man with that soft heart of his."

"Bart soft?" Verity exclaimed.

"None softer."

"My man!"

"Oh, for heaven's sake, girl! Anyway, that's what I wanted to say. Also" ... a careful pause ... "so sorry. If you can ever find it in you to forgive –"

"Of course I can, Adele."

"And forgive for Robbie, too?"

"I think," said Verity slowly, "perhaps I should thank you for Robbie."

"Do you know what," Adele said eagerly, "that's the nicest thing you could have said."

Then she did what she had never done before, she came and kissed Verity.

Verity, watching her go, found that she was liking her more than she ever would have thought possible ... that she was waving her good luck.

Bart was out of intensive care now, and certain selected restricted visitors were being permitted. Peter and Priscilla had gone on several occasions. Cassandra. Mrs. Prince was flying back from Canada and would be seeing her son next week. Grete had rung from Tetaparilly to say she was coming down to see her antiques man. – "For the first time," Priscilla had smilingly reported Grete confiding over the long distance, "I won't be concerned about mahogany or oak."

Priscilla also told Verity that Grete Dahlquist had told her that a Mr. Chris Boliver would be calling at the Castle.

"Chris," Verity nodded.

Priscilla and Peter were again hospital-visiting the day that Chris came to the shop, but then they went every afternoon now. Verity never attended, nor had she been asked to. She knew they were all waiting for her to follow up that "Mrs. Prince" of hers, that "wife to Bart", that until she did, they were too sensitive ... for her ... to broach the subject, to tell her to come. But how could she unless Bart broached it first?

When Chris came in she was so pleased to see him, she fairly raced across.

"Hi, what's this?" he laughed. "Not changed your mind?"

"No, Chris. Changed yours?"

He shook his head. "I'm going back to America, Verity. What you said to me that night on the Outcrop put everything right for me again. I can go home, face up."

"I'm sorry you're leaving, Chris dear, yet I'm glad at the same time for you. For home is home always." She was thoughtful a moment. "What about your cotton?"

"I've handed it as it is to **Big** Gunnar and Grete for their boys. My boys, too – I'll never have any family, Verity, so they can be my sons. Until young Gunnar and Ulf are old enough to handle the cotton, it can pay for their education at some good boarding school. Because" . . . a smile down at Verity . . . "I don't think you'll be back there, and those two imps have to learn something more than –"

"Howareyoumate. But, Chris, I could be going back."

"I'll never believe that, my dear."

He left soon after. He had a plane to catch.

"A plane," he said finally and happily, "to Elvie."

. . . Again Verity found herself waving someone good luck.

There was to be a third.

Matthew told her so the next day. Not actually a waving of luck, perhaps, but if possible a prod along the path to well-being. To achieve this for Bart . . . Bart, of course, it was, Matthew nodded . . . the doctor asked Verity to go with Peter and Priscilla on their next hospital visit.

"Remember how I said Bart would be a bad patient but that he would be a patient? Well, both have come true."

"Bart is a bad one?"

"A disappointing, even dismaying one. In short he's not progressing as he should. You did the trick last time, V, so do it again."

"Nonsense, Matthew, it was your medical know-how that achieved that. However" . . . at a shake of Matthew's head . . . "being capable of performing miracles is rather a flattering thought."

"It still wasn't medicine," Matthew persisted stubbornly. "It was you. You know" . . . quizzically . . . "you've *still* never said whether you were speaking the truth when you got yourself in as you did to see old Bart, and I'm still not asking you, but I am asking you . . .appealing to you . . . to see him again."

"I can't," Verity refused. "Any move now must come from him."

"Lying prone in hospital? Unable to move? Don't be unfair, girl. Oh, no, V, it must come once again from you."

"But why? *Why,* Matthew? He is doing well. You have said so."

"But not sufficiently well. Oh, he'll recover all right, we have no fears about that, but to what degree of recovery? Verity, you did something before, so repeat the trick."

"I don't know what I did," Verity honestly replied, for she still could not remember that day clearly, it was still a daze.

But she did eventually agree to visit Bart with Priscilla and Peter.

CHAPTER XIII

VERITY'S heart was beating almost to suffocation as she followed Peter and Priscilla down the corridor to the room where Bart was now established ... and would remain for many months ... the next week-end. Stubbornly, she had refused to go until then, making her excuse an unattended shop, knowing inwardly she had to have a breathing space, a time to prepare.

"Not unattended. We'll close it," they had chorused.

"Quite unnecessary when we're so close to Saturday."

"You're a funny one, Verity."

No, Verity could have said, just an uncertain one, uncertain of what's going to happen there.

She kept well behind the pair; she did not know whether Bart had been told to expect her, and for quite a while she could not bring herself to glance up to read his reaction. By then, his surprise, if any, was over. He simply sat up, propped with pillows, looking fairly fit, if too pale and too thin.

"Once the initial awful impact of me is over, you become quite used to the sight," he tossed carelessly to Verity. That was his only greeting to her. — So Bart had regained his old astringent self.

They all talked together, Verity offering nothing to the conversation ... until suddenly she realized that Peter and Priscilla had slipped out. That only she stood there.

"So you're back at the Castle?" Bart at length broke the awkward silence that had descended.

"Yes. That is until Peter and Priscilla ... until they ..."

"They'll probably need you even more then – keep in mind my dear parent's strong grand-maternal urge," he laughed shortly.

"I don't know if I'd stay," she told him.

"Back to Tetaparilly?"

"No."

"Then" ... with a show of impatience ... "the adjoining cotton field, seeing you like to be explicit."

"No. How could I when –"

"Yes?" he asked sharply.

"I couldn't," was all she returned.

There was another silence. Verity broke it with: "I never dreamed at any time it was – Peter and Priscilla."

"But I told you all along that Peter was accounted for."

"Perhaps ... but I still thought, at first, anyway, it was Prissie – and you."

He shrugged. "Probably my mother started the idea."

"And the glances you used to give Priscilla helped the idea along." Verity was not looking at him. "Bart" ... she said sensitively ... "I just want you to know that I've learned all about it ... I just want to say I'm sorry for what you must have gone through that time ... how you must have felt."

A look of remembered pain flicked across his face, but he managed a shrug. "I expect to a doctor, though I wasn't up to that I admit, a first death is always something that's never forgotten ... especially when it's a child."

Another silence.

Verity broke it determinedly; she felt she could not bear these pauses.

"Matthew says this first indicative operation has been completely successful, that it augurs well for any that will follow."

"Yes," said Bart, but carelessly, almost indifferently, "I, too, have been told that."

"Then afterwards," followed up Verity flippantly, for sud
denly she was afraid of seriousness, "you'll be able to reac
your heart's desire. If your brother Peter was here now he'
say 'That's a pretty speech.' " Her laugh was insincere.

She saw that he was not listening to anything Peter migh
say . . . only listening to what she had said.

"My heart's desire was never that," he corrected her. "Be
sides" . . . aimlessly . . . "I don't know if I want medicin
now."

"But Peter wants the Castle."

"And will undoubtedly make a much better go of it than
did."

"I wouldn't agree." Her defence was spontaneous. "Loo
at your lamp collection."

"And why should I look? Not one of those lamps ever she
any light for me."

"Light?"

"Lit up one moment of truth." He was quiet a moment, but
and she saw it and repressed a little shiver, quite angrily, al
most furiously so.

"Oh, for heaven's sake, Verity," he burst out at last, "let'
stop patting balls at each other."

"What do you mean?"

"Truth is your name, isn't it? Then why can't you deal with
that commodity, practise it just this once?"

"What do you mean?" she asked again.

"Why did you cancel out? Oh, I know you have a talent for
cancelling – first Peter, then Matt, Chris Boliver after me. But
why . . . *why* did you leave like that? Five words on a sheet of
paper. Why?"

She did not speak.

"I hadn't hurried you. I wasn't going to hurry you. Yet
you –"

568

"Yet I went," she nodded bleakly. "It was wrong of me. It was even abominable. I'm sorry – but I said all that before."

"You said it, but I didn't accept it. I don't accept it now. Why? Why did you do such a rotten thing?"

... Because I rang Adele and heard your voice, she thought: if you had told me before it could have been different ...

Aloud she said: "Because even though you had paid for me it didn't mean –"

"Stop it!" he came in.

"Well, you wanted to know."

"Stop it!"

After a while he spoke again. "Yes, I did pay for you, but I would still have waited until you had forgotten the money that came into it and only remembered the ..." His voice trailed off. He did not return to that theme. "When I found you'd left, I put it down to Robin," he told her. "I knew how close you two had been."

"It wasn't Robin."

"I could see that very clearly as you came back down that track that morning with Boliver. You had run away to find something, something that I could never give you, mean to you. You found it in Chris. That was obvious in your two faces. Well – fair enough. As you said, I had bought you, so I couldn't expect from you the same as I had to give."

He had to give? Bart? But Bart had never had anything to give but money. Oh, Priscilla had had her ideas, but Cilla –

"I should have stopped the caper earlier," he said it a little wearily. "Oh, yes, I could have, I knew where you had gone – heaven knows it was simple enough, you never even destroyed that newspaper ad. It was sheer luck, though, that I happened to be previously friendly with the Dahlquists, sheer luck that it was them whom you contacted. – Sheer luck, too, I dare to suggest . . . for you . . . that Boliver lived so handy, and that he turned out so unmistakably decent and presentable. Otherwise I might have —"

"Might have what, Bart?"

He shrugged. "Thought out a different ending for you instead."

"There is no ending," she told him. She added bleakly, "Not yet."

"That I can well believe, for if nothing else you would be a very circumspect little girl. You would never, for instance, take on Boliver while still . . . on record only, of course . . . a wedded woman."

"I never took on Chris, as you put it."

"And you never," he reminded her thinly, "became that wedded woman. And because of that, have no fear for a happy ending in a very gratifying time. There's a special clause for instances like ours."

"Bart . . . Bart, stop all this!" Her voice must have risen, for he stopped.

"Whatever you believed you saw in Chris and in me —" she went on.

"I saw it."

"Was there only because we'd both just spilled out our hearts to each other. No" . . . as he went to make an obviously astringent comment . . . "let me finish, Bart. You see, it's not as you think."

He did not speak now, but his brows had lifted.

"Chris Boliver was still married to his dead young wife. For a little while he had thought differently . . . but he was wrong. So wrong," she finished, "he's gone back to America again. To Elvie." She was silent a while, remembering Chris's smiling face, still with that tug of sadness to the mouth, for that would always be there, yet an acceptance as well. A serenity.

"Then I –" she went on.

"Then you?"

"That," admitted Verity uncertainly, "I didn't know ... though Chris seemed to think he did."

"Know what?" Bart's eyes were boring into hers.

"I don't know." Restlessly. "I tell you I don't know. – Oh, why are you probing me like this? Why has it to be your side all the time? Why can't I ask in my turn and be told? Ask how did you think I felt that day when I rang – and you answered?"

"Rang where? Answered what? What in heaven are you talking about, girl?"

"Rang Adele's apartment. The afternoon of Robbie's funeral. Only two days after –" But at that she stopped.

"Two days after a marriage that was not a marriage," he finished for her. He paused, his eyes narrowed now. "Couldn't that comprise your answer?"

"It could – and it did. That is – until Priscilla told me the truth. Told me about the cheque you handed Adele. Before that I thought –"

"Thought that Adele and I –?"

"Yes."

"You little fool!" Bart's voice was incredulous.

"I know now," she resumed shakily, "I know you paid her for the legacy she'll never receive ... will you put that down, too, in your little black book?"

"Don't talk like that, Verity."

"Then don't do any more buying of me," she cried.

"Why not? You bought me, didn't you? You bought me back."

571

"Bought you back?"

"From the devil, you must often have thought." A short laugh. "I was dying that day, Verity ... yes, I was actually dying. That sounds dramatic, but I knew as I lay there following the op that I was slipping out. And I would have – only you came and said it. You said it, Verity."

"Said what?"

Bart looked at her for a long moment ... a desperate, asking look ... then turned away.

But presently he turned back again, a little amused now, the old sharp Bart showing through.

"When you heard my voice from Dellie's," he baited, "was your pride badly hurt?"

"No, Bart" ... and she said it spontaneously ... "my heart." – Then she was looking at him in a caught-out surprise and Bart was looking back at her.

At once she was remembering sitting beside his darkened cot that day after the operation, staring down at him, trying to reach him, to keep him, then saying ... and she heard herself quite clearly now: "Bart, I'm here. Verity is here. Bart, your wife is here. I'm your wife."

"Why not?" she came back now. "Why not a heart, Bart? After all – I am your wife."

Along the corridor the first of the afternoon visitors were beginning to leave.

"Say that again," Bart was demanding hoarsely.

"Why not? Why not a heart –"

"No. No, Verity. Say – say the end."

The visitors were passing the half-opened door. Some glanced curiously in, but there was nothing to see. Bart was just looking across at Verity, and Verity was still struggling with words that somehow could not come.

"Say it," he said.

A nurse put her head round the door, glanced significantly at her watch, and intoned, "Time, please."

"Time doesn't matter," refused Bart when she had gone, "unless it's the present. I don't want to hear *then*, Verity, I don't want to hear *when*, I want to hear *now*. I want to hear it this moment." He waited.

"Very well." At last the drought was breaking. "Only you're getting it all, Bart. I was your wife. I am your wife. I will be – Oh, Bart –"

For either he had managed to lean over, or she had gone to him, but there was no distance between them at all.

"You do realize," he was whispering ruefully, "that between one thing and another, one therapy after another, it will be quite some time before you can really put signed, sealed and delivered to that wife, my girl?"

"You do realize," Verity was coming back, "that I don't believe it's going to be any time at all, my man."

"Time, please." The nurse was thinking that for long-term patient, or so she had been informed, the patient in fifteen looked a very short one. She particularly thought it as Verity was released at last from the patient's arms.

"You can still wriggle out," he warned her when the nurse had left again. "You spent a night at Adele's, remember. Then you deserted me the next day. There's such a thing as instant annulment for that."

"But there's still a night on the mountains to be accounted for," she smiled triumphantly back at him.

"Accounted for truthfully," he reminded her, "remember your name, Verity."

"I'd sooner," she admitted, "deal in fairytales than fact."

And as she went down the corridor, the nurse the winner at last, Verity found herself repeating those stories ... those childhood fantasies that she used to practise for Robbie, because Robbie had demanded that his tales be smoothly recited, no indecisions. – She found herself dealing with one particular story.

"... Once upon a time there were three princes, a gracious prince, a charming prince, a prince who was –"

A prince who was, who is, who always will be *my* prince. Verity stopped saying it to let her heart sing it instead. Something made her glance up to a window. Evidently Bart had persuaded the nurse – or another nurse – to wheel his bed there. He was waving to her. He was touching his hand to his lips to her.

She caught the kiss and imprisoned it.

Threw one back to him.

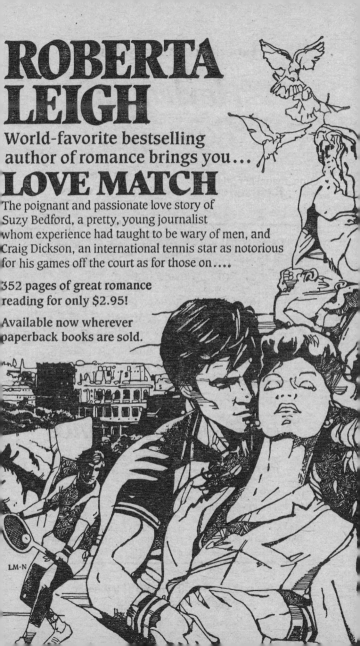